Robyn Grady was first contracted by Mills & Boon in 2006. Her books feature regularly on bestseller lists and at award ceremonies, including the National Readers' Choice Awards, Booksellers' Best Awards, CataRomance Reviewers' Choice Awards and Australia's prestigious Romantic Book of the Year.

Robyn lives on Australia's gorgeous Sunshine Coast, where she met and married her real-life hero. When she's not tapping out her next story, she enjoys the challenges of raising three very different daughters, going to the theatre, reading on the beach and dreaming about bumping into Stephen King during a month-long Mediterranean cruise.

Robyn knows that writing romance is the best job on the planet and she loves to hear from her readers! You can keep up with news on her latest releases at www.robyngrady.com

New York Times and *USA TODAY* bestselling author **Barbara Dunlop** has written more than forty novels for Mills & Boon, including the acclaimed Chicago Sons series for Mills & Boon Desire. Her sexy, lighthearted stories regularly hit bestseller lists. Barbara is a three-time finalist for the Romance Writers of America's RITA® Award.

ONE NIGHT WITH HIS RIVAL

ROBYN GRADY

THE DATING DARE

BARBARA DUNLOP

MILLS & BOON

First Published in Great Britain 2020
by Mills & Boon, an imprint of HarperCollinsPublishers,
1 London Bridge Street, London, SE1 9GF

One Night with His Rival © 2020 Robyn Grady
The Dating Dare © 2020 Barbara Dunlop

ISBN: 978-0-263-27918-4

0320

MIX
Paper from
responsible sources
FSC® C007454

This book is produced from independently certified FSC™ paper to ensure responsible forest management.

For more information visit: www.harpercollins.co.uk/green

Printed and bound in Spain
by CPI, Barcelona

ONE NIGHT WITH HIS RIVAL

ROBYN GRADY

With thanks to my wonderful editor,
Charles Griemsman, and literary agent
extraordinaire, Jessica Alvarez.
Professional, supportive and talented.
I just love working with you both.

One

Last night was the best and worst decision of her life. On the one hand, it was ecstasy. On the other hand, disaster.

Veda Darnel couldn't get her head around it. She had practically sold her soul to spend one sizzling night with a man who had reinvented the word *satisfaction*. A consummate charmer who'd caused her to swap out her common sense for the thrill of unparalleled pleasure.

Lying together now, front to naked front, Veda studied the cocky cowboy in question as he continued to grab some much-needed sleep. Primal instinct was keeping his hand glued to her behind, pressing her hips against his. Each time he breathed in, that mouthwatering chest expanded and wiry hairs teased her nipples. Whenever his lips twitched with a dream-induced grin, she longed for just one more kiss.

Just one more time.

Well, sorry, universe. Not happening. Not now. Not ever

again. Damn it, she knew better. In the future, would *do* better.

Still asleep, Ajax Rawson drew in a sharp breath at the same time the fingers on her butt flexed, then dug in more. Veda had to bite her lip to stem the groan; her Benedict Arnold body wanted those expert hands everywhere and all at once. And if he woke up now, that could very well be where they'd end up. Making love like nothing else mattered.

As if there weren't already enough prices to pay.

Tippy-toe quiet, she reached behind her and found the big, hot hand cupping her rear end. She carefully coiled her fingers around his wrist, then tried to lift and shift it.

Seriously? His arm must be made of lead.

Knuckling down, Veda tried again. When she'd finally managed to ease herself away, she held her breath. But he didn't stir. Not an inch.

So, slide off the bed, dive into your clothes, bolt out the hotel suite's front door and never look back. Never go *back.* Still, a knot of bittersweet longing kept her hanging. Ajax was the best she'd ever had—the best there ever was.

And how many other women had thought the exact same thing?

He sucked in another sharp breath, rolled onto his back and scooped his arm under his pillow while his other hand gave those ripped abs a languid rub or two. Then his brow pinched, eyelids flickered open, and Veda's stomach dropped.

Too late to run now.

Ajax frowned sleepily at the ceiling, getting his bearings, before turning his gaze onto her. When one corner of his wholly kissable mouth eased up—when his lungs expanded on a breath that said, "Oh, yeah... I remember you"—Veda's resolve to do better wobbled like a thimble full of Jell-O.

Ajax's dreamy ocean-deep blue eyes smiled into hers

as he spoke with a sexy growl that was equal parts playful and deadly serious.

"You need to come over here." He cocked an eyebrow, smiling wider as the sheet tented over his waist. "On second thought, I can't wait that long."

When he rolled back toward her, heat rushed through her blood, pooling deliciously low in her belly. But tempted as she was, Veda didn't lean in. Didn't surrender. Instead, she brought her portion of the sheet higher and sat up.

"Actually," she said, "I have to go."

Ajax paused, then leaned up on an elbow, head in hand, biceps bulging. "You mean to the bathroom or something?"

"No. Not that."

"Ah, you need food," he said. "Me, too. I'll order up. Maybe some green pepper omelets, hot-off-the-grill bacon and chocolate-chip-banana pancakes drowned in syrup. We can eat breakfast in bed." He came near enough to brush his gorgeous stubble against her cheek. "Lunch and dinner, too, if you want."

Ajax was never lost for words—more specifically, the right words. He gave off a vibe that confirmed that everything good fortune had to offer came to him naturally. Like he never had to even think about trying.

If only she could say the same for herself.

Years ago, and more than once, a much younger Veda had watched Ajax from afar while daydreaming about being in this exact situation. Back then, as well as now, she hated to think what her father might say. Drake Darnel had an ax or two to grind with the Rawsons, the first dating back decades to a time when Ajax's dad, Huxley Rawson, was known as a stud.

What was the saying?

Oh, yeah.

The apple never falls far from the tree.

Now, as Ajax maneuvered to claim that kiss—as his

musky scent flooded her senses and all her pulse points started to throb—Veda felt her resistance begin to ebb. Thankfully, somehow, she managed to shore herself up and pull back in time.

Ajax pulled back, too, studying her like he couldn't work out what the problem was for the life of him. After the way she'd allowed herself to be so completely adored these past hours…really, who could blame him?

"Have I done something wrong, Veda? Have I hurt you somehow?"

She shook her head. "No. Nothing like that." He'd been a total gentleman. An incredible lover.

"Do you have somewhere else to be?"

"Not particularly, no."

His pained expression only made him look hotter, if that was even possible.

"Is this about family? About our fathers not getting along?"

She winced. "It's kind of hard to ignore."

"We did just fine ignoring it last night."

They'd met at a glitzy Saratoga Springs charity event held at a well-known venue. An hour in, needing a break from the hype, Veda had wandered out onto a balcony. Wearing a tux that fit his dynamite build to perfection, Ajax had been standing by the railing, finishing a call. Veda had swallowed her breath and promptly turned on her silver high heel. But he was already putting the phone away and asking in a rumbling voice that reduced her to mush, "Haven't we met somewhere before?"

Lamest pickup line in the playbook. Except he wasn't playing. While they had never spoken, of course she might look familiar. For years, at various horse races she'd gone to with her dad, she had been a shadow hovering in the background, fawning over Ajax.

So, had they met before?

Feeling like a tongue-tied teen again, Veda had murmured, "Not, uh, physically." Those beautiful blue eyes crinkled at the corners as he chuckled and replied, "Well then, pleased to make your acquaintance—*physically.*"

After an exchange of names, of course the penny had dropped. She was a Darnel, he was a Rawson. Veda also mentioned that she had recently become friends with Lanie Rawson, his sister. Small world...and getting smaller.

With Ajax doing most of the talking, they had gotten to know each other more. Then had come the dancing and the kissing and, after midnight, *this.* The entire time, neither one had touched on the Darnel-Rawson feud. Frankly, Veda didn't want to spoil the mesmerizing mood. Apparently Ajax hadn't given the matter a whole lot of thought.

"Drake and Hux have butted heads over the years," Ajax reflected now, "but I can't remember the last time Dad even mentioned his name."

Was he joking? "I hear my father going on about Hux Rawson all the time."

"Wait. Didn't you say you're in New Jersey now?"

He was right. She hadn't lived here in New York with her father for years. "We keep in touch...phone calls, emails. I visit when I can."

Like this weekend. In fact, she was meant to have been her father's plus-one last night. Feeling under the weather, he'd backed out at the last minute.

Way to go, fate.

"Oh. Well..." Running a hand through his delectably mussed dark blond hair, Ajax blew out a breath. "I'm sorry to hear that."

"Sorry to hear that we keep in touch?"

"Sorry that your dad hasn't moved on. Must be tough holding on to a grudge like that."

Veda's cheeks heated up more. Drake Darnel was a whole bunch of things. *But c'mon now. Let's be fair.*

"I guess it would be difficult to move on when someone swoops in to steal the love of your life. The woman you'd planned to marry."

Ajax's tilted his cleft chin. "Did you say *steal*?"

"My father gave her a ring. Then Hux made his move and voilà." Game over.

"Uh, Drake *offered* a ring, which my mom declined. I heard that directly from her, by the way. And with regard to Dad casting some kind of a spell... Veda, it takes two to tango."

He gave the room a sweeping gaze, as if to say "case in point."

Veda wasn't finished. If they were doing this, she wanted to make the connection between then and now. Between player father and chip off the old block. Just one more reason last night had been a bad idea.

"I believe Hux had quite a reputation in those days."

Ajax frowned slightly. "He was a dude who dated before finding the right one and settling down."

Drake preferred to explain Hux's bachelor past in terms like *skirt-chaser, Casanova, cheat*, although that last dig was aimed more at the Rawsons' questionable business ethics. On top of the issue of how Hux had stolen Drake's would-be bride, the Rawsons and Darnels owned competing Thoroughbred stables. More often than not, Drake's horses were beaten by a nose by a Rawson ride.

Better training? Sporting luck? Or was something more going on behind the scenes with regard to performance?

As far as Veda was concerned, the entire horse racing industry was unethical. Cruel. That didn't even touch on the social pitfalls of gambling, where in some cases, entire paychecks were burned practically every week, leaving families in crisis. Long ago she had made a promise to herself. The day her father passed on, a for-sale sign would go up outside the front gates of the Darnel Stables and every horse would find a home without the threat of whips, injury or being shipped off to the glue factory when it was past its use-by date.

Shuddering, Veda refocused. Ajax was still talking about his folks.

"My mother and father were deeply in love. They were committed to each other and their family. Mom made a choice all those years ago. One she wouldn't hesitate to stand by if she was alive today."

Veda was sorry that Mrs. Rawson had died when Ajax was still a boy. Losing a parent at a young age changed who you were, how you coped. Every day Veda wished that her own mom was still around. She wished her childhood had been different—normal—rather than the screwup she had muddled and struggled through.

But now was not the time to go down that particular rabbit hole. She was vulnerable enough as it was.

Veda wound her hands tighter into the bedsheet she was holding close to her breasts. "I guess we'll just have to agree to disagree," she said.

"I guess we will." Ajax's gaze dropped to her lips as he added, "And if you want to leave… I get it. I do. Just please know that I don't have anything personal against your dad."

She wasn't done with being ticked off. The Rawsons had a lot to answer for. Still, Ajax's olive branch seemed so genuine, and the apologetic expression in his eyes looked so real… It wouldn't hurt to concede at least a small point.

"I don't hate your dad, either. I haven't even met the man."

"But you will. I presume Lanie invited you to her big birthday bash at home next month."

She nodded. "Should be good."

Though she wasn't looking forward to her father's reaction when he heard the news. While Drake knew that she and Lanie Rawson were more than acquaintances now, he was far from happy about it. He wouldn't care to hear that his daughter was looking forward to celebrating with her friend at her party.

And, of course, Ajax would be there, too, looking as magma-hot as he did right now.

His smile was just so easy and inviting.

"Wow. The Darnels and Rawsons finally coming together," he said. "Just goes to show, things change, huh?"

Veda gave in to a smile, too.

Just goes to show...

And because Ajax always seemed to know precisely when and exactly how to act, he chose that moment to lean in again. And when he slid that big warm hand around the back of her neck, this time Veda didn't resist. She simply closed her eyes and inwardly sighed as he pushed his fingers up through her hair and his mouth finally claimed hers the way it was always meant to. For better or worse, the way she must have wanted all along.

Two

"Eyes off. That means hands, too, partner."

Recognizing the voice at his back, Ajax edged around. Birthday girl Lanie Rawson stood there in a bright haute couture gown, hands on hips, a vigilant eyebrow raised.

Ajax played dumb. "Eyes and hands off *who* exactly?"

"If you don't already know, the bombshell you're ogling over there is Veda Darnel," his sister replied. "Drake Darnel's daughter *and* a good friend of mine."

When Ajax had gotten together with Veda four weeks ago in Saratoga, she had mentioned something about her and Lanie being tight. Frankly, in those initial few moments, he hadn't focused on anything much other than her amazing red hair and stunning lavender evening dress. Tonight, with that hair swept over one creamy shoulder and rocking a shimmering lipstick-red number, Veda looked even more heart-stopping.

Eyes off?

Never gonna happen.

Hands off?

We'll see.

Crossing his arms, Ajax rocked back on his boot heels. He'd had a full day at the stables before racing out to the track in time for the "riders up" call. After a thundering win, he'd made his way to the winner's circle to congratulate the jockey, the assistant trainer and their most recent champion, Someone's Prince Charming. Man, he loved that horse. Then he'd shot back to the on-site office to check messages and shower before driving the extra half mile here to don a tux. But first, he'd decided to take a peek at the party that was already getting under way in a glittering tented pavilion in the backyard of the estate.

Now, before he went inside to change, he had a question or two for Miss Lanie Bossy-Pants.

"How did you and Veda Darnel become pals?"

"We met at a women's business luncheon last year," Lanie explained, slipping her hands into the hidden pockets of her Cinderella gown. "Veda's a life coach. She talked about personal change through action rather than words. It was brief but powerful. Actually, I was blown away. Later, she said she recalled seeing us as kids at race meets when she tagged along with her dad. And then I remembered her, too. Or, at least, I remembered her hair."

Like the color of leaves in late fall, Ajax thought, doing some remembering of his own, particularly images of her moving beneath him in bed that night a month ago.

"Back then," Lanie went on, "Veda was like a mouse in a corner. Now she knows exactly what she wants. And I'm pretty darn sure that doesn't include being any man's flavor of the month."

Ajax chuckled to cover up the wince. "I'm not that bad."

Lanie had a skeptical if-you-say-so expression on her face.

"Anyway, I'm glad Veda didn't buy into her father's BS about all Rawsons being scum," she said. "You know she told me once that Drake is still steaming over Mom dumping him for Dad all those years ago. Just so sad."

Sad was one word. But Ajax didn't agree with Lanie. Veda had absolutely drunk the Kool-Aid when it came to believing her father's version of events.

During their one night together, she had gone to the mat for her father. According to Daddy Dearest, Hux was a slimy villain who had stolen Drake's girl. Ajax had set the record straight. His mom had made her own decision—because, duh, it was hers to make—after which she had married the far better man.

Veda had softened toward him again after that, and before vacating their suite around noon, they'd exchanged numbers. The next day, he'd sent flowers to her Best Life Now office address in Jersey. After a week not hearing from her, he'd called and left a message. A few days later, he'd sent a bigger bunch. Dialed again.

No response.

"She's smart, tough and to the point," Lanie said, looking Veda's way through the glittering party crowd. "Not someone who's desperate for a roll in the hay."

When Lanie pinned him with another look that said, *Don't go there*, Ajax coughed out a laugh. "You're seriously the sex police now?"

His sister tossed back her long dark hair the way she did whenever she was excited, angry or digging her spurs in. "I want to make sure that we're clear before I let you out to graze."

He threw her a salute. "Anything you say, Officer."

Lanie groaned. "Just go get changed. Not that the ladies won't drool over you in your boots." Walking off, his sister offered a fond grin when she added, "You're such a tart."

After parking in the designated area out in front of the Rawson property, Veda had followed a torchlit path that wove around the majestic Victorian mansion to a tent filled with conversation and music. She'd been taking in the swagged ceilings, which were awash with a million fairy lights, and looking out for anyone she might know when, larger than life, Ajax appeared at the entrance.

With hands bracing either side of his belt, Ajax was wearing a white business shirt rolled up enough at the sleeves to reveal his strong, tanned forearms. A sexy five-o'clock shadow highlighted the natural thrust of his jaw and cleft chin. Even from this distance, even in this light, his eyes radiated a hue that brought to mind ocean-deep waters sparkling with midsummer sunshine.

Following that whirlwind night in Saratoga, he'd sent two enormous bouquets of flowers. Both times when he called, Veda had ached to pick up. At some stage tonight, they were destined to run into each other. When they did, would Ajax try to reconnect? Were any sparks left on his side of the equation, or after her snub, was she already a speck in Ajax Rawson's rearview mirror?

Before he'd been able to spot her, Veda had inserted herself into a nearby circle of guests. Now she sneaked another look his way.

Lanie had joined him; given his sister's expression, their discussion wasn't particularly lighthearted. When Lanie walked off, Ajax left and Veda released a pent-up breath. She was safe—at least for now. Then Lanie headed Veda's way, which raised another question.

She and Lanie hadn't been in touch for weeks. Had Ajax mentioned anything to his sister about Saratoga? Lanie knew Veda wasn't the type to fall into bed with a guy for the heck of it. But after years of wondering, she had taken the opportunity to at last scratch her Ajax Rawson itch. And as much as she tried—as much as she knew she probably should—Veda couldn't regret a moment of the amazing time they had spent together.

When Lanie was a few feet away, she was joined by a man Veda recognized. Hux Rawson was tall and broad through the shoulders like his son, with neat steel-gray hair, complete with a widow's peak. He dropped a kiss on his daughter's cheek before he hooked an arm through hers and escorted Lanie on her way.

Right toward Veda.

Her head began to spin. From the way Lanie had described her dad, Hux would be gracious, even in welcoming Drake Darnel's daughter. In similar circumstances, she doubted her father would be as polite. Although he was aware that she and Lanie were friends now, Drake still disapproved of all the Rawsons. Always had.

Always would.

Red carpet ready in a tiered canary-yellow tulle gown and smelling like rose petals, Lanie gave Veda a hug and exclaimed, "You look positively gorgeous."

Veda was never good with compliments, so she simply passed on her best wishes, adding, "I left something on the gift table."

A glossy hard copy of the history of women in equestrian sports. Nothing Veda would ever want herself, but coming across it in a Princeton bookstore, she had known dressage champion Lanie would love it.

Lanie saw to introductions. "Veda Darnel, meet the most important man in my life."

An easy smile lit her father's bright blue eyes. "Glad you could make it, Veda. I'm Hux."

For a man in his midsixties, Hux Rawson cut a fine figure in his pristine tuxedo. The tanned face and smile lines bracketing his mouth suggested a long run of good health and personal happiness. Veda's father only ever looked annoyed—unless he was in his stables. Nothing against the horses, but there was more to life than work and stewing over the past.

Tacking up a smile, Veda replied, "It's great to be here."

"Hard to believe my little girl is twenty-seven today." Hux gave his daughter a wink. "So beautiful *and* conquering the world."

Lanie pretended to wither. "Pressure much?"

"You know I'm proud of you," Hux said, obviously referring to more than her riding achievements. "I know your mother would be proud of you, too."

Lanie's expression softened before something over her dad's shoulder caught her eye. Bouncing up on her toes, she signaled to a couple entering the tent.

"Will you two excuse me?" She snatched a champagne flute from a passing waiter's tray. "A hostess's job is never done."

Hux smiled as he watched his daughter hurry off, then returned his attention to Veda. There was a moment of uncertainty about kicking off the conversation again, which wasn't uncommon between newly introduced people. Except this man wasn't exactly a stranger. His decisions before Veda was even born had affected her life on so many levels, in ways he couldn't possibly know—in ways that could still leave her feeling a little lost.

Like now.

Looking directly into her eyes, feeling the weight of the past pressing in…

She wasn't surprised when a chill scuttled up her spine, then slithered around her throat—and squeezed.

The sensation wasn't new. It went back as far as elementary school when she had tried to learn her letters; they looked more like squiggling tadpoles in a white sea, no matter what her teacher had said. In later grades, whenever she was pushed to read in class or was feeling stressed, her ears would begin to ring and her throat would close. Feeling everyone's eyes on her, she would literally freeze, unable to speak. Whispers and open snipes followed her everywhere, even in her dreams.

Lazy.

Dumb.

Weirdo.

After a diagnosis of dyslexia in her teens, Veda had worked hard on herself. Not only was she determined to walk back all the damage that came from hellish anxiety, lack of confidence, few friends and less hope, she had vowed to be stronger for it. And looking on the brighter side, finding ways to reclaim her self-esteem had laid the foundations for her career as a life coach, the most rewarding job on the planet. While she still battled nerves and always would, Veda could speak in front of an auditorium full of people now. She hadn't suffered one of her attacks where she strangled on her words in years.

Until now.

Ringing ears…closing throat…freezing brain.

"This has been weeks in the making," Hux said, looking around at the tented pavilion and its high-end fairy-tale trimmings. "Lanie and Susan's efforts, of course, not mine. Have you met Susan yet? She came down early to make sure everything was set."

As Hux waited for a reply, Veda's throat remained squeezed shut. Cheeks flushed, she forced a smile and shook her head.

"Susan's a godsend," Hux went on. "Been with us for such a long time. She's phenomenal with the house and meals and, well, everything family."

Focused, trying to relax, Veda managed to squeak out, "I see."

Hux's smile dipped before he tried again. "When she arrived here, Susan knew nothing about horses or this kind of life. She loves the place now, of course, but she doesn't get much involved with that side of things."

Veda's mind was stuck. Words refused to come. And deep in her gut, tendrils of panic were spreading.

Lazy.

Dumb.

Weirdo.

Hux's eyes narrowed the barest amount before he tried a different approach. "I suppose you like horses, Veda? You've been around them most of your life."

"I… Horses are…beautiful."

He nodded like he hadn't worked her out yet and maybe didn't want to. "How's your dad doing?"

"Good. Busy." *Breathe, Veda. Just breathe.* "I'm staying there…this weekend."

"Right. The Darnel Stables aren't so far from here."

When she nodded again and took a sip from her champagne flute, Hux searched her eyes and then threw a look around. "Well, I'll let you get back to the party. Nice meeting you, Veda. Enjoy the night."

As he walked away, Veda let her smile and shoulders sag. Knowing next to no one here hadn't fazed her. She could even deal with seeing Ajax again, however that turned out. But being left alone to talk with the man who years ago had let loose a storm of demons that had ultimately torn her family apart…

Veda didn't like to dwell on how much she'd cried when her parents had split, let alone the bombshell that had landed after that. But now, snapshots of events leading up to her mother's death broke through. And with the music getting louder and the crowd starting to press in—

She needed some space, some air, and she needed it now.

Setting her glass on a nearby table, Veda escaped through one of the pavilion's back exits, and she didn't stop going until she was cloaked in shadows and certain she was alone. Out here, the night air was so fresh and freeing.

The beat of the music and drag of dark memories seemed just far enough away.

She was herding together more positive thoughts when, out of the shadows, a figure appeared. Dressed in a tuxedo now, Ajax was cutting the distance between them with a commanding gait. And the closer he got, the clearer the message grew in his gorgeous blue eyes.

You can run, sweetheart, it said, *but don't ever think you can hide.*

"If you want to leave, you're going the wrong way," Ajax said, tipping his head toward the house. "Cars are parked over there."

Taken aback, Veda blinked a few times before responding. "I wasn't leaving. I needed some air."

He forced a grin. "Like you needed air the night we met on that balcony a month ago."

Her knockout dress shimmered in the moonlight as she straightened. "Has it been that long?"

"Yup. That long."

After changing, Ajax had returned to the party pavilion in time to catch a flash of lipstick red as Veda dashed out the back. Of course, he had followed. He wanted to make sure she was all right. And, yes, he had also seen an opportunity to broach another sensitive matter. Namely, what the hell had happened after Saratoga? Why hadn't she accepted his calls?

Clearly, Veda wanted to avoid the subject.

"So, what are you doing out here in the dark?" she asked.

Ajax slid both hands into his pants pockets. "Psyching up for party mode?"

"Well, at least you're dressed for it now."

His smile was slow. "You saw me earlier?"

Her gorgeous green eyes widened before she visibly

gathered herself again and offered a cool reply. "You got changed in record time."

"I'd already showered at the office." Grinning, he propped a shoulder against a nearby oak and crossed one ankle over the other. "I don't mind the smell of hay and horse, but I'm not sure the guests would appreciate it much."

When her gaze dipped to his mouth, he remembered back to that night and words she had murmured while nuzzling him from his chest all the way down.

You smell so good. And taste even better.

As if she was remembering, too, Veda threw a glance toward the lights and music. "I should get back."

"I'll walk with you." He pushed off the oak before adding, "If that's okay."

After a second's hesitation, she made a face like it was no big deal. "Sure," she said. "Why not."

As they headed back down a lit path, he set a leisurely pace. After the flowers and phone messages—after the multiple times she had come apart in his arms that wild night—had she even considered dropping him a line?

He studied her profile—straight nose, lush lips, laser-beam focus. And then there was that jaw-dropping dress. He couldn't help but imagine sliding the fabric from her shoulders, tracing the contours of her breasts with his lips... with his tongue...

Focus, damn it.

"Did you get my messages?" he asked after clearing his throat. "I left a couple."

"I did. The flowers, too. They were lovely."

Uh-huh.

"I wanted to let you know how much I enjoyed our time together."

Gaze still ahead, she nodded. "Thank you."

He nodded, too, scratched his ear. "We left Saratoga on pretty good terms, wouldn't you say?"

Her heels clicked a little faster on the path. "We should get back to the party."

"I thought we could talk."

"Maybe later."

He pulled up. *Maybe now.*

"Is this still about your dad, Veda? Because I thought we'd worked through that."

The train of her red gown swirled as she spun back around. "We agreed to disagree. Not the same thing."

Really? "That conversation happened right before we made love again. Before you said, 'I wish we never had to leave.'"

Her nostrils flared as she crossed her arms. "If you're trying to embarrass me, it won't work."

For the love of God. "I'm trying to understand why you didn't pick up the phone."

He didn't get how she could be all prickly one second and turned on to the hilt the next. Was she an ice queen or too hot to be believed?

She hesitated before taking two steps closer. "I'm guessing you didn't tell Lanie about that night."

What the—?

"Of course not. That's between you and me."

Cringing, she darted a look toward the party pavilion. "So put away the megaphone already."

He rubbed the back of his neck, lowered his voice. "I'm confused, okay? We don't need our parents' consent. We're not kids."

"Right. We're adults making up our own minds."

He groaned. "Still confused."

"I don't regret what happened between us that night. In fact, I'll remember it as long as I live."

So he hadn't imagined it. He wasn't going insane. But when he stepped closer, happy to get back on track, her hands shot up, stopping him dead.

"Ajax, you are wonderful in every conceivable way," she said. "I love spending time with you. The problem is… I'm not the only one. You're always in news feeds with models, actresses, designers, female ranch hands, trainers… There's been an endless string of women over the years. For God's sake, you're known as the Stud."

Ajax exhaled. First he'd had Lanie bleating in his ear. Now this?

Sure, his brothers had ribbed him about that *stud* label, a name some features reporter had come up with for a story a while back. But Griff and Jacob knew who he was.

"I'm a normal and, let me emphasize, *single* guy. Like you're a normal single woman. Dating is not a crime." His shoulders went back. "And there's nothing wrong with us wanting to see each other again."

"Wanting something doesn't necessarily make it good for you."

"Unless it is."

She tried another tack. "I don't approve of the business that you're in."

Say what now?

"You mean the stud farm? Which has stables for race-horses, which is the exact same business that your father is in."

"That doesn't mean *I* like it." She asked him, "Do you have any idea how many people lose their shirts at the track?"

"Veda, I can't help that."

"Like a dealer can't help an addict who continues to use?"

"Not the same thing."

"I'll fill you in on the definition of addiction someday." She went on. "The worst part is the number of horses that are manipulated and hurt, too. Just last week, one of your own was put down after a fall."

He stiffened. "And let me tell you, I was upset about it."

"Not as upset as the horse."

He opened his mouth, stopped, and then sought clarification. "So you don't want to see me again because I own horses?"

"You *use* horses."

Whatever you want to call it. "That's not gonna change."

"No shit."

He had to grin. Veda could be direct when she wanted to be.

"Just please set me straight on one thing," he said. "You don't approve of keeping horses, but I don't hear you bawling out your bestie, the dressage champion."

"Lanie? That's...well, it's—"

"Please don't say *different*."

"Ajax, I'm not sleeping with your sister."

"Right." Stepping closer, he lowered his head over hers and ground out, "You're sleeping with me."

His whole body was a heartbeat as she gazed up with eyes flooding with questions. Veda might have her reasons for staying away, but he could tell a big part of her wanted Saratoga again at least as much as he did.

Finally she stepped back, took a breath.

"We're here for Lanie. This is her night."

He cast a look toward the twinkling pavilion and nodded. "Agreed."

"So we need to put this aside."

"That won't work."

"At least for now. For your sister's sake."

He slowly smiled. "You're a shrewd negotiator, Darnel."

"And you're a persistent SOB."

"One way to fix persistentness...because that's absolutely a word."

She didn't hide her grin. "Okay."

"The point is, yes, we should rejoin the party, *and* have one drink together."

She cocked her head. "One drink?"

"Don't know about you, but I'm drier than a dust storm."

They continued down the path until Ajax had another thought and stopped again. "One more thing before we go in."

Veda sighed. "I'm going to regret this, aren't I?"

"I need to say how amazing you look tonight. That dress. Your hair." He slapped a hand over his heart. "And that's all I'll say on the subject. No more compliments."

And he meant it. Foot on the brake.

But one drink could always lead to two. Could maybe lead to…more.

Three

The woman who stopped beside Veda at the tent's buffet table came right out and said it.

"He's something else, isn't he?"

When the woman sent Ajax an approving look—he was talking with guests by the birthday cake—Veda's cheeks went warm. While looking over the desserts, every so often she had flickered a glance his way, obviously not as discreetly as she had thought.

And who was asking, anyway?

The woman was somewhere in her fifties and dressed in an elegant peach-colored sequined sheath. Her shoulder-length auburn hair was tucked behind an ear, revealing a dazzling teardrop diamond stud. Based on the woman's maternal smile as she continued to watch Ajax, Veda took a guess.

"You're Susan, aren't you? Hux Rawson's…housekeeper."

After many years, it was known among relevant circles

that the pair was less employee and boss these days and more a couple without the legal formalities.

Susan's dimpled smile grew. "I met Ajax when he was a teen. Now he's like my own. The other kids, too."

After Veda introduced herself—leaving out her last name, which might complicate things at this time of night—Susan looked Ajax's way again. As she leaned back against a column, her expression deepened. "Did you know that boy is the reason I'm here?"

"Really? How's that?"

The lights dimmed at the same time Veda settled in for what promised to be an interesting conversation.

"After their mom passed away," Susan explained, "the family was devastated, as you can imagine. With his father so lost in his grief, Ajax decided to step up to the plate. He placed an advertisement in the local paper. *We need a housekeeper*, the ad read. *Someone who would like a family to look after. On my word, we will look after you right back.*"

Veda's heart squeezed. "That is so sweet."

"I'd been going through some difficulties myself. Not a death, thank heaven. But enough to spin my world around 'til I didn't know which way was up. Life can be like that sometimes. Downright dizzying." Straightening, she resurrected her gentle smile. "I got the job and haven't looked back since. I've never felt more fulfilled. I'd always wanted children of my own, so those kids were the icing on my cake. Griff, Ajax, Lanie and, of course, Jacob."

Lanie had mentioned Griff, the Wall Street kingpin, as well as her adopted brother, whom she idolized as much as the other two. "Jacob's a lawyer, right?"

"With an outstanding reputation. He came to us through a juvie program." She toyed with the diamond stud as she clarified, "For years, Huxley ran a scheme here for boys in trouble who might benefit from fresh scenery and a little guidance. While they helped with chores, they learned about responsibility as well as what they were capable of and, more importantly, what they deserved out of life. Jacob had a terrible childhood, but Huxley saw something very special in that boy. He decided to fill the void and give him a real home."

Veda's chest tightened and expanded all at once. It was easy to tell that Susan had a generous heart, like Veda's mom, who had always been willing to see the best in people. Sometimes that kind of faith was uplifting. At other times, it was naive. Even foolish.

As the music segued into a slower, older tune, Susan glanced up at speakers hidden among the fairy lights. "Oh, I love this song."

The lyrics spoke of stars falling from the sky and longing to be close to someone.

Veda smiled. "I know it."

"I was so young when it came out. Back then I couldn't imagine having a gray hair or wrinkle. Time's so precious. The most precious thing we have." She held Veda's gaze when she emphasized, "Once it's gone, there's no getting it back."

Just then, Veda felt Ajax glance her way. While his gaze, curious and hot, locked with hers through the crowd, Susan straightened.

"Well, I'm going to find someone to share this dance with." As she headed off, Susan gave Veda a wink. "Maybe you should, too."

Perhaps it was the commanding picture Ajax painted in that crisp tuxedo, the knowing smile hovering at the corners of his mouth, or simply the song that amplified the moment. For whatever reason, when Ajax looked between her and the dance floor and then raised his brows in suggestion, Veda felt slightly light-headed. A little too eager to agree.

Since sharing that drink earlier, the anticipation had

only built…delicious, taut and unrelenting. Now, as Ajax extended his arms in the air in front of him like he was already slow-dancing with her, Veda felt an unraveling. Like a corset being unlaced. Like she could finally breathe out and relax.

Time *was* precious, and this night and its challenges were almost over. Wasn't this an appropriate and mature way to say goodbye?

She walked toward him. He met her halfway. After taking her hand in his much larger, far warmer one, he turned to escort her to the dance floor. Once they were surrounded by other couples, Ajax positioned their joined hands higher near his lapel while his free palm slid around to rest against the sensitive small of her back. As he smiled into her eyes, she quivered with the same kind of longing the song spoke about. Which was only to be expected, and nothing she couldn't handle. And when they began to move, his expert steps guiding hers, she was okay with his strength and his touch. She had no trouble owning her body's response to his scent and his heat.

"You met Susan," he said.

"She's a big fan of yours."

"Ah, she likes everyone. Heart of gold."

"She said you're the reason she's here."

His smile kicked up one corner of his mouth again. "The first time we met, I knew she'd fit in. Turns out, even better than I hoped. She and Dad have more than a professional relationship now. They're more than friends."

"But they never married."

While he thought that through, his hot palm shifted on her back—moving slightly lower, pressing harder. "I've never asked why. Not my business. They're happy. That's what it's all about."

As his gaze brushed her cheek, then her lips, the sexual pull tugged even more strongly. Everything about him was soothing, beguiling, on top of being sexy to a giddy fault. If he ever took a page from his father's book and settled down, all Veda could say was that his wife would be a very lucky girl.

Lanie was dancing nearby, but she didn't seem to notice them, or anyone else for that matter. Rather she looked besotted with her partner, a classic tall, dark and incredibly handsome type. Interesting. Lanie was supposed to be into her career way more than the opposite sex. It was one of the things the two women had bonded over.

Veda asked Ajax, "Who's Lanie dancing with?"

Ajax didn't turn around to check. Instead the two couples drifted farther apart.

"Lanie has a lot of friends."

Veda nodded at the crowd. "At least a couple hundred."

"You wouldn't know it now, but once upon a time she was shy. Guess we all outgrow that childhood stuff."

Veda recalled Susan's story about the kid who had taken over the reins in an effort to help his grieving family. She couldn't imagine Ajax ever being awkward, lacking confidence, doubting himself or not having just the right words. Having just the right *everything*.

The song finished up. As the DJ cued his upcoming selection, the moment stretched out. Veda and Ajax looked into each other's eyes and invisible strings worked to tug them even closer together. When the DJ played a faster, louder song, Ajax led her through the crowd to a quieter semi-hidden corner where blinking lights didn't quite penetrate and only the most curious eyes might see. As they faced each other again, with his hand still holding hers, the physical awareness zapping between them became fully charged. She imagined what might come next...

Would Ajax lift her chin and claim his first kiss of the evening?

If she let that happen, she'd be lost.

Sucking down a breath, Veda shored herself up and announced, "I'm going to call it a night."

His head went back. "You mean *now*?"

"It's getting late." They had less than an hour until midnight. "No one's left that I know."

"You know *me*."

Intimately. But better to avoid that fact.

"Lanie's obviously occupied for a while." Veda remembered how entranced her friend had looked with her dance partner. She wouldn't interrupt that chemistry to say goodnight. "I'll call and check in with her tomorrow."

"You're not staying over? I thought Lanie might have offered you a—"

"I'm staying at Dad's tonight."

A couple of days ago, she had called to give her father a heads-up. When she'd dropped in there earlier today to stash her overnight bag and change, he had been reading a book in his favorite chair. He had complimented her gown, adding, "It must be a swanky event." When Veda admitted that she was going to help celebrate Lanie's birthday at the Rawson property, her father's fingers had tightened around the book. He had restrained himself from trying to talk her out of entering enemy territory, although he had made it clear that he would be waiting up.

Now, from their tucked-away vantage point, Ajax studied the scene again. The party had changed gears, entering the phase when formalities were over. Plenty of guests were still here, happy to let loose. Plenty of women with whom Ajax could become well acquainted.

But he only tugged at his bow tie and released a couple of shirt buttons as he said, "I should call it a night, too. Big day tomorrow. I'll walk you to your car."

It had rained earlier. Crossing from the shelter of the tent onto a wet path, Veda scooped up as much of her mermaid dress train as she could. After a few steps, however, some of it slipped, dropping right into a puddle. She was about to dive and rescue what she could, but Ajax had already gone into action.

As if she weighed no more than a bagful of petals, he scooped her up into his arms. When Veda flipped the fabric up and over her lap, Ajax's gaze caught hers.

"All good?" he asked.

She almost sighed. "All good."

As they left the party noise behind, rather than focus on her body's reaction to being pressed up against so much Rawson muscle and heat, she did her best to concentrate on something else.

"When was the family house built?" she asked, studying the majestic shingle-style Victorian.

"The original place was built a hundred and forty years ago," he said, his big shoulders rolling as she gently rocked to the swing of his step. "It's still standing just a little north of here."

Veda wondered if it was anything like the original Darnel house, a gorgeous but pint-size stone structure that she used whenever she stayed over now.

"This house," Ajax went on, "was built around ten years later. It's been extended and modernized, but its heart is the same. Earthy. Solid."

Through some living room windows, she saw a wall filled with family portraits—some recent, others obviously going back years. There wasn't a single photo displayed in her father's house anywhere—not of family or graduation. Certainly not of a wedding.

As those portraits slid out of view, Veda sighed. "Lots of happy memories."

"Oh, man, I had the *best* childhood. This was a great place to grow up, and with fantastic parents." As they passed beneath an overhead light, Veda watched a pulse begin to beat in his jaw as his grin faded. "Things changed after Mom died, of course. But we got through it. In some ways, we're even stronger."

Veda was happy for them. Was even envious, as a matter of fact. What she wouldn't give to have been part of a big, happy family. How different her life would have been.

"I didn't get to meet Griff or Jacob tonight," she said, "but they looked proud standing behind Lanie with you all before the cake was cut." After a brief speech, she had thanked everyone for coming; some guests were from as far away as Argentina, Australia and the Netherlands. Lanie's dressage events took her all over the world.

"Yeah. Great night. And tomorrow morning, over a huge breakfast, all the highlights will be rehashed and new stories shared...until we're all asking about lunch."

When he chuckled, Veda noticed that her hand had come to rest upon his chest. Along with the gravelly vibration, she could actually feel his heartbeat against her palm. Then he looked down into her eyes and everything else receded into the background at the same time his gorgeous grin seemed to gravitate a smidgeon closer.

If I wound my fingers into his lapel... she thought, *...if I edged up a little and he edged down...*

Then—thank God—they arrived at her SUV. Ajax lowered her onto her feet and, as Veda admired his profile—the high brow, hawkish nose and shadowed granite jaw—he gave a thumbs-up to the ad panel for her business painted on the door.

"Best Life Now," he said. "I like it. Real catchy." He nodded like he was invested. Like he sincerely wanted to know more. "So how does a person do that—have their best life now? Do you give talks? Teach classes?"

"I do both." She delivered her automatic line for anyone who showed interest. "You ought to come along to a self-improvement seminar sometime."

Not that she could possibly tutor him on anything in

that regard. Ajax had his life all sorted out. He was exactly where, and how, he wanted to be.

He crossed his arms and assumed a stance that said she had his full attention. "Give me the elevator pitch."

"You can achieve your best life now by behaving your way to happiness and success," she replied. "Start with healthy habits and surround yourself with the best. The best friends, the best information, the best advice, *and* be smart enough to take it. You should also go after the things that matter to you the most. Everyone needs to get behind themselves and push."

"Sure." He shrugged. "Get up in the morning and get things done."

Spoken like someone who'd always had his shit together.

"Did you know that some people struggle to even roll out of bed in the morning? And you need to look beyond the rationale of just being lazy."

"Look beyond it to what?"

"Maybe past trauma, dysfunctional family, learned helplessness."

His eyebrows drew together. "You can learn to be helpless?"

"Sure. It can happen if a person feels like they can't stop the bad stuff from happening, so they just give up."

The same way Veda had wanted to give up after her mom had died. She wasn't able to save the person she had loved most in the world. Worse, she had felt responsible for the accident. Constant feelings of worthlessness coupled with guilt had added up to a *why the hell bother?* mind-set.

Ajax's expression changed as his eyes searched hers. "There's a whole lot more to you, isn't there, Darnel?"

"A few layers. Like most people."

The perfect Ajax comeback line might be, *And I want to peel back every one, starting here, tonight.* But there were parts of Veda no one would ever know. Not her father or

Lanie. Not Veda's Best Life Now clients or blog followers. And certainly not Ajax Rawson…family rival, player extraordinaire and proponent of an industry that she wished would disappear.

As if he'd read her mind, Ajax's jaw tightened and his chin kicked up. Then, rather than delivering a line, he did something that pulled the rug right out from under her feet. He took a measured step back, slipped both hands under his jacket and into his pants pockets. The body language was clear.

Nothing more to say. Won't hold you up.

After a recalibrating moment, Veda got her rubbery mouth to work. "Well, Ajax…it was good to see you again."

"You, too, Veda. Take care. Stay well."

When he didn't offer a platonic kiss on her cheek—when he only pushed his hands deeper into his pockets—she gave a definitive nod before climbing into her car. But she hadn't started the engine before his face appeared inches away from her window.

The nerves in Veda's stomach knotted even tighter. Damn, she had to give it to this man. He'd waited until the very last minute, wanting to catch her completely off guard to ask if he could see her again.

Channeling *aloof*, Veda pressed a button. As the window whirred down, she got ready for an extra-smooth delivery. But Ajax only pointed down the driveway.

"Take it slow down the hill," he said. "There's a sharp bend near the office."

She blinked. "A bend?"

"It'll be wet after the rain."

When he stepped back again, Veda took a moment before winding the window back up, starting the car and driving away.

So…

Score, right?

Rather than trying to charm or argue with her, Ajax had given her what she wanted. A cut-and-dried goodbye. And the bonus: she wasn't the one receding in Ajax's rearview mirror. *He* was receding in *hers*. In fact, watching his reflection now, she saw how he was literally walking away.

Sighing, Veda settled in for the drive home—or tried to. After being so close to Ajax and his drugging scent, the car smelled stale, and following hours of music and conversation, the cabin was too quiet. Veda flicked on the radio, but she only heard that song playing in her head…the one she and Ajax had danced to all of ten minutes ago.

She shook herself. Thought ahead.

In thirty minutes, she would be turning into the Darnel driveway. She would find her father reclined in his tufted high-backed chair by an unlit fire. After inquiring about her evening, he would calmly regurgitate how he felt about his daughter consorting with the enemy. The Rawsons were cheats who would have their comeuppance. Drake never tired of admitting that he couldn't wait for the day.

Veda sat forward and looked up. Raindrops were falling again, big and hard on the windshield. She switched on the wipers, imagining her father's reaction should he ever discover the truth. Not only was his daughter friends with a Rawson, she had also—shock, horror!—slept with one. In his chilling way, Drake would let her know his verdict. She was no better than the woman he had loved *or* the woman he had married. To his mind, both had betrayed him with a cowboy. Then her father would disown his daughter, the same way he had disowned his wife. And there wouldn't be a thing she could do about it.

You are dead to me.

Dead. Dead. Dead.

Suddenly that tricky bend was right there in front of her. About to overshoot, Veda wrenched the wheel, slammed on the brake. As her tires slid out, she pulled the wheel the other way and the SUV overcorrected. A surreal moment later, it came to a jolting stop on the grass shoulder, at right angles to a heavy railed fence and the sweeping river of asphalt.

With those wipers beating endlessly back and forth, Veda white-knuckled the wheel, cursing her inattention. Her stupidity. But thankfully, she hadn't crashed. There was nothing that couldn't be undone. *So pull up your big-girl panties and get back on the road!* And she would...as soon as she'd dealt with the tsunami of déjà vu rolling in.

Mom sitting in the front seat of a growling pickup truck. Her cowboy boyfriend looking over his shoulder at Veda in back. A terrifying screech. A crashing, blinding jolt—

When her ears started to ring, Veda pushed open her door and scrambled out.

There were plenty of motels around. Or maybe she should simply drive on through to Jersey. She was under no obligation to see her father tonight. Damn it, her only obligation was to herself.

Not my fault, not my fault, not my fault.

At that moment, just as the skies opened up in earnest, a pair of big hands clamped down on her shoulders and spun her around. With hair whipping over her eyes, it took a moment to recognize the masculine figure, and then the concerned face streaming with rain.

Ajax raised his voice over the downpour. "What the hell are you doing?"

Veda thought about it and shrugged. "I don't know."

His brows snapped together before he threw open the back car door and waved an arm.

Get in.

The next second, he was behind the wheel, getting the vehicle back onto the driveway before turning, not toward the house or the main road, but into an offshoot lane. A moment later, they'd pulled up outside a building. After helping Veda out, he handed over her evening clutch from the front passenger seat and led the way to the building's main entrance.

Soaked through, her soles sliding in their heels, she asked over the noise of the rain, "Where are we?"

"Somewhere safe."

And yet, as Ajax punched numbers into a control pad by the door, the sign mounted next to it seemed to both mock and warn her.

Rawson Studs.

Satisfaction guaranteed.

Four

Entering the office reception area and flicking on the lights, Ajax was torn between a slump of relief and thinking, what the hell?

So much for carrying Veda over those puddles earlier. Now her hair and dress were drenched. Worse—and no surprise—she was visibly shaken. He could practically hear her teeth chattering. Had she been playing with her phone or simply off with the fairies when she'd overrun that bend? The bend he'd specifically told her to watch out for.

With Veda close behind, he strode down the corridor, past some other offices and into his private office suite— his home away from home. Running a hand through his dripping hair, he took it down a notch. And then two. The last thing she needed was a grilling. Far better that he shake it off.

"I vote scotch," he said, making a beeline for the wet bar and pouring two stiff ones. But when he brought hers over, Veda's nostrils flared like he was offering week-old hog feed.

"I don't drink hard liquor," she said.

"Fine." He lifted the glass and tossed it back. "Bottoms up."

After the heat hit his gut, Ajax found the bar again. "I'll get you a wine."

"Just water," she said. "Although… I've probably had enough of that for one night."

Enough water? Because of the rain and almost killing herself? But he didn't laugh.

Despite dancing together and their too-hot-to-ignore connection, by the time he'd escorted—no, literally carried—her to her vehicle, he'd made a decision. If Veda really wanted him to take a hike, he would comply, at least for now. So he had played nice and said good-night. Thank God he turned back around when he did. Seeing her almost take out that fence had scared the living daylights out of him. Veda must have gotten the fright of her life.

But now as she accepted the tumbler of water, he noticed her hands had stopped shaking. After taking a long sip, she let her head rock back and eased out a breath.

"I'm sorry, Ajax," she said, looking so vulnerable and bedraggled and all the more beautiful because of it.

With the tightness easing in his chest, he hitched up a shoulder and swirled his drink. "Ah, you're not hurt. That's what matters."

"I'll get out of your hair as soon as the rain stops. Promise. I don't want to hold you up."

Veda wasn't an inconvenience. He wished she'd just relax. That was sure as hell what he intended to do.

She pushed aside the wet hair clinging to her cheek and neck. "Do you mind if I take my shoes off?"

"Be my guest."

While she sat down on the couch to slip off her heels, Ajax shed his jacket and plucked at his soaked shirt.

"I need to change." He considered her soggy dress. "I can offer you a towel and a clean shirt."

Getting to her bare feet, she held up the waterlogged hem of her dress. "I'll take it."

Ajax slipped into the attached private suite where he spent most nights, and grabbed a freshly pressed shirt from the walk-in closet next to the bed. Back in the main area, he held the button-down out to Veda.

"How's this?"

"It's dry—so, perfect."

He pointed her to a guest bathroom with plenty of towels. As soon as she disappeared behind the door, he headed for his room again, ripping his shirt off as he went. After ditching everything else in a corner—shoes, socks, pants— he towel-dried his hair in the attached bathroom, then found a pair of drawstring pants. That's when his phone sounded in the next room. He recognized the ringtone.

Griff.

Hopping as he slotted each leg into the pants, he recovered the phone from his jacket's inside pocket.

"Your lights are on," Griff said when Ajax connected. "Want company? I have some stuff to unpack."

Glancing toward the guest bathroom, Ajax lowered his voice. "What's wrong?"

"Not so much outright wrong as possibly troubling."

"To do with family or business?"

"Both. I'll come down and we'll hash it out."

Ajax grasped for an excuse. "It's raining."

Silence on the other end of the line ended with a grunt.

"Okay. Got it. You have someone squirreled away with you down there."

Ajax was shaking his head. "Not what you think."

"Bro, you don't need to play Boy Scout with me."

"She had a little accident going down."

Griff cleared his throat. "Okay. Not touching that one."

"Going down the entrance road. Her car skidded out."

Griff's tone changed. "Is she all right?"

"Shaken, but otherwise fine."

"I'd ask if there was anything I can do but I'm sure you've got it in hand. Or she has."

He and Griff were of a similar mind where the opposite sex was concerned. Unlike their brother Jacob, who had recently found the girl of his dreams, neither Ajax nor Griff was ready to settle down. They dated freely and widely and, more often than not, were with women who shared the same philosophy.

Given what Lanie had said earlier, and Veda's comments about men with reputations, his current guest did not subscribe to that particular point of view, which didn't gel with her enthusiasm in Saratoga, but whatever.

Absently pulling the string on his pants tighter, Ajax said again, "Griff, this is not a hookup."

"So you two definitely won't end up naked together tonight."

Ajax looked down at his bare chest at the same time he imagined Veda's dress puddled on that bathroom floor as Griff went on. "Look, we'll catch up over breakfast. You ought to bring her along."

"Why would I do that?"

"Gee, I don't know. Manners? Food?"

"Veda won't be here in the morning."

Even if he and Veda *did* spend the night together—say, she curled up on a couch, shut her eyes and fell dead asleep—neither would want that kind of morning-after scrutiny. Yes, they were adults who were more than capable of making adult decisions. But after that "eyes and hands off" talk, Princess Lanie would blow a gasket if he walked into the house with her bestie hanging off his arm.

And Veda had that thing going on in her head about Hux—the story where he was supposed to have stolen Drake's future bride. *As if.*

"Wait a minute," Griff said. "Did you say Veda? As in Darnel's daughter?"

Ajax groaned. "Don't tell me you've got problems with that, too?"

"I, uh…" Griff exhaled. "Jax, we'll talk in the morning, okay?"

Ajax was signing off when the guest bathroom door fanned open. As Veda stepped out, every cell in his body stood to attention. The button-down shirt she wore was ten sizes too big, her towel-dried hair was a flaming mess, and what he could see of her legs made his mouth water. The unconscious way she used both hands to push back all that hair told him she felt more relaxed. Then she stopped, her eyes grew to saucers, and Ajax remembered.

She was the only one wearing a shirt.

He'd swear on the Bible that was not intentional.

"I, uh, got caught up on a call," he said, waving the phone.

Veda's gaze slid up from his chest.

"It was Griff," he said. "My brother. He saw the lights on here, so I filled him in."

"As in, I'm an idiot?"

"As in we need reflector lights on that curve."

When her eyes dipped to his chest again, Ajax reevaluated his position. He definitely had *not* brought Veda here to seduce her. Before his phone had rung, he'd had every intention of slipping on a T-shirt. But now he got the distinct impression that Veda wasn't about to freak at his lack of clothing. Hell, she'd seen him in way less than this.

Veda was crossing over to his desk. He'd left his hat by a stack of papers. Now she ran a finger around the black brim, then sent a bland glance his way.

"Every cowboy needs one."

"At *least* one. That particular hat's for dressing up." Like for meetings, events. He nodded at another Stetson on a vintage hat stand. "That one's for work." For when he was hands-on in the stables with the horses and his team.

She picked up the formal hat and sussed out its lines as he wandered over.

"I reckon it'd suit you," he said.

"Pretty sure you're wrong."

He took the hat, but when he placed it on her head, the brim fell low enough to cover her nose. He saw her grin before repositioning the inner band so that it was propped against the front of her crown.

"There now," he said. "Not too big at all."

"All I need is a set of spurs and a big ol' buckle on my belt—"

The hat slipped again. As she caught it and pushed it back up, he angled her around toward some mirrored wall tiles. Setting her hands on her hips, she struck an Annie Oakley pose, then pulled a face.

"Yeah, nah." She lifted the hat off her head as she turned back around. "Bend down."

She set the Stetson square on his head, then stepped back to inspect her work. As she took him in from top to tail, her grin changed from light and playful to *we're having too much fun here.*

Putting her weight on one leg, she crossed her arms. "Your other hat's black, too."

"Yep. All of them from day one."

"Which was…?"

"When did I get my first real cowboy hat?" He scratched his temple under the brim. "I can't remember ever being without one." When her lips twitched, like he'd said something funny, he frowned. "What's the joke?"

"It's just…at the risk of inflating your ego, you look like you ought to be on a billboard right now."

He flicked a glance up at the brim. "You like the hat that much?"

"I like the overall picture. Who wouldn't?" She seemed to gather herself, adjusting the oversize shirt's collar, before assuming an indifferent expression. "Just an observation."

Ajax's smile grew. "An observation, huh?"

"The hat, the smile. You know…" She fluttered her hands at his chest.

Chewing his inner lip, Ajax grinned more.

"I think you're flirting with me," he said.

She rolled her eyes. "I am not."

"You definitely are, and you know it."

"Ajax, I've never said you weren't sexy."

"Double negative, but go on."

"That's it." She glanced at his chest *again*, then, just as fast, looked away. "You can stop fishing for compliments."

"Well, I have something to say."

"Of course you do."

"You seem okay now. After that incident in your car."

"I am. Thanks again."

"And one other thing."

"Let me guess. You think I'm sexy, too."

Well, yeah. But that aside…

"Just thought you'd like to know—" he nodded toward the window "—the rain stopped five minutes ago."

Ohmigod!

He was doing it again. Being all mind-bendingly gorgeous, having her believe he was about to make a big move, and then—

And then—

Veda spun toward the window.

The rain had stopped?

"I thought it was still pouring."

"Nope." He rubbed his knuckles over his shadowed jaw as he peered out the window, too. "Guess it could start again, though."

Before she thought to stop herself, Veda smiled. "Yes, it could."

"But you said you wanted to leave as soon as it eased off. So, to be safe, you should probably make a break for it now."

That teasing grin, the mischievous glint in his dreamy blue eyes... He was just so full of it.

"You love playing with me, don't you?"

His smoldering grin spread wider. "I'll go with yes."

She'd put it another way. "You don't really want me to go."

"Wait. *You* were the one who said you wanted to leave. I'm merely respecting your wishes. Keeping you up to date. Making sure any possibility of you and me getting together again tonight is categorically off the table." He shrugged his broncobusting shoulders. "That *is* what you want, right?"

While his chin tilted downward so that the brim of his hat almost covered the gleam in his eyes, Veda froze. What was the right response? She wasn't completely sure anymore. The spinout in her car had brought back some ugly memories. Now she was with the man who had stormed down that hill in the rain to rescue her, which had made her feel not just good but safe.

And yet Ajax was the furthest thing from that. He was a prince in the art of seduction. He was in love with an industry she loathed.

For God's sake, he was a Rawson.

"I can see you're frustrated," he went on.

She grunted and shifted on her feet. "A little."

"Would you like me to fix that for you?"

Like how? By kissing her senseless?

He was blindly laying the hat on the desk while he studied her face and hair like she was a fine piece of art. Like he could devour her whole in one big-bad-wolf bite.

"Veda? You okay?"

She held her nervy stomach. "I'm not sure."

His gaze raked over her again, drawing out the moment, leaving her to wince and wonder and wait.

"You know," he finally said, "I wasn't going to push it, but we need to do this. We need to quit playing games."

"Playing games?"

"Come on, Veda. You know what I'm talking about. Just be honest and say it—"

"Okay, okay! We do. We need to talk."

A muscle in his jaw jumped before he gave a slow, approving nod. "So you agree. We need to be open about how we feel."

"And then what?"

"Then we need to do something about it."

"You mean the same something we did in Saratoga."

He moved closer, until his breath warmed her brow and the energy arcing from his body to hers could be measured in megawatts.

In his lowest, sexiest voice, he said, "I'm going to kiss you now."

Her insides began to throb. To beg. "Why…why are you telling me that?"

"I want to know you're okay with it."

"You didn't ask the first time you kissed me."

"Did you want me to?"

"No."

"And now?"

She blinked, then gave it up. "I suppose you can tell me what to expect."

His lidded gaze dropped and locked on her mouth. "This kiss will be soft and light. Just a taste. Just in case. Then, if you're absolutely sure, I'll kiss you again. Deeper and longer next time."

She croaked, "And then…?"

"Then…" He studied her shirt. "That'll need to go."

She swallowed and pushed out a quivery breath.

"Ajax…?"

"Yes, Veda?"

"I'm not wearing anything underneath."

His grin grew. "I was hoping you'd say that."

Five

This time four weeks ago, she and Ajax had been in Saratoga Springs. As they strolled around a garden after the charity event, there hadn't been a cloud in the jasmine-scented moonlit sky. She remembered how he had stopped to cup her face and then kiss her like no woman had ever been kissed before. In that instant, it was all over.

She was his.

For years, she had dreamed of Ajax Rawson telling her she was beautiful, making her blush. But that night he'd done so much more than that. He had lifted her up. Helped her to fly.

After parting ways, she'd decided that had to be a one-time-only experience. And yet, as his lips met hers now and sparks began to ignite, Veda only wanted to know that kind of ecstasy again. Suddenly all she cared about was Ajax, all night long.

That didn't change when his mouth claimed hers and she found out he had lied. This wasn't soft and light, or just a taste just in case. This was as deliberate as any kiss got. And then his arms wound around her, urging her in, and her hands found his chest, hard and hot just as she remembered. When her fingertips grazed his nipples, she felt his grin before he deepened the kiss…so penetrating and skilled, her blood felt on fire.

While she reacquainted herself with his shoulders and pecs, his hands trailed down her back until they were under her shirttails, kneading her buns. After each loving squeeze, his fingers slid together, scooping between the backs of her thighs. When Veda lifted a knee against the outside of his leg, his tongue stopped stroking hers for a beat before his touch went deeper, sliding along her sex. Each time he dipped a finger inside, pressing on just the right spot, she inched that knee a little higher and held on that bit tighter.

"I've thought about you every day," he murmured against her lips.

"Me, too," she sighed. "I've thought of you."

His jaw grazed her cheek. "Next time, you'll answer my calls."

She couldn't stop grinning. "Just try to get me off the phone."

He hooked both hands between the backs of her thighs, coaxing her legs apart as he effortlessly raised her up. As her feet left the floor and her legs looped around him, she clung to his neck before his mouth took hers again. Cradling her seat, he rotated her hips, pressing her closer, stoking that heat.

And as his hold grew firmer and the grinding got more intense, the friction began to climb…dear Lord, it began to blaze.

That night in Saratoga, Veda had given herself to him completely despite being nervous as hell. Ajax remembered how she had blushed while he'd gotten her out of that dress…how she had hesitated that first time climbing on top. Being with Veda had felt different.

Had felt…new.

Tonight, however, the training wheels were off. In no time, they had gone from kissing to full steam ahead. Now her legs were lashed around his hips, and every time he pushed in against her, the bulge in his pants just grew and grew.

Breaking the kiss, he set his chin on her forehead, found his breath and drilled down on necessities.

"Protection," he said.

Her teeth grazed his Adam's apple. "We need that."

As he resumed their kiss, her hand dipped under his waistband and coiled around his erection. It felt good. *Very* good. Dropping her weight a little, he balanced her on his thighs to give her a little more room.

A moment later, he fought through the pheromone fog to ask and be sure. "You're on the pill, though, right?"

Her grip on his neck slipped. At the same time he caught her, he moved to brace a palm against the nearest wall. A heartbeat later, she eased up and positioned the tip of his shaft precisely where it needed to be.

After that initial bolt of pleasure, he began to move. Not in careful, gentle *we'll get there* pumps. Tonight she obviously didn't need slow and steady, and you'd better believe, neither did he.

Her fingers were in his hair, knotting through the back, plowing up the sides, and he was wishing it hadn't been so long between encounters because nothing felt like this… Veda here with him now and all brakes off, letting him know that her reasons for staying away didn't matter anymore.

Or at least didn't matter tonight.

As her legs vised tighter and his hold on her butt grew

firmer, perspiration broke out on his brow, down his back. And then the responsible side of his brain kicked in again. *No glove, bro, no love.* Being inside her again was better than anything. But he needed to rein it in. For a start, he wanted to satisfy her first.

But it seemed, on that score, she was way ahead of him.

He was about to pull out when she ground in that much harder, deeper, at the same time her legs locked around him extra tight. When her head arced back, she shuddered and convulsed as her mouth dropped open and her nails bit into his neck.

God! There was so much steam and energy. Such intensity and blinding, shooting heat.

That was the second Ajax realized he'd just crossed the finish line, too.

Six

Amazing wasn't the right word. It wasn't nearly big or, well, *real* enough. With early-morning light filtering in through the windows, and Veda still asleep, the best Ajax could come up with to describe last night's reunion was explosive.

Lying beside her, facing her, he played with a wave of her hair as he recalled the conflagration when they'd come together. He'd been acutely aware of the heat as it built, the speed with which it had grown. But that tandem climax had caught him completely off guard.

Afterward, Ajax had carried her in here to the bedroom where they'd scrapped her shirt and his pants and played around in a warm sudsy shower. There'd been plenty of exaggerated lathering and just as much kissing. But after toweling off, they'd slipped under these sheets, snuggled up and fallen asleep.

As he'd drifted off, Ajax had embraced the feeling. Absolutely, without question, he'd been satisfied like never before. Now he wanted to coax her awake and not only re-capture it all, but go harder and deeper.

He wanted to know so much more.

Veda stirred. Tangles of red hair glistened in the muted light as she stretched and sighed and eventually blinked open her eyes. She smelled of soap, remnants of her citrusy perfume and a natural scent that aroused him possibly even more than the sight of her breasts peeking above the rumpled sheet. He wanted to trace the tip of his tongue around each nipple, nip and gently suck the tips.

Instead he brushed his lips over hers. When she sighed again, sleepily smiling into his eyes, he ran a palm up her side. As he found her breast, she slid her fingers back through his hair.

Angling his head, he kissed her slowly and emphatically while he rolled her nipple between a finger and thumb. Then, moving closer, he pressed in against her belly, letting her know how darn turned on he was. He loved making her come, making her happy. He couldn't think of a better way to kick off a lazy Sunday morning. Hell, if it was up to him, he'd spend the whole day here. The whole week.

Then Veda paused and shifted onto her back. Maybe she wanted him to use his mouth instead. He was only too happy to oblige.

But as he moved to go down, she caught his shoulder. Her voice was croaky but firm.

"What time is it?"

Ajax leaned in to circle the tip of his nose around hers. "Doesn't matter."

"It *so* matters."

A few moments earlier, he'd caught the time on his wristwatch on the bedside table. "A little after seven."

She shut her eyes and groaned. "I need to go."

"You do not need to go." He knew where she was headed with this, but right now they needed the outside world to butt out. "If you're worried about what anyone might think—" like Lanie or Hux, or Griff, who'd called it last night on the phone "—this is none of their business."

"It would just be so much easier—"

"You know what would be easier?" he cut in, edging closer. "If we finished what we're doing now. And later, you come up to the house and have breakfast."

She blinked like he was talking Mandarin. And, yes, he'd baulked at that breakfast idea, too, when Griff had suggested it. But now, after being with Veda again, extending that invitation seemed like the obvious thing to do. He didn't want to shoo Veda off like he was ashamed or some kind of prick.

"Sorry," she said, pushing up onto an elbow. "I don't work that way. I'm not going to flaunt it."

Ah, hell. He'd come right out and say it then. "You mean because your father wouldn't approve?"

Her eyes widened. "My father wouldn't be the only one knocked off his chair." She stopped, seemed to remember something and then cursed under her breath. "I forgot to call to say not to wait up."

"Your father was waiting up for you?" Really? How old was she again?

"It's his house. I am his daughter."

"And you're over twenty-one."

She switched tacks. "What about Lanie? What's she going to think?"

When she found out that her friend and brother had spent the night together? "Lanie wouldn't expect this. But she'll support you because that's what friends do. Siblings, too, for that matter."

He pushed up to sit against the headboard. Veda took her time but finally joined him. Wrapping his arm around her, he nuzzled her sweet-smelling hair and waited. He'd said enough. Time for her speak.

Bit by bit, he felt her relax. Eventually, she laid a palm on his chest.

"When I drove away last night," she said, "I was…distracted. Thinking about Dad and how he would react if he knew…"

Drake might get his nose out of joint, but dude. Suck it up. Except Veda didn't need to hear that.

Ajax stroked her arm, nuzzled her again.

"I'm sorry," he said.

"Sorry we got together, or sorry that my father's against anything Rawson?"

"Veda, I don't care what Drake thinks about me or my family. I care about how you feel."

She paused before she rubbed her cheek against his shoulder, nodding.

"I want to tell you something else," she said.

He held her a little tighter. "Shoot."

"When we were younger, I had a massive crush on you. I'd go to a race with my father and see you there with your dad. You were this tall, blond, muscle-ripped dream. Always smiling and talking. But I think an even bigger part of the attraction was knowing you were taboo. Forbidden. And even though I've moved away and have my own place and my own views, I always felt that was a place I could never go."

Ajax's gut was in knots. Imagine growing up in the cold shadow of a father like Drake Darnel. Sure, Ajax liked having his own father's approval, particularly when it came to looking after the farm and the business. Hux's middle name was High Standards. But they were still their own people who enjoyed a mutual respect. There was trust. A certain understanding.

Which was obviously not the case where Veda and Drake were concerned.

"So don't tell your father," he said. The silly old coot didn't need to know.

"It's too late for that. My car is parked right out front. Whether or not I sit down for breakfast with your family, rumors will spread. They always do."

"My family isn't into gossip, Veda."

"Maybe not. But you have how many employees? Riders, assistant trainers, grooms, barn and breeding managers? I just want to get in my car and drive away." She winced before giving a small, surrendering smile. "But I guess I'll stand tall and stay."

He got that this was hard for her, and maybe she was right. Maybe she should just jump in her car and forget the whole breakfast-with-the-Rawsons thing.

"Are you sure?" he asked.

A wave of red fell over her cheek as she nodded. "Except… I can't wear an evening dress or a man's shirt to your family's table."

"Well, I know how to fix that."

She was already onto it. "You mean contact Lanie and ask if she's got anything I can borrow."

Veda looked like she'd rather pull out her toenails.

"I can do it," he said.

"Thanks, but it'd seem less weird coming from me."

Just then his phone sounded. A text.

"Princess Lanie's morning ride must have taken her by here," he said, putting aside the phone after reading his sister's message.

Veda slumped. "She saw my car."

"She says that she just dropped off a selection of clothes at my front door, and she expects to see us both at breakfast." He cocked a brow. "Or else."

People openly talked about anxiety these days. No matter how infrequently, everyone experienced the sensations.

Racing heartbeat. Increased blood flow. Feeling uneasy, flustered. Even panicked.

On her blog, Veda often addressed the issue. Her philosophy? Accept that you're only human and embrace the idea that you can work through it. Having grown up with a learning disability, a self-absorbed father and a mother who "loved too much," Veda felt as if she had earned the right to give advice on the subject.

As an adult, she continued to feel the fear and come out the other side, like last night when she'd been left alone to speak with Hux Rawson. Or now, walking into the Rawsons' dining room with Ajax as everyone's attention turned their way. Even the golden retriever lying by the closed porch door lifted its head to check her out. Just like last night with Hux, Veda's throat closed while her heart punched her ribs like a heavyweight champ. But she would get through it.

She always did.

The stunned silence ended when Lanie called out from a separate buffet table adorned with silver-domed platters.

"You guys want a coffee?" she asked. Her attitude was, *Nothing to see here, folks. Just my lady-killer brother with his latest conquest, who just happens to be my friend and a Darnel.*

As promised in the text, Lanie had left an assortment of clothes on Ajax's office doorstep; Veda had chosen a mustard-colored sundress and matching sandals. And yet as Lanie laid two brimming coffee cups in front of a pair of vacant chairs, she avoided Veda's gaze. Didn't so much as try to return the smile.

As if Veda hadn't felt awkward enough.

From his vantage point at the head of the massive table, Hux Rawson nodded a greeting as Veda and Ajax took their seats to his left. Brother Griff raised his cup and muttered, "Morning," while Jacob offered an easy smile, as did the beautiful woman beside him. A high chair sat between the pair, occupied by a little boy playing "squish" with a banana.

Veda expected Hux to rise above any perceived awkwardness and say something inclusive...welcoming. But he was looking off toward an adjoining doorway—perhaps the kitchen—as if someone had just called his name.

As relaxed and charming as ever, Ajax did the honors.

"Everyone, for those who don't know, this is Veda."

No surname supplied, which set off a tug-of-war in the pit of Veda's gut. She would rather Darnel wasn't mentioned, but like it or not, it was a big part of who she was.

Jacob was the first to speak up.

"I didn't get over to say hi last night. I'm Jacob." He ruffled the boy's mop of dark hair, an identical shade to his own. "This is my son, Buddy. And next to him, the other love of my life."

The woman's eyes sparkled with obvious affection for them both before she met Veda's gaze. "I'm Teagan. Great to meet you, Veda. Can I just say—I love your hair."

Veda had brought a small comb in her evening purse. Not nearly enough to get through this morning's whole new level of tangle. Then she had used Ajax's brush to sort through as many knots as she could, which still hadn't taken care of things.

Smiling, Veda ran two fingers around a thick wave. "There's lots of it, and it's all red."

The oldest Rawson brother introduced himself. "I'm Griff."

Veda returned his smile, which looked a little wooden.

"Nice to meet you, Griff," she said.

"Did you have a nice time last night, Veda?" Hux asked as Susan entered the room. Upon seeing the additional guest, she hesitated before recovering to take a seat alongside Hux.

"It was a lovely evening," Veda replied without a stumble, although her hands in her lap were clutched tight enough to strangle someone. "Just beautiful."

"I got to bed around three." Having set down her plate of hash browns and avocado toast, Lanie took her seat between Susan and Ajax at the same time she blew a kiss to her dad. "Positively the best night ever."

Susan was looking past Lanie and Ajax to Veda. "We discussed a song, you and I."

Veda nodded and smiled. Susan was such a sweet lady. "It's still doing rounds in my head."

Ajax finished swallowing a mouthful of coffee. "What song?"

Susan sang a couple of lines about creating a dream come true, and then winked at Hux while everyone else either chuckled or grinned. Veda felt her own smile warm her right through. Yes, this was awkward. She and Lanie would need to talk later. But the overall energy said *togetherness*…said family ties and lots of love.

When Ajax pushed back his chair and nodded toward the buffet table, Veda followed his lead and stood up. While she put some strawberries and a lemon muffin on her plate, Ajax gathered enough food to stock her refrigerator for a week. Meanwhile, at the table, the Rawsons were back to discussing the party. The focus was off her, thank God.

While taking their seats again, Hux kicked off a different conversation, speaking directly to Ajax.

"I've had an interesting chat with Yvette Maloney. She wants to buy a few acres that butt up against her property, and for an eye-popping price, I gotta say."

"You mean the parcel with the original house," Ajax said, squeezing a pool of ketchup onto his plate. "Not for sale."

"That old place needed a bulldozer when Dad was a kid," Griff said.

"Not anymore." Ajax collected his silverware. "I've done some work on it over the years."

Hux's eyebrows shot up. "Where'd you find the time?"

"A day here and there." Ajax cut into a fat sausage. "In my opinion, those acres are the best we have. Yvette Maloney knows that."

The men back-and-forthed for a while. When the subject ran out of steam, Jacob took a fork and pinged it against his glass.

"Everyone, I have an announcement to make."

Hux swallowed a mouthful of waffle. "We're all ears, son."

Jacob reached past the high chair to squeeze his partner's shoulder. "I gave Teagan a ring this morning." He caught her gaze and smiled like only a man in love could. "We've set a date."

The room erupted as everyone got to their feet to give Teagan hugs while Buddy's plump cheeks pinked up with excitement and he slapped banana all over his bib. Veda remembered Lanie mentioning their situation. Jacob had been given full custody by Buddy's mother while Teagan— a billionaire's daughter, no less—was relatively new to such a family dynamic.

Veda didn't insert herself among the well-wishers. She simply smiled, letting the newly engaged couple know how happy she was for them both. The way they gazed at each other—with respect and pure adoration—it was clear they had a wonderful future ahead of them.

Suddenly the backs of Veda's eyes began to prickle. It happened sometimes when she thought about marriage. Kids. Of course all that was way down on her to-do list. Right now her focus was on her work and helping her Best Life Now clients achieve their goals. But one day she *would* like a family of her own.

And, boy oh boy, would she do it right.

Jacob reached across and lifted Teagan's left hand; a multi-carat emerald-cut diamond sparkled on her third finger. Standing behind the couple, Ajax glanced across the table and caught Veda's gaze. His brows nudged together and his head slanted before he returned his attention to the happy couple and their child.

"We'll need to celebrate," Susan said, drifting back to her seat. "An engagement party."

"My father wants to give us a party in Australia," Teagan said, mopping up banana from around Buddy's mouth. "You're all welcome, of course."

"A trip Down Under." Griff scratched his head. "What's that? A twenty-two-hour flight?"

"From this side of the country," Teagan replied. "I live in Seattle. Or *did* live there."

Jacob explained for Veda's sake. "Teagan's moved to Connecticut to be with Buddy and me."

There was more talk about the wedding, which would take place on the Rawson property, the same kind of elaborate party pavilion-style event as last night's birthday do. Veda thought about the distant future and the possibility of having a wedding at the Darnel estate. Her father was often so cynical and miserable, she couldn't see him offering his home, let alone being truly happy for her no matter who she married. Drake didn't believe in that kind of love.

Everyone returned to their seats and their various conversations. But Lanie still avoided Veda. Was her friend that taken aback at this turn of events between Ajax and Veda or was she simply annoyed?

Ajax was finishing the last of his hash browns when Griff caught his attention from the other side of the table.

"Ajax, you got a minute?"

Dabbing his mouth, Ajax looked Veda's way. She nodded. Of course he should go talk with his brother. It opened the door for her and Lanie to have a chat, which would include an explanation of how Ajax and she had first met. Simply put, she had fallen for Ajax Rawson's charms not once now, but twice. He made her feel so good. Like when they were alone, and in the zone, she didn't have to try.

Didn't have to think.

And, yes, she knew he'd made a lot of women feel that way.

Someone's phone was ringing. Hux pulled a device out of his top pocket and studied the caller ID with a quizzical look on his face.

Getting to his feet, Griff asked, "Who is it, Dad?"

"Matt Quibell. From the State Gaming Commission."

Veda didn't miss the look Griff slid Ajax's way before he said, "Maybe you should call him back."

But Hux was connecting the call. "Matt's a friend. He might want to congratulate us on yesterday's win."

Griff lowered himself back into his seat and motioned for Ajax to do the same as Hux Rawson swiped his phone screen to pick up. Lanie and Teagan talked across the table while Buddy sucked a piece of toast and Jacob looked between Griff and Ajax. Veda got that receiving a call from anyone at the Commission, particularly on a Sunday morning, was a big deal. But Hux had said this guy was a friend.

However, by the time Hux finished the call, with only a few mumbled words from his end, his face was gray. He dropped the phone on the table and fell back in his chair like he'd caught a bullet in the chest. Susan reached to hold his hand.

"What happened?" she asked. "Huxley, what's wrong?"

"Yesterday after the race, an objection was lodged regarding our runner in the twelfth," he said.

Ajax gave a slanted grin. "It was a dry track. A clean race."

"Matt wanted me to know the objection relates to allegations of horse doping." Hux's brows knitted as he eye-balled his son. "Those allegations, Ajax, are against you."

Ajax was lost for words.

He felt everyone's questions drilling into him and, holy shit, he had them, too. Overmedicating, doping…no question, it happened in the industry. But everyone knew that Ajax Rawson's horses won fair and square or not at all.

Shaking his head again, he tried to resurrect his smile, shake everything off, because this was crazier than purple snowflakes in June. It was crazy to think he would throw away his sterling reputation, and for what? A Grade 1 purse? Yes, his was a nice cut. But Rawson horses had won plenty and would win plenty more.

"That's a crock." Ajax scanned the table of shocked faces and shrugged. "It's a mistake."

Jacob asked their father, "Who made the allegation?" like he was already taking notes in his head for a legal defense.

"An assistant trainer." Hux was focused on Ajax. "He claims he saw your float driver, Paul Booshang, using a syringe."

Ajax heard Veda's sharp intake of air as he held up a hand. "Stop right there. Paul is a good guy. I trust him like everyone I allow near my horses. That assistant trainer is full of it."

"You left right after the usual samples were taken from Someone's Prince Charming," Hux said.

"Sure." Ajax shrugged. "I needed to get back for the party."

"Later, Booshang was questioned by a steward. Apparently he wanted to come clean. He said you'd done this kind of thing before. That you must've gotten away with false negatives in the past. Or you'd paid someone off."

Ajax's heart was pounding in his chest and in his ears.

Gravity wanted to suck him back down into his seat. But he lifted his chin and stood firm, even as steam rose from around his collar. Even as his hands fisted into mallets by his sides.

"I need to talk to Paul." Now.

"Good luck finding him, because I'd bet my right leg he won't be anywhere around here." Hux threw his linen napkin on his plate. "Expect a call after the EDTP results are in."

Ajax heard Teagan ask Jacob in a near whisper, "What's EDTP?"

In a low voice, Jacob replied, "New York's Equine Drug Testing Program. Postrace testing is performed by Morrisville State College under contract with the Gaming Commission."

While Ajax digested the news, Hux looked somehow resigned. Or was that disappointed? Impossible. Ajax's ethics were as sound as his father's. Hux couldn't possibly believe…not for one second…

Ajax remembered Veda sitting beside him. She was gripping the edge of the table, looking up at him like he'd grown a pair of horns. Like he was already guilty as charged. And if for any reason those results came back positive for banned substances, as owner and trainer, he would be held legally responsible. Whether he was involved or not, the buck stopped with him.

Sitting forward, Griff clasped his hands on the table. "I don't think Booshang acted on his own."

"He's in this with someone else?" Jacob's amber-gold gaze burned into his brother's. "Why would you think that?"

Griff's jaw flexed. "I overhead something at the party last night."

Ajax's head snapped back. *My God.* "You knew this was coming, didn't you?"

That's why Griff had wanted to talk last night. Why he'd been so eager to get him away from the table a minute ago. He wanted a huddle before this all hit.

When he was thirteen, Griff had decided to befriend a stallion named Devil's Fire. Now he absently rubbed the scar above his left eye that had resulted from a secret bare-back mount and subsequent fall.

"I caught a few words of a conversation between two guests you'd invited, Dad," Griff said. "One had a horse in the same race. I heard him say that a steward was speaking with one of our drivers who had links to…certain people."

Hux's voice rose. "Speak up, son. Links to who?"

Griff averted his gaze when he ground out, "Drake Darnel."

As blood drained from his head, Ajax shut his eyes. Booshang had worked for other stables in the past, including Darnel's. Obviously he hadn't held it against the guy. But now Ajax was boiling mad inside. Not only had Booshang abused his trust on so many levels, now Drake Darnel was involved? Was he that jealous of Rawson's impeccable reputation and list of wins that he would try to frame them? Or was this some warped form of revenge for Hux supposedly stealing Drake's girl all those years ago?

Like, seriously—get a life!

Ajax strode for the door. "I'm going to find Booshang, wherever the hell he is, and tell him he's got two choices. Talk, and fast, or—"

"Being a hothead won't solve anything," Jacob said, shooting to his feet. "We need some kind of strategy going forward."

Ajax took a breath. When Jacob had first arrived at the farm all those years ago, Ajax had been less than taken with the juvie kid from Brooklyn. Jacob had been defensive, on the edge. But Hux had seen something in the troubled teen.

Jacob had had to work to gain their father's trust but, hey, hadn't they all?

Hux pushed back his chair. "Let's get on it then. We'll need vet records for a start. And a detective to dig around and see if there's anything to a Darnel connection." He squeezed Susan's hand before he stood and nodded toward his den at the back of the house. "Giddyap, boys."

When Ajax saw Jacob ruffling his son's hair and kissing his fiancée, he remembered Veda again. He strode back over and took her hand. Hux's dog, Chester, scrambled out of the way as Ajax swung open the door and ushered Veda outside onto the porch.

"And you thought this wasn't going to be easy," he joked as he shut the connecting door for privacy's sake.

Releasing his hand, Veda continued to give him an unimpressed look.

"I need to go."

Ajax couldn't argue. He had business to take care of, no getting around that. And, irrespective of whether her nutjob father was actually involved in this mess, now Veda needed some time and space.

"I'll walk you down to your car."

"I can walk myself." Her stony mask eased a little. "I wanted to talk to Lanie, but that can wait."

What a mess. This morning couldn't have ended worse. "I'm sorry this happened."

"It's almost poetic justice, don't you think?"

"Meaning…?"

"You and I…not the best idea."

His chest tightened, but he managed a stoic smile. "Let me sort this out."

When he took her hands, she pulled away.

"Do what you need to do. I don't want to be involved."

He held her gaze. "Just so we're clear, I don't dope my horses."

"You mean with steroids? Or just with too much of the legal stuff? Everyone knows it happens, and way more than the establishment cares to admit. No one even talks about the jockeys' lives that are put at risk when a juiced-up horse breaks down."

Ajax shot back, "In case you missed it, your father could be implicated." Her comment stung, and he couldn't help himself.

"Go ahead and join the dots for me." She crossed her arms. "I know you want to."

"Booshang worked at Darnel Stables in the past. Given how much your father hates Hux, maybe it's a frame job."

"Why would Booshang risk his job and a fine to help set you up?"

"Geez, I don't know. Maybe *money*? Your father is loaded. And he still has it out for Hux. Poor jealous bastard."

When her eyes flashed and nostrils flared, Ajax knew he'd gone too far.

"I need the entry code to get into the office building," she said.

To get her belongings. He'd left his private suite unlocked, so fine.

But then Ajax paused. He couldn't be sure if Booshang was indeed still on Drake's payroll. Regardless, Veda wasn't involved. And the vast majority of his records were electronic. But if he allowed her unsupervised access to his office, to his hard files, would she be tempted to snoop? Not that she would find anything untoward. And he had cameras installed outside so he could check the footage later if need be.

He passed on the code and watched her stride off, red hair swishing, before he kicked a porch post as hard as he could. But he had to focus on his number one priority now.

He needed to clear his name, and if that meant taking down Drake Darnel as an accomplice in this lie...

Ring the bell.

Bring it on.

Veda felt as if she had escaped a war zone. Breakfast with the Rawsons was supposed to have been a little shaky but ultimately fine. She should never have agreed to go. She should never have gotten with Ajax again, full stop. For whatever reason—and there were a few—it was always going to end badly.

She took a shortcut to the Rawson office through a lush connecting paddock. Inhaling fresh air mixed with the smell of horse, she held each of her cheeks in turn, trying to pat away the heat. She had no prior knowledge of this doping incident. As for her father? Drake hated the Rawsons, but he wouldn't stoop to criminal behavior to discredit them. Absolutely not.

The Rawsons were the ones incriminated here, not the Darnels.

As for Booshang being the one at the heart of this matter...she wasn't about to blurt out her personal association with Paul in front of Ajax or anyone else; how suspicious would that look? She didn't know whether Ajax had worked with Booshang to dope that horse, whether he'd done it before, and she didn't *want* to know. As far as she was concerned, this was the end. Ajax could send as many flowers as he liked. He could call her until his redial finger dropped off. She would never buckle and see him again.

She couldn't get out of here fast enough.

Using the code, Veda let herself into the building. She grabbed her gown, shoes and purse and headed for the door again. But then a series of glaring thoughts stopped her dead.

Ajax's denial of involvement had seemed genuine, but

if he *was* involved, she doubted he would simply throw up his hands and confess, particularly in front of his family. His father. Could Paul Booshang prove Ajax's involvement? Might there be some kind of evidence hidden away within these walls? A signed contract between the two men, maybe? But where would a person begin to look? If she dared, how much might she find?

Veda's ears pricked up. Through the open door, she heard a dog bark and hooves galloping nearer. She hurried out.

On the back of a magnificent black Thoroughbred, Lanie was closing the distance between them, her long dark hair streaming behind her.

Lanie had been kind enough to lend her these clothes. Her friend had also offered a welcoming comment when she and Ajax had entered the Rawsons' dining room earlier, but she hadn't met Veda's gaze once. Obviously she wasn't happy about her friend's overnight arrangements. How much less impressed would Lanie be when she found out that this wasn't the first time?

With an armful of red evening gown, Veda was opening her car door when Lanie jumped out of her saddle.

"I thought you and I should talk," she said, tossing the reins over a rail as the Rawsons' golden retriever scooted to a stop on her heels.

"This isn't the best time," Veda said, dumping her belongings on the back seat.

"You stayed with Ajax last night." She was stroking her horse's neck. "I had assumed he wasn't your type."

"But then Ajax is every girl's type, right?"

Lanie's hand dropped. "Who exactly are you angry with?"

"I'm angry with myself."

"Because you made a mistake?"

"Because I made *two*." When Lanie's eyebrows shot

up, Veda slammed the door shut. "Don't look at me like that."

"Well, see, here's the funny part. Early last night, I caught him looking at you like a wolf might drool over a juicy lamb chop. I told him you were off-limits."

So Lanie had been looking out for her, defending her from her stud brother, while Veda had lied to her friend by omission.

Veda slumped back against the car. "I should have told you."

"You don't owe me an explanation. Women find my brother exceedingly attractive—irresistible, in fact—and he knows it."

"That makes me feel so much better."

"As long as the two parties involved are consenting adults who know the stakes, it's off to the races, as they say."

Veda opened the driver's-side door. "I don't intend to see him again."

"Because of this doping business?"

"Among other things."

"Playing hard to get will only make him chase you more."

Veda sank in behind the wheel. "I'm not playing."

The glint in Lanie's bright blue gaze softened. "You're my friend, no matter what happens between you and Ajax. And remember... I'm his sister, not his keeper. I don't control what he does, how he feels. No one does." Lanie shrugged. "And who knows? Maybe in you, the mighty Ajax will finally meet his match."

Veda was buckling her seat belt. "Don't be facetious."

"I'm serious. Although if it's proven that your dad is behind this doping plot..."

"My father is *not* involved."

Lanie's smile was wry. "For everyone's sake, I hope not."

As Lanie rode off over the hill, Veda counted to ten. She liked Lanie but she didn't like the conversation they'd just had. It brought back memories of her first-grade teacher, and others, telling her that she needed to be smarter. Try harder. It made her feel like she wasn't sure about their friendship anymore.

Like maybe all the Rawsons were more trouble than they were worth.

Seven

Ajax got to his feet as Veda made her way through the sea of round tables set up for the Best Life Now "Motivation Is Key" seminar.

"Surprise," he said as she jolted to a dead stop in front of him.

Veda's eyes were wide and her mouth was hanging open like she'd just seen the ghost of lovers past. Two weeks had gone by since Lanie's party, which had ended with him and Veda enjoying one hell of a reunion. While he hadn't phoned or sent flowers, he hadn't forgotten her. Along with the pain-in-the-butt doping scandal that hadn't found a resolution yet, Veda had been at the forefront of his mind, particularly when he lay in bed at night. It would have driven him nuts if he hadn't come up with this plan B.

Veda's presentation had ended ten minutes ago. While she had spoken with interested attendees who wanted to personally introduce themselves, the majority of the audience had left the room. Now Veda flickered a glance around, taking in the stragglers while running a palm down the side of her emerald-green pantsuit.

"What are you doing here?" she asked in a hushed, harried tone.

"You invited me," Ajax explained.

Her eyes widened again as she hissed, "I so did not invite you."

"You said I ought to come along to one of your seminars. I looked up your website, saw this gig, in beautiful Barbados no less, and ta-da!" He held out his hands. "Here I am."

Her chest rose and fell a few more times before she returned a smile laced with venom. "Well, I hope you found my talk enlightening. Now, if you'll excuse me…"

As she breezed past him and through one of the opened doors, Ajax drank in the vision of her swaying hips before he nodded goodbye to the kind and still curious ladies who had allowed him to join their table when he had arrived halfway through Veda's talk.

"If you're through for the day," he said, catching up, "I thought we could have a drink."

Veda smiled at attendees who nodded and waved at the same time she cut Ajax a response.

"I think not."

"Veda, we need to talk."

She hitched the strap of her carryall higher on her shoulder. "Nothing to discuss."

"You're not curious about the horse doping thing?"

Her step faltered before she strode on, chin even higher. "Not curious enough to get involved."

When they had spoken last, he'd said Booshang might be on the take with her father offering the bribe. He still had no proof of that, and there'd been some kind of delay with the test results. He only knew that given Drake's grudge, a conspiracy theory fit, and his family agreed.

Veda pushed open another door. Ajax was ready to follow her inside until the restroom sign stopped him dead.

Five or so minutes later, Veda emerged from the women's bathroom and strode past again, this time heading for the elevators. If she got inside, that was his cutoff point. He'd come here to talk, not to flat-out stalk. He was slowing his pace, backing off, when she ducked behind a huge framed poster set up in a largely unpopulated corner of the lobby. Then her arm slid out and a curling finger beckoned him over. Ajax darted a look around, wondering if this was some kind of trap, and joined her.

"I'll be clear," she said. "Ajax, I don't want to see you again."

Given the circumstances under which they had parted, he'd expected that. Now was the time to lay all his cards on the table. No holding back.

"I came here in person to let you know face-to-face how I feel about you. How I feel about *us*."

She looked unmoved. "I already know how you feel. You think we're good in bed."

"We aren't *good* in bed, Veda. We're *phenomenal*."

"Like you haven't said that to a woman before."

"I know you feel it, too," he said, ignoring that last dig. "Maybe it's because we both grew up in families who own stables. Or maybe because we're opposites in lots of ways, and opposites are meant to attract."

"Sometimes they repel. Like water and really oily slime."

He wouldn't take offense. "That's not how this is." He edged closer. "That's not you and me."

She hesitated like he might be getting through, but then she straightened and seemed to shake it off. "It doesn't matter that we share an attraction."

Damn it. "The point is I miss you. And I think you miss me."

When she didn't try to deny it, Ajax felt pressure as

well as relief. Taking in every beautiful inch of her face—apple cheeks, cute nose and lips that were parted the barest amount—he knew this was the moment to act. So he set a palm against the wall near her head and oh so carefully leaned in. When he thought she might surrender, before he could actually connect, she dodged under his arm and was gone.

But when he emerged from their hidey-hole behind the poster, he found that she hadn't run away. Her expression wasn't *I'm yours*, but she didn't look like she wanted his balls on a chopping block anymore, either.

She adjusted her bag strap again and conceded, "I guess…now that you're here…"

Ajax tried to hide his grin when he prodded.

"Yes, Veda?"

She blew out a resigned breath. "Well, I guess you can buy me one drink."

While they found a table in an open-air bar with a spectacular view of the ocean, Veda told herself to calm the heck down. Her hands wanted to shake. Her heart was pumping like a steam train piston. After two weeks with no word, she had assumed Ajax had lost interest. Which had hurt—a lot—but was better than the alternative, which entailed finding the wherewithal not to answer if he called.

She'd been beyond shocked—and pissed—that he had taken it upon himself to show up at this exclusive seminar out of the blue. How rude. How presumptuous. On the other hand, yes, she was also a teeny bit flattered. He had obviously been thinking about her, and God knows she'd been thinking about him, too…in more ways than one.

"So, you really don't want to know what's happening with that ridiculous doping allegation?" Ajax asked, like he'd read her mind.

"Let me guess." Sitting across from him, she inhaled the

fresh, beach-scented air and set her bag down. "Your lawyer brother hasn't found any link to my father."

The gleam in his eyes said *not yet*. "Although Drake was happy to make a comment to the press when asked."

"Unfavorable, I suppose."

"You could say that." He sat back, looking like a dream in a shirt the same color as the water, a light breeze combing through his hair. "Jacob has tried to speak with Booshang. He's not cooperating."

"Which doesn't let you off the hook."

Paul Booshang had implicated Ajax, but he had worked for the Darnel Stables in the past, when she was a girl. Back then, if her father had ever found out that Paul was up to no good, he'd have been out on his ear.

Then again, Drake didn't know everything, did he?

"So I presume the results were positive," she said.

"They haven't come back yet. Some kind of delay at the lab. In the meantime, Jacob has his people digging around, trying to get to the bottom of it all. Other than Booshang's claim that I organized the whole deal, there's not a shred of evidence."

"Or evidence to the contrary."

"And thanks for the continued vote of confidence."

Her smile was tight. "You're welcome."

An impeccably dressed waiter appeared, setting down the drinks as Ajax asked, "Have you spoken to your father?"

"I dropped in before driving home that morning. Word travels fast in the racing industry. He'd already heard."

"And he asked you to pass on his best wishes, right?"

"Actually, he said that he'd always known this kind of thing would come out."

"Particularly if he helped set us up."

She stirred her creamy mocktail with her straw. "When

you find out that my father had nothing to do with this, I'll accept your apology."

"I'll look forward to his apology as well."

That would never happen. Never in a hundred years. In a million.

"So have you and Lanie spoken?" he asked, changing the subject as he picked up his glass.

Veda remembered their talk outside the Rawsons' office building that morning.

"She said whatever happened between us was our business. But she wasn't exactly cheering from the sidelines. She said she is in no way responsible for your behavior."

He paused before setting his beer back down. "I don't need to defend myself."

"Then don't."

He got back on point. "I care about you, Veda. I wouldn't be here if I didn't."

Veda remembered Lanie's parting remark about her being the one who might bring the mighty Ajax Rawson down. Before that, Lanie had said that playing hard to get would only make Ajax more determined to see her again. She hadn't been playing, and yet here he was.

Which raised an obvious question.

"You must have pursued other women," she said, stirring her drink some more.

"The point is I'm pursuing *you*. Pursuing *us*."

With those seductive blue eyes smiling into hers, he looked so convincing. But if Lanie was right, Ajax's relationships were largely about the chase. Veda had been putty in his hands the first time; she'd been won over the second. If she gave in a third time *and* let him think that she was seriously falling for him, would the Stud pull back on his reins? If she upped the ante and said she wanted a future together, would he turn tail and run?

Pursuing him rather than the other way around was an

insane idea. Even dangerous as far as her heart was concerned. But now she couldn't help but wonder.

Ajax cared about her?

Exactly how much, and for how long?

"The seminar's organizers are putting on a dinner tonight," she said, really curious now. "I can take someone."

His eyebrows shot up. "You're asking me?"

"You want to spend time together, right?"

"Right. Except…"

Except, suddenly this was too easy?

"You don't want to come?" she asked, feeling bolder now.

He gave her a smoldering, lopsided grin. "Of course I want to come."

Veda's stomach jumped before she manufactured an encouraging smile.

"So, dinner tonight?"

His cocky grin widened. "It just so happens that I'm free."

Eight

Ajax finished fastening the Tiffany cuff links before swinging the formal jacket off its hanger and slotting his arms into the sleeves. Standing before his hotel suite's full-length mirror, he ran his fingers through his shower-damp hair, then blew out a long breath.

To the starting gates, boys.

Following Veda here to Barbados had seemed like a no-brainer. It was either make a big gesture or continue to have her sail right out of his life. He couldn't let that happen. Not without giving it his all. But he hadn't thought that getting her back would be this, well, easy.

As he sat on the edge of the bed, slipping his feet in his shoes, Ajax remembered how he'd imagined Veda's initial reaction: shock followed by a flip of the bird. He'd been stoked when she caved and agreed to a drink instead. Tying the first shoelace, he recalled how she'd warmed up more at the bar. Not only had she agreed to see him again, she'd invited him to this dinner. It had crossed his mind to suggest that she come up to his room beforehand, because by that time, he'd gotten the impression she wouldn't say no.

Pulling the second shoelace taut, it snapped right off in his hand. Ajax tossed the piece aside and got on the phone to the concierge.

"Strange request. I need a shoelace," he said as his gaze landed on the king-size bed. He imagined Veda lying there naked among the cushions, calling him over, and couldn't they please stay the whole week?

The concierge was saying it could take up to thirty minutes to have a shoelace delivered.

"I'll come down and grab one. Thanks."

This would be a good night, Ajax reaffirmed to himself as he left the room with one loose shoe. Better than their night in Saratoga. Even better than after Lanie's birthday party.

And tomorrow morning…?

The elevator doors slid open. After stepping inside, he dug his socked toes into that loose shoe while visualizing the most obvious outcome. Tomorrow morning they would make love for the third or fourth time since returning from dinner. Then they would talk, probably about setting a date to see each other again.

But he was snowed under at the moment. It didn't make things easier that Hux had been weird since that phone call from his pal at the Commission. And Drake's recent comments to the press questioning the legitimacy of Rawson's long list of wins certainly didn't help.

For years, his father had left the majority of business decisions to Ajax. These past couple of weeks, however, Hux was always in the office or hanging around the stables. Asking questions. Going over things. Once he'd even enquired about Veda, and not in a supportive way.

When Ajax left the elevator, he finally lost the unlaced shoe. Picking it up, he continued across the extensive lobby floor. He didn't want to think about that other situation back home now. He wanted to focus on Veda because he absolutely couldn't wait to see her again. The thought of her made him buzz all over, like his blood was vibrating, it was pumping that hard.

Sure, he liked playing the field, like Griff. And, yes, like their father when he was younger, although that had changed when Hux had met "the one." Apparently, back then, Ajax's mom had let her future husband know early on that she wasn't letting go. Hux said that after a couple of dates he had known it would be until death do us part.

Gripping that shoe, Ajax shivered to his bones. Committing to a woman for life was one thing. Having her taken away far too soon was something else again. Losing his sweetheart had broken Hux in two. Ajax had never contemplated testing fate the same way. He had never imagined himself, well…risking that much.

One lousy misstep and everything could be lost.

A man behind the reception desk ambled over. After Ajax had explained about the shoelace, the clerk went off to hunt one down and Ajax's thoughts returned to Veda. When he'd texted earlier, she'd said they should meet here in the lobby. He smiled to himself wondering what she would be wearing? The lipstick-red number was a hard one to beat, but then Veda looked amazing no matter what she had on. In fact, his favorite getup had to be that oversize men's shirt and black cowboy hat.

What man in his right mind would pass that up? Who wouldn't want to grab on and never let go?

Still holding the shoe, Ajax crossed his arms and exhaled. What a night that had been. It made him wonder how this evening would compare. Guess he'd find out soon enough.

And in the morning…

Tomorrow morning…

* * *

Leaving the elevators, Veda saw him standing by the front desk—holding a shoe?

Ajax looked particularly gorgeous in a dark blue suit that accentuated those beautiful broad shoulders all the way down his long, strong legs. But his usual cheeky grin was nowhere to be seen. In fact, his eyebrows were drawn together and his freshly shaved jaw was thrust forward.

She couldn't have anticipated Ajax showing up uninvited, for all intents and purposes, at the seminar. The bigger shock was her asking him—and in record time—to be her date for this evening's dinner. But she was determined to go through with her plan. Either way, this had to end. Better it be sooner rather than later and with her in the driver's seat.

Following Lanie Rawson's insider opinion, when a woman pursued Ajax rather than the other way around, he lost interest. This class of male was all about the chase. When she fully leaned in to grab Ajax's charms with both hands—when she let him think that she was ready to be his happily-ever-after—he would choke and retreat. Problem solved.

Of course, in order for this plan to play out, she would need to end up in his bed again. She wouldn't complain. Nor would she hold back. Tonight she had a valid reason to really let loose. In the afterglow, she would bring up the possibility of marriage.

Come tomorrow morning, Ajax Rawson would be running for the hills.

After a uniformed man behind the desk passed something over to Ajax, he took a seat in the lobby lounge. Now she could see that he was rethreading his shoe with a new lace. Drawing nearer, Veda watched the jacket stretch taut across his broad back as he worked. Even doing such a mundane chore, his moves were close to hypnotic.

She was closing the distance, almost upon him, when he looked up and sent over the slowest, sexiest smile. Veda flushed—cheeks, breasts. *Everything.*

As he got to his feet, she put her plan in motion, giving him an openly salacious once-over. When his smile faltered, she read his thoughts. *What exactly is going on here?* he was wondering. Then she stepped into the space separating them, set her hand on his lapel, pushed up on tiptoe and brushed her lips over the fine-sandpaper feel of his jaw.

"God, you look hot," she murmured near his ear.

When she pulled back, she could barely contain her grin. Ajax looked shell-shocked. It would sting like hell when this ended, but in the meantime she was good with having an obscene amount of fun. Call it payback for all the girls who had been left behind in the Stud's wake.

He cleared his throat, resumed that dynamite smile and acknowledged her dress—a sheath made from a shimmering Caribbean print fabric with a corset back. She had planned to wear a matching cap-sleeved bolero jacket, but in this case, less was definitely more.

"And you look absolutely beautiful," he said. "Breathtaking, in fact."

Playing it up, she glanced down at her bust. "You don't think it's too…snug?"

She had laced herself up extra tight to get the maximum advantage from her cleavage.

"Not too snug," he assured her. "Just right."

She glanced down at his feet. "You had some kind of problem?"

"Would you believe I threw a shoe. All fixed now, though." He stomped like a horse and then offered her his arm. "Shall we?"As they walked to the elevators, she was aware of heads turning, men's as well as women's. Aside from looking like Hollywood's top leading man,

Ajax oozed charisma and smelled divine. This might not end well, but right now it felt good to be the one on his arm.

A woman joined them in the elevator going up. Her bobbed honey-blond hair and black evening gown with its halter neckline made for a stunning combination. But all of Ajax's attention was focused on his date. On Veda. Given the famished look in his eyes, she wondered whether he might tell her there was a change of plans. That he was taking her straight up to his room and staying there.

When the doors slid open, Veda let out her breath. She'd been full of confidence earlier, but he was the one with all the experience. Had she bitten off more than she could chew?

They followed the woman out and headed toward the ballroom's open doors.

"I've already told you how beautiful you look, haven't I?" he asked in a voice that suddenly sounded deeper and slightly rougher.

She pressed a palm against her stomach to ease her nerves. "Breathtaking, you said, and not too snug."

"You smell beautiful, too," he said as they entered the room. "What is that? Something French?"

"It's domestic." And hardly expensive.

"Want to know something?"

He looked so intense and sincere, like he had a juicy big secret he needed to share. She smiled, nodded. "Sure."

"I want to thank you."

"Thank me for what?"

"For trusting me. For not walking away."

It was on the tip of her tongue…snide and a little bitter. *Has any woman ever walked away, Ajax?* But tonight was all about an experiment that had only one logical conclusion. She would continue to come on to him, strong and relentless, and be the victor when she scared him away.

* * *

Throughout the evening, Ajax tried to look interested. And he had to admit, there were some high points. Like the main course, which featured the freshest lobster on earth. Veda seemed happy with her vegetarian option. He guessed tofu actually worked for some palates.

The conversation around the table was...interesting. Their dinner companions were well-heeled folks involved in the self-help business. There was a psychologist guru and his wife, a personal budget planning person and her high-profile chiropractor partner. The rest were people who had enjoyed being part of the exclusive seminar audience today.

While awards for best this and most acclaimed that were presented, Ajax tried to remain present. Rather than let his mind wander to the challenges that awaited him back home, he focused on Veda. Along with that dress, which was stimulation enough, she was doing all kinds of suggestive things, like when she'd held his eyes while licking her dessert spoon real slow and all around. Or when she'd "accidentally" missed her mouth and spilled water between her spectacular cleavage. Either Veda was trying hard to let him know something or he was losing his grip.

A waiter was removing their dessert plates when Veda settled her hand high on his thigh. And squeezed. Ajax slid her a pointed look while what was behind his zipper paid attention, too.

"I guess you're ready to go then?" he asked as her nails circled, then slid higher.

Her smile said, *You'd better believe it.*

He was pushing back his chair when she said, "I need to have a word with someone first. I won't be long. Can you wait a couple of minutes?"

He scooted his chair back in. A couple of minutes? Sure. "I'll be here."

He watched her weave between the tables and people milling about, some leaving, others heading for the dance floor. He would have liked a cheek-to-cheek but she was obviously keen to slide into home base. Which, of course, ratcheted up his anticipation levels. Because this was a sure bet.

Like really, *really* sure.

"Excuse me. I saw you earlier in the elevator."

He focused on the woman standing by his chair. "Oh," he said. "Hi."

"But I feel as if I've seen you before that," she went on.

He smiled. Shrugged. "I'm not sure."

She took Veda's vacant chair. "Maybe in a movie or a magazine."

Ajax chuckled. "Afraid not."

"Perhaps I've seen you at a previous event."

"This is a first for me."

Ajax flicked a glance Veda's way. She was deep in conversation with a couple on the other side of the room.

"The woman you're with…"

He replied, "Veda Darnel from Best Life Now. She spoke today."

She glanced at his left hand. "You two aren't married."

He shook his head. Definitely not married. "Veda and I are…good friends."

Her eyes suddenly rounded. "Oh, now I know where I've seen you before. You're Ajax Rawson. The Stud."

Ajax gave a wry grin. Would he ever live that tag down? "I'm Ajax. Right."

"You own a big ranch. A stable." She sighed. "I love horses. I went to the Kentucky Derby last year. What an amazing day."

He paused, then turned a little toward her. "We lost by a nose last year." He mentioned the name of the horse.

"Oh, so close!" she agreed before arching a brow. "So which Rawson ride should I keep an eye out for next?"

"Actually, I have a good tip for the Breeders' Cup."

"So hopefully an Eclipse Award, too."

He looked Veda's way again. She was still talking. So he settled back and continued to share his tips.

When Veda turned back toward the table, her stomach dropped. Her falling-all-over-Ajax plan was working better, and faster, than she had even hoped. He was talking with a woman—the same woman who had shared the elevator ride from the lobby up to this floor—and looking more animated than he had all night. Like this woman was so entertaining, he couldn't get enough of her conversation. Like he was already over Veda after she'd lavished attention on him.

With measured steps, she approached their table and, gritting her teeth, joined them. It took a second for Ajax to realize she was there.

"Oh. Veda. This is Charlotte."

Charlotte continued to smile into Ajax's eyes and explain for Veda's benefit, "I'm a huge horse racing fan."

Perfect.

As Veda collected her purse off the table, Ajax got to his feet. "Did you catch up with your friends?"

"I did." Veda exhaled. "I think I'm done here."

When Charlotte got to her feet, too, Veda fought the urge to push her back down. "Please," she said. "Keep talking."

Charlotte tipped her head Ajax's way. "Your call."

Ajax actually took a moment before he replied. "It was great meeting you. Might see you at the Derby one year."

As Charlotte took her leave, Ajax reached to take Veda's hand. She stepped away. Frankly, she wanted to kick his shin. Lanie was right about her brother in spades. All about the chase.

"I really don't want to get in the way," she said, overly sweet.

He had the audacity to look confused. "What…you mean get in the way of me and that woman?" His grin was pure charm. "I met her two minutes ago."

"Well, you do work fast."

His look said *you've lost a screw*. Like she was cranking the crazy for believing her eyes, knowing his record the way she did. Her plan tonight had been to come on so strong that he lost interest. But now she wondered. Would he have flirted with that woman regardless?

"Veda," he said calmly, sincerely, "she came over and recognized me. I was filling in time, waiting for you."

As she studied those blue, blue eyes, her throat began to close. Irrespective of whether that was true, she felt like a loser. Like a lost, misunderstood teenager again.

She blew out a shaky breath. "Ajax… You do my head in."

He kept his gaze on hers, looking as if, for once, he didn't know what to say. It was her move to make, and she knew what to do. What she should have done when he'd shown up unannounced earlier.

She walked away.

"I'm going to bed," she said, and then added, "*alone*."

An hour later, she had changed into her pj's and was staring blindly out over the quiet moonlit waters, feeling lower than low, when she heard a knock. Knowing who it was, she walked to the door, opened up. Ajax stood there, his tie hanging loose, shirt half-undone, making *remorseful* look so sexy that she quivered.

"I'm sorry I hurt you," he said. "I honestly didn't mean to."

While her heart continued to break, she took a long, agonizing moment and finally stepped aside.

He crossed the threshold and, before the door had even

swung shut, somehow she was back in his arms, both hating and consoling herself for wanting this man more than ever.

After Veda had left him in that ballroom, Ajax went down to the bar and thought the whole thing through over a double scotch. She'd been open about her feelings and insecurities where his dating history was concerned. Talking to that woman… He hadn't done anything wrong. But, hey, he got where Veda was coming from.

He could see, he supposed, why she'd been upset.

Finally, he'd knocked back that scotch and then knocked on her door. After his apology, she had buckled and let him in. As soon as their lips touched, she melted in his arms. And as the kiss deepened and he brought her closer, he felt a tremor run through her as if she was feeling the same relief that he did.

"I didn't want you to come back," she said against his lips. "I prayed you wouldn't because I knew I'd give in."

His hold on her shoulders tightened as his gut clenched. "Veda…don't you know how much I care about you?"

She cupped his cheek and almost smiled. "You should show me."

Ajax slipped the tie from his collar and let it fall on the floor. Veda wasn't asking for sex. She wanted him to make love to her. She needed to know she wasn't just one in a line. Now he needed to know that, too.

As she led him into the bedroom, he took a quick inventory…muted light, turned down bed. Then he held her face with both hands before brushing his lips over hers, feathering kisses on each side of her mouth until her eyes drifted shut and her hands covered his. Then he kissed her more deeply, but not the way he had at the door.

He stroked and teased her tongue with his, every now and then adjusting the angle and taking as much time as he could. When his lips finally left hers, her breathing was heavy and he was aching to move things along. But this wouldn't be like the last time when he'd jumped off that cliff way too early. He wanted to arouse her to the point of begging, then leave her satisfied beyond ever needing to question again.

He coaxed her around until her shoulder blades rested against his chest. After sweeping her hair to one side, he nuzzled a trail up the slope of her neck while his palm skimmed up and down over her pajama top. Nibbling her lobe, he undid three buttons and then slipped his hand in under the silk.

When Veda sucked in a breath, he shifted to rest his cheek against hers and slid his other hand into the opening, too. Veda's head fell back against his shoulder as she trembled and sighed. And when she pressed her behind against his thighs and undid the rest of the buttons herself, he coaxed her around to face him and kissed her again.

He blindly stepped her back until her legs met the bed. Then, easing the silk off her shoulders, he kissed her a little harder. When the sleeves caught at her elbows, he guided her down until she sat on the bed's edge. Lowering onto his knees, he drew one nipple into his mouth while she held on to his head, grazing the back of his leg with her toes.

"Take your shirt off, Veda," he said sometime later. "Honey, lie back flat on the bed."

Getting to his feet, he ditched the shirt and belt while taking in the picture of her doing as he'd asked. Her hair was a burnished halo. Her expression said, *I want to please as much as be pleased.* Leaning over her, one arm bracing his weight, he hooked three fingers into the waistband of her shorts and, little by little, tugged them down. Dropping the shorts by his feet, he studied that part of her he ached to know again.

Taking his time, he trailed a fingertip over her smooth, warm mound before tracing a teasing line down the center and between her thighs. Then, kneeling on the floor again, he caught her ankles and set her feet on the mattress. Savoring her sweet, heady scent, he used his thumbs to part and expose her further.

When he finally went down, she held his head while he stroked her with his tongue and slipped two fingers inside. It wasn't nearly long enough before she was gripping his ears, beginning to tremble. And as he reluctantly drew away, she held out her hand.

"Where are you going?"

He showed her the foil wrap he'd retrieved from his wallet before tossing it on the bed and ditching his clothes. When he stood before her again, she sat up and immediately coiled her fingers around the base of his shaft. Ajax groaned at the rush of heat as she angled him toward her mouth and ran her tongue around the tip three times. When she gripped his thigh, Ajax closed his eyes as, shifting forward and back, he cupped and held her moving jaw.

Before he got too close to that edge, he eased away and saw to the condom. He thought about swinging her on top of him but instead went the more traditional route. As she reached to link her arms around his neck, he positioned himself on top and eased inside…a long, deliberate stroke that felt like it lasted forever. Then he covered her mouth with his, matching the rhythm of the kiss to his thrusts.

When he thought she might be close again, he murmured a warning against her lips. "I wouldn't count on much sleep tonight."

On the brink, she grinned as she asked, "So what about the morning?"

He wanted to answer that question but he only picked up the pace.

Now just wasn't the time.

Nine

For as long as Ajax could remember, he was always up with the birds. And yet catching the time on his watch now—

Really? Was it after eight?

On any other day, he would be wrapping up track work and thinking ahead to checking on his foaling mares and attending to the books. But this morning he was with Veda. Although she was obviously already awake.

Ajax rubbed each eye and looked around the palatial plantation-style bedroom until his focus landed on the open door of the vast marble bathroom. Veda stood with her back to him, brushing out those gorgeous red waves. She was dressed in a romper that showed off her legs and was perfect for this setting. While relaxed, the resort was known for its luxury and pampering. Its facilities included three golf courses, a dozen spa treatment rooms, each with its own garden and plunge pool, and a massive, multi-layered swimming pool surrounded by coral-rock walls. There was plenty to do.

Right now Ajax was only interested in private pursuits.

As he pushed up on an elbow, every cell in his body told him he needed to get Veda back here in this bed. And later, when she wanted to talk about walking out on him after dinner last night, he'd happily listen.

She stopped brushing her hair midstroke and turned around. Finding his gaze, her expression stilled before a soft smile touched her lips and she headed back into the bedroom.

"Morning," she said.

"Morning back."

Getting ready for her to join him, he readjusted his position, sitting forward, resting his forearms on raised knees and lacing his fingers between his legs. But she crossed to the wardrobe instead, finding sandals to slip on her feet. Then she went through her open suitcase. Was she searching for sunscreen? A hat?

Or was she just filling in time?

"You're ahead of me this morning," he said, combing a hand through his bed hair.

"You should see the sky. So blue, it's unreal. The water, too."

Her tone matched his—light and easy. Which was in stark contrast to the intensity of their bedroom marathon the night before. And when she continued to fluff around in her suitcase and the silence got awkward, Ajax's thoughts returned to the previous day when he had wondered how things would be between them *this* particular morning after the night before.

Yesterday she had gone from *please disappear* to *I'm totally yours* in ten minutes flat. And she had continued in that steamy vein until that woman, Charlotte whoever, had sat down with him to share an innocent chat.

Veda had a thing about his "reputation." She didn't trust him. Apparently not for a New York minute. He had hoped that the time they'd spent together here last night would help, but now he wasn't getting that vibe.

As he got out of bed to pull on his pants, she wandered out onto the furnished terrace. When he joined her, he was taken aback by the view of golden sand and, farther out, turquoise water scattered with diamond drops of sunshine.

"I love the hills back home," he said, breathing in the warm salty air. "But this is pretty darn special."

"It's supposed to be hot today," she said, gazing out, too. "But I don't feel it. I think it'll be pretty mild."

He studied her profile, the small straight nose, elevated chin, determined green eyes that were sparkling as much as the water. Her hands were clutching the rail like nothing and no one could pry them free.

She was right. He wasn't feeling the heat, either. Not like last night.

Making love, he had wanted to give her more, give her everything. Physically, they had never been closer. And yet now, he was up against that wall of hers again.

He rested his hand next to hers on the rail. "What have we got planned for today?"

"I'm going to relax," she said, closing her eyes and tipping her face more toward the warmth of the sun.

"Relaxing sounds good."

She took in a deep breath but kept her eyes shut. "What are you going to do? I guess you need to get back. Work to do."

He took in a group of guests relaxing on sun loungers on the beach. "I'll stay on. Hang out."

When she finally opened her eyes and slid him a look, he moved to cover her hand with his. But she was already turning away, heading back inside. He frowned at his bare feet for a moment, weighing things up. Did she want him to simply say, *Thanks for the sex, see ya later,* and walk away? That would make her evaluation of him right, but it was an empty victory if you asked him.

Inside, he found her flicking through some hotel literature. Hitching up his shoulders, he shoved both hands in his pockets and got the words out.

"I meant what I said last night, Veda. The last thing I want to do is hurt you."

The brochure crinkled as her grip tightened. Then she shook her head slightly. "Doesn't matter."

"It matters."

Her eyes met his. "Don't you want to know why I was suddenly falling all over you yesterday?"

Well, yeah. "I was curious."

"I was testing a theory. The one that goes, 'girl full-on chases Ajax. Ajax gets bored and gets another girl.' It didn't take long."

"Veda, that woman and I were just talking. I wasn't bored."

She crossed her arms. "Really?"

He hesitated.

"Look, I've had more exciting evenings," he admitted, "but that had absolutely nothing to do with you." And about that theory… "You decided to throw yourself at me so I'd get bored? Why?"

"To speed up the inevitable. To prove the theory right. Just look at your track record. You *must* be all about the challenge."

He crossed over to her, took her hands and held on. "I came here to be with you. No one else."

"For however long that lasts."

"Well… Yeah. That's right."

Her eyebrows shot up. "At least you're admitting it now."

"Yesterday, after our drink at the bar," he explained, "I felt on edge. If we ended up in bed again, I wasn't sure how it would be the next day between us. I wasn't sure how I would feel come morning. Not because I was bored, Veda." He put it out there. "Because I haven't felt like this about anyone before."

She blinked several times, then pressed her lips together.

"That's another line," she said.

He smiled into her eyes. "Let's just go with the flow. See where this takes us."

"You mean despite my father despising your family, and Hux probably thinking I'm some kind of spy?"

"Don't forget the fact that you hate the profession that I love."

"And neither of us wants anything serious."

That got him. *Serious* was an interesting word.

And best not think about that now because he could see that he might have turned this ship around.

Her lips almost twitched. "So, what's your idea of going with the flow while we're here?"

Squeezing her hands, he winked.

"Put on your swimsuit," he said, "and I'll show you."

"Here's something you don't know about me," Ajax said, while they settled into a pair of sun lounges set up in a quiet nook of the extensive pool area. "It's my biggest secret. You'll never guess."

As Veda heeled off her sandals, she slid him a look. Now this could be interesting. Ajax was pretty straightforward. Openly charming. Explicitly sexy. Here for a good time, not a long time. Whether he was actually flirting with that woman last night wasn't the point. His history of short-but-sweet was the problem.

And yet when he had knocked on her door, Veda had looked into those dreamy blue eyes and rolled over. Which could be viewed as weak or simply taking what she wanted. And, of course, she hadn't been disappointed. Ajax had a way of bringing out the very best in her, with his hands and his tongue and his…well, *everything*. This morning, however, she'd been torn between wanting to jump on him again and wondering whether he was thinking she was way too easy.

And that's how she had ended up here, making the decision to simply relax in the Barbados sunshine with Ajax and his drool-worthy body. This man was her Achilles' heel, and ultimately, there would be a price to pay. But not today.

Not today.

He was talking about his biggest secret…

"Let's see." Pretending to think long and hard, she tapped her chin. "You love soppy movies?"

"Other than *The Longest Ride*, not a chance."

"You're an alien conspiracy diehard."

"Really good guess, but no tamale."

"You think only one game of football should be televised per week."

He chuckled. "My secret is that I used to be afraid of water. Couldn't swim. Not a stroke."

Veda slid her gaze from him to the pool, then back again. "You did say used to be, right? How'd you get over it?"

"Hux had the same fear when he was a kid," he said, flipping the lid open on the sunscreen. "Want me to do your shoulders?"

After ditching her wrap, she swept her hair to one side. Her swimsuit wasn't anything outrageously sexy—just a semi-fitted white tankini top that fell to her navel and black bikini bottoms that pretty much covered both cheeks.

"Is Griff afraid of water, too?" she asked, turning around. "I haven't heard Lanie ever mention it."

"Just me and Dad," he said as a big, hot, borderline rough hand smeared cream between her shoulder blades. "We have a huge pool at home. One summer when I was eight, he had me in there every day. It took a while but he was patient."

Veda's eyes drifted shut. He was using both hands now, working over her shoulders and down her arms.

Feeling a little dreamy, she asked, "So you went on to win every race at the school meets?"

"I never won a ribbon in the pool." He was close behind her now, reaching around to rub her thighs. "But I no longer freak out at the thought of my head going under, so all good." He made a shivering sound. "I'll never forget the feeling, though. Total panic."

"I can identify."

"You needed heavy-duty swimming lessons, too?"

"Heavy-duty *reading* lessons." She took a breath and let it all out. "I'm dyslexic." When she felt his hands draw away, she turned back around. "I get letters confused," she said. "Jumbled. Back to front."

"Dyslexic. Right." He nodded, then nodded again. "I mean, I've heard of it."

"It set me back when I was younger, in a whole lot of ways."

"You mean at school?"

"I didn't understand why other kids weren't turned off by books or writing the way I was. I didn't get how they put letters together to make words, let alone sentences. I actually thought it was some kind of joke and I was the punch line."

"So when did the teacher tell your parents?"

"I wasn't diagnosed until years later."

He rocked back. "You mean you went all the way through struggling like that?"

The sunscreen bottle lay on the lounger next to his leg. She grabbed it up and explained, "I did really well in math. Maybe it's a compensatory thing, but my brain does way better with numbers."

"Getting through something like that… It must be a huge inspiration for the people you coach."

She held off squirting sunscreen into her palm. "We were talking about secrets, remember?"

"Oh. So who else knows?"

"My dad. Now you. Turn around."

He swung his legs over to the lounger's other side and then there was his back...bare, broad and perfectly bronzed. As she rubbed the hot, smooth slopes on either side of his neck, she imagined him working in the sun with his horses, sans shirt, jeans riding low.

"So you're obviously over it," he said as she continued to stroke and rub.

"You don't get over dyslexia. But you can learn to work with it. In a lot of ways, I don't think of it as a disability. I had to try harder at a lot of things. Some of my grades sucked. But along the way I've learned other stuff like keeping things clear-cut and how to delegate. I've honed my concentration skills and try to listen to intuition."

His beautiful shoulders rolled back. "How did your parents react when they found out?"

Her stomach balled up before she squeezed more sunscreen into her palm. "It was after my mom died."

He paused before asking, "Did your dad help?"

"Not like yours with the swimming." Her father hadn't been hands-on. "He took me to professionals." For her dyslexia and also to help manage her grief. "He's never been big on communication." She rubbed Ajax's back again, painting a big circle, then sweeping her hand up and down. "Maybe that's where I get it from." Maybe Drake was dyslexic, too. Sure, she saw him with books, reading. That didn't mean it was easy.

"Veda, you're a great communicator. I was glued to my seat listening to you on that stage yesterday."

"Ha! You were not."

He turned back around. "No lie."

"Well, I'm not a natural at it. The big D held me back in

a lot of ways other than schoolwork. I was socially awkward through the roof. I never felt like I fit. Some kids at school made it way worse."

"You were bullied."

She nodded. "Whenever I got stressed, like if I had to read in front of class, my brain would freeze. It literally wouldn't work. I'd get this feeling like fingers closing around my throat. No words would come out. I was completely mute."

He leaned closer. "When was the last time it happened?"

"Not for ages. Until a little attack at Lanie's party when she introduced me to your dad and then left us alone."

"But Dad's easy to talk to."

"He is. But remember our family feud? Huge trigger. I got a few words out but by the time he left, Hux thought I was a kook. That's the other thing. When you have this problem, which is *not* the same as being shy, people don't know what to make of it. Make of you. Some wonder if you're just too stuck-up to talk to them, or maybe your IQ must be low." She winced. "Really not a nice place to be."

When he took her hand and smiled, her everything, inside and out, smiled, too.

"This is what we're going to do," he said. "We're going to swim out into the middle of that pool. I'm going to keep us afloat and listen while you tell me all about what's next on the Veda Darnel Kick Ass agenda."

Still smiling, she nodded. "I like that idea."

Hand in hand, they waded in and then freestyled out until the water was up to his chest and she couldn't touch the bottom. Then he wrapped his arms around her waist and twirled.

"Not feeling anxious?" she asked, holding on to his shoulders and winding her legs around his hips.

"Not in the least. Feeling good. Feeling *great*. And I'm listening."

"Well, if you really want to know, large scale, I do have a dream. I don't know when but I feel it'll happen some-time, even if it's when I need dentures and three naps a day. I would love to have a quiet acre or two for a rescue farm," she said.

"What kind of animals? Because I can't possibly guess."

"Right. Horses. But also sheep, chickens, ducks, pigs. Actually, did you know pigs are supposed to be more in-telligent than dogs?"

A sexy grin hooked his mouth. "I did not know that."

"Some say pigs are the fifth most intelligent animal in the world. They're capable of learning how to do simple jigsaw puzzles and work basic remote controls."

"*Sold*. We definitely need lots of pigs."

She laughed at his gorgeous smiling eyes. "Lots of ev-erything."

"You might need more than a couple acres then."

"Sure. Like I said. It's a ways off yet."

His hands were sliding up and down her back, making her tingle…making her hot.

"So, what are you going to call your first pet pig?"

"Well, Wilbur and Babe are already taken."

"Porky, too." Sliding and swirling, he touched his nose to hers. "I've got one for a sheep. Baa-bardos."

She smothered a bigger smile. "And people say you aren't funny."

"Oh, yeah? Want to hear a dirty joke?"

"Do I have a choice?"

"A white horse fell in a puddle of mud."

Before she could roll her eyes, he started tickling her ribs until she was splashing around, laughing so hard.

"I can do this all day," he said. "Take it back. Take it back."

"Okay, okay! You're funny. *So* funny."

"And you're beautiful. And really easy to tickle." He

came in to graze his lips over hers. His deep voice rumbled through her when he said, "I'm glad we're here together."

Catching her breath, easing out a sigh, she ran her palms over his warm, wet shoulders. "I'm glad we are, too."

As he held her by the hips, his eyes drifted shut. Then he nipped her lower lip and ran the tip of his tongue over the seam.

"What's your intuition saying now?" he murmured, staying close.

"That you need to prove just how good you are in the water."

When she found his arousal well below the surface, his mouth automatically claimed hers. By the time he broke the kiss, in Veda's mind, they were completely alone. In their own world.

She shivered as he nibbled that sensitive sweep of her neck.

"Veda?" he asked.

Eyes closed, she cupped his scratchy jaw. "Hmm?"

"I think we need to go back to the room."

And then he was kissing her again, and in that wet, steamy, crazy-for-you moment, she was already thinking about next time...dreaming about seeing her Ajax again.

Ten

Early the next morning, Veda and Ajax said a reluctant goodbye at the airport before boarding separate flights. Back in New Jersey hours later, still unpacking while smiling over the memories, Veda answered a knock on her condo door and almost fell over. This was the last person she expected to show up unannounced today. And, given her ongoing fling with Ajax, pretty much the last person she wanted to see.

"I was down this way," her father said, placing his tweed duckbill cap on the hatstand as he made a point of stepping around her to walk inside.

She took a moment to remember to breathe while Drake assessed the surroundings, taking a token interest in the bookshelf while running a fingertip over the self-help titles. He had asked for her address ages ago but had never arranged to visit, let alone simply dropped in.

"Well…can I get you something to drink?" she asked.

"Green tea?" He retrieved a handkerchief from his dress pants pocket and wiped his fingertip clean. "Very hot."

"I have coffee. Freshly brewed."

He took a moment to accept that option and then added, "No sugar, of course."

Walking to the kitchen, she felt rather than heard him behind her. For as long as she could remember, Drake had worn the same aftershave. More often than not, the scent stirred feelings of unease. As she had told Ajax yesterday, Drake wasn't a total monster; after her mother's accident, he had gotten her help. But he wasn't demonstrative as far as fatherly affection was concerned. He certainly hadn't shown love toward his wife.

Now the nostrils of his long thin nose flared like he was either opposed to the aroma of her coffee or, more likely, the space in general. Her condo was the polar opposite of Darnel Manor, as in modern and personal rather than ridiculously grand and, in so many ways, stuck in the past.

"There's a courtyard," she said, retrieving cups from the cabinet. "It's such a nice day out."

He nodded, then asked, "How long have you been here now?"

"Three years. It's home."

He grunted—the sound someone might make when they were on the verge of being bored stiff.

She led him through to the courtyard, which was littered with fallen leaves and petals from a vine. As she set down their cups on the tabletop, Drake snapped out his handkerchief again to dust down his seat.

"Are you staying in the city?" she asked, taking a chair. Drake had friends in Manhattan.

"I'm here to speak with you."

Veda caught something knowing lurking in the shadows of his eyes and then, of course, this shock visit made sense. Drake must have heard through the grapevine that she was romantically involved with a Rawson and couldn't wait to express his opinion. On the outside, he was his usual up-tight self. On the inside—oh, how it must bite.

His question, "Is it true?" confirmed her guess.

She wasn't after a fight. Nor would she lie or shrivel up in a corner.

"Yes." She lifted her cup. "It's true."

He carefully lowered himself into his chair. "You're asking for trouble. You know that, don't you? It was bad enough when you became friends with the girl."

"You mean Lanie Rawson."

"Yes. *Rawson*." His lips pursed and twitched. "I can't believe it. Can't believe it of my own daughter. You know the kind of people they are. The kind of *men*. The father has no scruples. And the sons…" He made a face like bile had risen in his throat. "I wouldn't be the least surprised if they all had diseases."

"Like Ebola?"

"Sexually transmitted."

After tsking, he took a mouthful of coffee, rather inelegantly, Veda thought.

"That boy is even worse than his father," he said.

"Worse?" She arched a brow. "Or better?"

Drake's chin began to quiver. Not because he was going to cry. Because he was livid and showing it.

"I didn't think you could ever betray me like this. Not like this."

Using that grudge from his past as an excuse to act out had been warped enough when he'd used it against her mother.

"You do realize that I'm your daughter, right? Not the woman who left you for Hux Rawson."

Getting to his feet, he retrieved something from his shirt pocket—a page torn from a magazine—and read it out loud.

"'Ajax Rawson, also known as the Stud, was spotted

with another beautiful female companion. Life coach Veda Darnel, daughter of longtime Rawsons critic Drake Darnel, looks smitten. We wish her luck.'"

Her father was coming around the table, standing beside her, almost begging.

"Veda…darling…he'll hurt you. Then he'll leave you."

She glared at him. "Because everyone leaves you, Dad?"

She and Drake had words after that. She said some things that she'd kept buried for way too long. And she was still pacing, fuming, long after he'd left.

She didn't owe that man an explanation. This was her life now, not her mother's and certainly not his. And yet in some ways she felt fourteen again, when her father could barely look at her because she had sided with her mom. Now she wondered more than ever: Would Drake have loved her less or more if he ever found out she was responsible for the death of his wife?

When her cell phone rang later that day, Veda had almost succeeded in pushing her father out of her mind. She needed positivity in her life, not smothering and controlling.

When she answered the call, an official-sounding woman asked to confirm with whom she was speaking. Then this woman passed on all the information that she had…said she was sorry…and, yes, most definitely…it would be wise to come to the hospital right away.

When Ajax arrived back at the farm, all kinds of shit was hitting the fan.

Even before entering the office building, he heard the raised voice. Striding through, he found his private door open. When he saw papers and files strewn all over the damn place, he was so taken aback, he couldn't contain the growl.

"What the hell is going on?"

Hux sat behind Ajax's desk, poring over an assortment

of splayed documents. When he looked up from the mess, his eyes were more unhinged than blue.

"What do you *think* is going on?" Hux fell back in the high-backed chair. "Did you even bother to open Jacob's messages?"

Charging forward, Ajax started stacking papers. "I spoke to Jacob an hour ago."

"So you know they want to look through your veterinary records."

"We went over them two weeks ago. There's nothing to see."

"The stewards have scheduled a meeting with you and Booshang this Friday. After the delay, the test results are expected to land that morning."

"We'll be ready. If there's a fine or suspension, we'll deal with it."

Hux shot to his feet. "Damn it, Ajax! This is serious." *For God's sake.* "My books and stables are *clean*."

"A Triple Crown trainer…and now your reputation will be—"

"Hux, get off my back!"

His father's eyes blazed before he moved to the window to gaze out over the stables. "Yesterday, two clients loaded their horses and took them away."

Which clients? What horses?

Exhaling, Ajax shoved the documents aside. "They'll come back when this is sorted out."

"And if there's a next time?"

Ajax studied his father and said it out loud.

"You can't seriously think I'm actually involved in this."

Hux slumped and shook his head. "No, no. Of course not."

"Then what were you thinking going through all this? There's nothing to find here. I told you. I'm clean…even if a lot of other trainers can't say the same."

Hux waved that away, but it was a valid point. As much as he loved horse racing, Veda was right. Everyone in the industry knew that doping, or at the very least overmedicating, was a problem.

Hux visibly gathered himself before asking, "Where were you this weekend?"

"I haven't had a day off in months. I needed a break."

"With the Darnel girl?"

"Her name is Veda." He grabbed his work hat, stuck it on his head. "And she's not a girl."

"Don't you think it's strange that she suddenly befriended Lanie and now you? When we spoke alone at the party, frankly I thought she was hiding something."

"Like she'd joined her father and Booshang in a vendetta against us?" *Oh, please.* Ajax headed for the door. "We don't know that Drake is involved in any way."

"Griff heard his name mentioned that night. Darnel is spouting off to the press."

Ajax had his doubts, too, but, "That's not proof. And it's certainly not any reason to ransack my office and send the hounds after Veda."

While Ajax stood at the door, his demeanor more than implying that Hux needed to leave, Hux's expression changed from frustration to something akin to enlightenment. His voice was a disbelieving rasp.

"My God. Ajax...you're serious about her, aren't you?"

"Dad, that's none of your business."

"You've always wanted to do things your own way," Hux said, moving closer. "Always wanted to lead the pack. Make an impression."

"If you mean like working my ass off to keep this place afloat when you could barely drag yourself out of bed—" Ajax thumped the door "—yeah, I lead the pack."

"Your mother had died—" Hux snapped his fingers "—just like that."

"She'd been sick for months." Ajax swallowed hard. "And she was my mother as much as your wife. Damn it, I was hurting, too. But I kept pushing forward." He gritted his teeth, shook his head and ground the words out. "I never understood why you resented that."

"I'm sure I've thanked you, and way more than once."

"With a clap on the back and a wage that hardly reflects what I bring in for this place. Griff just has to smile and you gush over how brilliant he is. I'll puke if I have to hear again how proud you are of Jacob."

Hux pulled a pained face. "You're jealous of your brothers?"

"I'm tired of bending over backward trying to please you." Ajax squared his shoulders. "This place would fall apart without me."

Hux's chin lifted. "Please don't think you're indispensable, because, I can assure you, none of us are."

When his father stormed out, Ajax fought the urge to follow and bawl him out some more. It hurt like hell to have that conversation. Hux was a good father, but this had been brewing for too long. Since his mother had passed away, rather than a son, Ajax had felt like an employee needing to jump through higher and higher hoops. Well, he was sick and tired of proving himself.

He slammed the door and wandered over to the window. An assistant trainer was working with a new boarder in the arena. In the lower paddock, a stallion was shaking his mane, enjoying the sunshine. Ajax loved this life, from keeping a close eye on foaling rates to writing up owner updates and finalizing racing nominations.

But what was his future here? He wanted his father to live to a hundred, but was he prepared to do pretty much all of the work only to be reminded in times like these that he wasn't really in charge? Had Hux ever truly considered handing over the reins one day?

And Veda...

No one would tell him whom he could or could not see. And if his father didn't like it—if Hux had suspicions with regard to Veda's motives—he could blow it out his pipe. Because Veda was not working with her father to bring them all down. She had way more integrity than that. He'd bet his life on it.

Ajax drew out his phone.

He might come across sounding needy, but he had to hear her voice about now. Although it had started off shaky, their time in Barbados has been the best. They had parted with an understanding that they would see each other again soon, and he appreciated that was a huge deal for her.

It was for him, too.

"Ajax?"

The boost he felt from hearing her say his name didn't last long. Rather than sounding pleased that he'd called, in that single word she sounded upset. Panicked even. He pressed the phone closer to his ear.

"Veda, are you okay?"

Obviously on speaker, she talked in a series of halting phrases. There'd been another phone call. She had left immediately. Would be there inside half an hour.

"Whoa. Hold on. You're driving up here? I'm guessing this has something to do with your dad."

"There's been an accident," she said, followed by a sharp intake of breath. "He's in the hospital."

Ajax's priorities did a one-eighty.

"Which hospital?" He was already rushing for the door, car remote in hand. "Don't worry, honey. I'll meet you there."

Eleven

Veda had kept it together the entire drive from Jersey, but when she saw Ajax waiting for her as she ran from her parked car to the hospital's entrance, all that built-up emotion threatened to break through. Being told that her father had been in a serious car accident had thrown her like nothing else could. Now she flung herself into Ajax's open arms and dissolved as he stroked her hair and murmured her name.

"It's okay, Veda. We'll go in together. I'm sure he'll be fine."

She dashed away tears she'd held back until now. "Apparently he was only a few minutes from home when he ran off the road. He said he thought he saw something…"

"So he's conscious?"

She nodded as they headed inside. "He hit a tree."

Walking to the elevator, Ajax held her hand so tight, it almost hurt. But she only gripped his hand back in return. God, how she needed an anchor…this depth of support.

Earlier on the phone, the administrator had passed on ward details. At the nurses' station, Veda provided her father's name, approximate time of arrival and reason for admittance. When the nurse looked up from the computer screen after checking, Veda knew something more was wrong.

The nurse adjusted her eyeglasses and tried on a smile as she got to her feet. "I'll see if I can find a doctor. Please, take a seat."

Veda's face began to tingle and go warm. As she turned to Ajax, the room seemed to slope and wobble on its axis. This wasn't the hospital her mom had been rushed to after that other accident, but it looked the same, smelled the same, and the look on that nurse's face...

Veda was aware of Ajax's hands bracing her upper arms as he rushed to reassure her. The nurse wouldn't be long. He was sure that Drake was all right. The entire drive here, Veda had told herself that same thing: as big a shock as this was, her father would be fine. But her thoughts were bombarded with phrases like *Fate can be cruel* and *History might not repeat itself but it often rhymes*. She seemed to have always been at war with Drake, but that didn't mean she wanted him taken from her, particularly the same way she had lost her mom.

A tall man with a lilting voice was introducing himself... the name badge said Dr. Wasley...or was that Sawley?

Veda couldn't wait a second longer. She had to know.

"Is he dead?"

The doctor's onyx eyes smiled as he reassured her. "Your father is very much alive. Apparently a deer leaped out and collided with his vehicle. No fractures, although we want to keep an eye on a minor head injury. A graze and bump on his head. He's a lucky man to have gotten off so lightly."

Ajax asked, "When can Veda see him?"

The doctor's mouth pressed into a harder line before he replied. "Ms. Darnel, your father has asked that he not be disturbed at this time."

Veda blinked, shook her head. "But does he know that I'm here?"

"He gave your name as next of kin." The doctor paused. "But I'm afraid he doesn't want visitors."

Veda was ready to ask that someone look into that again. But then the nurse's expression a moment ago began to make sense. She'd been reacting to the situation of a daughter rushing to an injured father who didn't want to see her. It was sad. Awkward.

The doctor tried to rationalize. "Oftentimes, people are embarrassed at having lost control of a vehicle. They might need time to overcome feelings of having let others down, as they perceive it." He offered a reassuring smile. "I'm certain he'll come around."

As the doctor left, Ajax looped his arms around her and Veda leaned in. He felt real when, at this moment, nothing else did.

"We'll hang around," Ajax said, stroking her arm as she nestled against him. "You can be here when he comes to his senses."

"And if that doesn't happen?"

"Like the doctor said…he's got issues with having screwed up."

"So he shuts me out. Typical." She stepped back. "Well, I'm not going to give him the satisfaction of being pathetic enough to wait."

Ajax's gaze softened further. "Maybe just a few minutes. He knows you're here. Let that sink in. He's obviously not thinking straight."

"He's thinking like he always does. About himself."

After their argument this morning, had Drake purposely wrecked his car for a sympathy vote? To snap his recalcitrant daughter back into line? Hell, she'd dropped everything to race here, hadn't she?

"Sorry," she told Ajax, heading off. "I've got to go."

"You can't drive back to Jersey," he said, catching up. "You shouldn't be driving anywhere right now. Your father might be acting like a dick, but you're smarter than that."

Stabbing the elevator call button, she tried to settle her emotions.

"You're right. I'll take a cab. Go back to Dad's place... catch my breath."

"I'll drive. And sit with you for a while."

She darted him a look. "You mean actually come into enemy territory?"

The corners of his mouth twitched. "Boy, wouldn't that piss him off."

Veda hesitated. Then she smiled. Finally she laughed because, hell, what else could she do.

As the elevator doors slid open, she linked her arm through Ajax's and, after this crazy, stress-filled morning, announced to the world, "Let's really tick Drake off. My God, let's make him howl!"

Veda had gotten her spark back before they'd left the hospital, but she'd gone quiet while he'd driven her car back to Darnel Manor. Obviously she was still dwelling on the accident, as well as Drake's latest dick move. He had manipulated a highly emotionally charged situation by refusing to see, and comfort, his own daughter.

Ajax didn't buy into the doctor's explanation about her father feeling embarrassed over totaling his car. Something major was up between father and daughter, and Ajax had the feeling it centered on him.

Passing through the open Darnel gates, he took note of the endless stream of soaring pines lining the drive. At the top of the first hill stood a massive stone-and-shingle structure that captured the essence of an over-the-top bygone era. After parking the SUV out front, he escorted Veda to the colossal cherrywood double entry doors. Looking around, Ajax couldn't make out any sign of the stables, arenas, paddocks—no horses or people were anywhere to be seen.

Then they stepped inside and Ajax almost lost his breakfast.

This place was the Gilded Age on steroids. The foyer was three stories of imported marble, gold trimmings and hardwood parquet flooring and had enough classical sculptures to man a football team.

He realized Veda was studying him and snapped his hanging jaw shut. "A wood shack this is not."

She hugged herself as if battling a chill. "It feels like a huge, creepy mausoleum, right?"

"I wasn't going to say that." *Out loud.*

"Mom never felt comfortable here. But that wasn't totally the house's fault."

"Must take an army of people to keep up appearances," he said, blowing imaginary dust off a Greek goddess's head.

"My father gets someone in three times a year to give everything a resounding polish. Other than that, I can't tell you whether anyone walks through those front doors anymore. Aside from me on occasion. And, I guess, someone to drop off groceries."

So Drake didn't allow his trainers, grooms, riders, farriers and other employees to enter his sanctuary. He preferred to conduct business at the stable office. A little Howard Hughes, but sure. Okay.

"Doesn't he at least have a cook?"

"Far too intrusive," she said with a manufactured air. "And he is the world's best chef. Just ask him." She cocked her head. "Ajax, are you hungry?"

Come to think of it. "I could squeeze in a little something."

She led him into a kitchen that continued the lavish theme, with an exclamation point. Compared to Susan's kitchen, this room looked so *big*. And lonely. The word *haunted* also came to mind.

Veda opened the refrigerator door and cobbled together ingredients for sandwiches. While he slapped mayo on the bread and she cut lettuce, tomato and cheese, he tried to picture her growing up in this place. He felt ill just thinking about it. But the stark formality fit with everything he knew about Drake Darnel, including his rebuff of Veda today.

He thought he was pretty darn special.

"I never felt like this was a home," she said, laying fillings on the bread. "I don't know how my mother suffered it for so long."

"What was the tipping point?"

"In the marriage? Drake accused her of having an affair with one of the stable hands. My father isn't much of a conversationalist at the best of times. After that, it was the silent treatment every night." Veda sliced the sandwiches, and while Ajax put them onto a plate, she found a chilled bottle of juice. "I challenge anyone to live in this kind of environment for any length of time," she said, leading the way through a door that connected with a colossal-sized sun room. "Slowly but surely, let me tell you, it drains the soul."

The hexagonal room was surrounded by soaring floor-to-ceiling French windows. Ajax could admit that the view of the hills was pretty—similar, of course, to a view from his home.

They sat together on an ornate red velvet couch and dug in while looking out over the vista. On his second bite, Ajax's phone rang. After checking the ID, he put the phone away.

"You can take it," Veda said. "Don't mind me."

"It was Hux."

"You didn't want to lie about where you were?"

"I don't give a crap whether he knows or not."

She lowered her sandwich. "That doesn't sound good."

Recalling their argument earlier that day was almost enough to put him off his food. "I love that man. He's a great father and mentor. But sometimes…he just doesn't get it."

"This is about that doping allegation."

"Yes. And no."

Ajax explained how he'd gotten home that morning to find Hux riffling through his office files, and then shared the news that a meeting regarding those allegations was scheduled for the end of the week, *and* some clients had decided to take their horses elsewhere.

"Hux and I have never had an argument like that before, and I'm over it. I love what I do, but sometimes, like today… He doesn't know how much I give."

Veda looked taken aback. "Sorry. I thought everything was hunky-dory in the Rawson camp."

"Ask the others and they'd agree. Griff, Lanie, Jacob… he supports and encourages them without a second thought. But me? I feel like I have to earn his approval every day."

"Have you always felt that way?"

"Since Mom passed. You know about me putting that ad up and finding Susan."

"That was so brave."

Ajax didn't see it as courageous but simply as necessity. "Everyone was so down. Someone had to get things moving again. I had to at least try to make people smile and forget." He flinched. "I sound like I'm whining, don't I?"

"No. Not at all." She smiled softly. "Ajax, you found a way to save your family. I think that is the noblest thing anyone can do."

His throat was suddenly thick. No one would ever know, and he would never forget, how desperate he'd felt at the time. He had wanted to save his family. What was left of it, at least.

"I felt so stifled living under my dad's say-so," Veda said, and then clarified, "I know Hux isn't anything like my father... Just saying."

"When did you leave?"

"Freshman year of college. Never looked back."

"I didn't do college. Too much to do at home."

"Did you want to go?"

"When I was young, I wanted to be a vet."

"Well, there you go!"

"That was a long time ago."

"Hey, there's nothing wrong with starting a little late." She thought a moment before squeezing his arm then getting to her feet. "I'd like to show you something. I mean if you're not in a hurry to get back or anything."

Ready to shake all the bad feelings out, he jumped up. "Veda, I'm all yours."

Seeing the tree house again brought back a flood of memories and emotions. Perched in a rambling old oak ten feet above the ground, the timber hideaway was the size of a modest bedroom and had once been home to Veda's favorite dolls and games. Here she had felt totally happy. Truly safe.

"I had a little dog growing up," Veda said as she and Ajax drew closer to the tree house. "Gus was my best friend. I used to climb up this ladder and he'd jump in that." She crossed over to a faded blue plastic bucket with a hairy old rope tied to its handle. "Then I'd pull him up."

"Gus... I'm thinking a beagle."

"A cream teacup poodle. He had apricot smudges on his cheeks like an old lady had done his makeup. Dad brought him home for me on my fifth birthday. I even caught Gus snuggled up on Drake's lap a few times."

Looking up at the tree house, Ajax grabbed a ladder rung. It snapped, rotten all the way through.

He winced. "I'll fix it for you."

"Don't worry. This must be fifty or sixty years old. An employee from the stables used to patch it up for me."

"Sounds like you had a friend."

She arched a brow. "It was Paul Booshang."

His head kicked back. "Get outta here."

"And he *was* a friend. Mom's, too. I don't think he liked the way Drake ignored my mother and me."

"I don't suppose you knew anything about him doping horses back then."

She shook her head. "And neither did my father, or Paul would've found a boot up his backside. In case you haven't noticed, my father is not a tolerant man, even where family is concerned. I'm sure Paul wasn't the only staff member to feel sorry for me and Mom. It got worse after she said we would leave if things didn't change. Once it got so heated, he slapped her."

She kicked the bucket and the old plastic split into brittle pieces at the same time Ajax drew up to his full intimidating height.

"Did he ever touch you?"

"Never. In fact, the night we packed up to leave, he asked me to stay." Remembering how torn she had felt... how lost... Veda shuddered. "Believe it or not, I cried walking out the door."

Ajax stepped closer. "I'm sorry you had such a hard time growing up. It must seem like a long time ago now."

Actually, it didn't feel that long ago at all.

"Dad came by to see me earlier," she said.

"You mean in New Jersey? Today?"

"We argued. And yes, it was about us."

He blinked as he put it together. "Veda, if you feel

guilty over your father's accident because he might've been upset—"

"I don't feel guilty." She fought down a shiver. "I absolutely don't."

Anyway, that was enough about Drake. Enough about the past.

"When I stay over now, I use the guesthouse." She nodded toward the beautiful old stone building. "It was here before the main house was built."

Following her gaze, Ajax's eyebrows shot up. "The Rawson original has a long way to go before it looks anywhere near as good as that." He brought out his phone and pulled up a few photos.

"Oh, it's sweet," she said, taking in the Cape Cod with its steep pitched roof and big front door centered below a massive chimney.

"I should show you around sometime," he said, slotting the phone away.

"My turn first," she said, grabbing his hand and heading toward the guesthouse.

"We'll need keys."

"Got them in my pocket."

He grinned. "I like how you think."

"I like how you feel…" Turning back and into his arms, she nuzzled his warm, salty neck. "How you taste."

When he kissed her, Veda felt her world shift that much more toward a new way of thinking and feeling. Once she had been happiest here alone, just her and little Gus. Now she was happiest when she was with Ajax. Right now, she felt safe.

Maybe even loved.

Twelve

When Ajax drove his truck up to the house early the next morning, an unfamiliar vehicle was parked in the guest area.

If Hux had company, Ajax was happy to take a coffee on the back porch and wait until his father was free. He'd been mad as hell after their argument. Since talking it through and spending the night with Veda, however, he had calmed down.

Not that his opinion had changed on anything, Ajax thought, taking the front steps two at a time. He hated the doping allegation hanging over his head. He was sorry that some clients had opted out. But he wasn't unhappy that this episode had brought to the fore his growing concerns regarding his standing here at Rawson's. He had felt like the hired help for too long.

So now it was crunch time, Ajax reaffirmed as he headed for the kitchen and the coffeepot. He and Hux would have a conversation today highlighting the fact that fair was fair.

He wanted a partnership agreement drawn up by the end of the week or he would need to consider his other options.

When he pushed through the swing doors, he found Susan standing by the center counter. Her eyes widened before her usual welcoming smile took over.

"Ajax. What good timing."

That's when he noticed their company. Five foot one. A hundred and ten pounds. Thick shoulder-length blond hair that she usually wore in a ponytail but was loose today. He was used to seeing her in training gear or jockey silks, not a dress. But her smile was the same. Big. Contagious.

He headed over and gave their guest a big, warm hug. She didn't smell a bit like leather and horse sweat. In fact, her scent brought to mind a summer garden.

"Fallon Kelly." Pulling back, he took his friend in again. "This is a surprise."

Fallon's chocolate-brown eyes were dancing. "I was driving through on my way to Vermont. I hoped y'all wouldn't mind if I dropped in."

Susan set a cup of coffee on the counter beside Ajax. "She looks well, doesn't she?"

"She looks *amazing*," Ajax replied.

Susan was headed for the swing doors. "You two get caught up while I tell Huxley you're here, Fallon. And I'll let him know you're home, Jax."

Susan and Hux didn't have secrets; she would know all about yesterday's blowup. Not that she ever inserted herself into family matters, which was nuts given she *was* family.

Ajax led Fallon out back and they took seats that offered a magic view of the hills. Dew was still glistening on everything green. The sky was a dome of early heaven-sent blue. If he squinted, he could even see the roof of the original house from here.

"It must be a year since we saw you last," he said. "Just after you gave up riding."

"Doesn't seem that long ago."

He thought about his own situation—about weighing up his choices—and asked, "Do you miss the racing scene?"

"I miss the special bond I have with a horse. I don't miss those early mornings and worrying about every little thing I put in my mouth."

Ajax hooked an arm over the back of the bench as he turned more toward her. "I'll never forget our big win at Belmont Park."

"I had a great ride. Kudos to the wonderful trainer." She tipped toward him, grinning.

And then, for just a second, her gaze dropped from his eyes to his lips, which prompted a whole other line of recollection. After that win and celebratory drinks, he and Fallon had gotten together—a single night that hadn't developed into anything more. Her career was her main focus. Or so he had thought. He'd been blindsided when she'd said that she wanted to pursue other goals.

"So what are you up to now?" he asked.

"I've been in Kentucky with family, thinking about starting a riding school. Nothing snooty. I'm more interested in being laid-back. In having fun."

Sounded good compared to the ruckus going on around here of late.

"What's been happening in your life, Jax?" she asked, before taking a long sip from her steaming cup.

"I'm surprised you haven't heard the rumblings, even all the way down in Louisville."

"You mean the rumor that you're into doping now?"

His grin was entirely humorless. "So, you *have* heard."

"I want you to know that I support you one hundred percent. And what the hell is with Paul Booshang anyway? I'd always thought he was a good guy. Trying to fix a race is bad enough. Dragging you into it is unbelievable." She took another sip and then asked, "Do you think Booshang is a lone wolf, hoping he could make a sure bet on the side, or is he in cahoots with someone else?"

"I'm not sure I should go into that."

Fallon's eyes rounded. "So there *is* someone else."

"Nothing's been proven. Not by a long shot." When she arched a brow, he grunted and gave it up. "We've heard Drake Darnel's name mentioned."

But after hearing Veda's tree house story, it didn't sound as if Booshang had ever been a fan of Drake's. So why would Paul work covertly with him now?

"Darnel Stables has an impeccable reputation. But as far as the man himself is concerned…" She visibly shuddered. "Do you know, after our win in Elmont, he flat-out scowled at me."

"His filly finished second."

"Drake Darnel is a stinking bad loser." She shrugged. "Still, I can't see him shooting his horses up. He's too darn self-righteous. But he does hate your dad. He'd tell anyone who listened that good training was not the reason your horses won."

"Meaning we had to be using performance enhancing drugs."

"I guess no one's surprised that his daughter thinks the same."

Ajax sat up. "Veda?"

"Uh-huh." Fallon sipped her coffee. "That's her name."

"So, you've heard that with your own ears? Veda saying that we break the law? Cheat?"

Fallon looked taken aback. "I've never spoken to her personally. But I think it's common knowledge what she thought of the industry."

Susan appeared at the door.

"Huxley is on a conference call," she told them. "He'll be a while. But I've pulled a batch of blueberry muffins out of the oven if anyone's interested."

Fallon smacked her lips. "I can smell them from here. Can you put one away for me?" she asked, getting to her feet. "I was hoping Ajax might take me on a tour of the stables while the sun's not too high in the sky."

"I'll let Huxley know where you're at," Susan said, heading back inside.

"I'll come and see him when we're through," Ajax said. His business with Hux could wait for now.

Walking along the path that led to the foaling barn, he and Fallon were stopped a couple of times, first by a rider and then a groom who wanted to say hi. She'd been popular with the team, and it had been a loss to his stables when she left.

"I miss this place," she said, gazing out over the hills and paddocks.

"Kentucky's pretty, too."

She nodded. "Dad still has half a dozen horses. Still rides every day."

Fallon's trainer father had enjoyed some success a couple of decades ago, which was how Fallon had found her way into the game.

"He always wanted you to ride in the Derby," Ajax recalled.

Fallon laughed. "I was never that good."

"You could have been if you'd kept going. Absolutely."

When she elbowed his ribs and laughed some more, Ajax got a funny feeling in his stomach. They'd always gotten on well. Common interests and parallel dreams. Which was hardly the case with Veda. But after yesterday, and particularly last night, they seemed to be overcoming their obstacles. Whenever they were together, he felt as if nothing else in the world existed. Like the only thing that mattered was making her happy.

But given the way she had cut him off at the knees in Barbados because of his innocent chat with that woman, how would Veda react if she saw him with Fallon when their relationship hadn't always been platonic?

Of course that was ancient history. Other than Griff, no one knew about their fling, and Ajax wouldn't go out of his way to mention it. Why upset Veda when there was absolutely nothing to worry about?

When they passed a stable hand leading a cream four-year-old, Ajax pulled him up.

"We need to check that left hind leg," he said, running a hand down the limb. "The hip's hiking when the leg hits the ground."

"The owner's already made up his mind about this one," the stable hand said.

Ajax frowned. "Made up his mind about what?"

"I thought he must've talked to you." The stable hand rubbed the horse's neck. "This guy's retiring. I'm about to load him up for the last time."

If a horse wasn't earning enough, an owner decided whether he would literally be put out to pasture, retrained for a new career or…that other lesser-talked-about alternative that meant a one-way trip to Canada or Mexico. When he spoke to the owner to square the accounts, he would make an offer for the cream.

If it wasn't too late.

"Come on," he said to Fallon, focusing on the now. "I'll introduce you to Someone's Prince Charming. I'm backing him for a Triple Crown next year. He's a star, and just so smart and wanting to give his all."

He'd certainly known a few in his time, but Ajax loved that horse like he had loved no other.

Ajax stopped and turned around. Hux was trotting down the path, calling out his name. When he arrived, Hux gave Fallon a hug.

"Is this a professional visit?" he asked. "Looking to get back into your silks?"

Fallon gave him a good-humored grin. "My racing days are over."

"Well, we all want to hear what you're up to, so you're staying for dinner," Hux said. "No arguments."

Fallon caught Ajax's gaze and nodded. "I'd love to."

"Do you mind if I steal Ajax for a second? There's some business we need to discuss."

"Sure. I'll catch you up at the stables," she told Ajax, heading off.

When she was out of earshot, Hux pinned his son with a look. "Nice of you to show up today."

Wow. "I'm actually taking some time off. So sue me."

"Don't speak too soon."

Was he referring to the doping business and possible sanctions?

Man, he was so over this.

Ajax was walking away when Hux added, "She must be good."

Bristling, Ajax slowly turned back. "If you're talking about Veda—"

"It could be part of Darnel's plan, you know," Hux said, cutting in. "Make sure you're sidetracked while it all crumples down around me."

"Around *you*? Like I don't put my heart and soul into this place?"

"Not lately. This time of year, you need to be here, doing your job. Once I didn't have to tell you that."

"Right. Once all I did was beg for every crumb of approval you'd toss my way."

As a groom hurried past, eyes cast down, Hux lowered his voice. "You need to get your head on straight."

"Which means?"

"Priorities. Open your eyes to what could be happening here."

As Hux strode off, Ajax remembered how good Veda

had felt in his arms last night, and then Fallon's recollection that Veda believed the Rawsons were unscrupulous, too. Perhaps that had come from her dislike of all things horse racing–related. It didn't mean that she would conspire to sell him out. Veda wouldn't do that.

No way, no how.

That evening, Veda was thinking she might have to leave a message when Ajax finally picked up.

"Hey there," he said, sounding beyond sexy.

"Hey, back." She set aside her laptop with images on the screen of teacup poodles available from rescue groups. "Just thought I'd check in and see how it went with your dad today."

"Hux is being a giant paranoid pain. I know we lost some business because of Booshang but…" He cursed under his breath. "I don't want to talk about any of that."

He sounded short, but she knew that wasn't about her. If she was in his position, she'd be stressed, too.

After an amazing night spent together here in the guest-house, after the way he had supported her yesterday when Drake was being so, well, *Drake*, she was feeling even better about her relationship with Ajax. There might be a mountain of things standing in their way, but at least now she felt more secure about his feelings for her. Yes, he'd been a stud in the past, but that didn't mean he would always play the field. Hux had settled down eventually, hadn't he? So maybe this liaison wasn't as doomed as she had once thought.

"Did you speak with your dad today?" he asked.

"After we drove down to the hospital to get your car, I hung around for a while but he was still sulking, so I just dropped off those personal items I knew he'd need. He should be out in the next few days. I'll stay here until then."

She clicked on an image and sighed as a pair of adorable baby-blue puppy eyes melted her heart.

"You know, talking about Gus the other day got me thinking," she said.

"Gus who?"

"My little poodle, remember?" she reminded him. "He was just so loving and cuddly and cute. I've always wanted another one."

"Do it," Ajax said. "Animals are great company."

"As a matter of fact, I could use a little human company right now." She shut her laptop lid. "Wanna hang out?"

There was a beat of silence.

"Actually, we had a visitor from Kentucky drop in out of the blue. Someone I haven't seen in a while."

Veda let out a breath as all her built-up anticipation deflated. The way he had kissed her goodbye this morning, the promise he'd made about seeing her again… Well, naturally she had hoped…she'd assumed…

But she didn't want to act like a clinging vine.

"Oh, sure," she said, opening her laptop again. "I understand. Did you work together?"

"Uh-huh. A jockey."

"Would I know his name?"

"Fallon Kelly. She retired last year. Hux invited her to stay for dinner."

Last year, after a Drake rant about being swindled out of a Belmont Stakes blue ribbon by a Rawson horse, Veda had googled the story. Fallon Kelly was not only a talented jockey, she was a beautiful and obviously self-possessed woman. In the story's accompanying picture of Fallon with Ajax, she had radiated confidence. They obviously made a great team.

Putting aside a twinge of unease, Veda said, "Well, I'll let you get back to your guest then."

"I'll call tomorrow."

There was a long silence when something else needed to be said. *Have fun* didn't fit. *Be good* was even worse. *Love you* was way too much, too soon. Although she was heading in that direction, which could hardly be a surprise. It was what she had feared from the start. Now...it was too late to try to push those growing feelings aside.

Finally he said, "Sleep tight. And good luck with the puppy search. Can't wait to meet him."

Veda put down the phone on a sigh. If the Rawsons and Darnels weren't enemies, he might have invited her over to meet his guest. She would feel included rather than shunted aside. But it was only one night. This time tomorrow Fallon Kelly would be gone and Veda would be in Ajax's arms once again.

Thirteen

Finally Drake deigned to see his daughter.

Sitting up in his hospital bed, Veda's father was freshly shaved, wearing the pajamas she had dropped off for him two days earlier. Other than a bruised color around his eyes, he looked remarkably well and more than prepared to hold court.

As Veda entered the private room, he kept his stony gaze glued to hers, but he didn't speak, which was clearly a tactic to make her sweat. Although Veda's stomach was churning, she didn't shrink away.

Taking a seat by the window, she let the seconds tick by as he continued the stare-off. Finally, his lips sucked in and he cleared his throat.

"I'm dry. Pour me a water, please."

Veda got to her feet, poured a glass from a jug and handed it over.

"The doctor said you can leave in a couple of days," she said while he sipped.

"I can find my own way," he said, and then covered his mouth to cough.

"If you're not feeling up to it, don't rush yourself." Making sure she looked unconcerned, she crossed her arms. "I imagine you've spoken to the stable manager and trainers so things would be sorted out there."

"Did your boyfriend want you to ask me that?"

Veda was so taken aback, she almost fell sideways.

"I beg your pardon?"

"You invited him onto my property, didn't you?" he bit out. "My God, a Rawson in my house. Did you think I wouldn't find out? That my people wouldn't pass on what they saw?"

She hadn't noticed anyone around. Had Drake sent someone over from the stables to literally spy?

"It was bad enough," he went on, "that you spend time with a Rawson boy. But it had to be Ajax, didn't it? The biggest bastard of the pack."

An impulse shot through her: she wanted to leap over and slap his face. But she wouldn't stoop to his level. Instead, she bit her lip and, outwardly cool, simply tipped her head.

"He makes me happy," she told him, recalling her mother saying the same thing about her cowboy once upon a time.

Drake sneered. "He's even worse than his father. Always charming the women. Seeing who he can fool. Rawson men don't care."

"Hux Rawson cared about the woman he married. I've been told that they loved each other deeply."

But this conversation was absurd.

"You've just survived a car accident, for God's sake. Can't you ever move on?"

Given his next question, clearly not.

"Married, you say?" Her father snickered. "Has Ajax asked you to marry him then?"

"Of course not!"

"Didn't think so."

Veda's hands fisted at her sides. "Bitterness destroys a person, Drake," she said. "It turns them rotten from the inside. It turns them bad."

Her father's eyes flashed at the same time he hurled his glass into a corner. As shards and water flew everywhere, Veda barely flinched. In fact, she stepped closer to the bed.

"Ajax is funny and laid-back. He's charming and brave. People are naturally attracted to men like that."

The corners of Drake's mouth pulled down more. His words were a harsh, hateful whisper. "You like to hurt me."

Veda withered. "You really are deluded."

When she was halfway out the door, he called out. "I'm going home tomorrow. Friday."

"Don't worry. I'll be gone."

"Veda."

She counted to ten before she turned back around. "What now?"

"I've changed my mind."

She looked at him hard. "Changed your mind about what exactly?"

"You can drive me home." He fluffed the sheet. "Be here by nine. Don't be late."

Lanie was lost in her thoughts when the cab driver kicked off a conversation.

"Said on the radio there's supposed to be a thunderstorm rolling in later today."

Glancing out the window, Lanie spotted a distant bank of clouds. "Rain is always nice."

"Oh, sure. As long as it's not too fierce." The driver added, "I have a vegetable patch at home so I take notice. Beets and peas and onions this year."

Lanie had gone back to her thoughts, trying to find a

solution to her nagging problem, when the driver spoke again.

"Was it fine weather where you flew in from today? The rest of the state's supposed to be clear."

"I'm just back from visiting a friend in Germany."

"That's a long way to visit a pal," he said with a gravelly chuckle.

"We have a lot in common. And it was a special occasion."

Lanie had met her German friend at the Dressage World Championship in Tryon, North Carolina. She wasn't able to attend Lanie's birthday party, but with good reason. She'd been preparing for her wedding, at which Lanie had just been a bridesmaid.

Although not too many people knew, Lanie really wanted a family someday, and the ceremony, which was held in the private courtyard of a centuries-old winery estate, had pulled all her romantic strings. Aside from the scenery and the couple's heartfelt vows, she couldn't help but remember the other special person she met during that trip to North Carolina. Kade Wilder had been a guest at one of the events held at the championships. He was handsome, articulate and passionate about running for Congress.

They had spent the night talking and later followed each other on social media. When Lanie had posted about her party, Kade had messaged he would be in town and would love to personally pass on his wishes. He had arrived late, but the dance they had shared was worth every second of the wait. As he'd held her in his arms, she had practically drowned in the dark blue pools of his eyes.

She wasn't the type to get goofy over a man, but her stomach had been filled with so many butterflies that night on the dance floor, and later when they had spoken alone. Perhaps the attraction was one-sided, though. Kade hadn't tried to kiss her that night, and he hadn't tried to contact her since.

"We'll be there in thirty," the driver said. "I've heard of Rawson's farm. They've had plenty of winners over the years."

"It was a great place to grow up, especially if you love horses."

Finding her phone, Lanie logged in to see whether Kade had posted anything since the last time she'd looked.

"So you're a Rawson kid?" the driver asked.

"I am."

"Must be hard right now with all those rumors about drugging and race-fixing floating around. Even money laundering. That's what some Darnel guy was hinting at on the radio this morning."

Lanie almost dropped her phone.

What the hell?

"Rawson's is one of the most reputable stables in the state. In the country."

The driver shrugged. "I'm sure it is, lady. Just sayin'."

Growling under her breath—at the situation, not the driver—Lanie swapped to another social media platform and swiped through the feed. She shouldn't be surprised that word of those doping allegations had leaked. People loved a scandal. But Hux and Ajax would have it sorted out soon enough. The Rawsons had overcome battles far tougher than this.

She stopped at a post from Veda. The caption indicated it was a view from Darnel Manor. The last time she and Veda had spoken was the morning after the party. Lanie had been stunned to learn that Ajax had scored that particular notch on his bedpost. Later, Veda had admitted that it hadn't been the first time.

Lanie had given her opinion on the subject, after which Veda had claimed that she wouldn't see Ajax again. Veda was a strong woman, but Ajax was a pro. If her brother set his mind to it, Lanie would bet her lucky saddle that Veda would fold.

Lanie focused on the photo again. If Veda was in town, they should catch up. Veda might want to talk about Ajax. Lanie could use a sounding board, too. Was it better to file her feelings for Kade away under Obviously Not Happening, or should she be the one to reach out this time?

Lanie speed-dialed her friend. Veda answered with her usual direct style.

"Lanie. I'm glad you called."

"I've just flown in and caught your feed. Are you visiting with your dad?"

"Kind of. He's been in a car accident."

Lanie gasped. "God. Is he okay?" She didn't personally know the man, and if she did, she probably wouldn't like him, but she still felt for her friend.

"He was lucky," Veda explained. "He's in the hospital, though, so I'm house-sitting between visits."

Lanie sat forward, peering out the windshield down the road ahead. "I'm not far away. I should drop by."

There was a grin in Veda's voice when she replied, "You definitely should."

Ten minutes later, Lanie was out of the cab and enjoying Veda's welcoming hug. Lanie came right out and said it.

"I need to unpack about a man."

Veda groaned. "Same."

While they sat out back with a glass of wine and the sun arcing more toward the dark clouds traveling in from the north, Veda and Lanie played rock-paper-scissors to decide who went first.

Lanie won.

After listening to the whole gorgeous-but-MIA-man story, Veda wanted to highlight a point.

"I saw you two on the dance floor the night of your party. You were literally floating on air."

Looking off, Lanie swirled her wine in her glass. "I don't carry on with something if the feelings aren't right. I was beginning to think I was incapable of going all weak at the knees."

Veda raised her glass. "Guess no one is immune."

"Which brings us to my brother. He's the man you want to talk about, right?"

Veda filled her friend in. She didn't leave anything out, including playing *not* hard to get in Barbados, followed by the *getting jealous over probably nothing* episode at that dinner. She wrapped up with how Ajax had met her at the hospital after her father's accident and, later, had come back here to keep her company.

"He stayed over that night, and we've spoken on the phone since."

Lanie prodded. "But?"

"We haven't seen each other since Tuesday morning." This was Thursday afternoon. "After having a long weekend, I know he'd be busy with work, catching up. And there's that Booshang thing to deal with. A stewards' meeting is set for tomorrow. On top of that, some Rawson clients have removed their horses from the stables."

Lanie grunted, surprised, and then tossed back her hair. "They'll be back."

When Veda only bit her lip, Lanie frowned and tipped closer.

"Wait. You don't think Ajax actually doped that horse, do you?"

Veda admitted, "I wasn't sure at the start. I mean that kind of stuff happens all the time."

"Not at Rawson's."

"But that's not technically true. Paul Booshang was working for Ajax when he was caught."

Lanie paused before she got to her feet and looked out over the hills like she was daring them to point out the facts, too.

"Ajax and Jacob will clear our name," she said. "Dad'll make sure of it."

"Ajax says that Hux is giving him a hard time, too."

Lanie swung around. "Well, it seems as if I came home just in time then. Far too much testosterone flying around."

When Lanie grinned, Veda smiled, too. "*Way* too much testosterone," she agreed before she sobered again. "Maybe I'm being selfish or needy, but I wish Ajax could find a minute to come over and see me."

Lowering back down into her seat, Lanie made a suggestion. The most outlandish notion in the history of anything.

"Why don't you come over and see him instead?"

Veda almost spluttered her wine. "That's such a bad idea."

"Veda, it's my home, too. You're my friend, and I'm inviting you."

"Forget about Ajax maybe feeling like we're treading on his toes. My father was mentioned in connection to those allegations. I'm sure Hux doesn't want a Darnel shoved in his face any time soon."

Or ever.

"My father is an alpha male who's not afraid to stand up for what's right. But Veda, he's not a tyrant. In fact, he can be a big ol' pussycat where I'm concerned." She took Veda's hand. "I know there's talk about your father being involved in this somehow. But even if that's true, it's no reason to hold it against you."

"I'm not so sure."

"Spurned by association? My mother dated Drake but Hux didn't hold it against her, did he?"

Veda had to think that through. "I guess not…"

"So it's settled." She took Veda's glass and set it down. "You're driving me home."

Veda's throat convulsed. "I'm still not sure that's a good idea. He has that meeting tomorrow, don't forget."

Lanie's determined expression softened. "From what you told me, you and Ajax are getting over your hurdles. I'm sure he would appreciate the visit. In fact, he'll probably be blown away."

Veda had something else she needed to say. "I'm sorry I didn't tell you about me and Ajax after that first time."

Lanie waved it off. "We're friends. Not Siamese twins."

"But we've always been open with each other."

"That hasn't changed."

"I'm just saying…if you ever found anything out about Ajax…something that you might think I ought to know…"

When Lanie read between the obvious lines, her expression filled with understanding as well as conviction. "No secrets between friends. Promise."

Smiling, Veda nodded. "I promise, too."

After another long day taking care of business, including rolling calls from clients who were growing ever more curious about those pending test results, Ajax was happy to kick back. When Fallon arrived at his office, saying that she had brought along two saddled horses that were raring to go, Ajax didn't waste a moment pulling the whistle on quitting time.

He needed to stop thinking about the stewards' meeting set for tomorrow. Jacob would be sitting beside him, and Griff was taking a day off work to show his support for the team. Of course, Hux would be there, too. Frankly, Ajax wished he would simply stay the hell away.

Since their confrontation earlier in the week, Hux's mood had tanked even more. No one knew what the test results would reveal, or what penalties would be handed down. But, yes, mud tended to stick, particularly when Drake Darnel was slinging it around every opportunity he got, like in that absurd radio interview this morning.

Money laundering.

What a crock.

None of that impacted his feelings for Veda, but it had held him back from seeing more of her these past days. At this point in time, Hux didn't need the added aggravation of having his son flaunt the fact that he was sleeping with the enemy's daughter. Hux had never let Drake get under his skin before, either professionally or personally, but this was a whole other ball game.

The big question was whether Darnel was shoveling his crap onto the Rawsons to divert attention from his own part in this doping episode. If that was the case, when would the truth be revealed?

Ajax was glad that Fallon had accepted Hux's invitation to stay on a few days. She understood the industry; whenever he vented about this, she was only ever supportive. And she helped in other ways, Ajax thought as he stepped outside and glanced at the clouds rolling in.

She came along on his rounds and helped out with track work. Best of all, she managed to bring the occasional smile to Hux's dour face.

Once those results were in, Ajax thought as Fallon spurred on her horse through the open paddock gate, everyone would be free to get on with their lives. He could properly pick up with Veda where they had left off. And if Hux wasn't happy about that state of affairs, too damn bad.

Ajax would always love and respect his father, but these past weeks had put a different spin on how he viewed their relationship. He'd given his heart, blood and soul to this place. Irrespective of those test results, he needed a partnership contract now. Tomorrow after the meeting, he would give Hux the news.

"Hey, Jax, I'll race ya!"

Fallon, who was handling that chestnut two-year-old like the pro she was, was already springing into a gallop. As she bolted off, throwing a goading look over her shoulder, Ajax swung into his saddle, and Someone's Prince Charming took off after them. Fallon was such a natural; hanging up her silks seemed a waste. Which brought to mind the other reason he was glad she had stayed. Having her own riding school was cool, but having their horse wear the Kentucky Derby's rose blanket next year would be monumental. And she, along with the Prince, had the goods to deliver.

Fallon just beat him to the oak at the top of the next slope. As her horse snorted and lowered his head to tear off some grass, Ajax pulled up, too. Breathing in air scented with approaching rain, he gazed out over the hills he called home.

"I'm going to miss this place," Fallon said as the sun disappeared behind the bank of rolling clouds.

"You don't have to go," Ajax said, leaning on his saddle's horn while she dismounted.

"I have a life to get back to."

"Don't you miss the one you left behind?"

Fallon swept up a wildflower and twirled the stem. "We've talked about that. I made a decision to move on. I don't regret it."

Climbing down to join her, Ajax asked, "Not even a teensy bit?"

"I need to do something different. Something for me."

"But you loved being a jockey," he said, stealing the flower and slotting the stem behind her ear.

"The truth is I did it for my father. It was always his dream."

Ajax blinked. "I didn't know that."

"As a boy, Dad dreamed of bringing home a Derby win, but he was never the right build to ride. I was."

"Winning the Kentucky Derby…" Ajax playfully punched her arm. "You could still do that. I have the ride right here."

While Ajax stroked his horse's warm, strong neck, Fallon searched his eyes for a long moment.

"Ajax, are you trying to talk *me* into staying or you?"

Muscles in his chest locked before he reevaluated those hills, which were fast becoming covered in shadow rather than sunlight.

Shaking his head, remembering how it used to be, Ajax growled. "I wish this had never happened." Booshang's behavior that day and his ridiculous allegations had turned the world upside down.

"This all could be a blessing in disguise," Fallon said. "A new opportunity for you. A new start."

If, or rather when, Hux signed that partnership agreement… "Yeah. I suppose it could."

"So you'll consider my suggestion."

"What suggestion?"

"That you help me with my riding school. We spoke about it the other night."

Over dinner. But they'd been joking around.

"I'm not saying give up what you do here, just lend a hand when you can. I think we could have fun." Fallon's smile changed as she adjusted the flower in her hair. "I think we could be happy."

A lightning bolt ignited the sky, cutting a jagged line through the churning clouds. Seconds later, an almighty clap of thunder split the air. Whinnying, Fallon's horse reared up, then charged back down the hill toward the safety of its stall. Ajax caught the Prince's reins as another bolt struck and an even worse clap shook the ground. The next second, hard rain began to fall.

Ajax jumped up into his saddle then threw out his hand to Fallon. "Want a lift?"

She caught his hand. "Bless your heart!"

She swung up behind him and they lit a trail back down the hill.

With rain hitting his face, Ajax let out a whoop. This was what life was about. Feeling free…even reckless. Like you could do anything when you decided nothing would hold you back.

Fallon was an amazing woman—beautiful, talented. He'd known that when she'd won the Stakes as well as later, when they had slipped away to be alone. He had loved catching up with her these past days.

But he had seen the look in her eyes a moment ago. When she'd said they could be happy, she was talking about more than working together on a riding school. If he had stepped into her space…if he'd kissed her…she wouldn't have pulled away.

But Fallon wasn't the one he wanted right now, and when they were under cover, he would be clear in letting her know exactly that.

Veda was driving up the Rawsons' private road, heading toward that fateful bend, when the heavens opened up and dumped big-time. As the sudden rain smashed against the windshield, Lanie readjusted her seat belt.

"This is one serious summer shower."

Veda switched on the wipers and shifted closer to the wheel. "Reminds me of the rain the night of your party."

"When your car spun out."

"Right here, actually," Veda said as the SUV rounded the corner and her stomach lurched.

"You must've been happy to see Ajax charging down to rescue you."

Remembering it all very well, Veda wanted to smile. But other older memories made her shudder instead.

"I wonder what would have happened," Veda said as

the vehicle climbed toward the house, "if it hadn't rained that night."

Lanie shrugged. "What's meant to be is meant to be."

Then the belting rain stopped as quickly as it had started, and the guest parking area appeared before them. As Veda pulled into a spot, she noticed some movement on an adjacent hill. Soaked through, Ajax was riding toward the house on the back of a magnificent-looking steed.

With his hair flying back and his shirt wet through, tugging against all those gorgeous muscles, he had never looked so handsome. So capable and in charge. She couldn't wait to feel those arms around her again.

Veda was hurrying to shut down the engine and jump out when, beside her, Lanie groaned out an expletive. Her eyes were bulging like she'd swallowed a toad. A chill rippled over Veda's skin as she reached across to hold her friend's shoulder.

"Lanie? God, what's wrong?"

"Nothing. Not a thing."

Lanie pasted on a limp smile that only made Veda worry more. She looked out through the windshield again as another chill swept over her. Ajax was bringing his horse to a showy stop. Someone was hooked up behind him. As he helped the other rider down, the woman looked up at him as if no one else compared.

As if he was the best.

Veda's scalp started crawling. She didn't want to jump to conclusions, be overdramatic. But come on. She wasn't a fool.

Without taking her eyes off the woman, she asked Lanie, "Is it someone from his past or someone new?"

Lanie exhaled. "You and Ajax should probably talk."

Veda clenched her jaw and drew down a big breath. *No secrets between friends.*

"If you know anything..."

Lanie shut her eyes and dropped her chin. "Griff mentioned something last year…"

Ajax was dismounting. He'd seen her car and was heading over with an uncharacteristically measured stride. She felt strangely hypnotized by the way those wet jeans clung to his thighs and his narrowed gaze held hers.

"What's her name?"

"Fallon Kelly," Lanie replied. "She's a jockey. Or was. She'd hung up her whip last I heard."

Veda felt as if she was folding in on herself and melting away. The surprise guest had stayed on longer than a night. Longer than Ajax had said she would or had mentioned in his calls.

By the time Ajax reached the car, the shock was ebbing. In its place, Veda felt those familiar fingers curl around her throat at the same time her brain began to shut down. But she needed to speak with Ajax. No games. No blinders. She simply wanted the truth.

Getting out of the car, she took in Ajax's plastic grin and the way his big shoulders in that chambray shirt slouched just a bit as he shook out his wet hands. He went to take a step closer, but then blinked and rocked back on his boot heels instead.

"Well, this is a double surprise," he said, acknowledging Lanie, who was out of the car now, too. "Veda." He jerked a thumb over his shoulder. "I mentioned Fallon Kelly was staying over. She used to ride for us."

Still standing by that magnificent horse, obviously realizing that Veda was Ajax's latest squeeze, Fallon sent over a half-hearted wave. Veda recognized her face from that story she'd read about her online. While Lanie joined Fallon, Veda and Ajax simply stood there, drilling into each other's eyes.

"You want to come down to the office?" he asked her.

"I'm not holding you up?" Veda replied.

His eyebrows drew together before he nodded toward the path. They walked side by side, neither saying a word the entire way. When they got inside, they moved through to his private office, and he shut the door.

She wanted him to talk first. Would he try to say this was completely innocent, or that it was all in her head? Maybe the time had come where he would simply say that he felt bad about them not working out. That would definitely fit.

"I know what you're thinking," he said.

"What's that?" she asked.

"That Fallon and I... That something's going on." He gave an exaggerated shrug. "We're just friends."

"If I could make an observation..."

He exhaled. "Go ahead."

"I would put my money on her wanting way more than friendship."

Veda almost expected him to deny knowing it, too. But he only searched her eyes as his bristled jaw worked from side to side. Veda's stomach went into free fall.

"We went for a ride," he said. "There was a clap of thunder. Fallon's horse freaked and galloped home. That's all there is to it."

Veda's throat was blocked with emotion. At the same time, she felt something akin to relief. This was really over. He didn't want to admit that he and Fallon Kelly had slept together in the past. And it sure as hell seemed like they were sleeping together now.

"Okay," she said.

His eyes narrowed. "Okay?"

"It doesn't matter."

"I'm getting the impression that it matters a lot."

She tried to ignore the tears pounding away at the backs of her eyes, threatening to break through.

"The bottom line is that I don't trust you."

His eyes grew darker as the line of his mouth hardened.

But his voice remained level. She guessed he might actually be hurt. The Stud always did the dumping, not the other way around.

"So I'm the only one who's supposed to embrace blind faith?"

She frowned. "What the hell are you talking about?"

"The Booshang fiasco. I keep defending you when other people think you might be involved."

Talk about deflection. How dare he throw that other stuff in her face now.

He cut her off before she got to the door.

"We need to talk, Veda."

Her unshed tears kept building up, but she held them back.

"I have nothing more to say."

"I don't know what you want from me." He drove both hands through his damp hair. "Galloping down that hill, I swear I was only thinking of you."

"Don't worry." She shoved past him. "You'll get over it."

Veda hated to think just how quick.

Fourteen

The next day, the stewards' meeting was over in record time.

As Ajax left the building, he didn't have a chance to re-hash the findings with his family before a tidal wave of reporters descended. There were TV cameras crowding him in while microphones got shoved in his face.

"How do you feel about the decision?" one reporter asked.

"What's your next move?" asked another.

"Clients have left Rawsons," someone cried out from the back of the mob. "How badly has this discredited your name?"

In his faultless attorney style, Jacob stepped forward and spoke for the family.

"This meeting was a courtesy to let Ajax Rawson know that samples taken from Someone's Prince Charming confirmed that no State Gaming Commission regulations were violated with regard to illegal drugs, medications or other substances. Furthermore, we would like to make clear that Mr. Rawson was not aware of Paul Booshang's questionable actions on the day under investigation."

A different reporter from a national network got her question in.

"Why did Paul Booshang implicate you, Ajax?"

Ajax stepped forward while his family arced around him. "You'd have to ask him. It seems bizarre and a total waste of time to me."

"Today Booshang implicated another big stable owner in multiple past misdeeds dating back decades," the same reporter said. "Will Drake Darnel be investigated?"

Hux fielded the question. "We can't speak for anyone else." He clapped Ajax on the shoulder. "We're just glad to get back to business as usual."

There were a few more questions asked and answered before Jacob stepped in again and closed the session.

"Well done," Hux said, shaking both his sons' hands as the reporters began to drift away. "And now that we're all law-and-ordered out, I suggest we put on our feed bags."

Wearing a smart pantsuit, Lanie piped up, "There's a new place opened around the corner. Grape pie's on the menu, I hear." She found Susan's gaze. "Not anywhere near as good as yours, of course. But it is the man of the hour's favorite."

Ajax loved grape pie almost as much as he loved the support his family was showing him. He couldn't have been more pleased with the outcome. But for once he wasn't particularly hungry. He was thinking about Veda. He couldn't get her out of his mind.

Jacob was hugging the women goodbye. "I gotta go. I promised Buddy and Tea I'd cook my world's best ever spaghetti tonight. Pasta from scratch. Sauce to die for."

Susan planted a big kiss on his cheek. "You need to give me the recipe."

"And we need to see the rest of the family up here again soon," Hux added as he drew Susan close. "There's nothing better."

Clearly Hux and Susan were in love—had been for many years. There was a familiarity and trust that radiated whenever they were together, and it didn't matter that they weren't as young as they once were. That kind of love just grew and grew. It was real and it was lasting.

"I'm going to shoot off, too," Griff said, checking his wristwatch.

"Big date tonight?" Jacob asked, nudging Ajax in the ribs as if to say, *We know this dude's game.*

"As a matter of fact…none of your business." Griff gave a wink as he headed off.

Which left four to enjoy that new place Lanie had recommended.

"Ajax, I need to apologize," Hux said as the women walked off ahead of them.

Ajax wasn't sure this was the right place or time.

"We can talk later, Dad."

"It's been weighing on my mind…how I expected too much of you, and even learned to depend on you. You're right. I don't show nearly enough gratitude for what you do. I haven't truly acknowledged how much you've sacrificed."

Ajax felt as if his chest just puffed out ten inches. He and Hux had said some things to each other they shouldn't have. It was good to hear his father open up this way.

"We wouldn't be nearly as successful," Hux went on, "if it weren't for all the hours you put in every week."

"Well, I love taking care of my team."

Susan was calling out, "You guys coming?"

Hux replied, "Be right there." Then he caught Ajax's gaze again and gave a definitive nod. "Jacob has his career. Griff and Lanie, too. And you, Ajax, have made a real name for yourself in this industry, not only as a trainer and businessman but as a gentleman."

Ajax ran a finger around the inside of his collar. "I wouldn't go that far."

"People enjoy your company. They want to work with you. Yes, we've had some losses these past weeks, but that won't take away from your legacy."

Legacy? "I'm not that old, am I?"

"Well, you're old enough for this." Hux reached into his jacket's inner pocket and drew out a folded document. "You deserve this, son. I should have taken care of it sooner."

When Ajax unfolded the paperwork, his stomach did a flip. He could barely believe his eyes. "This is a partnership agreement."

"Between you and me for the farm."

Ajax coughed out a laugh. This was precisely what he'd wanted. What he had decided to demand as long overdue. Inside he was kicking his heels, pumping both fists, because he was legitimately happy.

Yep.

He really was.

"It needs your signature," Hux explained as Ajax handed the contract back.

"Sure." He blew out a shaky breath over a smile and added, "Thanks. I really mean that."

"I know you do." Hux hesitated. "But I can see you're focused on something else right now."

Ajax rolled back his shoulders, shook his head. "You don't want to know."

"Let me guess. Veda Darnel." When Ajax nodded, Hux's expression deepened. "I owe you an apology there, too. I attacked that girl's character when, of course, she wasn't involved in the Booshang mess. Veda Darnel is important to you. I should have given that more consideration before running my mouth off. I was just pissed at her father shooting *his* mouth off to the press…pointing fingers…"

A reporter rushed over—the same guy who had asked about their next move.

"A heads-up," the reporter said. "We're all shooting over to get a statement from Darnel."

"You're out of luck," Ajax said. "Drake Darnel is in the hospital."

"Negative. My sources say he got out this morning. I'm not sure that he knows he's been implicated in the wrongdoing today." The reporter was striding away. "We're about to find out."

"They never let up," Hux said, removing his hat to dab his brow with a monogrammed handkerchief. "Hell, I almost feel sorry for Drake having to face it alone, and with no warning."

Ajax didn't care about Drake Darnel. As that reporter jumped into a news van and sped off, he was thinking about the one person who didn't deserve a grilling. The only person he cared about right now.

Veda.

Earlier that morning, when Veda had arrived, the doctor had yet to finish his rounds and give her father a green light to leave. In the waiting room, Veda had taken the time to reaffirm her decision, effective as of today.

To say Drake Darnel was a difficult man was an understatement. This week he had provoked not one but two significant disagreements. Rarely did he show that he cared. As far as fatherly affection was concerned, he'd missed practically every class. But that was on him.

Veda had her own life now.

The drive home from the hospital had been strained. Now as Drake walked into the house and headed for the kitchen, Veda took in his lanky figure. He was getting older…more gray hair and even more impatience. When she was a little girl, of course she had respected him. Growing up, she had no choice but to endure his miserable moods. Even as an adult, she had taken his BS. But now, if Drake wasn't on board with the whole mutual respect thing—if he wanted to continue with this crazy controlling crap— then she didn't need to be around him anymore.

She was done.

In the kitchen, he found his favorite Wedgwood cup and saucer. After the water boiled, he brewed his pungent green tea without a word or a look. She knew the drill. Her father dished out his silent treatment as often as sharks shed teeth.

As he lifted the cup, he sniffed and said, "Thank you for collecting me this morning."

Veda's reply was hollow. Automatic.

"You're welcome."

"The doctor said that I'm well enough to drive again now."

Meaning he didn't need her to taxi him around in one of his many cars housed in that huge, pristine garage.

Wonderful.

He took his time slicing a lemon and squeezing just enough into the brew before his gaze lifted to meet hers for the first time that day.

"This hasn't been a good week," he said.

"Tell me about it."

He grunted and squeezed some more lemon.

"Veda, are you still seeing that man?"

She stiffened. Firstly, she didn't want to think about Ajax right now. She wished she never had to think about him again. Secondly, her father needed to back off.

"I won't discuss Ajax Rawson with you," she replied.

"I think we need to talk about it," he said.

"I really don't."

"Come into the living room and we'll sit down."

As he moved toward her, Veda's patience expired and she held up her hand for him to stop.

"I won't do this anymore."

He frowned. "Do what?"

"I need to walk away. I mean *really* walk away. I should have done it a long time ago."

His brow furrowed before he scratched an ear and set his cup and saucer back down on the counter.

"I need to show you something," he said. "Something I see every day and yet never want to acknowledge."

Veda pushed out a heavy breath. "You're talking in riddles." Trying to manipulate her.

"A riddle… I suppose it is. Maybe we can solve it together."

Veda narrowed her eyes at him. She hadn't heard him use this tone before, or this tactic. "You aren't making any sense."

"Why don't you come and see for yourself?" When she continued to study him, trying to work out the trap, his eyebrows pinched before a small smile hooked one side of his mouth.

"Please, Veda?" he asked.

She couldn't remember a time when Drake had looked anything close to vulnerable. Whatever this riddle was, she had to see it.

She followed him through to the den, a large, well-appointed room with its own library, wet bar and assortment of fine art, including a full-sized bronze horse sculpture at the dead center of the room. Drake went to stand behind his ultra-tidy desk and waited for her to join him. When they were side by side, he slid open the top left-hand drawer, reached inside and pulled out three items…a pair of gold wedding rings and a photograph. A family photograph from when Veda was a little girl, prior to going to school.

He laid the rings in his palm and flipped over the

photo—the inscription on the back read, "Veda's three!"—before placing it faceup on the desk. In awe, she took in the image of father, mother and daughter sitting on the chesterfield in the living room. Drake was so young, with dark hair and no scowl lines. With her cheek pressed against Veda's, her beautiful mom was beaming. The room was packed with people smiling for the camera or looking adoringly at the lucky girl with her striking cloud of red curls. Drake was holding a kids' picture book—a birthday gift, Veda assumed.

As she let the image sink in, Veda's throat ached with emotion. There was gratitude that she had once known this kind of support coupled with a near-desperate longing to know it again. She was still digesting the fact that Drake had kept those wedding rings and this happy family snapshot when he drew a fourth item from the drawer. It was an old book.

The one in the photo.

"I wanted you to grow up to be smart and happy," he said, focusing on the cartoon barn animal scene on the book's cover.

Absorbing every detail of the cover, with its two horses, cow, three pigs and fluffy little dog, Veda got this warm, rippling feeling. She couldn't be sure, but it was so similar to the picture she'd had in her mind for so long…an image of how her own animal farm might look.

Her father cleared his throat but then studied the photograph again with a smile she had never seen on him before…like he not only remembered but also cherished having had that joy in his life.

"I spent practically all my time on the business," he said, "making sure you were both well provided for…that you could grow up with everything you needed and deserved. The trouble started the day after this party. She asked me to spend more time with you both. As the years went by, her patience turned into irritation and, ultimately, despair."

Veda picked up the musty-smelling photo and looked into her mother's smiling eyes. So many times she remembered her saying that she had only ever wanted three things: a happy child, a nice home and a good husband. Was that too much to ask?

"The more your mom insisted I put work second," he went on, "the more I retreated and looked back, clutching on to something—some*one*—who had never truly been mine. To take my mind off fixing a real problem, being less selfish, I began to focus on that aspect of my life. I picked and picked until I felt it like a scab on my heart."

He was talking about the woman Hux Rawson had fallen in love with and married. The mother Ajax had lost around the same time Veda's own mom had died.

"I was an uncompromising fool, stuck in my ways." Drake eyes were glistening. "I threw it all away."

Veda had never heard her father speak like this before… with insight and humility. Like a human being rather than a cracked and bitter shell.

"I saw you slap her once," she said.

He cringed like he remembered it well. "She had stopped talking to me. Stopping caring altogether. I thought she might have someone else." He shook his head hard. "I was wrong. There's no excuse. None."

Veda had half expected him to deny the entire incident, so she got something else off her chest. "I can't remember you ever really talking to me."

"I kept it all in. Blocked everyone out. And this week, I've pushed you even further away. I know if I don't change, and change now, I'll lose you again, and this time for good." Holding that book to his chest, he turned more toward her and lowered his chin. "I don't want that to happen. Veda.

It's hard for me to say, but—" he swallowed deeply "—I need your help."

This conversation just kept getting weirder. "You want *my* help?"

"I see from your blog, you're a bit of an expert at that."

Veda's mouth dropped open. She must have heard wrong. "You read my blog?"

"Every post. It's to the point. Extremely informative." His eyes shone as he smiled. "I haven't told you for so many years. I'm proud of you, Veda. I know your mother would be proud of you, too."

Those words... The night of that party, she remembered Hux saying them to Lanie.

The right thing to do was wrap her arms around her father and tell him everything was forgiven...to let go of the uncertainty, the fear and all the frustration. Letting go was a choice, after all. But she needed time to come to terms with this sudden change of heart and accept that her father might actually, well, love her.

So she held off on gushing. Instead, she returned her father's smile and nodded as if to say, *Let's see what happens from here. Fingers crossed.*

A speculative gleam appeared in his eye.

"Now we really do need to speak about Ajax Rawson."

She groaned. "Dad, can we not?"

"I was only going to say that we should have him over for dinner sometime." He anticipated her reaction. "Yes, it will be a little awkward. The Rawsons and Darnels are far from friends. I've done some things I'm ashamed of, particularly this week. I'm not sure Ajax would even accept an invitation. But I can try, Veda. *We* can try."

If the offer had come a week earlier, she would have considered it. But her on-again, off-again relationship with Ajax had been permanently laid to rest. Any notion of extending olive branches between the families was too late.

So, should she let her father know about the breakup? Would his eyes fill with sympathy—support—or would he simply say *I told you so*?

The sound of the knocker hitting the front door echoed through the house. But her father didn't react. He had more to say.

"How does a man who has lost what's most important get it back?" he asked. "That's the riddle."

She didn't have the whole answer, but said, "He starts by saying I'm sorry and meaning it."

Drake hung his head before finding her eyes again. "I'm so sorry, Veda. Sorry for driving your mother away. Sorry for putting up that wall and not appreciating what I had."

The knocker sounded again.

Veda swept away a tear before it fell. "We should probably get that."

He tried on a smile. "To be continued, then?"

Before she could answer, Veda's ears pricked up to a different sound. "Do you hear that?"

Drake's eyes narrowed as he looked out the den's window, which gave a partial view of the front of the house. "There are vans pulling up." He headed for the door. "I'll go see what's happening."

Veda set the photograph down and told him, "I'm going with you."

Out in front of the Darnel mansion, the Rawson truck skidded to a stop. With Hux riding shotgun—Lanie and Susan had decided to stay in town and leave this showdown to the men—Ajax had arrived here in record time but, unfortunately, not soon enough.

Reporters were congregated on the lawn, the same pack Jacob had handled so well earlier. Cameras were pointed like cannons at the front door, and questions were being thrown like knives. Facing the onslaught, standing at the center of his extravagant stone porch, Drake Darnel looked completely blindsided.

Ajax didn't care about Drake. Only Veda. She was standing beside her father, chin high, loyal to the bitter end.

Ajax threw open the car door, growling, "I'm going to save my girl."

"This all ends now," Hux replied, growling, too. "*All* of it."

Together, father and son strode up and cut through the media mob. Ajax was ready to tell them all to back the hell off and go home. But then Hux did something downright extraordinary. Something that had Ajax doubting his own eyes and ears.

Hux trotted up those porch steps. When he came to stand beside his old enemy, Drake's shocked expression deepened and Veda's eyes practically popped out of her skull. Then, turning to confront the mob, Hux waved his arms. When the barrage of questions quietened, he took a breath while Drake and Veda gaped on.

"My family spoke with you people earlier," Hux said. "You all know the score on those dud test results. As you are all obviously aware, this morning Paul Booshang, a former employee, went on to implicate Drake Darnel in similar illegal activities."

"Mr. Darnel!" a reporter called out. "Sir, what is your relationship with Paul Booshang?"

"Has the State Gaming Commission been in touch regarding this matter?" asked another.

Drake took a halting step forward. "The Darnel Stables… I have never…would…never…"

Hux edged closer to Drake's side and, catching his gaze, tried to share a stalwart smile.

"Let me be honest here. These stables are among the best and most reputable in the state," Hux said. "In the country." His voice took on a solemn tone. "Our families have known each other many years. I would like to go on the record as standing alongside our neighbors against these baseless allegations."

Ajax was watching Veda watching Hux. She looked like a child tasting ice cream for the first time—there was a second of surprise quickly followed by delight.

Hux went on. "Mr. Darnel has returned from the hospital only a short time ago. I'm sure you all agree, we need to walk it back and respect his privacy right now." He offered a meaningful smile to Drake. "It's time we all moved on."

Talk about taking the high road.

As the reporters and cameramen drifted off toward their vehicles, Ajax made his way up the porch steps. He wasn't sure what he was going to say to Hux, let alone Drake; this morning had certainly been one for the books.

But more importantly, he needed to talk with Veda. The last time they had spoken, she hadn't pulled any punches. He didn't have what she needed, and he would move on soon enough.

Ajax hadn't agreed then, and he didn't agree now. He needed one more chance to have her hear why.

Hux put out his arm to welcome his son as he climbed the steps. "Drake, I don't know if you've had the pleasure of meeting my boy."

As the other man's watery gaze narrowed, Ajax held his breath. Drake knew he had been seeing Veda. Given Drake's screwy way of looking at the world, he might view that as stealing his daughter, just as Hux had "stolen" the woman Drake had loved so many years ago.

But now Drake only surrendered a genuine smile and put out his hand.

"I'm pleased to meet you… Ajax, isn't it?"

Ajax's knees almost buckled. He had to be dreaming.

But when Drake's smile not only held but grew, Ajax accepted the fact that miracles did happen. Which was great news, because he sure as hell could use another one right about now.

There was a brief exchange about this morning's meeting and Hux's handling of the media before Drake invited them all inside for a cool drink. Ajax had felt Veda's eyes on him the entire time. Had this unfolding scene softened her stand against him? Ready or not, time to find out.

"A cool drink would be nice," he told Drake before focusing on Veda. "But I'd like to speak with your daughter first, if that's all right."

After an awkward beat, in which Drake and Veda exchanged looks, Drake headed for the open front door, tossing over his shoulder, "Huxley, shall we?"

When he and Veda were alone, Ajax tried on a *well, here we all are smile* while she scooped her hair back behind her ear, searching his eyes, looking more beautiful than ever before.

"I appreciate you and Hux coming today," she said. "We were totally unprepared for reporters."

"They'd just finished with us when we got word they were on their way here."

She titled her head. "So, congratulations on the test results."

"Yeah, well, it was an experience, and not without consequences."

"Have any more clients bailed?"

"One. But we've had a lot of support, as well."

She nodded. "Full steam ahead then."

"Which brings me to some other news. You remember how I wanted Hux to consider a partnership? I was saving the discussion until this was all over, but Dad was a step ahead of me. Right after the meeting this morning, he presented me with a document—fifty-fifty."

Her eyebrows edged up. "Bet you couldn't find a pen fast enough."

A week ago, that would have been the smart bet. As it turned out, he had handed the contract back, leaving it unsigned. For now.

When Veda slid a look toward the front door, he anticipated her next words. She would either suggest that they join their fathers or, more likely, that she would leave the men alone to talk. Neither option worked. He wanted more time with her alone. He needed to somehow make this right.

He spoke again before she could.

"So your dad got the all clear from the doctor?"

She nodded an unusually long time as if she wasn't sure if she should fill him in more.

"Actually, Dad and I had a discussion this morning," she finally said. "A real talk like I can't remember ever happening before."

"That's *huge*. Seems like it's a day for progress."

"Well, it's a start." She surrendered a smile. "I think a good start."

There was another loaded silence during which Ajax thought he saw a glimmer of anticipation in her eyes…a spark of *Say the right thing now and maybe I'll agree to see where this goes.* He had nothing to lose and pretty much everything to gain.

He'd get the tricky part out of the way first.

"Fallon's gone. She wanted me to pass on that she's sorry if she caused any trouble between you and me."

Other than crossing her arms, Veda gave no response. Not a word.

He forced the admission out. "I want to tell you that years ago, she and I spent a night together. Just one."

"I know."

"You…know?"

"Lanie told me."

"How did she—?"

"Griff."

He grunted. "So much for a brother's confidence."

"Oh, Ajax, I'm sure he's not the only one who knew."

He got back to the point. "Now Fallon is a friend," he said. "That's it. Friend. Period."

When Veda continued with the bland stare, he pushed on. He could feel his time running out. He needed to act, bring her close, show her just how he felt.

"Veda, I want to see you again."

Her jaw tightened before she shook her head.

No?

"Our fathers have put aside their differences," he said. "Can't we at least try to do the same?"

"I'm glad everyone's talking again. Dad and Hux. Me and my father. You and your dad."

He stepped forward, close enough to feel her warmth and for her to feel his.

"I'm way more interested in the two of us," he said.

She shook her head again.

"It's just… I feel very strongly about this," he went on. "About us."

"I know it's hard when you're so used to winning."

Every muscle in his body tensed. He had never known a woman like her. She never gave him a pass.

And then, as if she wanted to prove him wrong, she unfolded her arms and made a concession.

"I believe you about Fallon Kelly," she said.

He sparked up. "You do?"

When she looked almost disappointed, like she thought he was surprised that he had pulled the wool over her eyes, he took it down a notch.

"It's the truth. Veda, I would never do that to you."

She seemed to gather her thoughts before moving to the railing. When he joined her, her eyes were narrowed on the horizon like she was trying to see into the future. Or maybe back into the past.

"I'm not a fan of cowboys," she said. "Particularly the smooth-talking kind."

"You've made that pretty clear."

"Do you want to know why? The truest, deepest, most terrifying reason?"

As she faced him, he searched her resigned expression and nodded. "I really do."

"You know that my mother died in a car accident," she began.

"That was the word at the time."

"I was in the back seat."

He straightened as his stomach pitched. "God, Veda... were you hurt?"

"Not a scratch." Her grin was wry. "Isn't that something?"

More than ever, he wanted to reassure her somehow. But the best way to do that now was to sit tight and listen.

"After Mom left my dad, she hooked up with a man. A cowboy with a silver tongue. Or at least where my mother was concerned. Dad didn't keep in touch as such, but he sent money. Lots of it. Her cowboy was as sweet as he needed to be to get Mom to pay all the bills, including his gambling debts."

Ajax shuddered. He knew about Veda's problems with her dad and dyslexia. But this story was shaping up to be even worse.

"There were times when I was alone with him. He was nice until he started drinking. When he found out I couldn't read that well, he liked to put me down. He'd make out like he was joking, calling me Dumbo, flapping his hands at the sides of his head."

Oh, Ajax was mad now. Was this asshole still alive? He wanted to track him down and teach him a lesson about picking on someone his own size.

"The night of the accident," Veda went on, "he was

drinking from a flask with a pair of bull's horns etched into the tin. Mom was driving. He wanted to see Vegas, so Vegas it was. He'd never been mean to me in front of her before. Only ever sweet like he was with her, even when she accused him of being with another woman. *It's all in your head, darlin'. I would never do that to you.* But he told me once—said it straight-out—Mom was just his latest."

Ajax felt as if he were shrinking into the floor. The link was obvious.

But he wasn't that cowboy. He wasn't that kind of man.

He dug his hands deeper into his pockets. "You didn't tell your mom how he was with you?"

"I wanted to, but I didn't want to take her happiness away. She was so in love with the guy."

The absolute wrong guy.

While Ajax ground his teeth, Veda continued her story.

"We were in the car that night when he started on about my grades. I needed to try harder, he said. Do better. Then he called me Dumbo, softly at first, but getting louder. Growing meaner."

Veda's hands were laced together so tight, the knuckles were white.

"I didn't want to cry," she said. "I wanted to tell him to shut up. That he wasn't any better than me. But I was frozen…couldn't get the words out. Mom was ripping into him, though. Telling him to back off or get out."

Ajax felt sick to his stomach. There really were some first-class pricks in the world. Men who got their kicks from hurting kids and women. Lowlifes who had zero respect for themselves or anyone else.

"I was sitting in the back seat," Veda said, "throat closed, only choked sobs getting out. Then…all I remember is the bull horns on that flask and the oncoming headlights getting closer through the rain."

Ajax had heard enough. He brought Veda close and held her until she had finished shaking.

"The thing is," she went on, "when we lived here, I blamed myself for my mother being unhappy so much of the time. She wanted to keep the family together. I was the reason she stayed so long. And, of course, I blamed myself for the accident. For her death. She'd been distracted, trying to protect the dumb, mute weirdo who had never learned to defend herself."

Ajax dredged up a heavy smile. "But, boy, you can stand up for yourself now."

She straightened. "I know who I am. Even if it's hard sometimes, I know what I need to feel good about myself, and I can't afford to ever go back." Cupping his cheek, she searched his eyes and told him, "Ajax, not even for you."

Fifteen

Since that afternoon two weeks ago when she and Ajax Rawson had said goodbye for good, Veda had fallen into a slump. She had gotten involved with the wrong man and fallen in love. Now she was paying the price.

Today, after seeing off a new client at the door of her Jersey condo, Veda pulled up her sleeves and made a decision. She needed to regain a sense of control and, as nervous as she was about it, she thought she knew how. Time to step up, put it out there and reclaim that final piece of her power.

Veda opened her laptop and pulled up her Best Life Now blog on the screen. Over the years, she had discussed life's many challenges here: family, health, education and, of course, relationship issues. But this morning's post would go deeper and hopefully help even more.

I always try to be honest, Veda wrote under the header "A Life Coach's Best Advice." *That's the way to build trust in relationships and get good results. Except I haven't been completely open here. I have a big secret, you see. One that I'm finally ready to share.*

My brain has trouble with letters and associated sounds. Things can get jumbled and blend together all wrong. In school, I really struggled to read. Then, whenever I got stressed, I would freeze up. Zone out.

Think of a possum playing dead. Nothing to see here, folks!

Once I got my dyslexia diagnosis, things improved. I had a word and reason that explained my daily struggles, as well as tools to help me cope. After some hard work, I found my way out of that hole. Now I try to help others climb out of theirs. And guess what. Some of my Best Life Now clients have been dyslexic just like me.

But here's the kicker. The bare bones truth without a wrapper.

I never let any of them know. A part of me was still embarrassed. Ashamed. And yes, even scared.

I won't do that anymore.

So, what's this life coach's best advice?

When you feel like hiding away or flat-out giving up, remind yourself that none of us is perfect. Everyone is spectacularly unique. Then stand up, fill your lungs and shout from the rooftops.

If I want to be free, I need to be me!

Ajax and his team were finishing up for the afternoon when Hux walked into the stables.

"Another blistering win for this one last week," Hux said, eyeing Someone's Prince Charming's whiteboard chart. "Good job, son."

After making a note about feed, Ajax set down the pen. "Things are certainly getting back to normal."

Hux entered the stall to check Prince's hooves.

"I heard from Matt today," he said, rubbing a fingertip around one of the plates. "Paul Booshang finally came clean. Apparently over the years, he'd lost everything at the track. He said if he couldn't take down horse racing in its entirety, he wanted to at least cause a stir for some guys at the top. He had a personal gripe with Darnel…the way he'd treated his family…something about a tree house." Hux straightened. "Apparently a TV network has offered him a fortune for the story."

Ajax recalled one of Veda's arguments against the industry. "Losing your shirt… I wonder how many people can identify."

"Son, you can't help people like that. They have no control."

That's what Ajax had always thought, but that was kind of the point, wasn't it? "You have to admit we're at least part of the problem."

"We don't twist anyone's arm. We don't force anyone to get into bed with a loan shark."

Ajax paraphrased Veda. "A drug dealer doesn't force an addict to keep using, either."

Hux was on to the last hoof. "Hardly the same thing. Horse racing generates billions of dollars for the state's economy. It's a tradition." Joining Ajax again, Hux pushed on with another topic of conversation as he looked up and down the stalls. "So, update me on any new plans you have, partner."

Ajax had signed that contract. Half the land and half the profits were now his. A huge achievement, particularly knowing that he truly had his father's respect.

Only…he had thought it would feel better than this. That he might feel, well, really whole now. Complete.

"The new walker's almost finished," he said, grabbing his hat and heading to the door with Hux. "I put on another vet this morning. The very best credentials, and we're on the same page with regard to overmedicating."

All too often in the industry, horses were given powerful medications that allowed them to race despite their injuries.

Hux dropped his hat on his head. "Good. Good. We want a fair race."

"And healthy horses."

Hux's smile deepened as they headed out into the sunshine. "I'm so fortunate to have a son who wants nothing more than to carry on the family tradition. You've always been so dedicated. Such a natural."

Looking around the place, Ajax held his hat in his hands. "I've been at it a long time."

"And will be for a long time to come."

That had always been the plan, and Ajax hadn't wanted anything more. Now... Well, he had other things on his mind, all to do with a strong-minded redhead who had put up a wall he couldn't find a way to break down.

"Something troubling you?" Hux asked. "Maybe something to do with Veda Darnel?"

Ajax tried to shrug it off. "I'm good."

Hux gave a thoughtful nod. "Well, you know what they say."

"No. What do they say?"

"Plenty more fish in the sea."

Ajax shut one eye as he winced. "I don't see Veda as a fish."

"I'm only saying that she must not be the one. But one day you'll find your special someone, no doubt about it. And when you do, you'll know. And so will she."

When Hux hailed a groom on his way to a tack room, Ajax headed back to the office with his father's words still ringing in his ears. Hux didn't know what he and Veda had discussed that day on Drake's porch. Her story was as private, and haunting, as they come. Ajax couldn't stop thinking about the circumstances surrounding her mom's death. That cowboy had been lower than a bottom-feeder. No wonder Veda had developed a lifelong aversion to that type.

But Ajax reassured himself again: he was nothing like that. He could never treat anyone that way. *Never*.

And yet those lines kept circling.

It's all in your head, darlin'.

I would never do that to you.

Yes, he had known a few women in his life, but as he had explained to Veda, he had never parted with anyone on bad terms. Fallon Kelly was a case in point. Except...

If he were to be 100 percent honest, he had always gotten out early for just that reason—to avoid the possibility of an ugly breakup. Put another way: he liked to have his cake and eat it, too. He wanted to enjoy the intimate company of a beautiful, engaging woman without the drag of making anything official.

But with Veda, that way of thinking—of feeling—just didn't seem to fit. Where she was concerned, the idea of commitment didn't spook him. In fact, he couldn't fathom a time when he didn't want to be with her, and only her.

Things had changed.

He had changed.

As Ajax reached the main paddock, Chester came trotting down from the house like he usually did this time of day. Trying to clear his head, Ajax deliberated on a chestnut prancing about, tossing her mane, while a buckskin colt capered up, his tail elevated and strong neck curved. Farther down, in the next paddock, two retired horses were grazing, stomping a hoof every now and then to shoo away flies. Over the years, he'd given away others to good and caring homes.

Scenes like this had filled and shaped his life. He'd grown up hankering for the next bustling day at the track. From a young age, he'd always leaped out of bed before the birds to start the day. The horses in his care had grade-A food and exercise, as well as the best grooms, riders, farriers and veterinary care.

He loved his horses. They were treated like kings.

But there were still injuries, some of them fatal. More than once he had watched, heartsick, as one of his own had gone down. The latest statistics said over fifty horses had died or been euthanized on New York State racecourses just this year.

He'd been one of the blinder-wearing crowd who argued that those numbers were built into the system. But what did that mean exactly? For the owners...for the horses...

Which side was he really on?

When Chester started wagging his tail, Ajax realized they had company. Susan was strolling over, a covered plate in her hand. He could smell the pie from here.

"Just pulled this out of the oven," she said, removing the cover to reveal a fat slice of his favorite: grape pie.

Ajax accepted the plate. "You're a honey, do you know that?"

Susan gave a big dimpled grin before she turned to study the horses.

"Sometimes I still can't believe I actually found my way here," she said. "This truly is my safe haven home."

Ajax had always believed this was his safe haven, too. That he would always feel rooted and cared for here. But lately trying to hold on to that had left a cold, heavy knot in his gut. He was hardly a kid anymore but still a long way from hanging up his reins. Was there more for him somewhere out there?

"You must be glad all that doping business is behind you," she said, leaning down to ruffle Chester's ears while his tail batted the ground. "And I'm so relieved that feud between Hux and Drake Darnel is finally over," she added. "Just goes to show. Differences can be worked out even when we might think there's no hope." She slid him a look. "I'm sure Veda would agree. She seems like a lovely girl."

"She is lovely. And smart." He paused, then added, "And strong."

"Yes, indeed," Susan said, looking out over the paddock again. "Diamonds are definitely out there. My ex-husband, however...well, he was a grimy lump of coal."

Ajax recalled that Veda's mother had stayed with Drake for the sake of the family. But Susan hadn't had children with her ex-husband. Why had she stayed so long? He hoped she wouldn't mind if he asked.

"Why didn't you leave the guy sooner?"

"Well, I married young. Taking those vows... I thought I had to stay. But over the years, of course the abuse wore me down, to the point I could barely think straight. Hux helped bring me back. I truly am a different person because of his love." She thought that through more and added, "Or maybe not different so much as... I think the right word is authentic. He's so lovely. And smart. And strong."

Ajax grinned. *Lovely. Smart. Strong.* Those words were a common link between Susan's love for Hux and his own thoughts on Veda. And Hux might have helped Susan, but she'd done just as much for him. Maybe more.

So, what would have happened to Hux, to their family, if Susan hadn't come along? Ajax wanted to believe that his father would have come out of that thick dark fog on his own. But he wondered....

And if *he* fell in love, married, had kids, and something happened to his wife—if she died... How would he deal? Would he cope or simply want to give in?

After Susan left with Chester bounding off ahead of her, Ajax took his pie into the office. As he sat behind his desk and opened his laptop, he mulled over Susan's words.

She had helped settle what he'd been struggling with for weeks. He needed to reach out to Veda again because he couldn't dance around the truth anymore. Earlier Hux had given sound advice about a person knowing when they had found their special someone. Ajax *did* know. He had to believe that Veda knew, too.

But he'd run out of things to say.

What could he do to convince her?

He set the pie aside to search Best Life Now. The link to Veda's website popped up. He checked out each page and ended up on her blog. The latest post had him riveted. He could literally hear her speaking to him, giving him advice.

If I want to be free, I need to be me.

Ajax thought back on those words the following weekend at the track. Someone's Prince Charming was two lengths ahead when he stumbled and broke down.

The examining veterinarian reported catastrophic fractures to both front ankles. The jockey, who had sustained serious injuries, was carried away on a stretcher. When the order was given to euthanize the horse, Ajax was there, kneeling at his friend's side.

On the drive home, his chest and eyes were burning so much, Ajax had to pull over. A bottle of Scotch kept him company through the night. By morning, he'd crossed that line and made up his mind.

To hell with anyone who didn't agree.

Sixteen

Veda heard it first from her dad.

The previous week when they'd talked on FaceTime, Drake had mentioned the "big news concerning the Rawsons." Veda had coughed out a laugh and told him point-blank he was wrong. But her father insisted; a Darnel farrier had confirmed the rumor just that day.

Ajax Rawson was no longer associated with Rawson Studs. No one knew for sure what big plans he had for himself, although talk was that he was still on the property working things through.

Veda hadn't spoken with Ajax since that day on her father's porch two whole months ago when she had opened up more about her past and made her position crystal clear. She had survived some tough breaks. Now that she was in a good place, there was no turning back, only going forward.

At the time, Ajax had looked disappointed, but obviously he had accepted her decision and moved on. Of course, the breakup had brought her down. Coming out on her blog had helped build her sense of self up again, as did personally sharing her dyslexia experiences later with each of her clients. And if she ever felt like curling up into a ball, she reminded herself that she wouldn't feel this way forever. Over time, her love for Ajax would fade.

Unfortunately she couldn't see that happening anytime soon.

Before ending that FaceTime call, Drake had suggested she visit again. How about this weekend? She had smiled and said good idea. It felt weird actually looking forward to spending time with her dad. Even weirder to anticipate driving right past the Rawson property knowing that Ajax was probably still there.

Now, as she traveled on the interstate, getting closer to the Rawsons' connecting road, Veda told her heart to quit pumping so hard. But memories from the night her car had spun out were coming thick and fast. Ajax racing down through the rain to rescue her still felt like something out of a dream.

Her hands were damp on the steering wheel by the time the Rawsons' billboard-size sign came into view. Would things have been different between her and Ajax if that doping scandal hadn't hit? But of course, realistically, they were never going to make it. He had his life and, yes, she had hers.

Veda stepped on the accelerator and forced herself to look straight ahead. She was going to visit her father. When she arrived, Drake would welcome her with a smile and perhaps even a hug. Going through to the kitchen, he would brew his tea while she poured herself a wine. Then they would venture out to the same spot where she and Ajax had relaxed after he had driven her home from the hospital that day. She could see the tree house from there.

Veda slammed on the brakes and caught her breath as another *new* sign came into view.

Welcome to Giddy Up Safe Haven.

The letters were multicolored and cartoonish like the ones from that old birthday book. A drawing of a grinning horse, standing with his front legs crossed, made her smile even harder. Then she spotted something else in a corner. A blue bucket with a dog sitting up inside it. It was small and fluffy with apricot dots on each cheek.

A blasting horn sent Veda jumping out of her seat. As the flatbed truck swerved around her, she turned onto the shoulder of the entrance road. Her heart was slamming against her ribs, and she couldn't contain the grin because this was more than a coincidence.

The Rawsons owned hundreds of acres, including this hill. Ajax knew she had a dream of having a farm where animals didn't have to work or breed or die. A sanctuary. A safe haven. That puppy—little Gus in his bucket—was the bow that tied this all together.

Ajax had created Giddy Up Safe Haven, and he'd done it with her in mind.

Bubbling with excitement, she turned into the entrance road and drove to the crest of that hill. On the plateau, a freshly painted Cape Cod cabin appeared, as well as post-and-rail paddocks, a big old barn and then…

Well, suddenly all those warm, bubbly feelings began to pop and evaporate because on top of being a magnificent example of the male species, Veda knew the truth. Ajax was also a pro in the art of seduction. Lanie had said that he was all about the chase. And it had certainly been true where they were concerned. So, what was really going on here?

Braking, Veda saw movement up ahead. Three horses—a gray, a brindle and a cream—were trotting up to a fence. Ajax was holding two buckets, presumably full of feed. But beneath the wide brim of his black hat, his undivided attention was fixed on her approach.

A yearning, almost desperate heat filled Veda in an instant. In his white button-down, his shoulders looked even bigger. The vee below his open collar was definitely more bronzed. The weight of the buckets strained his gorgeous forearms, highlighting the corded muscle. She could imagine his crooning voice now, saying how beautiful she was, how good she smelled, how much he had missed her and...

"Well, dang, Veda baby. I knew you'd be back."

He had promoted a rumor that suggested he had given up the Rawson brand, his career and the prestige. But seriously? A couple of rescue horses and a rickety old cabin wouldn't hold his attention. That said, she was almost flattered that he'd gone to so much trouble to set up such an elaborate prop.

As he set down the buckets and sauntered over, rocking a pair of worn blue jeans like no other man could, Veda bit her lip to divert the pain that was filling her all the way to the top. He thought he could charm her, fool her, by using a dream she held so dear to her heart?

Setting her jaw, she threw open the car door.

Sorry, cowboy.

Guess again.

As Ajax dropped the buckets and headed over to the Best Life Now vehicle, his thumping heart nearly burst out of his chest. Veda must have seen the Giddy Up sign on her way to her father's place. Her showing up out of the blue gave this move a special seal of approval. He knew his mom was smiling down, cheering him on, giving her blessing.

Just as Hux had done when Ajax had explained why he needed to move on.

He had loved his life growing up. He would always hold dear memories of the farm through his years from a child to a man. But now more than ever, he knew he'd made the right choice. And as Veda got out of the car and her gaze meshed with his, it all felt so damn good, he broke into a jog.

Drawing closer, he watched the breeze play through her hair, making it dance while it pushed that summer dress against her body, emphasizing every delicious sweep and curve. Her green eyes were sparkling in the sunshine, and the beautiful lips he longed to taste again were…

Turned down?

Ajax pulled back.

Veda had found her way here but she wasn't happy? Surely it wasn't anything he could have done. Not this time. Perhaps she'd had another argument with Drake. Maybe there'd been bad news with regard to her business.

Well, if she was looking for a shoulder to lean on, two arms to bring her close and lift her up, she had come to the right place.

He picked up the pace again until he was running right at her. As he swept by, he grabbed her around the waist, hoisted her up against him and twirled her around. He felt her stiffen because of course she was caught off guard. And when he stopped spinning and let her slide down against him, he kept the surprises coming. As soon as her mouth was within range, he kissed her like he'd dreamed of doing every minute of every day since he'd let her walk away.

Now she was back.

You'd better believe she was here to stay.

Ajax worked the kiss, cupping the back of her head while he held her snug against him. Feeling her feet flap in the air, he pressed in deeper as every starving part of him hardened and cried out for more. Veda was gripping what she could of his shoulders, her fingers digging into his shirt while her lower half pressed against his belt. While working on this place these past weeks, he had routinely lost himself in daydreams about a reunion…how steamy and flat-out joyous the makeup sex would be. But this moment was about way more than anything physical. This connection was real, and no matter how many challenges the future threw their way, they would make it through together. To the depths of his soul, he knew that.

But then…

Well, something changed.

Veda didn't seem to be gripping his shirt so much as trying to shove him away. And while he was certain she'd been kissing him back a moment ago, now her mouth was closed, shutting him out.

Pulling back, he searched her eyes. They were shining with emotion. But he wouldn't call it love.

"Let me down!" She pushed him again. "What are you doing? Are you crazy?"

It took another second for those words to sink in. After setting her down, he tried to figure out how the hell he had read it so wrong.

"I get out of my car and you literally jump on me," she was saying. "You really have a problem, you know that?"

He blinked several times, rubbed his brow. "I presumed you were here to see me."

"I was curious," she said, rearranging her dress, which was askew after that amazing midair kiss.

His lips were still burning, begging for more. But he needed to stay focused and rewind to a time before he had believed she had actually wanted him to sweep her off her feet.

"Okay." Holding up both hands, he took in a deep breath, blew it out. "What's going on?"

"I was driving by," she explained, "when I saw the sign. I'd heard rumors."

"That I'd walked away from Rawsons. Correct."

Her eyes widened. "You really did?"

"I decided that I needed to do something different. Something where I could be around horses but…"

His words trailed off because this had all taken such a sharp turn in the wrong direction. What was she so pissed about? What had he done wrong now?

He threw a glance at the new paddock railings he'd put up, then at the cabin roof he'd almost finished repairing. The old barn was big enough to house twenty retired race-horses.

Veda was looking around, too, like she was waiting to be ambushed or expecting a big rock to crash on her head.

"You've really put a lot of work into this," she finally said, obviously remembering the pictures he'd shown her on his phone.

"Yeah." His mouth twisted as the backs of his eyes kind of prickled. "I did."

She crossed her arms. "But if this is all for me, you shouldn't have bothered."

He just looked at her now because...*wow*.

Just.

Wow.

"If you want to know, this wasn't just for you," he said over the god-awful lump in his throat. "It was for *us*. You were the one who said to go after the things that matter most. I thought I could make us both happy. In fact, when I set my mind to it, I felt so good, so sure, I thought you'd be blown away."

She hesitated, then said, "You really thought that I'd trust you?"

"Right." He stepped back into her space. "Because if this is going to work, and I know that it can, we need to trust each other. That's what love is about, damn it!"

He clenched his jaw and dialed it back. She obviously wasn't ready for this. Would she ever be?

Raking a hand through his hair, he groaned. "I need to shut up now—"

"No," she said as quick as a whip. Then the corners of

her mouth twitched. It wasn't exactly a smile but not an outright scowl, either.

He tried to corral the emotions needing to break free. But he couldn't contain the way he felt about her. Right now, this minute, he needed her to know it all.

"I enrolled in college. A bachelor's degree in animal biology. Vet school is another four years at least on top of that, so maybe not—"

"Maybe *yes*." She came forward. "That's so amazing. You always wanted to do that."

Ajax remembered the day when Someone's Prince Charming had broken down. He hadn't been able to save him. But he'd made his decision very soon after that.

"And I took some advice from your blog," he said.

Her eyes widened. "You read my blog?"

"I've done way more than that." He let it all out. "I've fallen in love with you, Veda. But it's more than that, too." He held her arms. "I know I want to spend the rest of my days with you."

When her lips quivered with a growing smile and her eyes filled with what he hoped were happy tears, he looped his arms around her waist and tugged her close again.

"I've brought over my retirees," he said, flickering a glance at the trio. "There'll be more to come. And there's plenty of room for pet pigs and sheep and a fluffy little dog we'll call Gus, too."

She still wasn't talking. Not a croak. Not a peep.

But the tears in her eyes were close to falling, and her lips were definitely calling to him again. So he leaned that bit closer, held her that much tighter and laid out the last of his speech.

"This is who I am," he told her. "This is who I want to be. With you every damn day for as long as we live."

This time when they kissed, Ajax felt a sense of certainty spiral through him, filling him up in a way that reaffirmed what he already knew. He had made the right choice. Veda would always be his sweetheart.

Veda was "the one."

When he slowly broke the kiss, her eyes were heavy with the same wonderful emotions he was feeling.

"Veda," he said, "you are the best thing that's ever happened to me."

"You really mean that? The *best*?"

She looked too choked up to get more words out. But then she took a breath, and asked in a near whisper, "Ajax?"

He smiled and brought her closer. "Yes, Veda."

"I love you, too. I'm pretty sure I loved you from the start."

Then he was kissing her again, lifting her higher, loving her even more. And he knew this time they had done it.

Theirs would be the best life ever.

The best there ever was.

* * * * *

THE DATING DARE

BARBARA DUNLOP

For all my friends at the office.

One

It wasn't like I was completely alone.

I had friends at work. Well, acquaintances really. But some of us exchanged Christmas gifts. We went to lunch. We even stopped for drinks in the evening before heading home.

My lifelong friends Layla and Brooklyn might have moved out of Seattle, but I'd rebound from that. People rebounded from absent friendships all the time. They filled their lives with other things, new experiences and new companions.

The companions didn't even have to be people.

I liked cats. I especially liked kittens. I'd heard once that kittens should be adopted in pairs, littermates if you could get them. That way, they kept themselves company when you were away.

A librarian with two cats.

Perfect.

Exactly how I hoped my life would end up.

I was at the Harbor Tennis Club in downtown Seattle contemplating the latest text message from Sophie Crush, the fourth close friend in our circle. Several games were underway on the indoor courts below me. The frequent sound of balls popping hollowly against the painted surface faded into the background while my herbal tea cooled on a round polished beech wood table in the lounge.

I liked herbal tea. It was a comfort drink, and I didn't want to give it up. All the same, I was thinking I might have to choose between tea and cats to keep from becoming a cliché.

I had acquaintances here at the Harbor Club, too. I'd been a member since I was a teenager. I'd taken lessons and played matches over the years with most of the other members in my age range.

But acquaintances weren't close friends. They weren't the people you could call up to spend a lazy Saturday afternoon with dressed in yoga pants, eating gourmet ice cream and loaded nachos, adding wine as soon as the clocked ticked over to four o'clock. They weren't the people you could count on when you were feeling down.

I was feeling down.

I told myself it was normal. And it was. I didn't begrudge Layla and Brooklyn their happily-ever-afters. I was happy for them. But it was hard to be happy for me right now.

I checked my cell phone screen again. The text from Sophie stared back at me.

Her lunch was running late—her lunch with her new guy was running late.

I surmised from the grinning emoji that lunch with the new guy was going great.

I was happy for her, too. Again, just not for me.

She'd canceled our Saturday tennis game at the last minute, so here I was sitting alone in my tennis shorts, my racket by my side, with no plans for the afternoon and none for the evening, either. I found myself wondering how late the animal shelter was open on weekends.

It felt pathetic again, the cat thing. I did like cats. What I didn't like was what they represented, like I'd given up and started that long, long journey through stoic mediocrity to… I don't know…retirement or death.

Wow.

I tried to laugh at myself. I'd just gone from a canceled tennis date to death in under thirty minutes. Maybe I needed tequila instead of tea.

One of the games below me ended. Two men shook hands and walked off the court.

I recognized James Gillen—Layla Kendrick's, née Gillen's, older brother. If I had to say, he was the one person in the club worse off than me.

I didn't know if that made me feel worse or better. Better for me, I suppose, since I'm human and not a saint. But worse for him—I definitely felt worse for him. Again, since I was human and capable of empathy.

I wouldn't wish his life on anyone.

James had been high-school sweethearts with my gorgeous and much sought-after friend Brooklyn. And up until this July, they'd been blissfully engaged.

They'd spent a full year planning one of the greatest weddings in the history of weddings. It would have been magnificent. In fact, it was magnificent—at least at the start, right up to the moment Brooklyn left James at the altar in front of five hundred guests and a stringer for the local newspaper.

I didn't blame Brooklyn, at least not completely. By all accounts her handsome, successful new husband, Colton Kendrick, was a real catch.

It hadn't surprised me at all that Brooklyn would have two great guys competing to marry her. Brooklyn sparkled. She always had, and I expected she always would. And that sparkle drew men—flies to honey and all that. It was a gift.

I wished I had that gift.

I pretended for a second that I did. I gave a Brooklynesque smile at my faint reflection in the tennis court viewing window. I tried to toss my hair the way she did, but it was fastened back in a tight braid, so my toss didn't work out.

I gave a real smile then, a laughing-at-myself smile. I took a sip of the lukewarm tea, wishing it really was tequila.

Librarians didn't sparkle. We weren't supposed to sparkle. We were practical and dependable, admirable qualities for sure. But there were no flies coming to my honey.

I removed my sports glasses and reached for my everyday pair as a couple strolled into the lounge. With my glasses back in place, I recognized them. My besieged heart sank another big notch.

It was Henry Reginald Paulson III with his pretty, bubbly girlfriend clinging to his arm.

She was tall, thin and blonde, with shiny white teeth and luscious eyelashes that seemed to blink too often. I thought her name was Kaylee or Candi or something. I'd never seen her play tennis, but nobody cared about her tennis skills. Athletic ability was obviously not on the top of Henry's wish list for a girlfriend.

The Paulson family, with Henry's parents at the center, practically ran the Harbor Club, hosting fund-raisers and sitting on the board. They were third-and fourth-generation members of the private club. Henry was the crown prince.

He was also my ex. He'd unceremoniously dumped me back in May, May 25 to be exact. It was the same day the Northridge Library had celebrated my fifth anniversary as an employee. It meant I was entitled to an extra week's holiday leave, and I moved up to parking lot B—two blocks closer to the civic building. I'd looked forward to those perks, and I'd been excited to meet Henry to cap off the day.

But our celebratory dinner at the Tidal Rush Restaurant turned into a lonely cab ride home in my blue crepe dress before the appetizers had even been served. I'd tossed the Northridge plaque into my bottom drawer and left it there. .

Henry had said that night we'd stay friends. He told me I had many good qualities. He said he admired me and that one day I was going to make some man very happy.

He hadn't complained about my plain brown hair, my glasses, my understated wardrobe or my modest height. But since he'd replaced me with my physical and stylistic opposite, I could draw my own conclusions.

Henry spotted me from across the lounge.

He smiled and waved as if we had, in fact, remained friends. We hadn't even spoken since the breakup.

I wished I wasn't sitting alone right now.

I wished I was out on the court playing tennis with Sophie.

I wished I was anywhere or anything but—

"Hi, Nat." It was a man's voice directly beside my table.

I looked up to see James.

Thank you, James.

If James would only stand still and chat for a minute or two, then I wouldn't have to look completely pathetic while Henry and Kaylee joined a boisterous clique of members at a central table.

"Hi, James," I said.

"Waiting for someone?" he asked, with a glance around the expansive room.

I lifted my phone as evidence. "Sophie just canceled. I'll have to give up our court time."

"Is she okay?"

"She's fine. Something came up." Something better than me.

"Mind if I sit down?"

"No, please." I pointed to one of the other chairs at the table for four. I honestly could have kissed him right there and then.

"I'm dying of thirst," he said. He signaled to the waiter and glanced at my little teapot. "You want something else?"

The waiter promptly arrived.

"A beer," James said to him. "Whichever local one you have on tap today."

Then James looked to me, raising his brows in a question.

"Sounds good," I said.

It wasn't four o'clock yet, but on a day like this, I was in.

It took him a second to get settled into his chair.

"Good game?" I asked.

"Caleb's a strong player. I got a serious workout."

James had obviously taken a quick shower. His hair was slightly damp and he'd changed into a pair of charcoal slacks and a white dress shirt with the sleeves rolled up.

He was a good-looking man, tall and fit. He didn't have Henry's flamboyance or gregariousness. He wasn't tennis-club royalty. But he'd always been respected for his playing skills.

Now…well, now he had to contend with the tactless gossip over Brooklyn running from St. Fidelis in her wedding gown. Consensus had it that James had been marrying up, and it came as no huge surprise to some that Brooklyn had dumped him for a better offer.

I could only imagine they were saying similar things about me. My relationship with Henry had only lasted a few months, but people probably assumed I was a quick fling for him, a roll in the hay, a temporary detour to the short and mousy side.

I wondered when it would stop feeling so humiliating.

I hoped James hadn't heard the worst of the Brooklyn gossip. I really didn't subscribe to the misery-loves-company school of thought. Nope, the fewer people in the world who felt the way I did right now, the better.

"I might have to do some biking later to make up for the lost game," I said, switching my thoughts to something more productive.

I wasn't a fitness freak by any stretch, but I did count on my Saturday tennis games for a weekly workout.

"Where do you ride?" he asked.

"Along the Cadman lakeshore, mostly. My apartment's only a few blocks from Green Gardens."

"I've ridden there," he said. "It's nice in the fall."

The waiter arrived with two frosty mugs of beer.

"Can you cancel Ms. Remington's court time?" James asked as the waiter put coasters under the mugs.

"Certainly, sir."

I thanked them both with a smile. Then I gripped the handle of the generous mug. "It might not be a very long bike ride after I finish this."

James smiled at my joke and held his own beer in a toast.

I bargained with myself out loud. "Maybe I'll go tomorrow morning instead."

Then as I clinked my glass to his, I caught sight of Henry, his arm around Kaylee as he regaled the four other people at their table with some kind of a story.

"Something wrong?" James asked me.

I realized I was frowning. "No. Nothing." I turned my attention back to James.

But he looked over his shoulder and saw Henry.

"Ahhh, Paulson. That's got to be aggravating."

Aggravating wasn't exactly the word I'd use.

"It is," I said.

James's dark blue eyes turned sympathetic.

I didn't want his pity. And I didn't want him to think I was wallowing in my own misery, either—even though I was. To be fair, I was wallowing in more than just my breakup with Henry. I liked to think I'd made a bit of progress from the breakup. But on aggregate, there was a lot to wallow in about my life right now.

I tried to shake it off. "It's nothing compared to you."

The words were out before I realized how they were going to sound. I'd managed to be both tactless and insensitive all in one fell swoop. I tried to backtrack. "I mean… I didn't… I'm sorry."

"I'd rather you blurted it out than silently thought it—or whispered it like everybody else around here." He scanned the room. "And it *is* nothing compared to me. I was dumped on a much grander scale, an epic scale, the scale to end all scales here at the Harbor Club."

I wanted to disagree. I should probably disagree. But he was right, and if I said anything other than that, I'd be lying.

"How are you holding up?" I asked in a quieter tone.

"It's weird," he said. Then he took another drink. "I keep finding her stuff in my apartment. I don't know what to do with it. Do I send it to her? Do I store it for her? Do I burn it?"

"Burn it." The words had popped out. "Wait, I shouldn't have said that."

But James chuckled. "I like your style."

Brooklyn was my close friend. But even close friends did bad things. And James deserved to be angry with Brooklyn. He deserved to light something on fire.

"Then can you explain your gender to me?" I asked James. Somehow one beer had turned into two.

"I doubt it," he said.

"Are they just shallow?"

"Mostly."

"I mean, look at Candi over there."

"I think her name is Callie."

"Not Kaylee?"

"Should we ask?"

"No!"

James chuckled at my panicked-sounding tone. I wasn't really panicked. I was just…well, self-conscious about even caring who Henry-the-cad was dating now.

I lowered my voice and leaned in. "Is she really what all men want?"

James slid a surreptitious glance to their table. "Some do."

"Some or most?"

"Okay, lots."

I heaved a sigh. I wasn't exactly disappointed, since I'd known the answer all along. Still, it didn't renew my faith in men in any way.

"Women are no better," James said.

"We're not obsessed with looks."

"You're pretty obsessed with looks, but you're even more obsessed with power and prestige."

I couldn't completely disagree. "We also want compassion and a sense of humor."

"A sense of humor is pretty hard to quantify."

"I suppose. And you can't exactly see it coming from across the room."

James tapped his mug on the table as if for emphasis. "See? Women are just like men. It's human nature to start with looks. Maybe it's because they're the easiest benchmark when you first meet."

"I wish I had them." The minute I made the admission, I wanted to call it back.

James wasn't my best friend, and this wasn't a heart-to-heart Saturday afternoon talk in yoga pants.

Now he was scrutinizing me, and I wished the floor would open right up and swallow me whole.

"Why do you say that?" he asked.

The answer was painfully obvious. "Because it *would* be nice. You must get it. You were with Brooklyn all those years."

Anybody who fell for Brooklyn understood the appeal of a beautiful woman.

"I mean, why do you think you don't have them?"

It was my turn to stare back at him.

"Hello?" I said. I pointed to my chin. "Plain Jane librarian here."

"Well, you're not exactly glamorous," he said.

"Thank you for making my point." I tamped down the ego pinch. I hadn't really expected James to insist I was beautiful. Still, blunt honesty was hard to take sometimes.

"But you're pretty."

I shook my head. "Oh, no. You can't backpedal now. Your first reaction is your true reaction."

"My first reaction was that you have the raw material."

"Be still my beating heart."

He grinned at me.

I had been joking. Well, I was mostly joking. I could make light of my looks or I could get depressed about them. I wasn't going to get depressed.

Plain was fine. It was ordinary and normal, and people led perfectly happy lives with plain looks. In fact, most did—the vast, overwhelming majority of people had looks that were plain in some way or another. The bombshells among us were few and far between.

"You did get a look at the guy Brooklyn married, right?" James asked.

I definitely got a look at him. I hadn't attended Brooklyn's wedding to Colton Kendrick, but I'd gone to Layla's wedding right after when she married Colton's twin brother, Max. Colton and Max were rich, rugged and handsome. They also seemed to be truly great guys.

I nodded to James.

He made a sweeping gesture down his chest. "Then you can guess how I feel."

"You have the raw material," I said.

I tried not to smile. I knew heartbreak wasn't funny.

James shook his head and seemed to fight his own smile. "Are we going to sit here and wallow in it?"

"That's the opposite of what I want to do," I said.

"What do you want to do?" he asked.

I gave my racket a pointed look. "I wanted to play tennis."

"Not this minute. I mean more broadly, in life, going forward?"

"I was thinking about getting a cat."

"Seriously?"

"No. Not really."

"A cat's a big commitment."

"You don't like cats?"

He seemed to ponder the question. "I'd probably go for a dog. But I'd have to get a house first."

I knew he and Brooklyn had planned to go house shopping right after the wedding. I wasn't going to touch that one.

"A dog does need a yard," I said instead.

"Maybe I'll buy a house," he said. But he didn't look enthusiastic about it.

I wished I could afford a house. It would be years before I had a down payment saved up for even a condo. I'd be staying in my loft apartment for the foreseeable future.

"Real estate is a good investment," I said.

James was an economist. I didn't exactly know what he did on a day-to-day basis in his job, but it seemed to me economists would be interested in good investments.

"It's definitely a good time to lock in an interest rate."

"But?" I could hear the *but* in his sentence.

"It's hard to know what to look for when you can't picture your future."

The statement seemed particularly sad.

While I searched for the right response, my phone rang.

"Go ahead," James said, lifting his beer and sitting back in his chair.

"It's Sophie." I was curious about her lunch date, but I wasn't about to have an in-depth conversation here in front of James. I swiped to accept the call. "I'll tell her I'll call her back."

"You want privacy?" He made to leave.

"No." I shook my head. I didn't want to chase him away. "It's fine."

"Hi, Sophie," I said into the phone.

"Bryce has a friend," she said.

"Uh…that's nice. Listen, can I call you—"

"As in *a friend*," she said. She was talking fast, enthusiasm lighting her voice. "A friend for you, a guy who wants to meet you. We can go on a double date. Dinner tonight. Does tonight work for you?"

I found myself meeting James's gaze.

"Nat?" Sophie asked. "Are you there?"

"Yes, I'm here."

I didn't know why I was hesitating. No, I didn't have plans for Saturday night, and of course I wanted to meet a new guy. What single girl wouldn't want to meet a new guy?

It seemed like Bryce and Sophie were hitting it off. I knew Sophie had good taste in men. If Bryce was a good guy, it stood to reason that his friend would be a good guy. I'd like to meet a good guy.

"What time?" I asked.

"Seven. We'll swing by your place. You might want to meet us downstairs. I mean…you know…"

Sophie was not a fan of my utilitarian loft apartment. She bugged me about fixing it up all the time.

Myself, I didn't see the point in spending a lot of money on cosmetics. The place was perfectly functional. Then again, if the guy thought like her, I didn't want to put him off straightaway because of my questionable taste in decorating.

"Sure," I said. "Seven o'clock downstairs."

"Perfect!" She sounded really happy.

I ended the call.

"Sorry about that," I said.

James waved away my apology. "Girls' night out?"

"Not exactly. Double date."

James sat forward again. "Blind date?"

"Yes." I took a sip of my beer "I haven't been on one of those in a while."

"I guess your dry spell is over."

I didn't particularly like calling it a dry spell. It made me sound desperate—like I was thirsty for a man.

All I really wanted was to move completely and permanently on from Henry. I supposed that made me thirsty enough. There wasn't much point in dressing it up.

"That's one way to put it," I said to James.

He lifted his mug in another toast. "Well, congratulations."

I touched my mug to his again and laughed at myself. I'd just been moaning about my loneliness. I should be thrilled about having plans for tonight. I would be thrilled. I was thrilled.

"That's better," James said. "Smile and be happy."

Two

Since I hadn't thought to ask Sophie where we were going for dinner, I went middle of the road on an outfit—a pair of gray slacks and a monochrome animal print blouse. The blouse was V-necked, with long sleeves, and the rayon fabric was loose and comfortable. I liked the way it draped over my hips, asymmetrical from front to back.

I put my hair into a loose braid with a long tassel. My hair grew fast, and it had been a while since my last trim. If I left it completely loose, it felt wayward and messy, making it hard to relax while I ate. This way, it was up out of the way but still wispy around my face, so I didn't look too severe.

I wore a little more makeup than usual—though it was always disappointing when the carefully applied mascara got lost behind my glasses. I put in some dangling gold earrings Layla had given me for my last birthday, and went with a pair of medium heel, charcoal boots.

I threw a sweater over my arm since September weather was unpredictable, and I hooked my trusty brown leather tote over my shoulder. It was heavy. I often thought I should streamline the contents. But the truth was I liked to be prepared—wallet, keys, sunglasses, comb, lotion, tissues and wipes, hair elastics in case of unexpected wind, a couple of coins in each denomination, enough hidden cash for a taxi home within a twenty-five-mile radius, credit cards, my phone, a flash drive—because, well, these days you never knew when you might need to unexpectedly download data—and self-defense spray because, well, these days you just never knew.

When I met Sophie at the street entrance, I rethought my look. Then again, I usually rethought my look as soon as I saw how Sophie had dressed.

She was wearing a short black scooped-neck A-line dress with just enough swish to make it fun. Over top, she'd put a faded jean jacket with a few scattered rhinestones on the collar and shoulders. The sparkling gems echoed her choker and earrings. She carried a little clutch purse, and wore strappy black platform sandals.

Her highlighted light brown hair was thick and lustrous, framing her dark brown eyes and full lips.

"Hi, Nat," she said. "You look terrific."

I didn't feel terrific. Then again, I hadn't been going for terrific. So, there was that.

"You look fantastic," I said.

She linked her arm with mine. "Bryce is a super good guy. He got us a sedan instead of a taxi. Classy or what?"

"Classy," I said. "Where are we going?"

"Russo's on the waterfront."

"Nice," I said. Russo's was a very trendy Italian restaurant. "Do we have reservations?" Saturday nights were crowded everywhere downtown.

"You don't need to worry about that. Bryce can worry about that."

"So, you don't know if he made them or not." I wasn't being obsessive, merely practical.

"We're on a *date*, Nat. Let the guys do the planning."

"Okay." I was still curious, but I wasn't going to belabor the point.

Two men were standing in front of a black sedan parked at the curb.

"This is Bryce," Sophie said of the taller one.

Bryce was easily over six feet. His hair was thick and near jet-black. He had a classically handsome face with brown eyes and a nice smile. His shoulders were square beneath a sport jacket and a white shirt.

"Bryce is head chef at The Blue Fern," Sophie said.

"I didn't know you worked together," I said to Sophie.

She supervised food and beverage service at the local high-end restaurant. I'd had the impression Bryce was a customer she'd met while working.

"I'm sure I told you," Sophie said.

She hadn't. But I decided disputing her memory was pointless.

"Nice to meet you," I said to Bryce, offering to shake hands.

His grip was gentle, his hand broad. "Sophie talks a lot about you to me, but obviously not the other way around."

I couldn't tell if he was offended or not. I decided to take countermeasures just in case. "Our jobs are so different we really don't talk about work very much."

"Nice save," Bryce said, telling me he'd been at least slightly offended.

Sophie and I really didn't talk much about our work. But belaboring the point would only make things worse. I stopped talking.

"And this is Ethan," Sophie said, gesturing to the other man.

If she noticed she'd offended Bryce, she didn't seem particularly worried about it.

Ethan was shorter than Bryce, about Sophie's height in her high-heeled shoes—still a good bit taller than me.

His hair was a sandy blond with a copper hue. His face was on the round side, his eyes a pale blue.

"Nice to meet you too, Ethan," I said, giving him my best smile, since he was my date, and since a woman never knew when she might meet "the one." I tried to imagine Ethan as "the one." I wasn't quite seeing it, but the evening was young.

"Hi, Nat." His grip was firmer than Bryce's.

His mouth was shaped in a smile, but his eyes didn't quite seem to meet mine—odd. It looked like he was focused on my eyebrows.

It made me wonder when I'd last plucked them. Did they look messy? Bushy? I sure hoped those little blond hairs hadn't grown out in between them. That would be embarrassing.

"Do you work at The Blue Fern, too?" I asked him.

"Ethan is a computer engineer," Sophie said. "He has his own business."

"That's impressive," I said.

I'd never been strong in science and technology. Layla had always been the brainy one of the group.

"Our focus is robotics," Ethan said.

"He's a genius," Sophie said.

Ethan gave Sophie a warm smile at the compliment. "The team turns big ideas into reality. And Bryce and Sophie have presented some very exciting concepts."

I didn't understand, so I looked to Sophie for an explanation.

"We're technologically revolutionizing the food service industry," she said with a wide grin.

The way she said it sounded like she was joking, though I didn't completely get what was funny about a technological revolution of the food industry. In my mind I pictured robotic salad tossing.

The image was a little bit funny, so I smiled back at her. "You're turning The Blue Fern into *The Jetsons*? Jet packs and robot waiters?"

Their silence told me I'd got it wrong.

"You're mocking her?" Ethan asked.

I sobered. "No. I didn't… I mean…"

"It's a brave new world," Sophie said, clearly disappointed by my reaction. "You have to progress with the times."

I felt terrible.

"We should get going," Ethan said, his expression telling me I hadn't made a good first impression. So much for judging him. He was judging me.

If Sophie was serious about orchestrating a technological revolution, you'd think she might have mentioned it to her best friend.

Ethan took the front passenger seat while Sophie climbed into the back and pushed to the middle. Bryce made to climb in behind her, so I went around to the opposite door, feeling awkward and self-conscious.

"Bryce and Ethan went to high school together," Sophie said to me while I wrangled my seat belt into the clasp.

"You've been friends all this time?" I was happy to have the conversation move along.

"We weren't friends," Bryce said.

"Oh." I left it at that.

I decided to keep my responses short and sweet from here on in.

"Ethan was a nerd. I was more of a jock," Bryce said. "He went off to university, and I went to culinary school."

"You must have done well," I said. "I mean, if you're a head chef already."

"It's a small place," Bryce said.

"But we have really big plans," Sophie said.

"It sounds like," I said, leaving her an opening to elaborate.

"You've heard about 3-D printing?" she asked me.

I nodded. I didn't know a whole lot about it, library materials not normally being 3-D. Our printers were 2-D. We had color for a price, but that was as high-tech as we got.

The excitement level in Sophie's voice grew as she spoke. "The three of us are partnering on a tech start-up."

"Our patents are pending," Bryce said.

Patents?

"We've got a prototype," Ethan said from the front seat.

"You should see it, Nat," Sophie said.

"It's too big," Bryce said.

"I have some ideas on that," Ethan said.

"But you can't fault the quality," Bryce said.

"We'll need investors," Sophie said. "We need to scale up."

"Once it's perfected," Bryce said.

"We're very close," Ethan said.

I had about a thousand questions for her, starting with: *What the heck?*

"How long have you been at this?" I asked instead.

"A few months," Sophie replied. "I didn't want to jinx it, so I've kept really quiet."

"Even from me?" I felt even more isolated than I had this morning.

It looked like Bryce wasn't such a new guy in Sophie's

life, after all. I felt like I was at a business meeting instead of on a date.

"I did," Sophie said. "Sorry about that."

"Just so I'm clear," I said. "You are dating Bryce?"

Bryce threaded his arm through Sophie's. "We started off as colleagues, then friends, and now, well…we've discovered something very special."

"And Ethan brought the tech side," Sophie said.

I assumed Ethan brought the tech side to the business venture and not to the romantic relationship.

"Baker's confectionary is our domain," Ethan piped in. "We're upping the level of precision and sophistication with which restaurants, even small establishments, can conceive, refine, create and serve desserts of every variety."

"You're 3-D printing desserts?" I wasn't exactly wrapping my head around that.

I'd seen a news report once on 3-D printing action figures. They took a scan of a person's face, cartooned it, and created a personalized action figure.

I got how a printer could squirt colored plastic in a specific pattern. I wasn't seeing how it baked a cake.

"We couldn't even be thinking about this without Ethan," Sophie said. "Bryce brings the culinary expertise, and I'm bringing the business know-how. We're an awesome team."

She reached forward and squeezed Ethan's shoulder.

He put his hand over hers for a second.

"So, like cakes and pies?" I asked, still skeptical.

"Oh, so much more than that," Ethan said.

"You should see how beautiful they are." Sophie smiled and sat back.

"And delicious," Bryce added, looping his arm around her shoulders. "You can build in a level of precision for incredible consistency."

Sophie nodded, looking excited. I was happy for her. She'd always had boundless energy and enthusiasm, and an impressive sense of adventure. Growing up, it was always Sophie who came up with the ideas for our adventures.

It seemed she'd gotten bored at work—but in a good way. She was branching out to a brand-new venture, and it even came with a romance.

The driver pulled to a stop at the curb and I shifted my attention to Russo's front patio. It was a lovely building, decorated with tiny white lights on clusters of potted trees. The walkway and stairs were red cobblestones, and the front door was made of thick oak planks with gold embossed hinges and handles.

Bryce opened the car door and stepped out and turned to help Sophie.

I went out my side and walked over the uneven cobblestones around the back of the car, glad for the moment that I'd gone with sturdy boots.

In her spike high heels, Sophie hung on to Bryce's arm.

Ethan and I fell in behind them.

I felt awkward walking silently beside Ethan.

"You grew up in Seattle?" I asked to break the ice.

"I was three when we moved out from Boston."

"I was born here," I said, keeping the conversational ball rolling. "We lived in Queen Anne."

"Wallingford. My parents are university faculty members."

"His mom's a renowned chemistry professor," Sophie said over her shoulder.

Bryce opened the big door and we all walked into the dim interior of Russo's.

"That's very impressive," I said to Ethan.

"Professor Mary Quinn." He sounded quite proud. "She's published over thirty articles in technical journals. Perhaps you've read some of them?"

I didn't have an immediate response. I wasn't sure why he thought I'd be reading chemistry articles.

"Since you're a librarian," he prompted.

"I'm in the public library. We don't catalog many scientific journals."

He seemed surprised by that. "Really? Have you considered the importance of STEM to young readers? And, really, to any readers?" He took a beat. "STEM stands for science, technology, engineering and mathematics."

I knew what STEM stood for. "It's a matter of capacity. For technical works, I'd refer people to the university library, or maybe the State Association of Chemists."

We'd stopped in front of the reception desk.

"Do you have a reservation?" the hostess asked Bryce.

"Brookside for four," Bryce said.

Sophie turned to us, a little sigh in her voice. "I wish I was that smart."

"You are smart," I said to her.

She had a business degree. She was only twenty-six, and she was already a manager at one of the best boutique restaurants in the city.

"I'm not science smart."

"You're real-world smart, and that's much more practical."

Silence followed my words.

Again.

"There's nothing more practical than science," Ethan said.

"It takes a team," Bryce said.

Ethan kept talking. "Science is responsible for everything from advanced agriculture to green mining techniques to fabric dyes for fashion shows, and all the obvious technologies. Take your cell phone, for instance. It took generations of highly trained scientists to develop the concepts that make a smartphone run."

"And we're grateful for that," Bryce put in.

"Right this way," the hostess said to us.

"I do enjoy my cell phone." I took Bryce's lead and tried to lighten the conversation.

Bryce followed the hostess. Sophie went behind him as we wound our way through the tables.

I took up the rear.

The friendly woman showed us to a booth with a half-circle bench. It was on the second floor overlooking the harbor. After a bit of fumbling over the seating arrangements, I ended up on one end of the bench next to Ethan. Bryce took the other end, and Sophie was sandwiched between the two men.

"Drinks?" Bryce asked, opening the cocktail menu.

"Oh, a cranberry martini for me," Sophie said.

"I'll take one of those," Ethan said.

"I'm having a Canadian whiskey," Bryce said, looking to me.

"A glass of cabernet sauvignon," I said.

A glass now and a glass with dinner, I decided. Then I'd be nicely relaxed.

"This whole thing started when we lost our pastry chef," Sophie said. "And we were having trouble finding a new one with the skills and expertise."

"The ante keeps going up and up," Bryce said.

"Enter technology," Ethan said.

"I did an informal poll of our customers," Sophie explained. "And dessert was the number one determiner of restaurant choice among women. It was only number three for men. They like steak and seafood."

Ethan jumped back in. "Studies show that on a date, especially the first few dates, men go where women want to go."

"And the business world is drastically changing," Sophie said. "There are more women executives."

"They want great dessert on their expense accounts," Ethan said.

"Studies show?" I asked him.

"That's just logic," he said.

"The skill level, the prep area, the prep time," Bryce listed off on his fingers. "There's a reason most restaurants have limited dessert menus, especially the small establishments."

"We knew technology could help," Ethan said. "Hence, the inception of BRT Innovations."

"Our company," Sophie said, pointing to all three of them.

"I see." I didn't see everything yet. But I had a feeling I was going to learn a whole lot more before the night was through.

As a date, the evening hadn't gone particularly well. As a business meeting, it had gone quite a bit better.

I hadn't exactly kept up, but I'd learned how much time, thought and energy had gone into the idea for Sweet Tech. If everything they said came to fruition, my friend Sophie really was going to technologically revolutionize desserts.

They'd dropped me off at ten thirty.

Ethan had dutifully walked me to the lobby door. He hadn't kissed me, just said good-night and that he'd had a nice time.

I said I'd had a nice time, too. I suspected our level of enthusiasm for each other was about equal.

On the upside, the restaurant had been lovely, the food delicious.

I'd had the grilled sole with a spring greens salad, opting for a brandy instead of dessert. A good decision since, on top of the wine, it had lulled me into a lovely deep sleep.

I felt rested this morning, ready for my bike ride along the lakeshore.

No more jealousy over Sophie's adventure, I decided. No more moaning about being stood up for yesterday's tennis game. I felt like an independent woman in the morning sunshine, pedaling along the paved bike path, up little rises and down small hills, the wind whistling past my ears.

"Good on you." A voice came up on my left side.

I looked sideways and realized my glasses were sliding down my nose.

I pushed them into place and saw James coming up to pedal alongside me.

"I wasn't sure if you were serious," he said.

"I was serious. I like bike riding."

"I can see that."

I smiled. I was happy to see him. We'd joked quite a lot yesterday, and I'd had fun.

"I prefer rowing," he said.

I knew he'd been on a championship team in college. "Yet, here you are."

"Here I am. You inspired me."

The idea of inspiring James amused me. "Like your own

personal trainer? 'Get your butt out of that bed, Gillen! Gear up! Outside! Give me twenty!'"

James laughed at my imitation of a drill sergeant. "Twenty laps of the lake? That seems a bit ambitious."

"We probably should have packed a lunch," I said, feeling lighthearted in the fresh air and sunshine.

A woman and two children approached us riding the other way, a boy and a girl looking about ten years old. The kids had flushed cheeks and windblown hair and were pedaling hard to keep up with their mother.

James shifted in behind me to give them space to pass. We both stayed tight to the right side of the path.

"How was your date?" he asked after the family passed.

A man was throwing a ball for his dog on the grass beside us, and I kept a watch in front of me as the animal ran close to the path.

"It was fine," I answered.

"Fine as in good, or fine as in meh?"

"Fine as in…mediocre, I guess." Sophie's business plans were secret for now, so I wasn't going to talk about them.

It would have been nice if the date part had gone better. I'd wanted to like Ethan. I mean, he wasn't that bad. Other women might like him just fine.

"Sorry to hear that," James said. "Where did you go?"

"Russo's."

"That sounds nice. Did you have the prime rib?"

"The grilled sole."

"Their prime rib is to die for."

"I'll try that next time."

"Is there going to be a next time?"

"I hope so." Then I realized he meant a next date. "I don't know about a next date. But I'll definitely go back to Russo's."

"Nix the guy, stick with the restaurant. I do like your style, Nat."

"The guy seemed fine." I felt guilty dissing him. "His name was Ethan. He's a tech guy. He seems very smart."

"But no second date? Are you one of those picky women with a long list of qualities you want in a man?"

"What? No. I'm not like that. I don't have a list."

At least, I didn't have one that was written down. But I'd admit there were certain things I was looking for—a sense of humor, for example, a progressive worldview, maybe somewhat more humble than Ethan. And I wouldn't be wild about someone who smoked or drank to excess or who, say, had a gambling addiction.

"You're listing it off now," James said with a tone of amazement.

"I'm not…" But I was.

He'd caught me.

"It's not a long list," I said defensively.

"What's on it?"

"What's on yours?" I asked.

"Are you thirsty?" he asked.

We were coming to a snack bar near a sandy beach and a play area.

"Are you changing the subject?" I asked.

"No, I'm just thirsty."

"Okay. I'll take a sparkling water. But then I want to hear what's on your list."

We both slowed our bikes, coasting to the dark green bike rack set next to a scattered group of picnic tables.

I pushed my bike tire between two bars.

"Spill," I said, smoothing my windblown hair.

I'd pulled it back into a ponytail, but some strands had come loose around my face. I tried not to imagine what I looked like. Some women looked cute when they were all disheveled. I looked messy. On me, messy wasn't cute or sexy or anything other than messy.

"It's a short list," he said, dismounting.

"That should make it easy."

"Not Brooklyn."

I felt a lurch of guilt. I probably should have kept my big

mouth shut about relationships. James didn't need this on a leisurely Sunday morning bike ride. I felt terrible.

"Now you give me something," he said.

He didn't sound sad or upset.

I was grateful for that. Maybe I hadn't completely spoiled the morning.

"No gambling addiction," I said.

"Seriously?" he asked as we walked to the counter. "You felt the need to include that on a list?"

"You think I should date a guy with a gambling addiction?" I asked.

The teenage girl behind the counter gave us an odd look.

I thought about clarifying the statement, but it seemed silly to launch into an explanation for a stranger whose life would only intersect with mine for a matter of minutes.

"Two Sparkletts," James said to her. "Plain."

The teenager turned and moved to the cooler.

"I don't think you should date a serial killer, either," he said to me. "But you don't need to put that on a list anywhere. It's obvious."

"I'd rather date an addicted gambler than a serial killer."

The teenager heard that one too, and gave us another puzzled look. "That'll be seven fifty."

James handed her a ten. "No need for change. Thanks."

"Thank you," she said with an appreciative smile.

We each took one of the bottles. I couldn't help but wonder what the clerk thought as we walked away.

"That girl back there thinks I'm dating a gambling addict," I said, twisting off the bottle cap.

"She really doesn't care."

"I suppose not. Still, I hope I didn't accidently set a bad example."

"I think you're safe." James took a long drink. "Now, give me a real one."

"A real what."

"A real item on your list."

I wanted to tell him to give me a real item, too. I didn't

think "not Brooklyn" was legitimate. But I didn't want to risk upsetting him.

"Good sense of humor," I said.

"Too generic," he said.

"It's legitimate."

"What else?"

"A progressive worldview."

"What does that mean?"

"It means you're progressive." I kept my expression deadpan. "You know, in your worldview."

James grinned. "Touché."

"You give me one."

"Me? But I'm a sad sack recovering from utter heartbreak."

I took in his überinnocent expression. "I *knew* that was a ruse." I shoved him with my upper arm.

"Not buying it?" he asked.

"Dish."

"Okay, let me see…hardworking."

"And you say *I'm* too generic."

"You think I should date a lazy woman?"

"Depends. Exactly how good does she look eating bonbons in front of daytime television?"

"Nobody looks good doing that."

We came to our bikes and stood there while we finished our drinks.

"I don't know what I'm looking for," I said.

"Love?" James asked.

"Now, *that's* the generic answer."

"But true." He took my empty bottle from me.

I knew he was right. "But how do you find it?"

I was serious. I felt like it had always eluded me. I mean, I'd liked Henry a lot, but with him, even when things were going well, it sure didn't feel like the poems and stories said it would.

James headed for the recycle bin. "You look really hard," he called back over his shoulder.

He tossed the bottles and started back. "Meet a lot of people, I guess. Statistically speaking, that'll give you the best shot at falling in love."

We mounted up.

"There are people everywhere," James said as we continued down the path.

He pointed to the beach. "There's one, and another, and another. Take your pick."

I chuckled as I pedaled beside him. It was silly, and it was funny, and it felt good to laugh at life.

"What about her?" I asked as we came up on a pretty woman in a white bathing suit cover-up.

"Mommy, Mommy." A two-year-old boy threw himself in her arms.

"Taken," James said.

"Either of them?" I joked about two women in their sixties chatting in matching lawn chairs.

"Wrong era," he said.

"You're so fussy."

"Him?" James nodded to a shirtless jogger with a tiny dog on a leash.

The twentysomething man's chest was shaved, and his bulging pecs were shiny with oil.

"Too self-obsessed," I said.

"You can tell that just by looking?"

"You can't? How many hours a week at the gym do you suppose that takes?"

"I guess," James said.

"When would he mow the lawn or clean the gutters, or play with the children, or plan date night?"

"You *do* have a long list."

"I'm a practical woman. It's not like I won't help around the house. But I'm not cleaning the gutters all by myself."

"I can respect that," James said.

We pedaled along in our own thoughts until we reached the far end of the lake where the path curved sharply over a wooden bridge that cut across a burbling creek.

"You want to take a rest?" James asked.

A wooden bench was positioned on a concrete pier that jutted out into the lake.

"Sure."

We pulled our bikes onto a grassy patch and took the empty bench.

"I think we're coming at this all wrong," James said.

"Coming at what?" My first thought was the bike ride. Did he not like the lakeshore path?

"It really is a numbers game."

"Riding?"

"No, meeting the opposite sex. You need to meet a lot of eligible people to up your odds."

"Sure."

Who would argue with that? Not me. I might not be a science nerd, but I understood the law of large numbers.

"And we need to bring them to us."

"The eligible people?" I wasn't exactly seeing what he meant. Were we going back to the crowded beach?

"Think about Callie."

My face pinched up. "What about her? And are you sure it's not Kaylee?"

"We can call her whatever you want."

"I always thought she looked like a Candi."

"Candi." He paused in thought. "She does sort of look like a Candi."

"Don't drool," I said.

"I didn't mean it like that."

"Yes, you did."

James grinned unrepentantly. "Okay, we both agree most men would point at her from across the room."

"We do."

He was right. Candi was gorgeous and glamorous and eminently desirable.

"And we agree that most women would point at the Kendrick twins from across the room."

I was surprised he brought them up. "Yes."

Separate or together Colton and Max Kendrick were definitely pointworthy.

"Let's do that," James said.

I was really puzzled now. "Point at people from across the room?"

"No." James shook his head. "Get people to point at us."

Three

"Explain to me again how this works?" I said to James.

We'd finished our ride, locked up our bikes, and found ourselves a table on a deck overlooking the Orchid Club courtyard at the edge of the park.

"The view is perfect," James said. "Are you ready to take notes?"

"I can take notes." I had my phone. It had apps.

He glanced at his watch. "There'll be an event at the club tonight."

"What's the event?"

A waiter came by with a platter of nachos and two beers with quarters of lime stuck in the necks of the bottles. I'd also been eyeing the mini éclairs pictured on the menu. But I'd decide on that later. I was holding out hope the nachos would fill me up enough to take the éclairs off my mind.

"I don't know the event," James said. "It doesn't matter. Whatever it is, it'll be posh. People will be dressed up, looking fine. We're going to pick out our favorites."

"Please tell me we're not going to talk to them."

I was still wearing my yoga pants and an oversize T-shirt. And I was still slightly damp with sweat. The sun was going down, and I was grateful for the propane heater stationed next to our table.

"Were you not paying attention?" James asked, looking stern.

I looked to the club entrance. "Did I miss something?"

"*We're* not approaching them. *They're* going to approach us."

"Dressed like *this*?" I gestured to my chest.

"Not these people. Other people. Future people. Tonight, we pick out the pointworthy people and take notes on what makes them pointworthy. Then, we replicate it."

"What if it's genetics? I'm not getting plastic surgery."

A new hairstyle and a fancy dress were only going to get me so far. It's not like I'd never dressed up before. I'd dressed up plenty of times. Dressing up didn't turn me into Brooklyn or Sophie or anyone else.

James was giving me a horrified look. "Who said anything about plastic surgery?"

"What if we decide I need a new nose? Or…" I glanced down at my chest. "Upgraded breasts?"

"You don't need upgraded breasts!"

He gave a glance around at the other tables and moved his chair closer in, lowering his voice. "I told you, you already have the raw material."

"I'm not so sure about that. Wait. Look. There's a limo."

I pulled out my phone and hit the notes app. "Who is it?"

A man got out of the back seat.

He looked about fifty.

"Nice tux," I said.

"Formal wear gets your attention?" James asked.

"Formal wear is good, depending on the occasion. I wonder if this is a wedding."

"Could be the father of the bride," James said.

The man extended his hand and helped a middle-aged woman out of the limo.

She was followed by two younger men in business suits.

"Which one attracts your attention?" James asked. "Don't think, just blurt it out."

"The guy with dark hair."

"Why?"

"He's tall."

"I could put lifts in my shoes," James said.

"You're tall," I said to him.

"Other men are taller."

"You're tall enough."

James was well over six feet. I'd say six-two. A whole lot taller than that and the height started to be a detractor. There was a perfect sweet spot. He was in it.

"What else?" he asked me.

"His shoulders," I said. "They're broad, but it's more than that. There's something to the set of his shoulders. It makes him look confident. Confident is good."

"Confident shoulders." James flexed his.

I chuckled. "Yes. Confident shoulders."

Another vehicle pulled up. This was a big white SUV.

Four girls piled out wearing identical aquamarine dresses.

"Wedding," James said.

"Definitely."

We were both silent for a moment while they settled themselves into a group.

James munched on a nacho.

"So, which one?" I asked.

"Auburn hair," he said.

"You like auburn hair?"

He shook his head. "It's not the hair color. It's… I would say the shape of her figure and the brightness of her smile."

I jotted down "bright smile."

I found myself running my tongue over my teeth. I'd whitened them a few months ago. But maybe it was time to have it professionally done. I needed a dental checkup soon. I could easily get some whitening at the same time.

It couldn't hurt.

"She has a graceful walk," James said.

"I could practice that," I said.

He looked at me. "I never paid any attention to your walk. Walk somewhere and let me look."

The request made me super self-conscious. "No."

He pointed. "Over to the exit and back."

"I'm not going to walk for you."

"How can I help you if you won't let me assess you?"

Assess me? "I'd feel ridiculous."

"Well, get the heck over that. I'm going to do whatever you want."

I couldn't let that opportunity stay hanging. "What*ever* I want?"

"You know what I mean. I'll walk. I'll talk. I'll make confident shoulders. Come on, Nat. If this is going to work, we have to trust each other."

I realized he was right. Everything he'd said and done so far made me believe he was sincere. I should get over myself and take his help.

It was either that or cats, cats and tea, tea and cats until I was old and gray and alone.

I stood. "Don't you dare tell anyone about this, especially not Layla."

I'd be mortified if he told his sister that I was on a self-improvement binge.

"You think I want Layla to know what we're doing? You think I want *anyone* to know?"

"So, our secret?"

"Yes."

"To the grave?"

"You want me to pinky swear?"

"That would be good."

He solemnly held up his pinky.

I hooked mine around it, and we both broke into twin grins.

"I pinky swear," he said.

"So do I."

His hand was warm and strong, his skin rougher than mine. It felt odd to touch him, and I realized how rarely it happened.

I'd seen James hug Brooklyn countless times. He hugged Layla, of course. And I'd even seen him hug Sophie—who pulled pretty much everybody into hugs at one point or another.

James and I, on the other hand, had always kept a respectful distance.

I hadn't thought about it until now.

But now I was thinking about it.

He dropped his hand from mine.

"Walk," he said.

I turned, took a breath and walked straight to the exit. There I turned and walked back, trying really hard not to feel utterly stupid.

"More glide," he said when I got back to the table.

"What do you mean?"

"Smoother, don't clunk when you walk, and keep your feet closer together, more like you're walking on a line than on the two sides of a railroad track."

"A *railroad track*?" Just how unattractive was my walk?

"Do it again," he said.

It was on the tip of my tongue to refuse.

But I told myself to buck up. Maybe my ugly walk had been the problem all these years. I wondered why nobody had said anything before now.

I glanced around to make sure the people at the other tables weren't paying attention. They weren't.

I breathed again, really deep this time.

I turned and walked—glided, I hoped. I pretended I was on a balance beam, moving my feet together with each step.

I turned.

I couldn't look at James.

I picked a spot in the trees above his head and I did my best to glide back.

"Hmm," he said.

Embarrassed, I sat down before he could tell me to do it again.

"Hmm?" I mimicked. "I get a hmm?"

"It was better. I think."

"You *think*?"

"You seemed a bit stiff."

"Well, of *course* I was stiff. I could feel you watching me."

"We'll practice."

"We?"

"I'll do the shoulder thing."

I looked back down at the courtyard to see that three more vehicles had arrived. "Oh, I'm going to find something way better than the shoulder thing for you to practice."

I was definitely not going to be in this alone.

"Bring it on," he said.

I watched two more couples get out of their cars.

Valets had arrived and were moving the cars away as more people turned up.

"That guy," I said to James. "The one in the blue blazer."

"You like him?" James squinted. "Next time we should bring binoculars."

"We're going to be stalkers?"

"Private eyes. Investigators. We're investigators investigating beautiful people."

"It seems a bit invasive to me."

"What do you like about blue blazer guy?"

"He looks relaxed." I gazed at James to contrast the two men. "You look uptight."

"I do?"

I nodded. "You do. You look critical, like the world isn't quite measuring up to your standards and you're about to tell it why. That guy down there, he looks like he loves the world and can't wait to meet it and have fun with it."

James gazed at the courtyard. "Interesting. I'm not sure how I practice that."

"Tequila." The suggestion jumped out of my brain.

"I'm game." He munched on another nacho. "But I'm not sure how much tequila will help with your walking problem."

I smiled and reached for a nacho myself. "Are we really going to do this?"

He met my gaze. "I think we are."

"Embark on a secret mission to make ourselves irresistible to the opposite sex?" I bit down on the nacho. It was delicious, and I was hungry.

"Law of large numbers until we fall in love."

"Okay," I said.

This was by far the oddest thing I'd ever done. But however it turned out, it was going to be way better than cats.

"You *have* to come with us." Sophie shut the heavy door of my apartment behind her.

I lived in what was once an elementary school and had been converted to thirty apartments. I was on the third of three floors in a high-ceilinged loft under what were now murky skylights, with an aging wood floor partially covered in scattered worn rugs. The walls were gray-painted cinder blocks, enclosing a single big room, plus a bathroom.

I'd added a freestanding wooden divider to cordon off the bed. I didn't like making beds, and I didn't want the world to see my failing.

"Nat," Sophie said with an urgency to her tone.

"Did Ethan specifically ask you to invite me?" I was having a hard time believing Ethan wanted another date with me.

Sophie paced to the cluster of sofas and armchairs on one side of the room. "Of *course* he wants you to come. That's the whole point, that the four of us would have fun together again."

"I didn't think he had fun last time." I went to the kitchen area to get a pitcher of iced tea from the fridge.

"Sure he did. Didn't you?"

"I felt a little out of place." I dropped ice cubes into two glasses.

"Why?"

I turned to look at her. "Because all you talked about was the dessert project."

"We talked about other stuff."

I had to grin at that. "A little bit. But it was mostly about Sweet Tech."

"I'm sorry." She dropped down on the arm of one chair. "Are you mad at me?"

I poured the iced tea. "I'm not mad. I didn't say I was mad."

"We didn't mean to be boring. I'm sure Ethan didn't mean to be boring."

"You weren't boring." I crossed the room and handed her a glass. "You were excited. And I'm excited for you. I just don't think Ethan and I are going to work."

"You didn't really give him a chance."

"I didn't feel a spark." I sat down in my favorite burgundy armchair.

I'd moved it and the matching burgundy sofa from my parents' basement on the other side of the city. I bought my brown sofa and the two leather contour chairs from an online reseller. They all surrounded a square glass-topped coffee table.

Sophie took an end of the sofa cornerwise from mine.

"You barely had a chance to get to know him."

That might be true. But I was pretty confident in my impression.

"Did it take a long time with you and Bryce? Could you tell right away that you liked him?"

"We were always friendly," she said. Then she seemed to give it some thought. "I never disliked him. Do you dislike Ethan?"

"I don't know him well enough to dislike him."

She made a mock toast with her iced tea. "Thank you for making my point."

I sighed. I didn't feel like having this argument.

I'd only been home from work for about twenty minutes. But I'd already slipped into a loose cotton T-shirt and a pair of worn blue jeans. I was planning to make a bowl of soup, then putter around in my sundeck garden for a while. The heather was still nice, and the pansies and chrysanthemums would last a few more weeks. I wanted to enjoy my little patch of outdoors as long as the weather held.

Afterward, I was thinking I might search for a video on graceful walking. Surely, I wasn't the only woman in the world with that particular challenge. I didn't want James to frown at me and say *hmm* the next time I tried walking for him.

"My car's out front," Sophie said. "I'll tell Bryce we're going to meet them there. That way you don't have to rush to get ready, and we can come home whenever you want."

"I wasn't planning to celebrate Technology Week," I said.

"This is a fun event. It's not nerdy at all. It's the Things Festival—phones and tablets and home alarm systems. It's stuff you should be learning about anyway. Don't you want to see the hologram exhibit?"

"I was planning to garden after dinner." I knew there was a whine in my voice, but I was feeling a little whiny at the thought of going back out again tonight.

"Come on, Nat. You can garden any old time. And it's way more fun when you're there."

Now I felt selfish. Sophie obviously liked Bryce a lot. She wanted my support, and I should buck up and give it to her.

I glanced at my torn jeans. "Do I have to change?"

"It's definitely come-as-you-are. Flats are better for walking around."

"I haven't eaten yet."

"There'll be vendors."

"With 3-D printed food?" I joked.

She looked worried. "I sure hope not. We're trying to be ahead of the curve."

"That was a joke," I said.

"Oh. Good. It'll be more like burgers and nachos."

"I can live with that," I said, forcing myself to stand up and show some enthusiasm. "Give me a minute."

Leaving Sophie to finish her iced tea, I cut past my bed to the bathroom, freshened my face and tossed my hair into a ponytail.

Then I hoisted my shoulder bag from the bed. I hesitated, testing its weight in my hand for a moment. Deciding to play the odds and be more comfortable, I stuffed the essentials into my jeans pockets—my phone, a credit card, a little bit of money, a mini comb and a couple sticks of gum.

Back in the living area, I laced up my runners and tied a sweater around my waist. "I'm ready."

"You're fast," Sophie said, coming to her feet.

"Do you have to stop and change?" I asked.

She was wearing blue jeans and heeled black boots with a burgundy tunic sweater that had a loose cowl neck and a row of oversize buttons. Her hair was airy and fluffy and framed her face.

"I'll just go like this."

Once again, she looked chic to my utilitarian.

I wasn't going to let myself worry about that. It wasn't like I wanted to impress Ethan.

I locked up and we headed down the central staircase.

My phone buzzed against my butt and I retrieved it from my pocket.

It was James.

For some reason, my chest gave a little lift at the sight of his name.

I didn't want to answer in front of Sophie, but I didn't want to not answer, either. So I slowed my steps and let her get ahead.

"Hi," I said into the phone, sounding more breathless than I'd expected.

"Are you biking?" he asked.

"Heading down the stairs."

"Doing stairs. Good for you." He sounded impressed.

"No, not *doing* stairs, just going down them. I'm with Sophie."

"Oh. I misunderstood. Girls' night out?"

"No, another double date."

There was a pause on the line. "Oh... With mediocre guy?"

I hung back even farther. "I don't think you should call him that. But, yes, with Ethan again." I listened for a second. "James?"

"I shouldn't bother you, then."

"It's no bother. We're just heading out. What's up?"

"I was thinking about the weekend. But you probably have a date."

"I don't have a date." I didn't expect to have a date. I was going along tonight to support Sophie.

I came to the bottom of the stairs as Sophie was on her way out the door.

"What were you thinking?" I asked James.

I wouldn't mind having some plans for the weekend. I wouldn't mind it at all. If nothing else, it would give me a good answer on Friday when people asked what I was doing.

"That we could shop for some new clothes. I don't know anything about the right places or the right designers, but we could look that up. We have to start somewhere."

"We do," I agreed.

I'd never gone clothes shopping with a guy before. I usually went with Sophie and Brooklyn. Which, now that I thought about it, was usually about their clothes and not mine.

I pretty much had a set style: Miles Carerra for blazers and skirts, Nordin for slacks and Mistress Hinkle for blouses. I rarely bought dresses. I stuck with my classic standbys that I'd had for a few years now.

I picked up jeans, yoga pants and T-shirts at the outlet mall. I didn't much care who made them, as long as they fit.

"So?" James prompted.

Sophie had stopped. Holding the door open, she waited, watching me with a puzzled expression.

I tried to look like I was having a business conversation. "What time?"

"I'll text Saturday morning. Around nine?"

"That'll work. I better go. Sophie's waiting."

"Have a mediocre time."

I couldn't help but smile as I started walking. "That's kind of what I'm expecting."

"Who was that?" Sophie asked. "What are you expecting?"

"I'm expecting the Things Festival to be interesting," I said.

"That's the spirit."

She didn't press me for more information on the phone call, and I didn't volunteer. The James and Nat self-improvement project was going to stay a closely guarded secret.

As we climbed into Sophie's car, my phone pinged.

I checked to see the message was from James.

Enjoying the mediocrity?

I sent a smiley face back, because he'd made me smile.

"What's going on?" Sophie asked as she pulled into traffic.

"Work," I said.

I didn't explain what kind of work. And creating a whole new me was going to take a lot of work. It was going to take a *whole* lot of work.

So I reasoned that I wasn't lying. I was misdirecting. Misdirecting wasn't exactly noble, but it wasn't the worst sin in the world, either.

And I was being Sophie's wingman tonight—reluctantly but with good humor, I was helping a friend. I hoped the two things balanced each other out.

On Saturday morning, James picked me up in a low-slung red convertible.

It shone bright under the sunshine, looking out of place against the dusty curb.

"Is this new?" I asked, shading my eyes. My clip-on sunglasses were in my purse, and I decided I was going to need them.

As usual, I was glad to be prepared.

"I bought it yesterday," James said. "What do you think?"

I didn't know what I thought. Mostly I thought, *Holy cow!* "It's very red."

"Isn't it?"

"Yes."

"I went to the dealer at lunchtime."

"Uh-huh." I was trying to think of something positive to say.

The car was pretty ugly, low to the ground, a bit boxy. The black interior was harsh. It looked like something a gangster might have owned in the '70s. And I wasn't sure about owning a convertible in Seattle. We had plenty of nice days in the summer, I supposed. But we had plenty of rain, too. And the winters were a mixture of slush and ice. It was hard to tell how well the car would stay heated.

"I took a good look at everything they had," James said.

"And you picked this?"

"You hate it."

"I… It's… It definitely doesn't seem like something you'd pick."

"I know. That's the point. I picked the one I wouldn't have

picked. It's a *new me* car." He opened the passenger door to let me in.

"I suppose."

If we were changing who we were, I guessed what you drove was part of that.

I had a ten-year-old crossover, hunter green. It was serviceable if not beautiful. It definitely wasn't flashy.

I held on to the back of the bucket seat as I lowered myself inside. It was low, really low. If we had to hide under the trailer of a semi, we were going to fit just fine.

James shut the door, and I felt like I was sitting on the sidewalk.

He rounded the back and got in on the driver's side.

He popped a pair of sunglasses on his face and adjusted the rearview mirror.

"Do you like the way it drives?" I asked.

He started the engine, and it throbbed beneath us, roaring under the hood.

Since the top was down, I could hear every piston.

"It corners like a supercar," he said.

"I take it that's good?"

"It's very good."

"Okay," I said.

"Buckle up."

I snapped myself in.

The tires chirped as we jolted away. James wound out the engine in first, then grabbed second gear and we lurched forward.

I was sucked back against my seat.

He quickly braked, since we were coming to a red light.

"Comfortable?" he called to me above the noise and the wind.

"The seat's nice," I said.

"What?" He cupped his ear.

"The seat's nice!" I called out.

He nodded.

The light turned green and we lurched forward again.

It had good acceleration, I'd give it that.

We slowed and turned onto the I-5 on-ramp, and James pressed on the gas.

We were going faster than traffic and easily merged.

Something hit me in the forehead. It stung, and I flinched.

"What?" he asked me.

I reached up to find a smashed bug on my forehead.

I held it out to him. "I'm not crazy about having the top down."

He laughed at me.

The cad.

Okay, I'd admit it was kind of funny.

"You'd think the windshield would be a little higher," he said.

Then he flinched, and I saw a black spot on his cheek.

This time I laughed at him.

He geared down. He flipped on his signal and took an exit.

"This sucks," he said.

"It's a little bit funny," I said.

"This is a stupid car."

"You don't like it?" I wanted to ask if he'd even test-driven it before he bought it. It seemed like an awfully impulsive purchase.

"You hate it," he said.

"It's not about what I like."

"Okay, I hate it."

We were slowing down now, and the noise wasn't quite so oppressive.

"So why did you buy it?"

"Like I said, I didn't want to buy something I liked."

"Like a practical sedan?"

He turned onto a side street. "I've had one of those for years."

"Maybe you went too far the other way."

"Maybe."

"You know." I was thinking this through as I spoke. "We're going to have to like the people we turn into."

He turned into the empty lot of a small park. "The danger in that is that we'll stay exactly as we are. We have to expand."

"We can choose the direction we expand in."

"We can't trust our own instincts. Our own instincts are what brought us to where we are."

I had to admit, he had a point.

He brought the car to a halt in a parking spot facing a base-ball diamond.

"How about this," I said. "I'll trust your instincts, and you trust mine. That way we change it up, but we don't..." I gestured to the dashboard. "We don't do something completely stupid."

"Are you calling me stupid?"

"I'm calling this car stupid. It's going to be freezing in the winter, if you don't lose it in the first snowfall. I feel like a kindergarten kid sitting down so low. The black leather looks like something a gangster would own. And it's butt ugly, James. Fire-engine red? What, are you having a midlife crisis?"

James started to laugh.

"I'm just saying..."

"The dealership's only about five miles from here."

"Can you take it back?" That seemed like the best course of action to me—the very best course of action.

"I can probably exchange it for something else."

I breathed a sigh. "I think you should."

"I think I should, too. And I think you're picking the next one."

"What?"

He couldn't be serious.

He put it in Reverse. "We've determined we can't trust my taste."

"But... I can't pick you out a car. A pair of blue jeans, sure. Maybe a tux. Maybe even a hat."

"You think I need a hat."

"No. I'm not saying you need a hat. You don't need a hat. You have very nice hair."

He did have very nice hair, thick and dark, classically

cut in a way that showed off his square jaw and gorgeous blue eyes.

He headed for the parking lot exit. "You're picking the new one, Nat."

I tried to be helpful. "You just have to go... I don't know... a little less...flamboyant."

"I'm sure you will."

"I'm not doing it alone, James."

"Ah, but you are. You volunteered."

"I did not."

"And I quote—*you* trust *my* instincts."

He looked completely serious.

I considered for a moment the strategy of choosing something completely ridiculous, like a superlifted pickup truck. Then he'd have to overrule me. That could work.

"I can hear what you're thinking," he said as we tooled along a main road.

"You cannot."

"You're thinking if you botch it, I'll have to take over. I'm not going to take over. This one's on you."

"You've lost your mind."

"Nope. I've gained yours. I think I got the good end of that trade."

I couldn't help but smile. "Then are you going to pick *me* out a new car?"

He glanced over at me. "Absolutely."

I'd been joking. "I can't afford a new car."

"It doesn't have to be brand-new. But cars are like clothes. They introduce us to the world."

I gestured to the dashboard again. "And *this* is what you wanted to say?"

"I plead temporary insanity."

Four

I chose a gunmetal-gray SUV. It had sleek curves, a tough-looking black grille, diamond-shaped headlights, big durable wheels that would stand up to any weather conditions, and comfortable seats that made you feel like you were sitting on a cloud.

I didn't analyze my choice too closely. I just knew that if three men drove up, one in a sports car, one in a sedan and one in an SUV, I'd be most interested in the SUV guy.

Maybe it projected strength, or maybe there was room in the back for my eventual kids. It could easily have been anthropology and my primal brain influencing my decision. But I picked it, and James bought it, and we left a very happy salesman behind.

"This is way better," James said as we drove along I-5 and he fiddled with the controls on the dashboard.

"I can hear every word you say," I said. "It's like a miracle."

"Yeah, yeah. I get it. Your taste is better than my taste."

I felt a moment of doubt. "As long as you truly like it."

"I like it a lot." His smile turned warm and his tone was sincere.

I liked how his voice sounded in my ears. I liked how the warmth made me feel—like I'd done something right and he was happy about it.

"We're going downtown," he said. "I researched the 'it' places to buy a tux."

"You're seriously buying a tux? You can rent those, you know."

"Be honest, Nat. Do you go for the guy in an off-the-rack rented tux, or for the one in a perfectly cut, perfectly fitting *owned* tuxedo?"

"You can't just—"

"Answer the question, partner."

"Owned," I admitted. "But I'm not falling for a bankrupt guy, either."

James grinned. "I'm not going bankrupt."

"Bold words from a man spending like a drunken sailor."

"I don't need to cash in the 401(k) just yet."

"You have a 401(k)?"

"Why? Is that sexy?"

I batted my eyelashes at him. "Depends on the size. Women like a man who can provide."

"Should I have my tax status tattooed on my forehead?"

"A little too showy, I'd say. You'll have to work it into conversation."

"And that won't be showy?"

I patted the dashboard. "If you show up in this baby wearing your new tux, you won't have to brag about money."

"And you say men are shallow."

"I didn't say you were shallow. I said you were obsessed with looks."

He exited the interstate onto the downtown streets. "Fair enough. We pretty much are. But your gender seems all about money."

"It's not so much the money."

"Ha."

"It's the power, all the power things—good height, broad shoulders, confident stance, intelligent, good career and, as it turns out, a really nice SUV."

He deepened his tone to übersexy. "That's because it has tall tires and deep treads."

I raised my fingertips to my chest. "Be still my beating heart."

He grinned along with me.

We made our way into downtown and found a spot in an underground parkade. From there, James led the way to Brookswood, a high-end store near the waterfront. I'd never been inside it. I'd sure never planned to shop here.

"I assume they sell tuxes here," I said as we passed through a tall glass doorway into what felt like a rarefied environment.

It was nearly silent. The lighting was muted. The floor was a plush carpet. The displays and stands were placed far apart. It was clear to me that successful people came here to buy very expensive things.

We'd entered into the purse and shoe section.

I didn't see any price tags on the nearby merchandise. It was probably just as well. The prices would likely freak me out. Good thing we were shopping for James and not for me.

"I think they sell most things," he said.

We stopped and took in the lay of the store.

"How did you pick this place?" I asked.

"Fashion bloggers."

"Seriously?" It was hard to picture James browsing fashion blogs.

"They're pretty obsessive about shoes," he said. "And I have to say, I'm not about to wear any of those tight leather pants."

"I think you'd look awesome in tight leather pants," I said with a straight face.

"Bright red," he said with disgust. "Bright red leather, decorated with steel studs. I'd feel like it was Halloween."

"And you were going as a disco vampire?"

James shuddered.

A well-dressed man approached us.

We turned to greet him, and he offhandedly but obviously took in our outfits.

I was wearing black slacks, a green pullover and a pair of comfortable black flats.

James was dressed in a blue-and-white-striped dress shirt over dark gray slacks.

The store clerk didn't seem impressed by us.

"May I help you, sir?" he asked James.

The expression on the man's face said he thought we'd wandered into the wrong store.

"I hope so," James said. "I'd like to look at a tux."

"Bold start," I muttered under my breath.

James gave me a little shove with his arm.

I took it to mean I wasn't being serious enough.

"A tux?" the clerk echoed. He still seemed skeptical.

"A tux," James said with conviction.

"Then, right this way, sir." The man turned to lead us farther into the store.

"This is making me nervous," I said to James in a low tone.

Like the clerk, I couldn't shake the feeling we didn't belong here. At least, I didn't belong here. I shouldn't speak for James.

It was possible that he shopped at stores like this all the time.

I doubted it—based on what I'd seen of his wardrobe. But I didn't know for sure.

"You need to roll with it," James whispered to me.

"It's your credit card," I said back.

"You think you're getting away unscathed?" he asked, amusement coming into his tone.

"I—"

"They have a ladies' section."

I shook my head. "I can't afford a place like this."

"Think of it as an investment."

"An investment in what?" It wasn't like used clothing appreciated over time.

Vintage dresses in some cases, sure. But I'd have to be royalty or a movie star to have a realistic expectation of that happening.

I was neither.

I was very far from being either.

"In your future," James said.

We stepped onto an escalator.

"I don't need *this* much of an image upgrade," I said.

I thought about the balance in my savings account. I had some money, not a ton, but I'd rather spend it on a new car or a vacation. I knew I wouldn't get the same level of enjoyment out of new clothes.

"Go big or go home," James said.

"In that case, I might have to go home."

He frowned at me. "You bailing on me already, Nat?"

I felt bad about that. "I wasn't…" I tried to frame my thoughts. "I didn't mean it literally. I just didn't expect to drain my savings account on day one."

He seemed to think about that.

We stepped off the escalator and found ourselves in the men's clothing section.

"I'll buy you something," he said.

"Oh, no you won't." That wasn't where I'd been going at all.

I was trying to be realistic. I could change styles, but I couldn't drastically change price ranges like this.

"I didn't think about the cost," he said. "Don't get me wrong, I'm not floating in money. But my salary's got to be higher than yours, plus I get bonuses."

"There's no way you're buying me clothes," I said. "We'll find another way. We'll go to an outlet mall or something. If you do it right, you can get bargains on good stuff."

"You have to know what you're doing," James said.

When I didn't say anything back, he kept talking. "Face it, Nat, we don't know what we're doing."

I couldn't disagree with him on that. We each had zero clues about what we were doing. And zero plus zero was still zero.

"One outfit," he said.

I shook my head but he pretended not to see it.

"One outfit," he repeated. "Something we can take on a test-drive to decide if it's worth the investment."

The clerk stopped and turned to face us, looking rather bored. "In this section we have Remaldi. To the left is Dan Goldenberg. And over there is Mende and Saturday Sweet. Do you have a preference for a designer?"

"I wasn't thinking off-the-rack," James said.

He sounded so posh that I felt a burst of pride.

The clerk's expression faltered, and he seemed to reevaluate the situation.

At least, it seemed to me that he was reevaluating the situation.

If I was him, I'd be reevaluating the situation.

He'd written James off.

That was a mistake.

Okay, this was kind of fun.

"Of course, sir." The man's tone had changed. His shoulders squared, and his expression became more welcoming.

I was right.

I could tell by the amused twinkle in James's eyes that he saw it, too.

"Right this way," the clerk said. "I'll show you to our tailor. I'm Charles, by the way. Is your purchase for a specific event?"

"My firm has a number of formal and charitable events coming up this fall," James said as we fell into step with Charles.

It was my turn to elbow him.

He was getting a little carried away.

He looked down at me. "What?" he mouthed.

I shook my head and gave him a censorious look.

He just grinned.

The lack of price tags was making me nervous.

I was on my fifth, or maybe it was my sixth dress.

They were all pretty. Some of them fit better than others, but nothing I'd tried on so far was butt ugly.

I realized now as I stared into the mirror just how much I normally factored price into my buying decisions.

"Let's see it," James called to me from outside the fitting room.

We were separated by a heavy blue velvet curtain that hung in a semicircle from big wooden rings.

I stood on a soft carpet in a cubicle with a three-way mirror, a padded chair, and a set of six hooks along the curved wall.

A salesclerk named Naomi had picked out a dozen dresses for me to try.

I hadn't been allowed to pick my own. Oh, no. James insisted we couldn't trust my taste.

He reminded me that I got to pick out his new SUV. It was his turn to choose something for me.

We'd let Charles run wild with the tux.

Once Charles realized James was a serious customer, his enthusiasm level had risen to impressive heights. Along with the tailor, they'd measured every inch of James, consulted me on fabrics and cuts and accessories, until they finally seemed satisfied with the order.

James had remained stoic throughout the process.

I knew he'd spent a fortune. But he'd assured me he could afford it, and he insisted it was my turn next.

I told myself to forget about the prices. For once in my life, I was going to indulge without guilt.

I drew back the curtain.

James stood nearby. Naomi had offered him a chair and a drink, but he'd refused both.

"Well?" I asked, trying to gauge his expression.

"It's better than the last one."

"I liked the last one."

It had been black with a pretty lace bodice, a V-neck and an A-line skirt that draped to midcalf. You could dress it up or dress it down. It would be very versatile.

"That one was too librarian." There was a glint of humor in James's eyes.

"Ha ha," I said, grimacing in his direction.

"This one has more drama," Naomi said.

"You have to match my tux," James said.

"Match your tux?" I asked.

"For the test-drive."

"Your tux is coming with me?"

I don't know what I'd expected in a test-drive. But it wasn't a date with James.

But now I was thinking about a date with James.

I couldn't stop thinking about a date with James—tall, striking, handsome James, with the new shoulder set in his custom-fit tux, and his great new SUV.

The image was sexy.

He was sexy.

I found my gaze stuck on his sexiness.

It was more potent than I'd ever imagined.

How had I missed that?

"And me in the tux," he said, his deep tone only reinforcing my attraction to him.

Uh-oh. I was attracted to James. This was not good.

"Turn," he said to me.

I was happy to do it. It hid my expression. I didn't want him to figure out what I was thinking.

I couldn't be attracted to James.

James was Brooklyn's. Or at least, he used to be Brooklyn's. From the time we were teenagers, he had dated one of my best friends. And now we were buddies, pals, wing-persons for each other.

I didn't dare let attraction into the mix.

"That's nice," he said from behind me. "I like the crisscross, very sexy."

I felt my skin heat in reaction to his words.

He thought I was sexy.

No, no, no, a little voice said inside my head.

He thought the dress was sexy. It was the dress, not me.

It was shimmering green, with a scooped neckline and spaghetti straps that melded into a crisscross pattern over my bare back. It was fitted over my hips, the ankle-length skirt gently flaring out at my thighs. The fabric was light, and I liked the way it moved when I walked.

"Does it come in purple?" James asked.

I turned back to him. "Purple? Really?"

I wouldn't say I was a purple kind of person. I felt exotic enough going with the emerald green. I was already out of my comfort zone.

"A dark plum or maybe boysenberry," he said.

I stared at him in silence for a moment.

"We can have one made through our supplier," Naomi said. "It'll only take a couple of days."

"Boysenberry?" I asked. "That's a very specific color."

"I read," he said. "I learn from all those blogs. And boysenberry will look good with your eyes."

I got a little shiver, maybe a little thrill at the idea that James had been studying my eyes.

I was staring into his right now.

I was staring deeply into his. They were dark deep midnight blue, and they were making me warm all over.

"It'll bring out the highlights in her hair, too," Naomi said.

"I don't have highlights in my hair." All I really did with my hair was grow it.

"But you do," she said. "It's chestnut and gold and copper. You have great hair."

"Really?" I pulled the ends of my hair in front of my eyes.

"You have really great hair," Naomi said. "You should think about doing some layers around your face. Do you put it up?"

"Not really." I didn't think the looped ponytail I used during yoga class would count.

"Don't get rid of the length at the back," Naomi said, scrutinizing me as she talked. "You can do pretty much anything you want with it now. But soften it around your face a bit. It'll look awesome."

I'd never thought much about my hair, my plain brown straight hair. I'd never imagined someone would call it awesome.

"You could stand to lighten it a bit," James said.

I turned my attention back to him. "You don't like my hair."

"I like it a lot," he said. "But I thought you wanted something different."

He was right. I did.

"Go with something semipermanent," Naomi said. "That way you'll keep all the complexity and natural highlights. Just lighten it a shade or two."

"How do you know so much about hair?" I asked her.

"My sister's a hairdresser. Do you have contact lenses?"

I shook my head. I'd tried contacts once, but my eyes couldn't seem to get used to them. It hadn't seemed worth it at the time.

"Too bad," Naomi said. She leaned a little closer to me so

James wouldn't hear. "You might want to think about getting some." She canted her head in James's direction. "He likes your eyes."

I opened my mouth to explain the situation, but James jumped in.

"We should probably get your sister's name," he said to Naomi.

Sophie swung open her apartment door and froze.

Her eyes went wide as she stared at me. "What did you *do*?"

"You don't like it?" I was feeling incredibly self-conscious about my new hair and really weird about my contacts.

I got the haircut just this afternoon. Nobody but me and Naomi's sister had seen it so far. I'd been practicing with the contacts for three days now, but I still felt like I was blinking way too often. And I was fighting a constant urge to rub my eyes.

"Are you kidding?" Sophie asked. "I *love* the new you!"

She pulled me into a hug and she whispered in my ear. "Ethan's going to love it, too. Great move, Nat."

"Ethan?" I asked.

I didn't think I'd given Ethan a single thought since the end of our second "date," where he seemed about as interested in me as I was in him.

"Nice to see you again, Nat." It was Bryce's voice.

"Bryce is here?" I asked, pulling from Sophie's hug.

This was supposed to be girls' pizza night at Sophie's apartment.

"Surprise," Sophie said. "I knew it would be more fun with all four of us."

"All four?" Then I spotted Ethan.

He was sitting on one end of Sophie's cream-colored sofa.

Bryce had stood up from the love seat and was looking at me.

"Hi, Bryce," I said. "Hi, Ethan." I smiled to cover my disappointment.

I liked Bryce quite a lot. And Ethan was okay, too. But it

was a strain to carry on a conversation with them. And I really wasn't excited about another deep dive into the ongoing adventures of BRT Innovations.

I loved Sophie, I truly did. But hanging out for hours on end with three people who were working on the same all-encompassing project grew tiring.

I wanted to talk to Sophie, just Sophie. I had a lot going on in my life, too.

Not that I would tell her the reasons behind my makeover, or my deal with James, or my weird feelings about James. Still, I wanted girl talk, generic talk about men and relationships, maybe clothes and jewelry. I didn't know.

I did know that 3-D printed desserts wasn't where my head was at tonight.

I dropped my bag on her entry table and headed for the sofa. I would have kicked off my shoes, but everyone else still wore theirs.

I gave an inward sigh as I sat down.

Sophie and I had planned on making mango margaritas tonight, our secret recipe. I supposed that was off, too.

Bryce took his seat again.

"A Hawaiian and a pepperoni?" Sophie asked all three of us.

"Sounds good," Bryce said.

"I prefer vegetarian if nobody minds," Ethan said.

"I'm easy." The last thing I was worried about was the pizza toppings.

Sophie took out her phone. "Don't you love Nat's hair?" she asked as she pulled up the number.

Ethan looked at me, taking in my hair.

I resisted the urge to fluff it or toss my head. The actions seemed appropriate, but too lighthearted for the expression on his face.

"You changed it?" he asked.

"I like it," Bryce said.

"It's lighter," I said to Ethan. "Thanks," I said to Bryce.

"She cut it, too," Sophie said. "Where did you have it done?" Then she got distracted by something on her screen.

Bryce rose and pulled his wallet from his back pocket, extracting a credit card and handing it to Sophie.

I had to admit, it struck me as gentlemanly.

It reminded me of James and how we'd argued but he'd insisted on buying a pair of shoes to go with my dress.

The upshot was that I never did find out the prices. I probably never would.

"I don't know why women insist on doing that to their hair," Ethan said to no one in particular. "Ammonia, peroxide, p-phenylenediamine, diaminobenzene, toluene-2, 5-diamine, resorcinol. It's not exactly a healthy brew."

"Beauty," Sophie said without looking up.

Now I felt like my hair might just blanket the entire Pacific Northwest in a fog of noxious gas.

"If nobody did it," Ethan countered, "if you all went natural, all with the lowest common denominator, then nobody would have to put toxic chemicals on their head."

"I'll tweet that out," Sophie said. "Likely nobody's ever thought about it."

She made me smile.

"Did you hear back from North Capital?" Bryce asked.

"Nothing yet," Ethan said.

"It's after five. I thought the committee was deciding today."

"That was the schedule," Ethan said.

"That's not good," Bryce said.

I was curious, but I wasn't about to ask a naive question about their business, not after my experiences the last couple of times I'd tried.

"It's just one fund," Sophie said. "We shouldn't let it discourage us."

"If we don't get the investment ball rolling soon…" Bryce shook his head.

A light went on inside mine. North Capital was an investment firm. Ethan had said they were looking for investors into BRT Innovations.

There, I had it.

I felt better.

Wait. No. It didn't sound like it was good news.

"Maybe we'll hear tomorrow," Sophie said, obviously trying to be upbeat. "They would have been meeting all afternoon, right? They could have finished after business hours."

"I suppose," Bryce said. He paused. "You're right. Worrying is premature."

I was glad to hear that. I wanted Sophie to be successful. I might not want to hear every single detail of their progress, but I'd sure be her biggest cheerleader if their invention got traction.

"It's the same thing with shoes," Ethan said.

I looked at him in confusion along with everyone else.

He didn't seem to notice. "Do you know the physiological damage done by wearing high heels?"

I had a feeling he was going to explain it to us.

"Dude," Bryce said. "Don't talk them out of high heels."

"You're willing to risk permanent ankle injury so your girlfriend looks sexy?"

Bryce didn't seem to know how to answer that.

"It's okay," Sophie said to Bryce, patting his arm. "We can risk the ankle damage."

I didn't exactly disagree with Ethan. But as a woman who'd only just jumped into the sexy shoe world, I wasn't thrilled with the idea of having them suddenly go out of fashion.

"I'm just saying—" Ethan began.

"That looks don't matter," Sophie said. "Well, I don't believe you. If looks didn't matter to men, women wouldn't go to all the trouble."

"You dress for each other," Ethan said.

"That's not true," I said.

I had it on good authority, James's authority, that men liked glamorous women.

"Studies have confirmed it," Ethan said.

"You'll have to show me those studies," Sophie said. "Pizza will be here in twenty minutes."

I was glad of that, too.

I was hungry, and I was hoping we'd break out some kind of alcoholic beverage.

Ethan turned his attention to his phone.

"Are we making margaritas?" I asked Sophie.

She looked regretful. "Do you mind beer? Bryce brought some imported beer."

"Sure," I said.

Beer didn't strike me as strong enough, since I was pretty certain Ethan was looking up the studies that showed women dressed for each other.

I wasn't going through all this to impress other women.

I wanted to impress men, men like James.

I wanted to impress James.

Oh, man. This was getting bad.

I really needed that margarita.

Five

I felt like a movie star.

The feeling lasted for about thirty seconds. And then I felt like an impostor.

I'd never had my hair professionally styled before. I mean, sure, I'd had it cut plenty of times. But I'd never gone to a hairstylist to get it put up for a special event—not even the day I was supposed to be Brooklyn's bridesmaid.

I'd found myself liking Naomi's sister Madeline. She was upbeat and positive, and she pushed me just enough to be adventurous without completely freaking me out.

I'd gone back to her a second time, and she'd done an amazing job on my hair. It was soft around my face and gathered in a loose braid that somehow swirled into a messy bun at the back of my head. The new highlights really showed up under my bathroom lights and seemed to give it added texture.

Madeline had talked me into a mani-pedi—a new experience for me.

I'd thought about pedicures on a few spa days. But I preferred a good deep-tissue massage to almost anything else. I once had a facial, but I wasn't wild about them.

Now my finger-and toenails were perfectly shaped, perfectly even, and shimmering with a subtle purple Madeline had called oyster mauve. I was almost afraid to use my hands.

I didn't have a lot of jewelry to choose from, and the outfit seemed to need something more dramatic than my usual studs or hoops. I searched the bottom of my jewelry box and found a set of long dangling crystal chain earrings with a matching necklace. They worked, and I was set.

Thank goodness.

I only had five minutes to spare.

I carefully strapped on the exotic shoes James had bought for me. I'd never owned four-inch heels before. They were sharp black on the soles, silver on the inner heel, with silver straps dotted with white and purple crystals.

They were wild.

I stood up in them and practiced my new walking style. For a few seconds, I felt wild.

Then I was back to impostor again.

I took one last glimpse in my full-length mirror, telling myself I could do this. I could go out in public and nobody would guess this wasn't really me.

My stomach started jumping in protest, but there was a knock on my door, and I had no choice but to go.

I opened the door to James.

His eyes widened a bit and he sucked in a breath. It was hard to tell what that meant.

First I wondered if he was reacting to me. And then I wondered if he was actually looking past me into my apartment. He'd never been here before. And Sophie told me all the time that "early industrial" was not going to impress people.

Brooklyn's place had always been tasteful, up-to-date and immaculate. It stood to reason that James would prefer elegance to utilitarianism.

"Hi," I finally said to break the awkward silence.

"You…"

I glanced over my shoulder. "I know it's a bit unusual. But it's quite functional."

"Huh?" he asked.

"My place," I said, gesturing. "I know it's ugly."

He looked over my shoulder for a beat. Then he looked directly at me.

"You did it," he said.

"Did what?"

He gestured up and down. "That is *some* transformation."

Oh, we weren't talking about my apartment. That was probably good.

"Where are your glasses?" He moved closer. "You got contacts?" He broke into a smile. "That a girl. I'm impressed."

"They feel weird in my eyes." I would admit it wasn't as bad today as the first few days.

"Well, they look great."

"Thanks. You look good, too." I shook myself out of my self-absorption.

He looked fantastic.

His hair was different, too.

I took it in, did a walk-around, and came back to face him.

"The hair looks good." It was shorter on the sides, looking updated instead of classic.

And he'd let the stubble grow out on his chin, giving him a more rakish look, a dangerous look. I found myself wanting to reach out and stroke his face to see what it felt like.

I resisted the urge.

He held out his arms. "The haircut cost a lot less than the tux."

"The tux is off the charts."

His shirt was crisp white. His tie was straight, black with subtle inlaid gray diamonds. We'd gone with my choice on the suit fabric, onyx rather than jet-black. The style looked even better on James than it had on the model in the picture.

James had a perfect physique, tall with broad shoulders, a deep chest and what looked certain to be washboard abs.

I felt a rush of attraction. It felt unnervingly like arousal. I feared my face might be getting flushed with it.

"So, worth the money?" he asked, gesturing to the tux.

"I don't know what you paid, but I see a long lineup of eligible ladies in your future." I didn't like the picture, but I was more than sure it would be true.

He grinned. "Let's hope so. Do you need to get a coat?"

I shook my head. "I don't have anything that'll go with this dress. I'll have to hope the ballroom is heated."

"There'll be five hundred people there. I think you can count on it being warm. And I'll tell the driver to turn up the heat."

"You're not driving your new baby tonight?"

"The theme tonight is Mardi Gras. I see some drinks in my future."

"I could get into a hurricane," I said.

I was definitely partial to fruit juices, rum and blended ice.

I stepped into the hall and locked the door behind him.

"Love the shoes," James said.

"You better."

He'd given me some say in the shoes, but he'd definitely been the one to push for higher heels and the sparkle look.

"I have very good taste." He gazed down for a moment. "And you have even better feet."

"I had professional help," I said. "With the hair, too."

"It all looks good, very chic, very swanky. I predict a lineup of men wanting to dance with you."

We started for the staircase.

"I just hope I don't fall off the shoes," I said.

"A gentleman would hold you up." As he spoke, we came to the top of the staircase.

He offered me his arm.

I took it.

I had no desire to ruin the evening by falling down a flight of stairs.

His arm was strong and warm and reassuring. It felt like I was steadying myself against an immovable plank of wood.

I slid my opposite hand along the railing and felt completely secure all the way down.

We started across the foyer, but he stopped in the middle.

"Do you mind?" he asked.

"Mind what?"

"Just standing there for a minute."

I wondered for a second if he'd brought me a corsage. Then I wondered if it would ruin the line of my dress. Then I told myself I was being ungrateful.

If James had gone to the trouble to bring me a corsage, I was going to smile and thank him, then pin it on my dress no matter what color it might be.

He stepped away from me.

I wondered where he might have hidden the florist box.

But to my surprise, he walked around me in a circle, looking, watching, making me feel incredibly self-conscious.

"Well?" I asked as he completed the circle. I felt stupidly nervous and impatient.

"I hate to say it."

"Just spit it out."

If the outfit wasn't working, there was nothing I could do about it now. It wasn't like I had a closet of clothes back upstairs that I could wear to the ball. Like Cinderella, I only had one gown.

"We might be finished."

"For the night?" Maybe I didn't look perfect, but I thought I looked pretty good. I wasn't wild about undoing it all before anybody else even saw the effort.

"Finished making you over." He came closer. His voice went sexy low. "You're absolutely perfect."

I opened my mouth to say I didn't want the evening to be over this soon, but then his words penetrated.

"Wait, what?"

"You," he repeated. "Are perfect. Even your walk. The law of large numbers is going to be massively in your favor tonight. You'll probably fall in love."

I coughed out a laugh. "That's *really* not what I thought you were going to say."

"Well, that's what's true."

"It's a huge exaggeration. But it's nice of you to say so."

"We'll see," he said.

He offered me his arm again.

I took it.

I didn't need it anymore. But I liked holding on to him. I liked the feeling of connection.

He was my partner in crime, after all. He shared my secret, and he was helping me make my life better. It stood to reason those things would make me feel close to him.

"Wow," I said.

"You do go well with the room," James said.

"I'm afraid I might disappear."

Perimeter lights in the hotel ballroom glowed purple. Icicles of glass crystal hung in streamers from the ceiling. The cloths on stand-up tables were mauve, while tall, bulbous arrangements of white roses picked up the surrounding colors.

A quintet played on a low stage at one end, jazzy piano music wafting over the voices in the big room. Hundreds of people were already there, mixing and mingling, looking impressive in their formal clothes.

"Do you do this a lot?" I asked.

I would have stopped and stared, probably with my mouth hanging open.

But James kept walking. "Me?"

"Yes, you. Does your firm send you to parties like this all the time?"

"Never," he said.

My steps faltered for a moment. "Are we crashing?"

James stopped. "What? *No.* I bought tickets. But I don't usually like this kind of thing."

"I never do this kind of thing."

"Buck up, Nat. It's good as a test-drive."

I silently reminded myself why we were here and what we were doing.

I'd started feeling like this was a date.

It wasn't a date. I was James's wing-person, and he was mine.

I glanced around as we walked and noticed how many women were surreptitiously checking him out.

"Do you see that?" he asked.

"I sure do."

"They're impressed."

"They are definitely impressed." More and more women turned to watch him.

I leaned in closer to his ear. "It's the tux."

"The tux?"

"Yes." I knew it was more than just the tux. It was absolutely the man inside the tux. But I wanted James to know he was getting his money's worth on the purchase.

"They're not looking at me," he said.

"They're absolutely looking at you—all of you, the whole package of you."

"The *men*?"

"What men?"

"The men who are staring at you."

"Nobody's staring at me. I'm talking about the women. There are a dozen women looking at you right now."

"Well, there are two dozen men looking at you. One of them just pointed."

I threw James a subtle elbow. "Ha ha."

"I wasn't joking."

I moved my attention from the women to the men in the area.

It was true. A few of them were looking my way.

I didn't buy the pointing thing, but it was gratifying to know my dress was working.

"You're getting your money's worth out of the dress, too," I said.

"I'm not getting my money's worth. It's them who are getting my money's worth. Which, when I think about it, isn't really fair, it is?"

I could hear the smile in his voice.

"You want to stand back and point at me?" I asked in an equally teasing tone.

"I think I should abandon you."

I didn't know how to take that. "What? Are you annoyed about something?"

"So they can approach you, Nat. None of them are going to ask you to dance with me standing here."

I could see his point. But I wasn't exactly ready to be left alone here.

"Maybe in a few minutes," I said.

"You can do it."

"No. I can't. I really don't think I—"

He was walking away.

"James." I didn't want to shout.

No, scratch that. I did want to shout. I wanted to shout at him to get back here and help me. This wasn't our deal. My wingman wasn't supposed to fly off in the first thirty seconds.

But he was gone, swallowed by the crowd of people.

I stood still for a few minutes, wondering how not to look like an interloper.

Conversational groups surrounded me, two and three, some groups of up to six people. They seemed to know each other. They were chatting and laughing.

I wanted to sprint for the exit.

I thought about taking temporary refuge in the ladies' room. But then I ordered myself to buck up. I couldn't hide and meet men at the same time.

The law of large numbers. That's why I was here.

I caught sight of a bar lineup and decided it was a halfway measure. Lining up for a drink wasn't the same as hiding, and it would give me something to do other than standing here looking pathetically lonely.

I joined the longest line, hoping it would take a while.

The man in front of me turned.

He was about five-ten, dark blond hair, a very nice suit and a friendly face.

I smiled at him. "Hello."

He nodded. "Hi. Are you from the hospital?"

I wondered if I looked like a nurse. "The hospital?"

"St. Michaels…the recipient of tonight's fundraising."

"Oh."

Well, didn't I feel stupid. It hadn't occurred to me to ask James about the event. I was too focused on my dress and shoes.

"My date is with O'Neil Nybecker," I said.

Then I realized I'd just told him I had a date. Perfect. I was really starting off with a bang here.

"You haven't made it very far," a woman said to him, arriving to link arms with him.

"You were fast, sweetheart," he said to her.

He turned to me. "This is…"

"I'm Nat Remington. I was just saying my date is with O'Neil Nybecker."

Since he wasn't single, I was definitely glad to have claim to a date. I didn't want this man's date to get the wrong idea about me. I wasn't poaching.

"Nice to meet you," the woman said with a friendly smile. "Harold is on the St. Michaels board."

The man held his hand out to me. "Harold Schmidt."

I shook his hand. "Hello, Harold."

The line moved.

"Here we go," I said.

"Ah, yes. This is better," he said.

They both turned to move a few steps.

A man in line directly behind me spoke up. "Did I hear you say O'Neil Nybecker?"

I turned to look at him.

He was younger, maybe in his early twenties. He was clean-shaven, tall and fit. His hair was close cropped on the sides, shaved almost bald, while it was long at the top, thick and fluffed up.

He looked cocky and confident.

"I did," I answered.

The line moved again, and I moved with it.

"I'm from O'Neil Nybecker. Just started a couple of weeks ago. Do you work there, too?"

"I don't. I work in the public library."

He gave a winning smile. "So you came with someone from the firm. Do I dare hope you're here with a friend and not a lover?"

I wanted to tell him it was none of his business. The question was almost rudely blunt.

Then I told myself to chill. It might have been awkwardly phrased, but he was only trying to decide if I was attached. Probably so he didn't make the same mistake I'd just made and have my date show up all of a sudden.

Not that I'd been flirting with the guy in front of me. I was only making chitchat. Still, his "sweetheart" showing up like that had taken me by surprise.

"A friend," I said.

The man held out his hand to shake. "Aaron Simms. I'm an economist."

I shook. "Nat Remington."

"Nat is short for Natalie?"

"Natasha."

"Ohhhh." He made a point of looking impressed. "A beautiful name for a beautiful woman."

"Are you here with a date?" I asked in return.

If he was with a date, he probably shouldn't be flirting with me.

"I'm here on my own. It's a corporate thing. I want to impress the brass."

"The brass cares about this kind of thing, do they?" I couldn't help remembering that James said he never went to functions like this.

Aaron leaned in and lowered his voice. "I'm showing enthusiasm for the firm. You want to get ahead, you play all the angles."

"And this is an angle?" I had to admit, I was intrigued.

I'd never been one for office politics. Not that there were many politics in the public library. Then again, the last promotion I'd been in line for had unexpectedly gone to someone else. She was very socially astute, organizing outings and events for the staff.

Maybe I should pay more attention.

The line moved again, and I kept pace.

"I'm young, eager, a good conversationalist and dancer. I know which fork to use, and I know how to get the O'Neil Nybecker name out there. Why do you think they donate to the hospital?"

It seemed like a trick question. "To help sick people get well?"

Aaron chuckled as if I was delightfully naive. "Corporate reputation, darlin'."

Darlin'? Seriously, *darlin'?*

He kept talking. "They throw their money at prominent causes, especially those near and dear to the mayor's heart. It makes them look like they care, softens the edges of their hard-nosed corporate focus. Did you see the mayor? He's here with his wife. She's a big supporter of the arts center. Guess which cause O'Neil Nybecker's supporting next?"

Okay, I could get this one. "The arts center?" I asked, half-sarcastically.

"Now you're catching on."

I grimaced.

Luckily, the Schmidt couple were the only ones left in line in front of me. I'd be out of here soon.

"What are you drinking?" Aaron asked.

I truly did not want him to order my drink.

"I haven't decided yet."

"They do a great Sazerac."

"Oh." I wasn't sure what to say back.

I wasn't about to agree to his recommendation. I was having a hurricane. But I didn't want to disclose that, either. I could be wrong, but I was guessing his plan was to order our drinks together and use it as an excuse to walk away with me.

I didn't want my hair, dress and shoes to work on this guy. No thanks.

"*There* you are." James arrived and looped his arm around my waist.

I gave him a surprised look.

My first impression of Aaron might not have been great, but James couldn't know that.

It surprised me that he was breaking up the conversation.

"Hi, James," I said, framing a what-are-you-doing? question with my expression.

"Simms." James nodded to Aaron.

They knew each other. I guess that should have occurred to me. O'Neil Nybecker was a very big firm with a twenty-story office building, but I supposed there were meetings and a lunch room. People would pass each other in the halls.

"Hi, James." Aaron took in James's arm at my waist. Then he looked back at me. "Friends?" he asked, looking a little bit annoyed.

"Good friends," James said.

The Schmidts took their drinks and moved on.

"What would you like?" James asked me.

"A hurricane, please," I said.

"Coming up," James said.

"Was it what you hoped for?" I asked James as we made our way through the hotel lobby at the end of the evening.

"It was about what I expected." He didn't sound thrilled. "You?"

"It was fun walking in."

After James had rescued me from Aaron, I'd mixed and mingled some more. I'd even danced a few times. But I hadn't met anyone interesting. The law of large numbers seemed to have let me down tonight.

James smiled as we approached the front door of the hotel. "You caused a bit of a ripple with your entrance."

I agreed that I'd attracted a bit of attention. But James was the one who had women craning their necks.

"You caused a bigger ripple. Did those women approach you?"

"A few did. They seemed nice."

"But nothing to write home about?" I asked.

He pushed open the door for me. "Definitely nothing to write home about."

"Do you think we were doing something wrong? Or maybe my expectations were too high. I mean, we definitely look good and all."

"We look great," he said.

"Yeah, I think we do." I couldn't imagine any woman not falling all over James the way he looked tonight, that was for sure.

I'd fall all over him myself if I thought there was any chance he'd reciprocate. And that wasn't just the two hurricanes talking. He was hot.

"We'll have to try again," he said.

He looked both ways on the hotel driveway and signaled for our car.

"Try the same thing?" I asked.

"There'll be different people at a different event. I don't think we should abandon this approach just yet. O'Neil Nybecker is a sponsor of the arts-center fund-raiser coming up."

"Aaron mentioned that," I said.

James's brow went up. "Oh?"

"Uh-huh," I said.

There was a bit of an edge to James's voice. "What else did he say?"

"Is there something you don't like about Aaron?"

"There are a few things I don't like about Aaron. What did he say to you?"

I realized Aaron wasn't the most appealing person in the world. "He said he attended events like this to impress the brass."

James gave a cool laugh as the car pulled up in front of us. "That sounds like Aaron."

"He seemed harmless enough," I said. "A bit annoying maybe. A bit young."

James opened the back door. "A bit nakedly ambitious."

"Is ambitious bad?" I asked as I climbed into the car.

Aaron had been clear about wanting to climb the corporate ladder. But lots of people wanted to get ahead.

"Depends on how you do it." James closed my door and went around to the other side.

"How is Aaron doing it?" I asked while James got settled.

I remembered I was thinking about my own lost promotion while Aaron had been talking about his approach to his career development.

"Well, he's got a big leg up, that's for sure."

"Because he's smart? Hardworking? Ambitious?"

The car pulled smoothly away from the curb.

"Because he's a Simms."

"That's a good thing?" I guessed.

"His uncle is Horatio Simms, senior partner at O'Neil Nybecker. Word on the street is that it may soon become O'Neil Nybecker Simms."

"Ahhh," I said. *Ahhh* was how I felt hearing that information.

"Aaron is entitled and cavalier," James said with a frown. "And last week he became my special problem."

That piqued my curiosity. "Why? What did he do?"

"I've been asked to show him the ropes. He's an intern."

"He didn't tell me he was an intern."

Aaron hadn't sounded at all like he was in a training position.

"I'm not surprised," James said. "But let's stop talking about Aaron. I'll worry about him Monday morning."

"One last question?" I asked.

James frowned. "About Aaron?"

"Let's call it Aaron adjacent."

"All right. I'll give you one more. But only since you look so gorgeous."

I tried not to smile, but I couldn't help it. His teasing compliment made me feel good.

I should stop letting James make me feel good. I should at least try to stop it.

"He said the brass is impressed if you attend functions like this. But you said you never attend them. I wondered why not."

There was an edge to James's voice when he spoke. "Maybe I don't care about impressing the brass."

It was clear I'd asked the wrong question. But we'd pledged to be honest with each other. And I had to wonder if James's instincts might not be leading him astray on this one. Women were definitely attracted to money and power, and moving up in a firm like O'Neil Nybecker would only increase James's power and therefore his desirability to large numbers of women.

We were going after large numbers here.

"What would it hurt?" I pressed. "You went tonight. I mean, I know it wasn't the success we'd hoped for, but it wasn't exactly painful, either. Your bosses saw you there. If they liked it—"

"I'm an economist, not a show pony." His sharp response took me by surprise. "There are people who get ahead by playing games, and those who get ahead through solid, hard work. Maybe I don't want to compromise."

His reaction threw me.

"I thought that was the point of all this? I thought we were playing the image game. All we're doing here is compromising."

"In our personal lives," he said. "Not in our professional lives."

"I was thinking it might work for both. And maybe it only works if we do both. Maybe we need to change all the way through, not just on the surface, not just on the weekends or when we're together playing dress up."

"You want us to compromise all the way through?"

"I'm not saying we compromise our ethics or anything." I wasn't sure where I was going with this, but so far, it sounded okay. "I'm saying where's the harm in being more exciting on all levels? Look at me."

He did.

I gestured to the outfit. "I'm all dressed up. But I'm still librarian Nat Remington. I have her opinions. I have her hobbies. I have her attitude. I have her plain old name. Aaron said Natasha was a pretty name."

"Aaron again?"

"Stop. Seriously. Don't let Aaron mess with your mood. Natasha is a pretty name. But I went with Nat. Why did I go with Nat? Tasha is the better nickname. It's gorgeous. It's exotic. It's the name of someone who leads a wild and glamorous life."

"So change it," James said.

"I might."

"You should."

"I will." I felt empowered just making the pledge.

"Good."

"You change yours, too."

He gave me a look of skepticism. "How can you change James?"

"Jamie. You can be Jamie."

"I don't—"

I reached out and touched his arm. "You promised to trust my judgment. You need a new name, something less uptight than James."

"Seriously?"

"Yes."

"Okay."

"Really?" I couldn't help but feel excited.

"Yes, really. So, tell me, what are Jamie and Tasha going to do next?"

Six

We decided on a popular dance club.

James picked out my dress again, but this time I paid for it.

I kind of loved it. It was a shimmery gold-and-black geometric pattern, sleeveless, with a scoop neck. Tight to the waist, it had a gold metal belt over a pleated skirt. The soft skirt hung to my midthigh and swirled when I danced.

The following Friday, I left my hair down and found some dangling gold earrings that looked flashy enough for the occasion.

James argued for gold sandals, but we settled on black cutout ankle boots with tapered heels. They were easier to wear, but still had a funky, avant-garde appeal. I never would have considered them before now.

We stood in line for half an hour. The club was loud and crowded, with lots of techno music, flashing laser lights and haze from a fog machine behind the DJ.

It wasn't to my taste, but I danced a lot. I couldn't talk to any of my partners, so I had no idea if I liked them or not. Mostly, they grinned at me while we danced, then they bid me a silent adieu with a wave of their hand before moving on to another partner.

Finally, James touched my arm and pointed to the exit.

My ears were throbbing, the music following us outside as we found our way into the fresh air. It was misty, and a skiff of wet from some earlier rain made the black pavement shine under the lights.

He asked me a question, but I couldn't hear.

"What?" I asked in what I hoped was a loud voice. I couldn't hear myself very well, either.

He leaned into my ear. "What did you think?"

I gave him a shrug while we passed the lineup of more people crowding the sidewalk, waiting to go inside.

Some of the outfits made mine look tame.

"Not my thing," he said.

"Mine, either," I admitted, although it had been my suggestion.

We made our way down the block to the brighter lights of First Avenue.

"Let's scratch it off the list," he said.

"Consider it scratched."

My feet hurt, but I liked walking.

"Hungry?" he asked.

"Starving." I was.

He pointed to a brick café with big awnings and glowing lights. "Try that?"

"Yes, please."

The sooner I sat down, the happier I'd be.

A hostess showed us to a booth beside the window. It looked out on a patio that was empty now since rain was beginning to sprinkle down again.

"This is nice," I said, settling into the cushy seat and opening a big menu on the table in front of me.

James did the same. "So, did Tasha meet anyone?"

I grinned as I read my way through the burger selection, thinking a chocolate milkshake sounded awesome. "Tasha met a whole bunch of people."

"Did she like any of them?"

I glanced up to see his gaze on me.

"She couldn't tell. I didn't have a single conversation. What about Jamie? Anyone interesting for you?"

He shook his head. "Same thing. Lots of inanely grinning maniac dancers."

"Is Jamie being judgmental?"

"Jamie is being realistic. Dance clubs are *so* scratched off our list."

"I do like the outfit," I said, making a point of taking in his distressed jeans, white-and-gold foil-patterned T-shirt and short leather jacket.

"Never going to wear this shirt again," he said. "What are you having?"

"Maybe you could do yard work or paint in it or something."

"You're too practical for your own good."

"If you don't want it, I'll take it."

"You think it's girlie?"

"I didn't say that."

"It'll be way too big for you."

"I can sleep in it." As the words left my mouth, our gazes met. They meshed and melded and the air seemed to sizzle between us.

I didn't think I was imagining it.

"What can I get for you?" a waitress asked, stopping beside the table.

James broke the look.

He moved his attention to the menu. "I'll take a bacon mushroom burger with fries."

"Anything to drink?"

"Cola," he said.

I willed my heart rate to slow down.

I wished my skin didn't prickle. I knew I had goose bumps, and I knew exactly why. There was no point in even pretending I didn't have a crush on James… Jamie. It was Jamie now, and he was hot.

"And for you?" the waitress asked.

"Cheeseburger," I said. "With fries and a chocolate shake." I definitely needed the shake to cool me down. And drowning my arousal in delicious calories seemed like a really great idea right now.

"A shake sounds good," Jamie said. "Can I switch?"

"Certainly," the woman said. "Coming right up."

"Thanks," Jamie said, handing her his menu.

I did the same.

"We have to come up with something else," I said before we could take the conversation back to me sleeping in his shirt. Even though I was staring at the shirt, thinking of how it would feel skimming over my skin and how Jamie would look without it.

Whoa.

"Something else?" he asked.

"Another exciting activity for Jamie and Tasha." I forced a light note into my voice. "Exactly how brave are we? Are we going bungee jumping or skydiving?"

"Is that what you want to do?" He looked serious.

I'd been joking.

"Nah," I said, thinking it through. "It would be over so fast, and we wouldn't meet anyone on the way down."

He didn't answer, and his gaze focused outside the window.

The rain was increasing, bouncing off the tables and chairs on the patio and streaking through the bands from the street-lights.

Jamie frowned, and I wondered if he was worried about flagging a cab.

"Don't worry," I said.

He looked back at me. "About jumping out of a plane? I'll jump out of a plane if that's what you want."

"I thought you were worried about getting a cab."

He looked confused. "Why would I worry about that?"

"The rain," I offered.

"It's Seattle," he said. "The system can handle rain."

"Then why are you frowning?"

"I'm not frowning."

"You were. You frowned when you looked out the window just now."

"Oh, that frown."

"Did I say something wrong?" I went over the past couple of minutes inside my head, trying to figure out what it could have been.

"It wasn't you. I thought I saw someone out there."

I was relieved, but only a little bit. I didn't want Jamie to feel upset about something I said or about anyone else.

"Who was it?" I asked, hoping to make it better.

"It doesn't matter. It wasn't them."

I knew I shouldn't press, but I couldn't help but be curious. "You can talk to me. Remember, we're going to be honest with each other. You said it was the only way this was going to work."

"Fine," he said. "Sure. Why not."

I braced myself, not sure what to expect.

"I thought I saw Aaron."

Okay, that wasn't at all what I'd expected. "From your office Aaron?"

"That Aaron."

I'd met Aaron a second time on a night Jamie and I went shopping. It was clear he and Jamie didn't get along particularly well. But I didn't understand why merely seeing Aaron would annoy Jamie.

"We're not that far from O'Neil Nybecker," I said. "Maybe he was working late."

"I *wish* he was working late. He cut out early today… again."

I still wasn't seeing why Jamie cared. I tried to make a joke. "I take it you don't have flexible hours?"

"Not for interns. And not after the stunt he pulled this week."

Again, I was curious, but I didn't know if the incident would be confidential.

I waited, but Jamie didn't elaborate.

The waitress dropped off our milkshakes.

He was still frowning, and he didn't take a drink.

I sipped through the straw, and the milkshake was delicious.

"Do you want to talk about it?" I asked.

"I don't want to bore you."

"Go ahead. I'll tell you if I get bored."

Jamie tried his own milkshake.

"Good, huh?" I prompted.

"It is."

"So?" I wanted to know what had the power to make him frown like that.

"It sounds minor, but it's not. In a meeting with one of our biggest clients, where, as an intern, he's supposed to sit quietly and learn, Aaron pops up with a *suggestion*."

Jamie paused, and I waited.

I stirred my milkshake with the straw, pretending I wasn't dying of curiosity.

"He says," Jamie finally continued, "and I quote, 'Take the company public.'" Jamie's expression told me he was disgusted.

"And that's a bad idea?" I was guessing, of course. I didn't know anything about it.

"It's a risky idea," Jamie said. "Worse, it's a knee-jerk idea. It's a gut reaction. We don't do gut reactions. We do thoughtful and thorough analysis. Even if it was the best idea in the world, even if we'd done the research, you don't blurt it out in front of the client without a plan. The team had no plan."

"Would you ever go with your gut?" I asked. "Make a risky decision based on your instincts?"

"Never."

I'd never do that, either. At least Nat would never do that. I wasn't sure about Tasha. Tasha just might.

"What about Jamie?" I asked.

Jamie looked confused.

"I get that James is careful, but would Jamie take a flier on something?"

Jamie's eyes narrowed and the corners of his mouth went white. "Are you suggesting Jamie should be more like Aaron?"

I tried to figure out how to call the question back.

But the waitress appeared with two laden plates.

"One cheeseburger," she said, putting a plate down in front of me. "One bacon mushroom." She set Jamie's plate down. "Will there be anything else?"

I shook my head to answer her. I wasn't hungry anymore. I was feeling a little sick.

"We're good," Jamie said to her. "Thanks."

She walked away.

"I didn't mean that," I said.

"Jamie's not careless," he said.

"I'm sorry."

"Don't worry about it. Let's just eat."

But I was worried about it.

I took a bite of my burger and forced myself to eat some fries. But my heart wasn't in it.

Jamie might not be careless. But I was beginning to worry Tasha was.

I didn't hear from Jamie all week.

Sophie called to see if I would meet up Friday night. But I was afraid she'd bring Bryce and Ethan along, so I lied and said I had plans with the girls from work.

By Thursday, I couldn't bring myself to look at my new clothes. After work, I stuffed them to the back of my closet and changed into my oldest and most Nat-like outfit, deciding to garden until I was ready to go to sleep.

I pulled back my hair and tied it up in a scarf. Then I propped open the patio doors to let in the fresh air and tucked my hands into my floral-print garden gloves.

There was a knock on my door.

I ignored it at first, thinking it was probably Sophie. She might be frustrated that I'd turned down her invitation and decided to bring Bryce and Ethan directly to me.

Wouldn't she be surprised to have me greet them all like this? Ha. Ethan would be well and truly cured of any lingering desire to date me then.

The knock sounded again, this time more forcefully.

Fine.

If she wanted to surprise me, I would surprise her right back. For better or worse, this was Natasha Remington. I wear old clothes. I garden. I'm plain and boring, and I like it that way.

It would have been perfect if I already had a cat.

I went for the door, wrenching it open.

It was Jamie.

"Hey, Tasha." He breezed past me. "I have an idea."

I stood with the door wide-open, staring at him.

He glanced around at the decor but didn't react. He turned back to me. He didn't react to my outfit, either.

"I don't understand," I said.

"That's because I haven't told you yet."

"Told me what?"

"My idea. Didn't I just say I had an idea? That's why I'm here."

"But…"

"Rock climbing," he said.

I didn't have a response.

"Wait." He seemed to notice what I was wearing. "Are you…renovating?"

That I could answer. "Gardening. What do you mean rock climbing?"

"Want some help?"

I took in his slacks and dress shirt. "You don't look dressed to get dirty."

He glanced down at himself. "I suppose."

I closed the door behind me. "What are you saying about rock climbing?"

"You and me. Instead of jumping out of a plane, we take some training and go climbing. It'll be exciting and adventurous. And it'll get us out to meet regular people, not the club or ballroom set."

"Have you ever done it before?" I asked.

"Never. You?"

I shook my head.

"I saw a beginners class advertised. It starts on Saturday over near Ballard. We could sign up."

I took my gloves off. "Did I miss something?"

"Miss what?"

"I thought you were ticked off at me."

He looked puzzled. "Why?"

I really didn't want to bring it up again. "The argument… last weekend…at the café."

"I told you not to worry about that."

"You didn't sound sincere."

"Well, I was. Are you that thin-skinned?"

I felt my back go up. "Excuse me?"

"Do you want me to apologize for disagreeing with you?"

"No." I tossed the gloves down. "And I'm not thin-skinned. But you were clearly annoyed with me, and then you didn't call."

"Should I have called?"

"You're missing my point."

He moved a little closer. "I'm sorry. What's your point?"

"You got mad, and then you went silent, and I didn't know what to think."

"You're forgetting the 'don't worry about it' that came in between those two things."

"You can't just toss something off like that and expect it to land. I thought our project was over. I thought you were giving up."

"Are *you* giving up?"

"No." Well, I was. At least, I had been. But I didn't want to.

He gently took my hands. "I'm not giving up."

I felt his touch all the way up my arms and into my chest.

I had an overpowering urge to lean forward, to press my chest against his and to wrap my arms around him. I wanted to hug him. I wanted to kiss him. I wanted to... Oh, boy.

I swallowed.

"So, what do you say?" he asked.

Yes! I almost shouted.

"Shall we learn how to rock climb?" he asked.

"Yes," I said out loud. "Let's learn how to rock climb."

He hugged me.

He pulled me against his chest and wrapped his strong arms around me and hugged me to him.

My body sighed. It sang. I hugged him back, leaned my cheek against his chest, closed my eyes and absorbed the heat and the energy pulsing from him into me.

Time seemed to stop.

I felt his breath on my hair.

His chest expanded with a deep breath. Then his arms pulled more tightly around me.

I pretended it was attraction.

I let myself fantasize that he liked the feel of me, the scent of me, that he wanted to taste my lips the way I was dying to taste his.

Too soon, he drew back.

He turned away and cleared his throat.

I was mortified to think he could tell how I felt.

Had I hugged him too tight? The way my body had gone boneless and molded to his had to be a dead giveaway. He was embarrassed. He probably pitied me.

I pitied myself.

I had to get over this infatuation.

"Is there a website or something?" I asked, trying desperately to sound normal. "Where we sign up?"

His shoulders were tense, and he didn't turn. "I'll take care of it."

"I don't mind—"

"I'll take care of it."

"Okay." I waited for him to look at me, but he didn't.

"Uh, Jamie?"

"Yes."

I *so* didn't want to have this conversation, but I wouldn't be able to stand another two days of guessing his mood. I'd just done that, and it was awful.

"Is everything okay?" I asked, bracing myself.

"You bet." He turned then, and he smiled. He looked almost normal. "I'm glad you're willing to give it a try."

I was willing to give a whole lot of things a try right now.

But I couldn't tell him that.

Instead, I fought the lingering hum of attraction. I wished mind over matter worked better than it did. But it didn't. Despite logic, reason and my honest-to-goodness best efforts, I couldn't shake the desire to hurl myself into his arms.

"I'm glad you thought of it," I managed to say.

"The class starts at nine on Saturday. Can I pick you up at eight?"

"Yes. Sure. I'll be ready. Is there anything I need to bring?"

"There's a list of suggested attire on the website. I'll send you the link."

"Good. That sounds good." I felt like we were making small talk.

"See you Saturday." He headed for the door.

I stepped out of the way.

When the door closed behind him, I blew out a breath.

I knew I had to get gardening. I had to do something normal. But my feet didn't want to move.

My phone pinged with a text.

It was Jamie, and my heart lurched ridiculously at the sight of his name.

He was sending the link to the climbing website.

I felt like a foolish teenager mooning over that cute boy in math class.

I was way too old for this.

I took a vacation day on Friday.

I didn't really need the day off, and Nat would never take a sudden, random day off work on a lark. But it felt like something Tasha would do. So I did it. And I was glad.

I was a little restless, but I was still glad.

I sat staring at my gray cinder block walls. I'd lived here three years now, and they were the same color as when I'd first moved in. I'd hung two pictures on them, both in the spots where a previous tenant had drilled a hook.

They were watercolor portraits of four young girls—in one they were smiling, in the other they were thoughtful. Sophie had bought them for me as a housewarming present. She said they reminded her of the four of us: Layla, Brooklyn, her and me.

It was obvious that Brooklyn was the pretty, pink-cheeked blonde. Layla was the intent girl with auburn hair. I was the short brunette with glasses, always the glasses. That was me, always shorter, always a little mousier than the rest.

Sophie had been right. The paintings did look like a peaceful, rather angelic version of the four of us.

I wondered for a minute if actual photos might be even better. I thought I'd like to look at the real us instead of the paintings.

Maybe that was what I would do.

Something Jamie had said was ticking through my mind today.

It had been innocent enough.

I didn't think he meant it as a criticism.

But when he walked into my apartment last night, he'd asked if I was renovating. He clearly thought my apartment needed renovating.

It shouldn't have been a huge surprise to me. Pretty much everyone who knew me had advised renovating at one point or another.

But back then, they'd suggested it to Nat. Nobody had suggested it to Tasha before. I was thinking this morning that Tasha might like to renovate.

Not that Tasha had the slightest idea of where to start.

But painting the walls seemed reasonable. With the right color of paint, you could make a huge difference without spending a lot of money.

I had hundreds of photos on my computer. I liked some of them a lot.

If I painted the wall, say, a nice cream or pale gold.

"Shut up, Nat," I said out loud.

Tasha, Tasha, Tasha, I thought inside my head. *What color do you like?*

It occurred to me to ask Jamie. After all, we'd agreed that he would trust my judgment and I would trust his. But after last night, I felt really weird about contacting him.

Then again, how better to make the first contact after our awkwardness than over something an innocuous as paint color? It was probably the perfect question: bland, lightweight, easy to answer.

I picked up my phone to type the text.

I'm painting my walls. What color should I use? Tasha.

Before I could talk myself out of it, I hit Send.
His text came back.

Your apartment?

I wasn't sure what other walls he thought I might be talking about.

Yes.

Shouldn't you be at work?

"Reasonable question," I muttered to myself as I typed.

I took a vacation day.

And you decided to paint?

Tasha is impulsive.

He sent a smiley face.

I'll have to come by and take a look.

The smiley face was nice. I felt like we'd made it past the awkwardness. But the rest was disappointing.

I'd hoped he'd tell me mauve or burgundy or blue. I was all set to head out to buy paint, brushes and a drop sheet. I didn't want to sit here for the rest of the day and think about redecorating. I wanted to get started.

I told myself I could clear the decks. Painting was messy. I'd have to move the furniture to the middle of the room. I should roll up the rugs. If I was moving the furniture, I'd definitely need to vacuum underneath.

There was plenty I could do to get going.

I rose from the sofa, cleaned up the few breakfast dishes and changed into some old jeans and a battered sweatshirt.

The rugs were easy. I rolled them up and made a pile.

I decided I'd need about five feet in front of each wall. That meant moving one sofa up against the coffee table. It wouldn't be usable while I painted, but I wasn't planning on entertaining or anything.

I discovered I was right. Beneath the sofa there was quite an accumulation of dust and grit. I plugged in the vacuum and went to work. As it sucked up the debris, I studied the floor. It was in worse shape than the walls, all scratched and scuffed by about fifty years of students. If you looked closely, you could see the pattern of the desk rows, the little round dents from the desk legs and the worn paths where students trod in between.

I found myself smiling when I thought of all the kids that had learned in this room. When you thought about it, it was a nice provenance to have in a home. Maybe some of them had grown up to be doctors or pilots; maybe they were artists or athletes. I would bet a whole lot of them had kids and grand-kids by now, Sunday barbecues and family baseball games.

I heard a noise and shut down the vacuum.

I waited, and it came again—a knock on the door.

My first thought was the downstairs neighbor. They were a young family with twin toddlers and a baby. My noise could be disturbing nap time.

I crossed to the door and opened it.

I was startled to see Jamie in the hall.

"What?" I asked, somehow not able to be more specific. "Weren't you downtown at the office?"

"I came to check out your walls."

"In the middle of the day?"

"You're playing hooky."

I found myself insulted at the accusation. "I put in for vacation leave. It's legit."

"I'm on an early lunch."

"It's ten thirty."

"Hence the word *early*. Are you going to let me in?"

"Sure." I stepped back. "Of course."

It occurred to me then how I looked. Not pretty, that was for sure. I hadn't bothered with makeup. I hadn't even showered yet today. My hair was in a quick knot on the top of my head. My gray sweatshirt was stained and boxy, and I had holes in the knees of my jeans.

I resisted the urge to smooth my hair or check my cheeks for streaks of dust. If Jamie was going to show up out of the blue, he got what he got. Tasha might dress up for a night on the town, but she dressed down for painting her apartment.

And, hey, I was painting my apartment. There should be points for that effort.

"I figured Jamie would duck out of the office if he had a good excuse."

"Jamie thinks picking my paint color is a good excuse?"

"I'm here to support you, Tasha," he said in a smooth, silky voice that trickled all the way through me.

I was *not* going to let things get awkward again.

I put some space between us.

"In that case, Jamie, what color should I use?"

He looked around for a long minute. He took a step, changed his angle, turned around.

"This really is…" he said.

"Utilitarian," I said.

He nodded. "That and a few other adjectives."

"Are you going to insult my apartment?"

He fought a smile. "I'm going to say Tasha's instincts are right. Paint is a good idea. Along with…" He looked around some more.

"I was wondering what to do with the floors," I said.

He looked down. "Fresh paint on the walls will definitely make the floors look tacky."

"I'd be offended, but I agree with you. It's high time I did something with this place."

I pictured Sophie for a moment. I had a feeling I was quoting her. She was going to be over the moon when she heard I was redecorating.

Trouble was, she'd want a hand in it. And she had very strong opinions.

I wanted this to be Tasha's apartment, not something tasteful and lovely that was inspired by Sophie.

I'd have to move fast. I wanted to be past the point of no return before Sophie dropped by and caught me.

"So," I said. "How adventurous do you think Tasha is feeling today?"

"Butter yellow with a russet-brown feature wall and some tangerine trim to make it pop."

"That sounds delicious," I said, trying to picture it.

"Maybe not tangerine," he said. "Maybe pumpkin. It's a bit darker."

"Do I want to know how you know all this?"

"I confess, I've wandered from the fashion blogs into home decorating a time or two."

I broke into a grin.

"It'll look great. I'm stealing it from a design I saw last week. I'll send it to you."

I did like the sounds of butter yellow. And given the size of the room and the walls, a contrasting wall seemed to make sense. I didn't know what pumpkin orange looked like, so who was I to say no?

"You could put stone laminate on the floor and pick up the colors."

I looked down.

I really liked the idea of a new floor. But I doubted I could afford it.

"I was thinking about something you said," Jamie said into the silence.

His words piqued my curiosity, and I looked up.

"You asked if Jamie would go with his gut, make a risky decision based on instinct."

I didn't want to argue again, so I didn't say anything.

"He would," Jamie said. "Oh, not on behalf of a client, that would be irresponsible. But he'd take a risk for himself. I'm sure of it."

He had me intrigued. "You're going to take a risk?"

"I think I should."

I saw the chance for a joke. "And you've thought this through."

He grinned at me. "Yes, I'm going to thoroughly analyze my instinctive, impulsive action."

"Do tell," I said. I backed up a little and folded myself into one of the armchairs, motioning for him to do the same.

He sat down across from me. "Short-term trading. High-risk, short-term trading with the potential for large financial gains."

"You're going to play the stock market."

It made sense for an economist, I supposed.

"*We're* going to play the stock market," he said.

I felt an immediate sinking sensation. "I don't have any money to lose."

"I'll stake us," he said. "We can share the profits."

That wasn't fair. "But—"

"No buts, Tasha."

"You're the one with the money. You're the one with the know-how." I would be dead weight in this.

"We'll make the decisions together. I'll explain my thinking to you, but we'll decide together. If it goes well, you'll be able to afford a new floor."

I looked to the ugly floor again. "I don't feel right about this."

Jamie came to his feet. "No, Nat doesn't feel right about this. Tasha thinks it's a great idea."

He was right, and I could tell by his expression he knew it.

Tasha, me, *I* was excited at the prospect of buying and selling stocks with Jamie, of having more secrets with Jamie, of spending more time with handsome, sexy, desirable Jamie.

Nat yelled stop. She recognized the danger.

But Tasha said go. She didn't need a reason.

Tasha won.

Seven

Rock wall climbing wasn't nearly as hard as I'd expected.

I'd have to learn the knots, and I'd have to learn how to put on a harness, and I'd have to learn a whole bunch of technical things before I'd be anywhere near ready to go out on my own. But the actual climbing, finding a handhold, finding a foothold, pulling myself toward the ceiling on the big vertical wall so far was a whole lot of fun.

I'd thought Jamie would be way, way better than me. Oh, he was definitely good, really good. But while he had bigger muscles, he also had a higher body mass to lift. Thanks to my short stature and relatively lean frame, I could hold my own.

I couldn't help but feel proud of that.

It also turned out that I had no fear of heights. I'd never given it much thought before, but quite a few of the people in the class got nervous as they climbed higher. As long as my harness was tight, I just enjoyed the view.

"You're a natural," Jamie said as my feet came down on the mat.

I was facing the wall, and he put his hands on my hips, obviously to make sure I stayed steady.

His touch felt good. It felt strong and secure. I didn't really want him to let me go.

"Your girlfriend's impressive," the instructor, Paul, said to Jamie.

Jamie abruptly let go. He seemed to realize how the gesture had looked.

I was glad my face was warm from exertion, or I might have worried about blushing. It wasn't such a huge mistake, thinking I was Jamie's girlfriend. After all, we'd signed up together. That would be perfectly natural.

As it was, Paul's suggestion embarrassed me. I might secretly want to be Jamie's girlfriend. In fact, I was starting to fantasize about it.

But that wasn't the point. The point here was to make Jamie attractive to other women. I was his sidekick, his means to an end, the person helping him replace Brooklyn with someone equally glamorous and exciting.

"Thanks," Jamie said to Paul.

I couldn't help but note that Jamie made no correction, offered no explanation, and was simply appreciative.

I felt stupidly good about that.

It didn't change anything. But for a second there, I felt more important to Jamie than just a pal. I liked that.

It would hurt later, I knew. But for the moment I was going to bask in the idea that someone, or maybe more than just Paul, considered Jamie and me a couple.

"Want to go up once more?" Paul asked me.

"Is there time for that?"

The clock was inching toward noon.

"Only for one of you," Paul said.

"Go ahead," Jamie said.

"You don't want to?" I didn't want to be greedy.

We'd each had three climbs this morning, after sitting through a presentation on theory and practicing some basic knots. I could see there was a whole lot to learn about the sport.

"Go ahead," Jamie said. "I'll watch Paul on belay."

I waited while Paul double-checked my ropes and equipment. Then I set off again, with Paul on the ground holding the rope to anchor me in case I slipped. To change things up, I started from a different point.

There were three climbers on the wall with me, each working with a different instructor.

Paul had told me to watch my feet. My feet were way more important than my hands. It made sense to me. And since I didn't have a ton of strength in my arms and shoulders—not being a regular at the gym or anything—I was more than happy to depend on my leg muscles. All that bike riding and running around on the tennis court was serving me well.

"Keep your arms straight," Paul called from below.

I reminded myself of that one, looking for a handhold farther away.

I saw one and took it, then I concentrated on my feet, finding the next step.

By the time I made it back down, my legs and arms were quivering. I knew I'd be sore tomorrow, but in a good way. This morning had been a whole lot of fun, and very satisfying.

Now, when I met new people at parties or anywhere really, and they asked my hobbies, I could sound daring and exciting. Who wouldn't be impressed with the answer *rock climbing* if they asked me what I did for fun? It was better than *tennis*, and sounded a whole lot more impressive than *reading*.

"Hungry?" Jamie asked as we drove from the parking lot in his SUV.

"I am. That really works up an appetite."

"Should we go watch some pretty people while we eat?"

"Where?"

"Northland Country Club. Have you ever been there?"

I had, but only once.

It was the high-end clubhouse at a private golf course. The restaurant was open to the public, but the prices were sky-high.

"Dressed like this?" I asked, knowing we'd never fit in.

"You look awesome."

"I look casual and sweaty."

He waved a dismissive hand as we pulled into traffic. "It's only lunchtime. Think of it as being incognito."

"No one will ever suspect we're spies?"

"Exactly. And it's on the way home."

"Sure," I said. "That sounds great."

There was no doubt that successful, stylish people frequented the Northland Country Club. It attracted business tycoons, politicians and millionaires from around the state and beyond.

"I hope our stock portfolio is rising," I said as we made

our way through midday traffic. "I hear a cup of coffee costs sixteen dollars in that place."

Jamie tossed me his phone. "Check it out. The password is 8596."

I took a second to absorb the idea of Jamie giving me his password.

"You'll probably have to swipe over one screen. Open the Tracker app."

I entered the password, feeling like his girlfriend and telling myself to stop it already.

I swiped and tapped the app. Six lines came up with codes and numbers.

"What does it say?" he asked.

"CPW 27.32, LNN 2.06, QPP 32.17."

"Read that one again," he said.

"QPP?"

"Yes."

"QPP 32.17"

"Click on it."

I did.

"What do you see?"

"There's a graph."

"What does the trajectory look like?"

I didn't exactly understand the question.

"Long, slow start and sudden spike?" he asked.

"That's right."

"Hit the sell button."

I was kind of intimidated by the request. "Are you serious?"

"Completely. Go ahead."

"I'm selling stock?" I asked.

He grinned. "You are selling stock, Tasha."

"Okay." If he was sure, then I was game. I touched the sell button. "It's asking me to confirm."

"Confirm," he said.

I did. "Wow. That was exciting."

Jamie laughed.

"What did I just do?"

"You just paid for lunch."

"Really?" It felt pretty amazing.

"Lunch and a whole lot more," he said.

"How much did we make?"

"Ten percent."

"How much did we invest?"

"Ten thousand dollars."

I was speechless for a second. "That's... Jamie, we just made a thousand dollars?"

"I'm thinking champagne with lunch."

I looked back down at the phone. "But how...? It can't be that easy."

"It's not easy."

I felt like I'd insulted him, belittled his expertise and experience. "I know... I mean..."

The phone pinged in my hand and a text message came up. I automatically read it. "I'm sorry," I quickly said. "I didn't mean to pry."

"Who's it from?" he asked.

"Aaron."

"What did he say?"

"Are you sure you want me to—"

"You've already read it."

I couldn't tell if he was annoyed or not. "I didn't read it on purpose."

"I know that. What does it say?"

"It says Bernard postponed the IPO."

"Thank goodness," Jamie said.

"It's good?" I was glad it wasn't something to upset Jamie.

I wanted to go have lunch. I wanted to analyze beautiful people. I didn't want Jamie rushing off in a bad mood because of a problem at work.

"It means I talked them off the ledge. Aaron had their heads filled with ideas of quick riches and smooth sailing. It wasn't going to work that way."

"Maybe they should have thrown it all into QPP."

"There's nothing wrong with high risk when you're prepared to lose—whether it's a stock or an equity investment. I was prepared to lose on QPP. I doubt Bernard wants to risk losing control of his company."

"You were prepared to lose ten thousand dollars?" I couldn't wrap my head around that.

"We wouldn't have lost it all. Probably not. Likely not. But we could have lost some of it."

"You want me to read the rest of the numbers?" I asked, worried that we could be losing money on something else while we sat here talking.

"I'll check at lunch," he said. "For now, let's just bask in the win."

"Basking," I said as he swung into the country-club parking lot.

Once we'd cut in the edges, the painting went fast. Jamie was great with the roller, putting on an even coat. And with the roller extension, he could stand on the floor and paint all the way up to the high ceiling.

"What are we going to do up there?" he asked, looking at the ceiling.

I held on to the ladder and tipped my head. From up here, I could see more detail than I wanted to know about. "The skylights are really getting grungy."

"They definitely need to be replaced. Are they leaking?"

"No, thank goodness. Construction is way beyond my budget. I don't think the landlord would let me do it anyway."

"He would if it increased the value of his building."

"I suppose," I said.

"But he'd probably up your rent."

I went back to edging the russet-brown wall. I was on the last section cutting in the ceiling line.

"I'd have to get an agreement in advance," I said, thinking out loud.

"You should ask for a decrease in rent proportional with the amount you're putting into repairs."

"Would anyone go for that?"

It seemed like a good idea. But since I'd already started the work, I didn't see where I'd have leverage.

I could ask. I would ask. Maybe I wouldn't mention that I'd already done the painting.

"We should stop for the day," Jamie said.

I was tired, too. I met up with the final corner.

"I can't believe you did all this," I said, looking around.

The room looked brighter and fresher already.

We'd picked up the supplies after climbing yesterday, and Jamie had insisted on coming back to help me this morning.

I felt guilty then, and I felt even worse now, especially when I looked at my watch and saw that it was after six.

"We've been working for hours," I said.

He crossed the room and reached up toward me. "Hand me the paint can."

I bent over to get it to him. "I'm sorry I kept you all day."

He smiled, and his blue eyes warmed. At least, they warmed me. They warmed me a lot.

I had no idea whether or not he could tell.

Our hands brushed as I handed off the can, and the familiar charge of energy sped up my arm.

He looked sexy in his worn jeans, his faded T-shirt and scuffed work boots. I really liked the new scruffy look he seemed to have landed on. It emphasized his square chin, his strong, straight nose, his eyes that were honestly the most beautiful shade of blue. They were bright in the sun, midnight indoors, always startling, always striking.

His shoulders were broad under the snug shirt, his biceps taut and solid. Under a tux, he looked great. Dressed for construction, he looked spectacular.

"The brush," he prompted, pulling me out of my thoughts.

He was staring right at me, into my expression, into my eyes, and for a terrible second I thought he could read my mind. If he could see my thoughts, he'd know I was compromised. I wasn't his buddy, his pal, his wingman.

I was falling for him. And that wasn't even remotely what he'd signed up for here. He'd be disappointed if he knew. He might even be amused if he knew. Mousy little Nat Remington thought a veneer of makeup and a few new clothes would turn her into Brooklyn.

Sure.

Could happen.

In my dreams.

I leaned down to give him the paintbrush.

The ladder shifted. The brush slipped from my fingers.

The russet-brown end caught Jamie in the forehead. "Crap!" I cried out. The brush bounced to the floor. Jamie grasped the ladder, righting it, but dislodging me.

I lost my balance and fell into his arms, and he caught me, pulling me tight before my feet hit the floor.

The ladder wasn't so fortunate. It teetered, then tipped, then banged on the linoleum, the sound reverberating.

"Good thing we moved the paint can," he said.

I blew out a sigh of relief. "You caught me."

"I caught you," he said.

He shifted, and our gazes met.

They locked.

His arms flexed tight around me.

We stared at each other in silence while time suspended.

"Tasha," he whispered.

I wanted him.

I wanted to breathe him, to taste him, to feel him touch me anywhere and everywhere.

I was about to make a fool of myself.

If he didn't let me go, I was going to kiss him hard and long, and he'd know exactly how I'd been feeling all these days.

He kissed me.

Okay, that was unexpected.

I hadn't seen it going that way at all.

But there it was.

His lips were on mine. They were firm and tender and delicious, and this was the best kiss of my life, possibly the best kiss ever in the history of mankind.

I didn't want it to stop.

I cupped his cheeks, feeling the stubble like I'd been dying to do since he'd grown it out.

It felt rough and rugged, adding to my sensory overload.

My breasts were pressed against his chest, my thighs against his, my belly, his belly, his sex.

A roaring sound came up in my ears, as the kiss went on and on and on.

He pulled off my T-shirt, revealing my lacy bra.

We stared at each other, breathing hard. I think we were trying to figure out which of us was more shocked.

Only I wasn't shocked. Okay, I was shocked. But I was aroused more than shocked. I was aroused more than anything.

He removed my glasses. I peeled off his shirt, for the first time getting a look—though it was blurry—at his magnificent pecs, his bare shoulders, what I knew were gorgeous abs.

He reached for the clasp of my bra, and I knew we were gone. This was right out of control, and we weren't stopping for anything.

My doorknob rattled.

We simultaneously whipped our heads in that direction.

"Nat?" It was Sophie.

She knocked. "Nat? I can hear your music. Is everything okay?"

"She has a key," I hissed to Jamie.

He set me down.

I grabbed my T-shirt from the tipped ladder and threw it over my head.

"I'm coming," I called to her.

Jamie threw on his own T-shirt and ran his fingers through his hair.

We stared at each other for a second.

I had no idea what to say or do or even think.

We'd almost had sex.

I gave myself a shake and went for the door.

"What took you so long?" Sophie said as she marched in.

"I was up on the ladder," I said.

She saw Jamie first. Then she saw the ladder and the painted walls.

I could almost hear her brain humming as she took everything in.

"Hi, Sophie," Jamie said.

"What?" Sophie seemed at a loss for words as she looked around.

"James was helping me paint."

Sophie looked completely confused. "Why would he do that?"

As far as Sophie knew, Jamie and I barely talked to each other—which had always been true in the past.

"We were talking, uh, the other day," I said, my mind scrambling for something logical.

"At the tennis club," Jamie put in.

"Yes," I said. "At the tennis club. And I was asking, well, you know, all the stuff you and Bryce and Ethan told me." I went with the first and only thing that came into my mind—Sophie's new business. "And with James's job and all. Well, it got me to thinking, maybe, and I didn't want to say anything to you, because it wouldn't be fair. You know, if it didn't work out."

Sophie and Jamie were both staring at me as if I'd lost my mind.

Which I had. I apparently had completely lost my mind.

To be fair, my brain had overheated from Jamie's kiss.

After a kiss like that, a woman shouldn't be required to think anything coherent for at least a couple of hours, maybe all night long.

"Ethan was saying you needed investors," I plowed on. "James sometimes invests in things. So, I asked him." I looked at Jamie, trying to apologize with my eyes. "I asked him about your 3-D printer dessert thing, if it was maybe something that he could invest in."

"You did?" Sophie looked amazed and hopeful at the same time.

"But I don't think it's going to work out," I quickly said. "It's not the kind of thing that—"

"I'm going to need more information," Jamie said.

I gave him a warning look. My story was only a way to get us through this awkward moment. We couldn't let it go any further.

Sophie moved closer to where Jamie was standing. "We can give you anything you want."

"James usually makes short-term investments," I said from behind her, trying to shut it down. "Yours is at a really early stage. And it's going to take a long, long time."

"We're going to revolutionize the food service industry," Sophie said.

My gaze hit Jamie's, half apology, half warning.

"We're upping the level of precision and sophistication with which restaurants," Sophie said before I could slow her down, "even small establishments, can conceive, refine, create and serve desserts of all kinds with our technology."

What had I done?

"That was amazing," Sophie said, dropping down on the single sofa that wasn't covered by the painting drop sheets. "But why was James here? And why are you renovating? And why didn't you tell me?"

I decided to answer the easiest question. "It was a sudden decision."

"I could have helped. I can still help. What's your color scheme? What else are you doing besides the walls?"

I said a silent thank-you that we'd moved past James.

I pushed the passionate kiss from my mind. Could I call it a kiss? It was a whole lot more than a kiss—even if we hadn't technically gone any further than a kiss.

"Butter yellow." I did a circle point to the painted walls. "Plus a russet-brown feature wall. And we're… I'm thinking of adding some pumpkin accents."

Sophie stared unblinking at me. "Who are you and what have you done with my friend Nat?"

I wanted to say I was Tasha. But I kept the thought inside my head.

I did smile.

Sophie smiled back. "This is going to be fun."

I'd known that one would be coming.

"Have you thought about furniture?" she asked. "It would be so much fun shopping. This stuff is pretty tatty."

"I'll have to check my budget before I decide."

"It doesn't have to be right away. I mean, not all of it anyway. We can start with some small pieces. Honestly, Nat, anything would be an improvement."

"You keep telling me that."

"And you're finally *doing* it." She grinned. "We need to celebrate."

Then she went quiet for a moment, looking thoughtful.

I braced myself for another question about James. I hoped I could keep a straight face and that I wouldn't have to lie too much. I wasn't going to betray Jamie's confidence. But I was thinking I could talk a little bit about the changes I'd made to my own image—my hair, my contacts, my apartment.

People upgraded their lives all the time. It wasn't so weird.

"Do you think he'll do it?" Sophie asked.

I was guessing she meant Jamie.

"He said he'd talk to people," she continued. "I guess he must know those kinds of people. He works in a financial place, right?"

"He does." I didn't want to say more. I didn't want to get her hopes up.

It was impossible to tell if Jamie was being polite and trying to protect my cover story, or if he really did know people he could talk to about angel investment into a tech start-up company.

I would have liked to ask him—about the money, about the kiss. At least, I thought I'd like to ask him about the kiss.

It had been one incredible kiss. We'd practically torn off each other's clothes. We had chemistry together. That was for sure.

But I was nervous because this wasn't what Jamie had signed up for. And it could have been a momentary impulse.

Physical attraction could take you by surprise, and he might regret it already.

The best thing to do was to take his lead. That made sense to me. If he wanted to talk about it, we'd talk about it. If he wanted to pretend it never happened, I'd go along with that.

I didn't want to mess up our friendship or our deal to help each other. Both had become too important to me.

"Nat?" Sophie said. "What do you think?"

I ordered myself to stop obsessing. It was a kiss. It was over. Life was moving on.

"I don't want you to be disappointed," I said to her. It was my honest answer.

"I can't help but be hopeful. I should really call Ethan."

I was surprised Ethan was her first thought. "What about Bryce?"

"Oh, him, too. Of course, him, too. But Ethan's put his heart and soul into this. Bryce is a little bit on the sidelines with the recipes and all."

That hadn't been my impression. Bryce had seemed quite passionate about the project.

"We should meet them somewhere," Sophie said.

"It's Sunday night."

"It's not even eight o'clock. We can grab dinner and talk about the possibilities. Whatever happens, we should be prepared for it."

If I had to make a bet, I'd say nothing was going to come of this. And I really didn't feel like going out right now.

I made a show of looking down at myself. "I'm a mess."

"We won't go anywhere fancy. Comb you hair, put on some makeup, change your clothes."

That all sounded like a whole lot of work to me. I was exhausted.

"Angelo's at the Lake would be perfect. It's only five minutes from here."

"I'm really tired," I said. "And I have to work tomorrow."

"Come on, Nat. This is huge. I mean, I know it's not a sure thing. But I want to see Ethan's face when I tell him the news."

"There's no news yet," I pointed out.

"You have to eat," she said. "Summon up that peppy new gal who did all this redecorating and come out for dinner with your best friend."

When she put it that way, I felt like a cad saying no.

"Fine," I said.

Her grin made me feel a little more energized.

I pushed myself from the depths of the comfy armchair, telling myself I'd perk up once I got out in the fresh air.

While I got myself ready, Sophie texted Ethan and Bryce.

I combed out my hair, fighting a few globs of stubborn paint. It occurred to me that I should have worn a hat while I painted. I'd definitely do that next time.

I washed my face, brushed my teeth, and put on a little makeup before changing into black jeans and a dove-gray sweater with a silver thread running through the weave. The jeans were a gift from Brooklyn. They were tighter than the ones I usually bought, so I hadn't worn them often. But I was feeling very Tasha-y right now.

"They'll meet us there," Sophie called out.

"Okay," I called back.

I put a pair of silver hoops in my ears and decided I was ready.

I did feel a little more energized. And I was really hungry. Angelo's made fantastic seafood lasagna. I was going to treat myself to that.

I felt bad that I hadn't fed Jamie. I'd planned on ordering something in once we'd cleaned up. As it was, all I'd done was close the paint can and put the brushes and roller to soak while Jamie had talked to Sophie about investments.

"I'm all set," I said as I walked around the divider.

"That was fast." Sophie did a double take of me and then stared.

"What?" I asked, looking down at myself and craning my neck to see the back.

"You look great," she said.

"Thanks."

"No really... I mean...you look... Wow."

"I'm going to assume that's good."

Sophie took in her own outfit of blue jeans and a multicolored blouse. "I feel like I should change."

Her hair was windblown, and her makeup wasn't as fresh as it usually was, but she looked perfectly good.

"Don't be silly," I said. "You look awesome. It's not like you need to impress Bryce. He's impressed already."

I wasn't an expert on long-term relationships. My romance with Henry Paulson didn't qualify, since it had crashed and burned. But it seemed to me that at some point you could start relaxing your look around your boyfriend.

I thought about how I'd looked today with Jamie. I'd looked pretty casual, beyond casual. I'd looked downright functional—probably because I *was* downright functional.

Not that Jamie and I had anything romantic going.

Even that kiss hadn't been romantic. It had been passionate and erotic and exciting. But I wasn't foolish enough to equate those things with romantic.

Sophie still looked uncertain.

"You want to borrow some makeup?" I asked. "I'd offer my wardrobe, but you know what my clothes are like."

Sophie laughed at that. "That's a cute outfit, though."

"These are the jeans Brooklyn gave me last year."

"Oh, yeah. I remember. Why don't you wear them more often?"

"They're a bit snug."

"They fit perfect. You've got to get away from the early-matron look."

"I think you mean the early-librarian look." I was trying to get away from it.

It occurred to me that I should do some more shopping. Maybe Jamie would like to come with me. Maybe I was obsessing about Jamie. Maybe I should get a grip.

"Either." Sophie paused. "I think I will borrow a little mascara or something."

"Help yourself." I gestured to the bathroom.

While she was gone, I opened the closet and took in my shoe choices.

The black cutout ankle boots I'd bought for the dance club would go great with the jeans. I hesitated, knowing I would have to explain them to Sophie.

But I couldn't resist.

I put them on. Then I stood in front of my full-length mirror.

I looked sharp. I had that casual, "I don't really care about it, but I look pretty great" appearance that Brooklyn seemed to so effortlessly achieve.

Part of me was excited, and part of me couldn't truly believe it was me staring back from the mirror.

Eight

Jamie agreed to another shopping trip.

But there was something off in his texts. They were so brief and to the point. He seemed more formal somehow than usual. And then I thought I was imagining it. And then I thought I was still obsessing about the kiss—which I was—and I was reading things into his seven-word texts that simply weren't there.

After work on Wednesday, one of my coworkers dropped me off downtown. Jamie and I had agreed to meet at Brookswood. We'd barely scratched the surface of its ten floors when we bought his tux and my dress.

I'd decided to blow the clothing budget today. Our investment account profits were still climbing. I'd told Jamie quite a few times that it felt wrong for me to share in the profits, since he'd provided the seed money, and since it was his expertise making the trades.

But he wouldn't listen. He said he'd already made back the seed money and a deal was a deal. I was getting my half.

I'd given up fighting.

If he was going to insist, then I supposed I'd accept it. I pictured myself Christmas shopping this year with a lavish budget and so many choices to surprise my family and friends.

And maybe I'd buy a couple of fancy outfits. Or maybe some not-so-fancy outfits. I could buy some of those deceptively casual clothes that were high quality and well made. To other people, they simply looked good. The secret was that they made *you* look good.

I was beginning to realize that Brooklyn and Sophie were onto something. There was a difference in quality and flair as you moved up the price range. Sometimes it seemed subtle, but it was real.

Last Sunday when I wore the black jeans to Angelo's, a

dozen guys turned their heads when I walked to the ladies' room. Nobody had pointed, at least not that I saw. But many of them had followed me along, appreciative gazes on their faces.

Ironically, Ethan hadn't been one of them. Although Sophie kept trying, Ethan and I were never going to connect.

He connected better with Sophie than he did with me. I supposed that had a lot to do with their business venture. But still, his expression lit up for her and stayed flat for me.

Sometimes I thought Bryce saw that. Sometimes I thought Bryce got annoyed.

Sophie seemed like the only one who didn't notice.

After the outing at Angelo's, I vowed that if she suggested another double date, I was going to be frank with her and refuse. I wanted to spend girl time with Sophie. I wanted to hear more about her business venture. It was obvious she was really excited about that. But I hoped I could do it without spending another uncomfortable evening with Ethan.

I could tell Ethan had a crush on her. But I didn't want to throw that kind of a grenade into the Sweet Tech business venture. If Bryce didn't want to address it, there was no value in me addressing it. I would probably make things worse by telling her.

Jamie beat me to Brookswood and was waiting outside the main door.

"Hi," I said, feeling suddenly breathless.

He looked sexy, handsome and aloof.

"Hi," he said back and immediately turned for the door.

He held it open for me and I once again entered the rarefied environment of high-end shopping.

After a few steps, I opened the conversation. "Did you have a nice day?"

"It was fine." His strides were long and I had to hurry to keep up.

"So was mine."

"Good. Do you want to start with office wear, casual wear, a jacket? The weather's going to turn soon."

The weather? We were going to talk about the weather?

"Jamie?"

"Hmm?"

"What's going on?"

He looked down at me. But he wasn't seeing me, not really.

"What?" he asked.

"Something's wrong. What's wrong?"

"Nothing. We're shopping. You're right. We both need a more extensive new wardrobe. I hope you're not planning to bargain hunt."

"I'm not. You've convinced me to spend the investment profits. At least, you've convinced Tasha to spend the investment profits. Turns out she's not as scrupulous as me."

I expected him to laugh at my joke, but he didn't.

"You are Tasha," he said.

"You know what I mean."

"And it's not unscrupulous to spend money that belongs to you. What about shirtdresses? I read they're a thing."

"Jamie, stop."

He clamped his jaw, but he stopped.

"Look at me."

He turned, the aloof expression firmly in place.

"Is it the kiss?" I asked, tired of feeling jumpy, tired of trying to guess how he felt about it.

From the way he was acting, I could definitely guess he regretted it.

I pushed myself forward. "Are you being like this because we kissed each other?"

He didn't answer. And he sure didn't look happy that I'd brought it up.

I wanted to let him off the hook, to show him it was no big deal and I hadn't been obsessing about it—which, of course, I had, like every second since it happened.

"It was a kiss," I said. "A simple kiss. People do that. We were working together. We were happy. Plus, we've been, you know, turning each other into the image we think will attract the opposite sex." As I framed up my explanation, I decided it was pretty good. "All that kiss meant was that it's working. It's working, and that's a good thing. Hey, you should have seen the guys react to me at Angelo's on Sunday night."

Jamie sucked in a breath.

So did I. I needed oxygen to keep on talking. "They liked my look. A lot of them liked my look. As for you and me, well, it would be weird if we weren't a little bit attracted to each other. Don't you think that's true? And we were. And we kissed. And it's over. It doesn't have to mean a thing. It doesn't have to make you go all…" I gestured up and down at his posture. "I don't know, James-the-uptight on me."

"I'm not uptight." But he said it through teeth that were kind of clenched.

"I doesn't have to mean anything," I repeated. "It doesn't have to change anything. I don't want it to change anything."

I really, really didn't want anything to change between us, and I was afraid that I'd already blown it. These past few weeks had been the most enlightening, exciting and downright fun of my life. I didn't want to lose Jamie, and I desperately hoped my unbridled reaction to his kiss hadn't done just that.

He stayed silent for a moment. "It didn't change anything."

I felt a tiny hint of relief. "Then smile or something."

He tried, but it didn't come off.

I decided to keep it light and hope against hope that tactic would work. "Well, that's pathetic. The Jamie I know would blow past a little kiss in a heartbeat."

"You call that a little kiss?" he asked.

"I do."

We stared at each other for a moment.

He seemed to be daring me to do something or say something. But I couldn't tell what he wanted.

I took a stab. "I want to stay friends, Jamie. I really don't want to lose what we have."

His expression finally relaxed just a little bit. "Neither do I."

"Good." I was relieved, and I was glad. I didn't dare say anything more.

Instead, I glanced past him to the racks behind. "I don't really want a shirtdress."

"No shirtdress then," he said. "How about a jacket?"

I wouldn't say the shopping trip was the best time we'd ever had. We were still tippy-toeing around each other. But at least it was successful. We both left the store with armloads of new clothes, shoes and some jewelry for me.

Jamie got a text while we were paying and asked if I minded stopping at his office.

I easily agreed, not yet feeling like we were back on normal ground.

We drove over and parked in the company garage in a spot labeled for Jamie.

His key fob opened the doors, and an elevator whisked us to the thirty-second floor.

Aaron was sitting at a desk in the open office area.

There were a couple of other people in the distance, but otherwise the office was empty and quiet.

"Tell me exactly what Bernard said," Jamie said to Aaron.

"You didn't have to come all the way in," Aaron said.

"I assume it was you who changed his mind."

"A lot of things changed his mind. He thought about it, and he decided he's willing to take the chance."

"He never should have been put in this predicament in the first place. Watch and learn, Aaron. How hard is it to understand the concept of watch and learn?"

Jamie was angry.

I didn't know what to do with myself.

I felt awful just standing here listening to the argument, but there wasn't an easy way for me to escape. It was a long walk back to the elevators, and I wasn't sure where I would go from there. All the offices around the periphery of the space were closed. Not that I'd randomly walk into somebody's office.

"Rehashing it isn't going to help," Aaron said in obvious frustration.

Jamie clenched his jaw. "Then give me a path forward. You set this up. What's your solution?"

Aaron stood. "It's done, so we roll with it."

Jamie coughed out a laugh. "Go public on Monday without doing due diligence?"

"It's going to work, James." Aaron's tone was emphatic now. "I know in my gut that it's going to work."

"We're not trusting your gut. Your gut's only two months old."

"What about your gut?" Aaron asked.

The question seemed to throw Jamie.

"What does your gut tell you?"

I could see that Jamie didn't want to answer. I had to wonder if it was because he disagreed with Aaron or because he agreed with Aaron.

For some reason, he looked at me.

I tried to give him an encouraging smile, even though I had no idea what he was thinking.

The last thing he might want is for me to be happy when he was so obviously frustrated.

I wasn't happy about his frustration, of course.

But I was curious about the obvious struggle going on inside his head.

"I'm not recording this," Aaron said.

Jamie glared at him.

"Gut reaction." Aaron shrugged. "What could it hurt to say it out loud?"

"It'll work," Jamie said.

"There we go." Aaron smiled.

"No, there we *don't* go."

"Do you want me to explain gut reactions to you?" Aaron asked.

"No," Jamie drawled. "I do *not* want you to explain gut reactions to me."

"They're made up of subtle signals, information that you don't even know you know. It happens deep in your subconscious."

"What part of *no* did you miss?"

"It's not your gut working, James. It's your brain, your whole brain, the deep recesses of your entire brain. You know the answer. You just don't like working without the data on paper, driving without a seat belt."

"Jumping without a parachute," Jamie said. "And I change my mind all the time based on the data on paper."

"How do you do the short-term stuff?" I asked.

I thought I was being helpful, but Jamie shot me the same glare as he'd shot Aaron.

I wasn't being helpful.

"That's completely different," he said. "You know that. I explained that."

He had.

But I didn't see it being completely different. Then again, what did I know? I was a librarian, not an economist.

"Sorry," I said. I was.

"Bernard will ask for our recommendation in the morning," Aaron said.

Seconds ticked by.

"What do we say?" Aaron asked.

More seconds ticked by. I thought Jamie wasn't going to answer.

"Recommend the IPO," he said. His tone made the words sound painful.

"All right!" Aaron shouted and made a fist.

"Don't get cocky," Jamie said. "And if this goes bad…"

"It's on me." Aaron nodded.

"No, it's on me. Because that's the way it works."

Now I was nervous. I hated to think I might have pushed Jamie toward a decision he wasn't comfortable with.

"Jamie, if you're not—"

"Relax, Tasha. You didn't talk me into anything."

I swallowed.

Aaron spoke up. "The mighty James Gillen isn't one to take his girlfriend's advice."

Jamie's tone was cutting. "You don't know whose advice I'll take."

Then he turned to me. He looked tired, and his voice lost its edge. "Come on, Tasha. I'll drive you home."

* * *

Rock climbing training was uneventful on Saturday. It felt like our relationship was somewhat back on an even keel, and I told myself to be happy about that.

I didn't have any plans for Saturday night. I was disappointed that I wouldn't get to take any of my new, new clothes out for a test-drive. I'd bought this dusty blue tufted blouse and a short, blotchy, dusty-blue-and-pink-patterned skirt that I was dying to wear somewhere. It was set off with a wide black satin sash, and I'd bought oversize pearl earrings and a necklace to go with it.

It was softly romantic, and totally not me. I wasn't completely sure it was Tasha either, but I was willing to give it a shot. Both the salesclerk at Brookswood and Jamie had said it was a "must."

Who was I to say no to a "must"?

But it wasn't going to be this weekend.

I told myself it was just as well. I still had a lot of work to do on my apartment. If I pushed myself I could get the pumpkin—it turned out that was a very popular color—trim done today. Then I could put my furniture back and feel normal again.

Well, the new normal, of course.

I really did like the way the paint was turning out. It felt fresh and alive. I found it energizing to be at home.

If I worked hard, I'd be ready to start on the floors. I'd already picked up samples of stone and wood laminate. Not all of the brands were expensive, especially if you shopped carefully.

I liked the stone patterns best. It gave you the greatest range of color options.

So, Sunday morning, I dressed in paint clothes. I'd picked up a white cap at the hardware store, and I folded my hair underneath. I wasn't going to risk globs of pumpkin orange in my hair.

I'd masked stripes on the top and bottom of the walls, plus a wide box around each window.

I shook the paint bucket, pried it open, gave it a stir and then held my breath.

The butter yellow and russet brown were pretty low-risk colors. The orange on the other hand was going to pop. I felt like that first stroke was a momentous decision.

There was a knock on my door.

I gave myself a split second to wonder if it was a sign. Maybe I wasn't supposed to paint bright orange on my walls.

The knock came again.

I balanced the brush across the top of the open can, half-relieved by the interruption and half-annoyed that I was being given a chance to change my mind. I didn't want to change my mind. I wanted to dive wholeheartedly into my new bright orange life.

I opened the door to find Jamie standing there with two coffees and a paper bag from Penelope's Bakery.

His appearance took me by surprise. When he'd said good-bye yesterday he didn't say anything about helping me again. Not that I wouldn't say yes to the help. I'd really appreciate it.

Then again, he might not be here to help at all. He could be here for something completely unrelated to my apartment renovations. I shouldn't be so presumptuous.

"Hungry?" he asked.

"Why are you here?" I sounded rude. "I mean, sure, yes, I'm hungry."

He rattled the bag. "Fresh bagels."

I realized I hadn't eaten breakfast.

"I was just starting to paint," I said.

"Then I'm right on time." He moved forward, and I got out of the way.

"I didn't know you were coming," I said as I closed the door.

I was positive he hadn't said anything yesterday.

"Spur-of-the-moment. I stopped by Penelope's. The blue-berry bagels made me think of you."

"Blueberry bagels? Really?" I couldn't for the life of me see the connection.

"Okay, it was the giant éclair in the refrigerated case. It reminded me of that time at the Orchid Club."

I remembered the decadent dessert we'd shared on that first reconnaissance foray outside the Orchid Club. We'd ordered mini cream puffs drizzled with chocolate and caramel sauce. I'd eaten the lion's share, and Jamie had teased me about my enthusiasm.

"But I thought it might be a bit much for breakfast, so I went with the bagels."

"Too bad," I said, only half joking.

Chocolate and pastry cream was my weakness.

"I can go back," he said.

"No, probably a good call. I don't want to go into a sugar coma before I finish painting."

Jamie handed me one of the coffee cups and looked around. "Seems like you're all set to go."

I decided coffee and fresh bagels would be worth the delay in starting. I took one end of the uncovered sofa that was angled in the middle of the room.

Jamie sat on the other end and put the bag of bagels between us.

"I'm hoping to finish today," I said.

Then I remembered the flooring samples and hopped back up, going to the kitchen counter where I'd left them.

"Take a look at these," I said as I carried them over to him.

Jamie had opened the bag and extracted a bagel. Both his hands were occupied.

"After you finish," I said and helped myself to a bagel.

"You've inspired me," he said.

"With flooring samples?" I grinned as I took a bite. It was awesome. "Mmm."

"With your willingness to change your life," he said.

It wasn't all me. It was far from all me.

I swallowed. "You're changing yours just as much."

He shook his head. "Not as much. Not everything."

"What do you mean?"

"I mean I need a new house."

I gave another big swallow. Okay, that was pretty huge.

"Are you sure? I mean, we only paid a couple hundred dollars for the paint." As commitments went, sweat equity wasn't nearly as serious as a mortgage.

"I'm moving up," Jamie said. "Or I'm moving sideways. I mean, I'm moving to where Jamie wants to live."

"Do we know where Jamie wants to live?" I asked.

"We're going to find out."

"Wow. That's huge."

"I'm counting on your help."

The statement, along with his expression, made me nervous. My head started to shake all on its own. "I'm not picking out your house."

"You did a terrific job with my car."

My head shaking continued. "That's crazy. It's nuts. A house is a major life decision, maybe *the* major life decision. It's a huge, long-term commitment. You have to pick it out yourself."

"I checked our stock portfolio this morning." He paused. It seemed like he was going for dramatic effect.

I wasn't sure if I should take that as a good or a bad thing. Good, I had to think, if he was talking about it in conjunction with buying a house.

Then again, I didn't want to get my hopes up. He'd come up with the investment seed money without too much trouble. He probably also had a decent down payment waiting in the wings. The two things might have nothing to do with each other.

"And…" I prompted.

"And it's up."

"Good." I was relieved—more for Jamie than for me.

I didn't really have anything at stake in it. We'd already taken out the money for our clothes-buying binge. But Jamie still had his capital at risk. I knew that stocks could fall just as easily as they could rise. And we'd had an awfully good run of it lately.

"Way up," he said.

I could tell he was toying with me.

"Are we going to play this game all morning?" I asked.

He grinned. "Remember Street Wrangle, the wireless company?"

I did. "Yes."

"Remember how I said they'd inexplicably bought that property next to Newmister?"

I remembered that, too. Jamie had speculated that the companies might be talking about a merger.

"They merged?" I asked.

There was a light in Jamie's eyes that said this was big.

I lost interest in my bagel.

"They merged. The stock spiked. It's set to split first thing Monday morning. Traders are lining up to get in. I've never seen buzz like this."

"But we're already in."

Jamie held his coffee cup up in a toast. "We're already in."

"Did we invest a lot?"

"We were bold. We went with our gut."

My grin grew, feeling like it might split my cheeks. "Oh, I *do* like Jamie's audacity."

"Will you help me find a house?"

"I'm scared." This situation called for me to be completely honest.

"Don't be scared."

"I don't know the first thing about real estate. I'll screw it up."

"You won't screw it up."

I gave a chopped laugh of disbelief. There were a thousand ways for me to screw up a choice like this—from location to plumbing to the foundation to…well, everything.

"Don't be scared, Tasha," he said in the gentlest of tones. "You're smart and methodical. And you have great instincts. You have gut instincts that are incredibly impressive. Run with them. Be audacious." He paused and seemed to be thinking. "Plus, I love your taste. You know you found me a great vehicle. Look at it this way, I just moved into a whole new housing bracket." He smiled and reached out to give my hand a quick squeeze. "This is going to be *fun*."

I considered his words. They were heartwarming.

I was on my way to being convinced, but I wasn't quite there. "You have a warped idea of fun. This is going to be *stressful*."

"No, stressful is slapping pumpkin on a freshly painted wall and hoping it looks okay."

"Wait a minute. You were the one who picked out the orange paint."

"And you let me. That was very trusting of you."

"This is on you," I said.

I took a last bite of bagel.

"I'll take that risk." Jamie finished his bagel and tipped back his coffee.

We stowed the trash. Then we crouched down at opposite ends of a wall and started painting orange.

Four hours later, our paintbrushes met in the middle of the last window.

We both straightened up. We took a few backward steps and gazed around.

I was amazed.

It looked fantastic.

"How did you know?" I asked him.

"Know what?"

"That it would look this good?"

"I cheated," he said.

"Cheated how?"

"I stole the idea from a decorating website, remember?"

"Nice steal." I couldn't believe this stylish, sophisticated apartment was mine. Now I couldn't wait to get going on the flooring.

Nine

"If you can do this without flinching," Jamie said to me as we stared up the thirty-foot rock face, "then you can definitely pick me out a house."

We'd looked at three different houses on Thursday night. While I'd tried to drag Jamie's opinion out of him, he kept insisting it was my choice to make. I'd been afraid to say I liked anything for fear he'd pull out his checkbook right then and there.

"I can do *this* without flinching," I said. I was excited about our climb, not frightened.

Spending hundreds of thousands of someone else's dollars? Now, *that* was frightening.

We were on a field trip with Paul, the other instructors and the rest of our class. It was a graduation ceremony of sorts, although Jamie and I had already signed up for the next level of climbing class, as had most of the rest of the class. We weren't qualified to undertake more than an uphill hike or a scramble by ourselves at this point.

"Great," Jamie said.

"But you really do have to weigh in on the house."

We'd seen two more houses last night with the Realtor Emily-Ann. I'd liked the last one quite a lot.

"Go through your safety check," the head instructor called out.

I made sure my watch was zipped into my pocket. I checked my harness buckles, my leg loops, rope orientation and carabiner. Jamie and I double-checked each other's knots, then we waited for Paul to give us a thumbs-up. We both passed his check, and we were ready to go.

I was going first with Jamie on belay.

Each of three teams had chosen a different section of the rock face.

I was ready.

I was excited.

"On belay?" I called back to Jamie.

"On belay," he confirmed.

"Climbing," I called.

"Climb on," he answered.

I found my first foothold, flexing my toe. I'd learned most of the patterns on the climbing wall, and it was exciting to be trying something completely new.

I was connected by a top rope that looped from the top of the climb back to Jamie. I trusted Jamie, and Paul was supervising, so I focused on the foot-and handholds.

I dead-ended once and had to back down a few steps, but otherwise, I made it up without any mistakes.

When I looked back down, Jamie was beaming and giving me a clap.

He lowered me down, and I took belay while he climbed.

By the end of the morning, we were all stripping off our windbreakers under the beaming sun. Paul and the other instructors had brought along a light picnic and some celebratory champagne.

Jamie and I toasted each other in the fresh air, laughing at our accomplishments.

He pulled me into an unexpected hug.

I felt arousal buzz through me.

"Now, that was adventure," he whispered in my ear.

"We are wild and exciting," I whispered back.

"Who wouldn't want to point at us across a room?" he asked.

"Or fall madly in love with us?"

His hug tightened for a second.

"Anyone who wants to take the long way home…" the head instructor said in a loud voice. Then he pointed. "There's a trail from here that goes around the face. It leads to a viewpoint lookout. Farther up, you can get into Pebble Pond. Then the main trail loops around back to the parking lot."

"It's all about the views," Paul said.

Most people were shaking their heads. Everyone was already hot and tired.

Jamie drew back to look at me.

"Game?" he asked.

I was.

In the end, six of us changed into hiking shoes and walked the two miles to the viewpoint.

As Paul had said, the view was spectacular, sweeping green hillsides, spikes of evergreens, and snowcapped peaks surrounding a deep blue lake in the valley bottom.

The rest of the group turned around there.

Jamie wanted to keep going, and my exhilaration was giving me energy. I felt like I could hike all day.

My exhilaration was ebbing by the time we made it along the narrow path to Pebble Pond.

The picturesque and isolated spot was worth the hike, but I'd admit I was glad we'd be going downhill on the way back.

"I like this," Jamie said, gazing out at the blue-green water surrounded by towering rocks and lush grasses and shrubs. A few cedars clustered near one shore with a group of crows circling the tops, calling to one another in the silent wind.

We were on a tiny stretch of pebble-covered beach. The smooth little rocks were quite a pretty mix of white, blue gray, amber, green and black. Some were solid colors. Some were striped. And some were mottled. It was easy to see how the pond got its name.

It felt like we were all alone in the world.

Above us, an eagle took flight from the cedar trees, then another followed, chasing off the crows.

"Nature in the raw," I said, quoting something I'd once heard.

"My money's on the eagles," Jamie said.

"They must have a nest up there. Chicks do you think?"

"It seems late in the season. But they look like they're guarding something."

The eagles swooped in tandem, and the crows scattered.

The world fell silent again with the barest of breezes lifting the leaves around us.

"I'm sweltering," Jamie said.

I guessed the sun was reflecting off the surrounding rock faces. We did seem to be in a pocket of still heat.

Jamie stripped off his shirt.

My mouth went dry, and my brain paused for a beat. To be fair, I was dying of thirst. But the brain seize was all Jamie— his abs looked like they'd been sculpted from marble. His pecs and shoulders were firm, smooth and rounded. His biceps bulged, and his forearms were thick and sturdy.

I knew he had strong hands. I'd watched him work. But they looked stronger against the backdrop of nature.

Then he reached for the button of his khakis.

"Wh-what are you doing?" My stutter was mortifying.

"Taking a dip," he said, and dragged down his zipper. "Aren't you hot?"

I was hot. I was very hot. I was a whole lot hotter than I'd been two minutes ago.

"Don't look so worried," he said. "I'm not getting naked or anything. Come in with me. You're wearing underwear, aren't you?"

I was wearing underwear.

I was wearing Tasha underwear, sexy but very beautiful underwear. I wouldn't mind people seeing it.

Person, I corrected. I wouldn't mind a person seeing it. And that person was Jamie.

Oh, boy.

He kicked off his shoes, pulled off his socks and stripped down to a pair of black boxers.

This was Jamie all right. It was all Jamie. There wasn't an ounce of James left in this man.

My hands twitched with an urge to reach out and touch him.

But he started for the pond.

I had a ridiculous desire to call Brooklyn and ask her what on earth she thought she was doing. If Jamie had been waiting to marry me in the nave of St. Fidelis, I'd have been sprinting down the aisle, desperate to get going on the honeymoon.

"Come on, Tasha," he called over his shoulder. "Live a little."

I was living.

In this moment, I felt like I was *really* living.

I pulled my T-shirt over my head. I kicked off my runners, peeled off my sweaty socks and stepped out of my pants.

The pebbles were warm on my feet. They shifted as I walked to the shore.

Jamie dived under, resurfacing with a whoop that echoed off the cliff walls. He sent ripples across the surface of the pond.

"Cold?" I asked.

"Refreshing." He swiped his hand across his wet hair as he turned to look at me. He went still then, scanning me from my head to my toes.

I was acutely conscious of my burgundy bra and panties set. It covered everything that needed to be covered. But it covered it all in sexy, stylish satin and lace.

Jamie was definitely all Jamie today. And I was sure all Tasha underneath my climbing clothes.

I waded determinedly into the water, ignoring the cold, acutely conscious of Jamie watching me.

"Refreshing," I said as the water hit my shoulders.

Goose bumps came up on my skin.

He cleared his throat. "You'll get used to it in a second."

"I think you oversold the experience," I said.

He grinned. "Wimp."

"Hey, I just climbed a rock face."

"Want to climb another?" He looked meaningfully above us.

"Dressed like this? Without equipment? I don't think so."

"Live a little," he whispered.

"This *is* living a little."

In fact, it was living a lot. I was leading a hugely exciting

Tasha life here. A month ago, I couldn't have even imagined a Saturday like this.

"Up there," he said, pointing to a flat ledge about ten feet in the air. "I'm going to jump."

"Have fun."

"Come, too?"

"Scramble up that little goat track in bare feet just to jump off a rock?" I winced.

"Tasha..." he said, in the most cajoling tone I'd ever heard. He moved closer to me. "I know deep down inside your little heart is a wild woman trying to get out."

I looked around us. "This isn't wild enough?"

I was swimming in my underwear in early October.

"Not wild enough for the two of us." He waggled his brow. "It's not going to kill you."

I looked up at the ledge.

He was right. Jumping ten feet wasn't going to kill me.

I wasn't scared. And it would probably be fun. I honestly didn't know why I was so reluctant. Reflex, I supposed. Nat was used to saying no to anything that seemed weird or off-beat, anything she knew she didn't know how to do, anything that seemed frivolous or silly or without purpose.

Jumping off a rock ledge into a mountain pond was arguably silly and without purpose. But it was also arguably fun.

"Fine," I said.

Jamie looked surprised. Then he grinned. "Come on, Crazy Tasha." He started paddling to the edge of the pond.

"First I'm not wild enough, now I'm crazy? There's no pleasing you." But I followed him.

"I'm crazy, too," he called back. "In a good way."

He hoisted himself onto a space at the bottom of the rock face.

He stood and turned, offering his hand to me.

"There's a foothold about two feet under the water," he said.

I reached for his hand and found the foothold with my right foot.

His grip was strong around my hand. "Ready?"

I nodded.

Jamie hoisted. I pushed with my left. I pulled up with my free hand on the ledge, and in seconds I was out of the water standing beside him.

Our wet bodies brushed together.

I felt the glow of the contact right through to my bones.

Our gazes hit each other. They held for a sizzling moment. But then Jamie looked away, up the side of the rock, finding a path.

He marched away from me, then scrambled to the top.

"It's easy," he called back.

It looked easy. And he was right. It was easy.

In minutes we stood on the edge of the face looking down at the deep, blue-green water.

"Are you scared?" he asked.

"Not really." I might be a little nervous. Or maybe I was excited. Or maybe I was so fixated on the beauty of the man standing beside me, that I didn't really care about the long plunge into the water.

"By the way, did I tell you the latest on our stock account?" he asked.

"What happened?" I couldn't tell if it was good news or bad.

"September Innovations posted their R & D results."

"Good?" I asked cautiously.

We could stand to lose some money at this point. We could easily stand to lose some money. I knew Jamie hadn't dumped our entire portfolio into September Innovations, a wireless technology company. But he had made a substantive gamble on them.

"Come Monday morning, we'll be able to watch the graph go up and up. You should think about buying a condo."

The suggestion took me by surprise. "We just redecorated my apartment."

"You've built up a serious down payment," he said. "You should start setting up some equity now."

It was probably good advice. But my brain didn't want to

delve into equity and interest rates at the moment. I'd think about it later, when I was alone, when a half-naked Jamie wasn't crowding out all the logic inside my head.

"I'll think about it," I managed between processing the images of his rugged face, his sexy body and his clinging boxers.

"Good." He reached for my hand and squeezed it in his.

I loved the strength of his grip. His energy flowed up my arm and into my chest, and nothing else in the world mattered, not one little bit.

He nodded to the pond. "On three?"

I was thinking on ten, or maybe twenty, or maybe thirty. Or maybe we could just stand here in the sunshine forever holding hands on this perfect wild and wonderful Saturday afternoon. I didn't think life could get any better.

"On three," I said.

Jamie counted. "One..."

I joined him, and together we said. "Two...three."

We jumped.

I squeezed his hand tight as we flew through the air.

It felt like a long time, but it was only seconds before my feet hit the water, then my hips, my hands, and my head went under.

Cold engulfed my senses, and I lost hold of Jamie's hand.

I bobbed down a few feet, and then buoyancy took over, pushing me back up.

I broke the surface and blinked the water from my eyes to see Jamie grinning beside me.

"I like you, Tasha," he said, his warm gaze holding mine.

"I like you too, Jamie." I meant it in ways he couldn't possibly understand.

I bicycled my feet to stay afloat in the deep water, veering toward the shore.

He kicked toward me.

His expression sobered.

He touched my shoulder, and my whole body lit with desire.

"You are beautiful," he said.

I didn't know what to say to that.

The way he was looking at me made me feel beautiful.

He feathered his hand from my shoulder to the middle of my back.

His other arm went around my waist, anchoring me, and I realized he was standing on the bottom.

I stopped moving my legs.

"Tasha," he said.

"Jamie," I answered.

He tipped his head and slowly leaned in.

His lips touched mine, cool from the water. But they heated quickly.

His kiss sent waves of wanting through my arms, my legs, to my belly and breasts. My body tightened and quickened. Passion amped up as our kiss deepened.

I wrapped my arms around him, sliding them from his firm shoulders across his back, up to his neck. My fingers tangled in the base of his hairline as I held him to me.

My lips parted farther and his tongue touched mine.

Fireworks flashed behind my eyes. Under the water, my legs wrapped around him.

Somewhere deep in my brain stem, I understood what I was doing, the intimacy of the move, what I was signaling. But my conscious mind didn't care about that.

I wanted to get closer to Jamie. I needed to get closer to Jamie. Every inch of space between us should be erased and eradicated.

His hand closed over my breast, the wet fabric making no barrier at all. I moaned with the pleasure of his touch.

I tipped my head back to give him access.

His kissed his way along my neck.

I knew where this was going. I loved where this was going. I couldn't wait to get there.

He cupped my behind, holding me to him, pressing against me, spreading pulses of heat and power in all directions.

Then he quit the kiss and gave a chopped exclamation. "We can't."

He pulled back from me. "Tasha." He took a couple of deep breaths. "I don't—"

"It's fine," I managed. I was as mortified as I'd ever been in my life. "It's nothing."

"It's not—"

"You said it yourself." I disentangled my arms and legs and put some space between us. "I'm completely refreshed."

"Tasha, wait."

"Let's get back to the car." My feet found the bottom of the pond, so I was able to propel myself even faster toward the pebble shore.

"That's not what I meant," he called from behind me. "Tasha, stop."

I wasn't stopping. The last thing I was doing was stopping.

I'd made a colossal mistake. We'd both made a colossal mistake. There was still time to correct it, and that was good.

We'd gotten over the kiss. We'd get over this.

I felt his hand on my arm.

I tried to shake it off, but he refused to let go.

He turned me, and I nearly stumbled over in the waist-high water.

"I only meant—"

"Will you let me go?" I demanded.

Maybe his precious Tasha didn't care about dignity, but Nat still did. There was still enough Nat in me to want to get the heck out of this situation.

"I don't have anything." He stared meaningfully at me, moving close up. "I don't have a condom, Tasha. I wasn't saying we shouldn't, I was saying we couldn't, not here, not now, not without protection."

His words dropped to silence.

It was a very uncomfortable silence.

"Oh." My voice was tiny. I swallowed.

He raked a hand through his hair. "What is with you?"

I didn't have a ready answer for that.

He kept talking. "Do you think I behave like that when I *don't* want to make love?"

I found my voice again. "I don't know. I couldn't tell."

"Well, *tell* already. That's what raw, unbridled lust and passion look like. You're hot, Tasha. Any guy within fifty yards of you probably wants you. And none of them, definitely not me, is going to shut it down without a damn good reason."

"Oh," I said again, struggling to shift the emotional gears inside my head.

"We should go," he said.

"Okay." I had no idea where this left us.

He moved closer. His expression changed. And my uncertainty dropped a notch.

"To your place," he said with meaning. "As fast as we can get there."

I opened my apartment door to find Sophie inside.

We both stared at each other in shock, me on finding her in my apartment—which was not unheard of, but pretty unusual—and her likely wondering why my hair was wet and why Jamie was with me.

What on earth was I going to say about that?

"Oh, good," she said before I could form any kind of a coherent sentence. "You brought Jamie. I guess you heard?" Her eyes were alight with joy.

"Uh…"

"Aaron called. Bryce and Ethan are on their way over. I can't believe it." She started to pace. "I just can't believe it. How long have you two known?"

I looked at Jamie.

We must have had identical expressions of bafflement.

"I wish you'd told me yourself," Sophie said to me. She closed the space and wrapped me in a tight hug.

Then she seemed to notice my wet hair.

She looked at Jamie, then back at me. I could see it all unraveling right here in front of us.

"Were you at the club?" she asked us.

"Yes," Jamie said.

Sophie took a step back and put her hand on her forehead. She grinned and turned away. "We need champagne."

I gave Jamie a panicked look and mouthed the word *what?* He shrugged his shoulders.

"When Aaron told me it was five hundred thousand, I made him say it again. I couldn't believe it."

Five hundred thousand? Dollars? Did she mean *dollars?* She turned back. "We need champagne."

"Aaron talked to you about five hundred thousand dollars?" Jamie asked.

His tone was tense, his expression worried.

"Did I get the number wrong? Oh, I hope I didn't get it wrong because I told Bryce and Ethan. Did you talk to Horatio Simms?" Her question was directed at Jamie. "Did he say that was his investment? Oh, I sure hope I didn't mess up."

"Horatio Simms is investing five hundred thousand dollars in Sweet Tech?" Jamie asked.

"I know I have you to thank for that. I don't know what you did, but—"

"I didn't talk to Horatio," Jamie said.

Sophie looked confused.

"But Aaron told me…"

"I did talk to Aaron," Jamie said. I could hear the annoyance in his voice. "Aaron must have talked to Horatio."

Sophie breathed a sigh of relief. "Oh, then that makes sense."

Jamie went to his phone.

I didn't know what was happening, but I could tell we had a big problem. There was a knock on the door.

"That'll be Bryce and Ethan." Sophie brushed past me.

"Simms?" Jamie said into the phone. "I'm at Tasha's with Sophie and her crew."

I glanced to Sophie to see if she'd noticed Jamie calling me Tasha.

She hadn't.

"When you get this," Jamie said. "Call me. Or better still, get your butt over here and tell me *what is going on.*"

Jamie disconnected.

"What?" I whispered to him.

Jamie came close to my ear. "I specifically told Aaron that Sweet Tech wasn't ready for investment. It's way too high risk and we don't have a proper prospectus. I waved him off, and he pulled in his uncle instead? This is going to go *so* bad."

I didn't know what to say. I was awash with both guilt and worry. I hated the thought that I'd caused problems at work for Jamie.

"Bryce brought champagne!" Sophie said. "Get some glasses, Nat."

I forced a smile on my face. "Sure." I didn't know what else to do, so I started for the kitchen. "Can you tell me more about the deal?"

Maybe, at the very least, I could arm Jamie with some information before he talked to Aaron.

I found my champagne flutes in a high cupboard, and I passed them around.

Jamie tried to refuse, but I gave him a glare that told him to play along. There was no point in getting angry right now.

Sophie and her friends were oblivious to any problems. To them, Jamie was the hero who'd saved their fledgling business. All she could see was a bright and beautiful future of success and riches.

If it had to come crashing down, it had to come crashing down. But we should figure out exactly why before we gave her the bad news.

"To success," Sophie said, raising her glass. "And to James for all of his help."

For a second I thought Jamie might blurt something out. But he didn't, just took a drink of his champagne.

Sophie, Bryce and Ethan all started talking, fast and with plenty of emotion and excitement. I heard them say *scale up* and *distribution* and *markets*.

Before I could take Jamie aside again, there was another knock on the door.

I opened it to find Aaron.

He was grinning. "Hi, Natasha."

I could feel Jamie's presence right behind me. "Start talking, Simms."

"You heard."

"Of course I heard. Why, *why* would you tell Horatio about Sweet Tech?"

"Because I knew you were holding out on us, keeping it all to yourself."

Jamie shook his head. "That wasn't it. You knew that wasn't what was going on."

Aaron shot back, "No. I know that you told me it wasn't ready for investment."

"It wasn't. It isn't. And Horatio should know that. This isn't his kind of deal. How did you convince him to invest so much money?"

Aaron didn't answer.

"How?" Jamie repeated.

"I told him it was your recommendation."

"You *what*?" Jamie bellowed.

"I'm not an idiot, Gillen. You were going to invest. You might have wanted to dot the *i*'s and cross the *t*'s, but you know you were going to invest."

"I was *not* going to invest."

"Then why spend all that time, effort and energy on it?"

"I was doing a favor for a friend."

Aaron looked at me. "A *friend*."

His inference was clear.

"You've set your uncle up to lose money. And he's going to think I suggested it. You overconfident, cavalier little jerk."

"Nat?" Sophie's voice sounded shaky behind us.

My heart sank.

"What's going on?" Sophie asked.

There was a brittle silence. Finally, Jamie turned.

"Aaron made a mistake," Jamie said to Sophie.

"There's no mistake," Ethan said. "We have a handshake deal for five hundred thousand dollars."

Jamie shot Aaron a brief glare. "I need to talk to Horatio. He didn't have all the facts when he made that deal."

"You don't have faith in us?" Sophie asked Jamie.

Jamie didn't answer.

"It's not that," I said, trying to help.

"Tasha, don't," Jamie said.

Sophie gave him a puzzled look at the name Tasha.

"You're right," Jamie said to Sophie in a clipped, professional voice. "I don't have faith in you. The reason I don't have faith is that I'm a realist. You're at a very early stage. You need patient capital. Horatio is looking for a faster return on his investment. You're not going to be able to give it to him."

Ethan took a step forward. "Who says?"

"I say... Ethan, is it?"

"Ethan Tumble. I'm the technical brains behind this, and I know a good idea when I see one. This thing's got legs."

"I'm not saying it's not a good idea."

"We should close the door," I said.

I didn't have a lot of neighbors, but I didn't think this was a conversation we wanted people to overhear.

Jamie looked frustrated, but he stepped aside and Aaron came in.

I closed the door.

Jamie spoke again. "You may have the best idea in the world. Over the long term, you might all be headed for stellar success. And I hope you are. I really do. But it was presented to Horatio in a ridiculously irresponsible way. Aaron has to answer for that. And I have to answer for Aaron. And I will. *We* will. We'll tell Horatio the truth and take it from there."

"We're not getting the money," Sophie said, sounding completely dejected.

I didn't blame her, and I hated that I'd had a hand in setting up this debacle.

"Simms," Jamie said as he reopened the door. He gestured for Aaron to leave.

Aaron left, and Jamie followed him out.

Sophie looked like she might cry, and I realized Jamie had left me alone.

I mean, Sophie, Bryce and Ethan were still there. But Jamie was gone.

I'd come home from the hike with such high expectations for Jamie and me. This wasn't how the day was supposed to go.

The day was supposed to end with the two of us alone, together, in my bed with a condom and our pent-up passion for each other.

Ten

I wished I could have done a better job consoling Sophie. But I was fumbling in the dark. I had no idea what was going to happen next.

We speculated on the potential for Horatio's investment, and we talked about other investments that might replace it. I reminded her that she still had a good job. I told her she was young, just starting out. Things were going to go up, and things were going to go down. And I truly believed that.

Trouble was, she'd gotten her hopes way up. I knew it was hard to go from the top of the world to the depth of disappointment. It really sucked.

Privately, I wondered what Jamie and Aaron were going to say to Horatio—Aaron in favor of the investment and Jamie opposed was the best I could guess. And I really couldn't see how Horatio would be willing to invest in Sweet Tech by the end of that conversation.

A handshake deal was all well and good, but I doubted it would stand up in court. I honestly couldn't imagine Sophie suing anyone anyway.

She left at about ten thirty, after a couple of glasses of wine. We didn't have the heart to finish the champagne.

I showered the dried pond water out of my hair, using extra conditioner to get the softness back into it. Then I changed into the worn cotton shorts and T-shirt I usually wore to bed.

But I wasn't tired. I wasn't hungry. I didn't feel like watching a movie or reading a book. I wasn't even thirsty.

I prowled the apartment for a few minutes before I decided to surf around online.

I thought back on what Jamie had said about me buying a condo. I was feeling like I should get my life in order. This windfall from our investments might or might not last. I should put it to good use while I had the chance.

I'd be thirty in a couple of years. I should own my own real estate by then. That's what people did when they became full-fledged adults. They invested. They settled down. They started to build their lives.

I looked around my apartment and thought about moving. I really liked the work we'd done, the colors and the style. But it wasn't mine. It was a temporary stop for me. I considered how I could duplicate the colors and style if I bought my own condo.

Maybe I could get something on a ground floor. It would be nice not to have to lug groceries up the stairs every week. Not that it wasn't good exercise. It was very good exercise. But if I could find a place near the park, I could keep my bike handy and get exercise that way. Riding through the park would be more fun than lugging groceries up the stairs.

There was a knock on the door.

I got up to answer, my first thought being that Sophie was back. Like me, she was probably feeling way too blue to sleep. I hoped she hadn't driven her car after we'd had the wine.

Then I hesitated before opening the door.

It was really late, well after eleven. And why hadn't she texted me? She would have texted me if she was coming back.

I glanced to the dead bolt to make sure it was locked.

"Hello?" I said through the door.

"It's Jamie."

At the sound of his voice, my chest tightened with anticipation. I was glad that he'd come back, way too glad.

I quickly unlocked and opened the door.

"What happened?" I asked him, drinking in his handsome face but forcing my thoughts to Sophie. "Is it bad? Is it good? Have you talked to Sophie yet?"

He came inside. "I haven't talked to Sophie. It's too late to call her."

He was right about that. And bad news could always wait until morning. If Sophie was already asleep, it seemed cruel to wake her up only to make her more miserable.

"What happened?" I asked, hesitant to know, but knowing that not knowing wouldn't change a thing. I knew that much.

"Aaron and I talked to Horatio."

"And?" I backed away a little and braced myself.

I was pretty sure the outcome was inevitable. But once I heard the words, there was no more hope for Sophie. I felt terrible for being a part of boosting then dashing her dreams.

"It turned out badly for me," Jamie said, looking grim.

It wasn't the answer I'd expected. "I don't understand." I struggled to figure out what it might mean. "Oh, Jamie, what did Horatio do? Did you get fired"

"No. It wasn't that."

I felt a small measure of relief.

"But he won't walk away from the investment."

It took me a second to have the words make sense inside my head.

Jamie's expression was at odds with his words.

"But that's good," I said. "That means Sophie will get the money."

"No, that's bad. Yes, they'll get the money. And if they lose it, Aaron and I will be in big trouble."

I was confused. "You told Horatio the whole story, right? He knows you think it's risky. If he decided to stay in anyway—"

"Sure, I told him the whole story. Problem was, he didn't believe me."

I lowered myself into an armchair. "Why didn't he believe you?"

"He thinks I want the investment for myself."

"He thinks you'd lie to him?"

"Horatio is not exactly the trusting type. Aaron had him convinced he'd beaten me to the punch. He thinks the minute he pulls out, I'll jump in."

"Would you?" Even as I asked the question, it sounded silly.

Jamie didn't have five hundred thousand dollars to risk. And why would he put his money where it would be locked up for a long time, and where he thought he might lose it?

Why would anyone do that?

They wouldn't.

"It's still a risky investment," he said. "And if it goes bad on him, Horatio will save his reputation by putting the blame on us."

"I'm so sorry." I stood again. I was feeling worse by the minute.

"I hope I can help them. They need to get out of R & D, bring it to market and scale up."

"I'm sure you can," I said. Everything I'd seen Jamie touch had turned out well.

"Even if I can think of something, Ethan doesn't seem like the kind of guy to listen."

"You're a lot smarter than Ethan. And Sophie will listen to you."

Jamie gave a cool smile at that. "I appreciate the vote of confidence."

I didn't think Jamie needed me to tell him what he already knew. He was amazing, in so many ways. I thought it had to be obvious to the world.

We gazed at each other in silence.

Memories of our swim bloomed to life in my brain.

I wondered if he was remembering, too. I didn't know how to ask. I didn't know how to bring up the subject—the fact that I was sitting here wishing I could throw myself into his arms and pick up where we left off.

I didn't have any experience with this.

How did people tell a friend they wanted to sleep with them?

I was pretty sure they did it all the time. Friends with benefits was a thing. It was a big thing. People seemed quite taken with the concept.

It seemed like the kind of concept Tasha would like. Tasha would definitely like an arrangement like that—all the benefits and a friendship, too. Why wouldn't she want that?

And she'd ask. She'd just outright ask: *Hey, Jamie, how about we sleep together tonight?*

I snickered at myself.

"What's funny?" Jamie asked.

"Me," I said. "Tasha me."

His gaze went soft as he studied my face. "You are Tasha."

"Sometimes," I said.

I'd been very Tasha this afternoon when I jumped off that rock, then nearly jumped Jamie's bones. That had been very Tasha.

"Why is Tasha smiling?" he asked. "I'm assuming she's not amused by my predicament."

"Not at all. I'm really sorry about that."

He waved my words away. "Let's get back to the smile."

I stepped forward, bringing myself closer. It felt easier to say the words when there was some intimacy between us.

"You remember this afternoon?" I asked.

He moved too, closing the distance between us. "Is that a joke?"

"It's an opening line."

"Yes, I remember this afternoon."

I gathered every ounce of my courage and dived into the deep end. "Do you want to sleep with me?"

"Did I not make that obvious?"

"Because I want to sleep with you. There, I said it." I paused. "Okay, you probably already knew that." I recalibrated in my brain. "I'm thinking Tasha would just say it out loud. And so would Jamie. You know that Jamie would say it. If Tasha and Jamie wanted to be friends with benefits, they'd say so. They'd say it. They'd own it. They'd do it. And they'd enjoy it. No big thing. No big deal. They wouldn't dwell on whether or not it was a good idea. They're exciting. They're risk takers. They embrace life and enjoy every single moment of it. And there's no reason, none at all, why we shouldn't do exactly that. I have condoms, you know."

Jamie cracked a sudden smile. "Are you done?"

I took a breath.

Part of me couldn't believe I'd just blurted all that out.

Another part of me was darn proud for having done it. "I think so…yeah… I think that about does it."

"Yes," Jamie said.

I waited for more.

He didn't say anything else.

"That's it?" I asked.

"That's it. A solid, definitive, exciting, risk-taking yes."

I reached for his shirt.

He reached for mine.

We all but tore off each other's clothes.

Then we stopped. We stared at each other. We were mostly naked, both breathing deeply.

"I want to do this fast," Jamie said.

I was fine with fast. I was more than fine with fast. We had two perfectly good sofas within a few feet of where we were standing. And there were the armchairs. I'd make love on an armchair.

Or the floor. I'd happily make love with Jamie on the floor, too.

"But I want it to go slow." He reached out and feathered a touch on the tip of my bare shoulder.

Oh, yeah. Slow sounded marvelous.

His palm cupped my shoulder, and he drew me into a kiss.

It was long and deep and sexy sweet.

I stepped into him, my nipples brushing his chest. Tendrils of passion were winding through me, heating me straight to my core.

I wrapped my arms around his neck, leaning into the strength of him.

He cupped my rear with both hands, pulling me against him.

"But I can't do slow," he growled against my lip.

"Okay," I said.

"Slow later," he said and scooped me into his arms.

I didn't know where we were going, and I sure didn't care.

He rounded the divider in less than five seconds. Deposited me on the bed and followed me down, covering my body with his heat.

He kept up his kisses, and I molded my lips to his, thinking that he tasted good, really good, extraordinarily good. I didn't think a man's lips could taste so sweet.

His palm stroked its way up my side, over my ribs, onto my breast, settling there.

I arched my back, and a moan vibrated my lips.

His fingers wrapped my nipple, and the tingle told me it was beading in response.

"Tasha," he whispered, then stroked his tongue against mine.

I loved my name on his lips, my special, secret name that meant everything I was doing was okay. It was better than okay. It was fantastic and fun, and there wasn't a reason in the world I shouldn't be enjoying sex with Jamie.

We'd made a deal. And it was a good deal. It was a marvelous deal, and all I had to do was lie back and enjoy it.

I parted my legs to cradle him, and I stroked my hands down the length of his back, feeling the satin of his skin, the definition of his muscle, marveling at the texture and the masculine contours of his body.

I broke from his mouth to kiss his shoulder. I wanted to see if his skin tasted as good as his lips.

It did.

I kissed my way across his chest.

He threw his head back and groaned.

His fingers tightened on my nipple, sending quivers of desire rocketing down my body. I arched into him, my legs going around his waist.

"Condom," he whispered.

Good call. For a second I'd forgotten.

I would have remembered, I told myself as I reached out and pulled open the drawer of my bedside table.

The interruption was brief, and I watched his expression until he was done and met my eyes. His were dark blue, deep and intent.

"You're gorgeous," I said.

He smiled. "You're the gorgeous one." His arms slid back

around me, and he held me so tenderly close that I felt a random tear slip from the corner of my eye.

I wasn't crying. I wasn't sad. I was very, very far from sad. If anything, I wanted to whoop with joy.

"You ready?" he asked.

I'd been ready for quite a few days now.

"Yes," I said and angled toward him.

He pressed into me.

I closed my eyes, savoring every inch and every second, until we were together and desire was rocketing through my body.

He pulled, and I gasped.

His voice was a groan again near my ear. "This is *so* not going to be slow."

"Good," I said.

Slow could come later. At least, I hoped slow would come later. If making love with Jamie felt like this all the time, I didn't know how we'd ever stop.

His body met mine, and I synced our rhythm. His hands were everywhere, plucking my passion, drawing out sensations I hadn't known existed.

A colored haze took over my brain, green then blue then yellow and orange. We flew high and crested fast.

I cried out. I dived into the sun. Waves of pure ecstasy all but lifted me from the bed.

Jamie groaned, and our bodies pulsed together for long minutes.

Then I felt the tension drain from him. I melted into every touch, every sensation. My skin was slick against his. The air finally felt cool on my limbs.

"Wow," Jamie said.

"Wow," I said back.

"That was fantastic."

"It was," I agreed wholeheartedly.

"We have to do that again."

I smiled at that. I loved the conviction in his voice. "Right this second?"

"Tonight. Definitely again tonight."

His words made me think about tomorrow.

But I wasn't going to think about tomorrow. I was Tasha, and I was daring and confident, and I was going to take this moment, this night for what it was. A supergood time with a man who was becoming a supergood friend. There was absolutely no value in worrying beyond that.

It was Sunday, and I opened my apartment door to Sophie.

I was expecting Jamie in an hour, and until I saw her standing there I'd hoped the knock meant he was early. I'd hoped he was as anxious to see me as I was to see him. Then I hoped Sophie couldn't see the disappointment on my face.

She didn't.

She looked tired and frustrated.

"It's hard trying to get rich," she said and moved past me.

She was dressed in jeans and flats. Her light brown hair was swooped up in a ponytail that looked hasty. And her sparkly T-shirt hung lose over her jeans—no half tuck, no saucy knot, no nothing. This wasn't like Sophie.

"No orders yet?" I knew they'd all been contacting potential customers.

I told myself I was sympathetic. And I reminded myself how important the success of BRT Innovations was to Sophie and everyone else, including Jamie. I reminded myself that sex with Jamie was secondary to his own career and to Sophie's future.

Still, I couldn't stop thinking about his arrival. And I couldn't help hoping Sophie would be gone by then. Most of all, I couldn't help picturing Jamie naked.

"We've been at it for *months*," she said. "We're all working doubly hard now, and Jamie is helping, but there's no interest from the market. I'm talking zero interest, Nat. And it's starting to terrify me."

I closed the door. "These things take time." I knew that had to be true.

She took a couple of steps and then turned to face me. "It

would be different if we had some maybes, if people liked the idea but maybe couldn't afford Sweet Tech. If they thought they might want to buy one in the future. But nobody wants to buy one in the future. They won't even consider the possibilities."

I knew I'd be a terrible salesperson. I couldn't even imagine how demoralizing it must be to face so much rejection.

"We're moving pretty fast, spending, spending, spending," she said, looking even more worried as she said it. "Ethan's put together ten more prototypes."

"You need those for sure," I said, trying to sound optimistic but feeling as worried as Sophie looked.

She gave a nervous laugh. "You have to spend money to make money?"

"I've heard that." I didn't have much else to offer.

"We're spending Horatio's money now. And the things Aaron's said about his uncle make me feel like we're indebted to a criminal—like he'll break our legs or something if we don't pay it back."

"Nobody's breaking anyone's legs." I thought about my half of the money Jamie and I had amassed and wondered if contributing it would help.

I could wait for a condo. I could be happy in my apartment for a few more years. At least it looked great now. It wasn't ugly anymore. I had that going for me.

Another knock came on the door.

My brain and my heart rooted for it to be Jamie. I couldn't help the feelings, even though I knew they were selfish.

"Aaron was going to meet me here," Sophie said.

More disappointment for me.

As I walked to the door, I told myself to stop being so self-absorbed.

Last night with Jamie had been beyond amazing, and I couldn't wait to be alone with him again, to kiss him, make love with him, to talk, to laugh, to whatever with him. I was greedy for every second we could have together.

I was greedy. And I needed to stop. Sophie needed my support right now.

I opened the door, and it was Jamie.

My heart lifted.

"Hi, Tasha," he said, his eyes warm, his lips breaking into a smile.

"Why do you call her that?" Sophie appeared at my right shoulder.

Jamie was obviously surprised to see her.

"It's short for Natasha," he said.

"So is Nat." She looked from him to me and back again. "And what are you doing here?"

Jamie didn't answer.

I opened my mouth, hoping something logical would come out of it. No reasonable explanation was forming inside my head.

Then Aaron appeared in the hallway.

"Did Aaron call you?" Sophie asked Jamie.

"He didn't have to call me," Jamie said, brushing past the awkward moment. "We work in the same office. What's going on?"

As Jamie moved past me, he purposefully brushed his hand against mine.

My skin tingled and my heart thudded.

It had been a busy week, and I was impatient to get to the benefits part of our friendship again. I was feeling *really* impatient. Clearly, I wasn't a very good friend to Sophie.

"We have to get this under control," Aaron said as he walked in the door. "We can't keep bleeding money with nothing to show for it. We need a plan to get some orders under our belt."

Bryce and Ethan arrived behind him, and my apartment filled up with the entire gang.

"We need to open some doors," Aaron said. "Nobody is taking us seriously."

"Because Sweet Tech has no track record," Jamie said, sounding impatient. "BRT Innovations has no track record. That's been my point all along."

"An 'I told you so' isn't going to help," Aaron said.

"Even if it makes you feel like the big man," Ethan tossed in.

"Ethan," I snapped.

Aaron was right. But Jamie was right, too. And Ethan being rude wasn't going to help any of it.

Jamie's eyes were annoyed, but his voice was calm. "Who have you been targeting, and where have you gone so far?"

I was impressed with his apparent self-control. Then again, I was pretty biased when it came to Jamie. I knew he had flaws, but I was hard-pressed to see any of them. He was one incredible package of a man.

I realized we'd turned him into exactly what he'd wanted—the guy that women pointed to from across the room, the guy every woman wanted to meet. And now that we'd succeeded, I didn't want it at all.

Why hadn't I just spoken up way back then, way back when no other women were looking? Why hadn't I just said, "Hey, James, date me, let's see what happens?"

I could tell myself that Nat would never have done that. But she should have done that. I should have done that. Now I felt like our time together was ticking down.

"Suppliers," Sophie said. "We've done trade shows from LA to New York. Bryce and I have taken two weeks' vacation to focus."

I was surprised to hear that. Sophie hadn't said anything to me about using up her vacation time.

"I've been through a Rolodex of suppliers," Bryce said.

"Have you tried individual restaurants?" Jamie asked. "Who are the trendsetters?"

"They can't get a return going retail," Aaron said.

"They can prove the concept," Jamie said. "And trendsetters move things on social media."

"I've tried that approach," Bryce said. "I made appointments during my downtime in New York City. I couldn't get any takers. I'd try locally, but nobody in Seattle has a big enough national profile."

Jamie paced to the kitchen corner and then turned. "Give me your elevator pitch again?"

"Perfection," Bryce said. "Zero labor, no waste, consistency and perfection."

"Who likes perfection?" Jamie asked.

Everybody looked at each other, but nobody answered.

"High-end places," Ethan suggested.

"That's where I've been *trying*," Bryce said.

"This is getting us nowhere." Aaron frowned and dropped onto a sofa.

"Nationally," Jamie said.

I could tell by his quirk of a smile that he'd thought of something.

He kept talking. "Our focus is too narrow. What about international? Who likes perfection? The French? Food is a really big deal in Paris."

"The French are all about taste," Bryce said. "They cater to sophisticated palates. The look isn't so important."

"Italy?" Jamie asked. "Asia?"

"I see what you're thinking," Bryce said. Then he gave a chopped laugh. "Japan."

"That's good," Jamie said.

"Japan?" Aaron mocked. "Your solution is to try doing business in Japan?"

"They're technology leaders themselves," Ethan said, though he looked skeptical.

"Has a Japanese company come out with a comparable product?" Jamie asked.

Ethan looked uncomfortable. "I don't know."

"Well, find out," Jamie said. "If New York doesn't want to be a trendsetter, maybe Tokyo does."

"I don't have a single contact in Japan." Sophie looked like she was close to tears.

"I have a few," Jamie said.

I couldn't help but look at him in surprise again, and maybe in awe, and maybe with an even bigger crush than I'd had ten minutes ago.

Was there anything he couldn't do?

Jamie had his phone out and was pressing buttons. "Ethan,

you need to get a prototype packed and ready to ship with us. Bryce, keep working on individual restaurants. They may end up being our only hope. Try LA next. They must have trend-setters in LA. Sophie?"

Sophie glanced at him. "Yes?"

"Want to go to New York with me?"

"Me?" she asked, looking surprised, beautiful and sur-prised.

I was surprised, too. Not that I didn't trust Sophie's busi-ness acumen. I did. But Bryce was the chef and Ethan was the tech specialist.

"Rina Nanami is in New York City right now. The Nanami family is a client, and they own a chain of high-end restaurants in Japan. Our best bet is for her to meet one of the owners in person. It has to be Sophie because Rina will like that she's a woman entrepreneur. That's our ticket in through the door."

I fought a lump in my throat.

I was glad that Jamie had an idea. I was excited for Sophie and for everyone.

And I wouldn't be jealous of Sophie going to New York with Jamie. I got that she was the business owner and not me. Be-sides, Sophie wasn't interested in Jamie. She was with Bryce.

And, anyway, Jamie and I were just friends. I didn't have the right to be jealous of him with anyone.

But I wanted it to be me in New York, me with Jamie, me on a cross-country flight in his company.

He looked at me then.

I could tell what he was thinking. At least, I hoped I could tell what he was thinking. What I wanted him to be thinking was that he'd miss me. Better still, I wanted him to be think-ing he'd stay here tonight, that he'd wait until everyone else left and then he and I could have benefits again.

I wanted him to spend the night this time. I wanted to watch the dawn break in his arms, share coffee in my little rooftop garden, laugh together over toast or eggs or blueberry bagels.

I wanted Jamie to myself.

I didn't want him to fly off with Sophie.

The countdown on our relationship felt like it was ticking louder than ever.

"It'll be a whirlwind trip," he said to me. "I'm…" After a second, he clamped his jaw, seeming to become aware that all gazes were on him.

"Good luck," I said in the brightest voice I could muster.

"I want to be there by morning," he said. "It'll give us the best chance of catching Rina."

He was talking to everyone, but his gaze was still on me.

I thought he was apologizing. At least, I hoped he was apologizing. I wanted him to be as disappointed about tonight as I was. But I couldn't be sure that was happening. It was impossible to know.

It was bad enough to be jealous of Sophie.

I'd spent two days being jealous of Sophie.

But as I walked into the O'Neil Nybecker offices, I had a whole new reason to be jealous.

I'd felt good leaving home to drive over here. Jamie was back, and he'd asked me to meet him at the office. I assumed we were going out for dinner, maybe we'd do a little downtown shopping, or maybe we'd look at houses again. Whatever it was, I'd like being back on track.

As long as we ended up back at my place later on, or maybe his place this time. Friends with benefits was way more fun when you found time for the benefits.

I'd put on a pale blue crepe dress with a flowing gray speckled sweater over top. Both hung to midthigh, leaving a length of bare leg to show off my shimmery, dusty-blue ankle boots. They weren't perfect for walking, but they were better than spike-heeled sandals or pumps. I'd topped the dress off with a chunky bright blue necklace.

I'd felt chic and funky, quite pretty, really. That is, until I spotted Sophie laughing next to Jamie in a royal blue cocktail dress. It was fitted and sleek, with a straight neckline and wide shoulder straps. Sophie looked ready for a night on the town.

Worse, on the other side of Jamie was a lovely, petite Japanese woman. She wore a short, jewel-encrusted jacket over a pleated white skirt. Her dark hair was swooped up, and her jewels looked like real diamonds. She had her hand on Jamie's arm, and he was whispering something in her ear.

They looked fantastic together, a power couple out to conquer the world.

I tried to capture the feeling I'd had when I gazed in the mirror earlier. But it was gone. The sweater that had seemed so fashion forward then felt dowdy now.

"Natasha." It was Aaron who spotted me first. "Did you hear the good news?"

I hadn't heard any news. Although Jamie had definitely sounded upbeat when he'd called and asked me to meet him at the office.

"What's going on?" I asked Aaron.

"We're about to pop the champagne."

"For?" I prompted.

"The contract, of course."

"Of course," I said.

"And all the rest," he said with a grin.

Sophie spotted me then and rushed forward. "Nat. There you are!"

I was grateful for her enthusiastic greeting, but I couldn't help wanting Jamie to notice me, too. So far he was still absorbed in conversation with the pretty woman who still had her hand on his arm.

"Isn't it fantastic?" Sophie asked.

"I don't know what's going on," I told her.

"We got a deal. Rina Nanami, well, her family, the Nanami Corporation, have put in an order for Sweet Tech. A *big* order for their restaurant equipment distribution company in Tokyo. They have customers all over Asia, their own restaurants and a bunch of others. James is thrilled. He says Horatio is thrilled."

Aaron reappeared and handed Sophie and I each a flute of champagne.

I was a little surprised that O'Neil Nybecker would pull out the stops like this to celebrate the sale. I mean, it was fantastic for Sophie and BRT Innovations. But it couldn't be that big of a deal to O'Neil Nybecker. I mean, in the greater scheme of things.

Just then, an older man appeared from a corner office. He was quickly handed a glass of champagne, and the attention all turned to him.

"That's Horatio," Sophie whispered to me.

When I compared him to Aaron, I could see the family resemblance.

Everyone went quiet.

"Thank you all for helping us to celebrate today," he said to the assembled crowd.

I glanced around at executives of all ages in suits, skirt suits and classic dresses.

"To O'Neil Nybecker's newly expanded relationship with Nanami Corporation. Thank you to James Gillen and Rina Nanami for getting the ball rolling. We look forward to our firms' future together in technology and beyond. Ms. Nanami, please extend my sincerest thank-you to your grandfather. We look forward to visiting Tokyo soon."

Horatio held up his glass.

Everyone followed suit and took a drink.

It took me a second to remember to take a sip.

Clearly, there was more going on here than a contract for Sweet Tech.

"Good trip?" I asked Sophie. My tone sounded darker than I'd intended.

She gave me an odd look. "Fantastic, of course."

Jamie still hadn't looked at me. Rina Nanami had all of his attention. I was wishing I'd stayed home.

"I take it James did more than the Sweet Tech contract?"

"Is something wrong?" Sophie asked.

"No. Why would anything be wrong?"

"You tell me. Are you jealous?"

I almost spilled my champagne. I couldn't believe Sophie had pegged me so fast. What had I said? How had I given away my feelings? This was mortifying.

"I'm not a millionaire yet or anything," Sophie said. There was a teasing tone to her voice. "It was a good sale, but you and I are still friends." She gave me a nudge on the arm. "And, anyway, I'll still hang out with you when I'm filthy rich."

I managed a smile. It was a smile of relief. My secret was still safe.

"I'm not jealous," I told her. "And I don't want to be filthy rich."

"I'll take us on a cruise," she said. "You and me in the South Pacific, hanging out on the beach, barefoot waiters bringing us blender drinks."

"You just used up all your vacation." I ordered myself not to look at Jamie.

"After we make the first million, I'm quitting my job."

I managed a chuckle at that. "What about Bryce? Won't he want to go on a cruise with you?"

She waved a dismissive hand. "Oh, that's not going anywhere."

"What? I thought it was a thing. He seems really nice." I couldn't help it. My thoughts went to Jamie again. Was it Sophie I needed to worry about and not Rina Nanami?

I hated myself for thinking that way.

"We decided not to mix business and a relationship," Sophie said.

"You didn't meet someone else?" I hated to ask, but I didn't want to have to wonder. Wondering would be painful.

The alternative was asking Jamie. And I didn't think I could bring myself to do that.

"*When* would I have met someone else?" she asked.

"Oh. Okay." I felt worse. No, I felt better. No, I felt stupidly selfish and suspicious. "Are you okay about it?" Remembering I was her best friend, I checked her expression for signs of heartbreak.

"I'm fine. It was a mutual decision."

"How mutual?" Like me, Sophie had bemoaned her single status after Layla and Brooklyn each got married.

"*Very* mutual. I'll be more than happy to go on a girlfriend cruise. I won't mope around."

My gaze moved to Jamie. I was afraid I might mope around without him.

He caught my eye then, and he smiled. A big, not-a-care-in-the-world smile as if he hadn't been standing there flirting with Rina Nanami and ignoring me for the past fifteen minutes.

He said something to her, maybe excusing himself, maybe telling her he'd be right back, maybe setting a time to meet up with her later…at his place…for wild and crazy sex in his king-size bed.

I knew my imagination was out of control. And I knew I was being stupid, stupid, stupid about my friend with benefits. My job was to help him become attractive to women. If the past few minutes were anything to go by, I could check that one as a success.

But I couldn't help but wonder what had happened between them in New York. They'd been together there for two whole days and seemed to have made the business deal of the year. Clearly, they respected each other. Maybe they admired each other. Obviously they liked each other, quite a lot I had to imagine.

You didn't make the business deal of the year with someone unless you liked them a lot. And Rina Nanami seemed perfect for the new Jamie. She was worldly, successful, sophisticated, exciting. Men definitely pointed at her from across the room. They'd be jealous of Jamie if she was by his side.

They might have had a whirlwind romance in New York. Maybe there'd be no more benefits for me. Maybe Jamie was now taken.

I knew I could ask Sophie if something had happened between Jamie and Rina, but I'd give myself away for sure if I started quizzing her on that.

"Hi, Tasha," he said.

He didn't hug me. He didn't kiss me. He didn't even shake my hand.

I didn't like that.

"Did Sophie tell you we're all going to dinner?"

"All of us?" I asked.

Jamie paused for a second. "Yes. All of us. It's a celebration."

"Great," I said, forcing a note of cheer into my voice. "That's great."

Sophie motioned to Bryce and Ethan.

What? Jamie mouthed to me.

"Nice trip?" I asked him.

I tried to stop myself, but my gaze went to Rina Nanami. Jamie followed my gaze.

"Sophie told you?" he asked.

The bottom fell right out of my stomach. I was stunned for a moment. I wanted to ask him why he'd bothered inviting me here. Did he want to show off Rina Nanami? Was she proof that our little experiment worked, that our little game together was over?

"I didn't think she'd do that," he said.

"No reason not to," I said.

Sophie didn't know I was falling for Jamie. Heck, Jamie didn't know I was falling for Jamie. I was completely alone here in my heartbreak.

"It's really my news," he said.

"Okay." I waited for him to give it to me with both barrels. I told myself I'd take it well. I'd congratulate him and make an excuse to go home. Maybe I had a headache. I did have a headache. At least, I was developing a headache. I'd have one soon, I could tell.

"Head office is a huge step," he said. "Guys wait decades for an offer like the one they gave me."

I blinked at him.

I might have also cocked my head sideways in confusion.

I dropped my mouth open, hoping for logical words to come out. Nothing did.

Eleven

I sat next to Sophie at dinner.

It was an oversize round table that made it feel like we were slightly too far apart. Aaron was on the other side of Sophie, then Bryce, Jamie, Rina around to Ethan next to me.

Sophie leaned close, keeping her voice low. "Tell me again why Brooklyn didn't marry James."

The question made me look at Jamie. Looking at Jamie made me want him.

After hearing Jamie's big news was a promotion to the head office in LA, I wasn't as jealous of Rina. But it was still clear she liked him. She liked him a lot. As did both waitresses, and I thought the hostess might try to give him her number before we left.

"She met Colton," I said to Sophie, my voice equally low. "She fell in love with Colton."

"I suppose," Sophie said. "But why she'd go looking, I'll never understand."

I didn't want to be jealous of Sophie again. I hated that feeling.

I told myself admiring Jamie was a long way from making a serious play for him. I didn't think Sophie would do that, not given his history with Brooklyn.

I shouldn't be doing it, either.

I wasn't doing it. Not really.

I was just mooning over him, wishing I could sleep with him again and trying to keep my feelings under control. That wasn't the same as making a serious play for him.

"I don't know why she did, either," I said to Sophie.

It wasn't the first time I'd wondered about Brooklyn's decision.

If I was with Jamie, really with Jamie, not a friend, not a coconspirator on a life-improvement quest, but with him like Brooklyn had been with him, I'd never look at another man.

"Do you think he dates?" Sophie said.

I was pretty sure he didn't. At least, he'd never said anything about dates he'd had since Brooklyn. I knew he'd like to date. That was the whole point of everything we'd been doing.

I wished right then I could tell Sophie about me and Jamie. I wanted to share my confusion and fear, and the thrill I'd felt sleeping with him. Those were the kinds of things best friends shared.

"I expect he wants to move on," I said to her instead.

"I'd date him," she said.

My fork dropped from my hand.

"I mean," she continued, "if he asked, and if there was a spark, if I could stop thinking of him as a brother." She heaved a sigh. "Man, I wish I could stop thinking about him as a brother."

Relief washed over me. At least I didn't have to worry about Sophie.

I picked up my fork.

"Why do you suppose you feel that way?" I was curious. Especially since it turned out I didn't think of Jamie as a brother at all.

"I've known him since I was four, I suppose. And he's kind of always been there in the background, helping us build that playhouse, driving us to the movies, moving our stuff into the college dorms. You know, brother stuff."

I also thought it was all-around great guy stuff. But I wasn't about to start waxing poetic about him.

I caught his gaze across the table. But it only lasted for a split second. Rina was talking, and his attention went back to her.

"Does she seem like his type?" I asked Sophie.

"She's pretty," Sophie said.

"Brooklyn's pretty, too."

Both Rina and Brooklyn were ultrafeminine. I couldn't help wondering how my athletic rock climbing and practical apartment renovation pursuits came across to him. Did he think of me as feminine, or maybe sturdy…sturdy and plain? It occurred to me that, when all was said and done, Tasha might not be all that far from Nat.

"He's a great-looking guy. Great-looking guys date pretty women."

I wanted to change the subject now. "Bryce is a good-looking guy," I said in a low tone.

"Are you interested in Bryce?"

Sophie's response took me aback. I hadn't been thinking that at all. Bryce seemed nice. He seemed fine. He seemed, well, brotherly really when I thought about it. I had no romantic interest in Bryce whatsoever.

"That wasn't what I meant," I said.

"Well, you didn't warm up to Ethan."

"Are you saying I'm picky?"

Sophie grinned. "Very picky. But in a good way. You should be picky. You're wonderful."

I wished I felt wonderful. But this wasn't a wonderful-feeling kind of evening.

Jamie laughed at something Rina said. On her other side, Ethan laughed, too.

"I'm going to the ladies' room," I said to Sophie.

I felt like I needed to stretch my legs and breathe for a minute.

"Do you want dessert?" Sophie asked. "Should I order you something if the waitress asks?"

"Sure," I said. "Pick something decadent."

I'd seen a few desserts go by, destined for other tables, and they looked fantastic. I wasn't above consoling myself with sugar.

I left the table and retreated to the elegant quiet of the ladies' room. In the powder area I took my time, washing my hands, combing my hair, taking my sweater off for a minute to see if I liked the look better in just the dress. It was different, but I wouldn't say better. I should have gone with a more fitted dress, and maybe jazzier earrings. Strappy sandals wouldn't have been the worst idea, either.

When I'd dressed, I'd thought we might be going house shopping for Jamie. I'd thought I might be walking a lot. I didn't want to walk through houses in spike heels. But I could have done spike heels across a restaurant, easy.

When I decided I couldn't put it off any longer, I left the powder room, coming into the hallway back to the dining room.

Jamie suddenly appeared.

He grasped my hand and pulled me against him, stepping back into a small alcove.

He kissed me there. It was a deep, long, tender kiss that had my entire body sighing with joy.

His arms went around me, and mine went around him. I molded myself to the breadth of his chest and his sturdy thighs.

He cradled my hair and tucked my face into the crook of his shoulder.

"This isn't what I wanted," he said.

I really hoped he didn't mean the kiss.

He kept talking. "Nanami is a huge, huge account."

"I got that." I had.

There was nothing Jamie could have done to get out of this dinner. And he shouldn't have done anything. He'd made huge strides for Sweet Tech and for O'Neil Nybecker. He'd done everything right.

I felt a little guilty for sulking.

He kissed me again, and I felt nothing but wonderful.

But then we heard voices and footsteps.

We broke apart. We weren't alone in the hallway anymore.

I went one way, back to the table. And Jamie went the other toward the men's room.

"You okay?" Sophie asked as I sat back down.

"Fine," I said, assuming she was worried about how long I'd been gone.

"You look flushed."

I felt flushed. "It's a bit hot in here. Plus the glass of wine. You know."

She was still peering closely at my face.

"Did you order dessert?" I asked to change the subject.

"Raspberry chocolate mousse."

"Sounds perfect."

I watched Jamie sit back down.

The waiter put a beautifully decorated plate in front of me. But I knew the mousse wouldn't be anywhere near as sweet as Jamie's kiss.

I wished I could have left the restaurant with Jamie. But I had my car, and he had his. It made the most sense for me to drop off Sophie and Ethan. And Jamie was acting as host for Rina.

I told myself not to be jealous. Jamie's kiss in the hallway had gone a long way to making me feel desirable. It was a fantastic kiss. It showed me how much I'd missed him.

If I wanted to worry about something, I should worry about that.

He wasn't mine to miss, but my heart had started pretending he was.

I'd have to watch that. I'd have to watch it very closely. Maybe not Rina, but someday, likely someday soon, Jamie was going to meet Brooklyn's replacement, and I was going to be collateral damage when that happened.

It was good that I'd come home alone.

Good, I told myself as I came to the top of the staircase in my building. So good. "Really frickin' good," I muttered.

Something moved in the shadows of the hall.

I froze.

"I hope I wasn't too presumptuous," Jamie said, stepping into view from my doorway.

My heart nearly thumped from my chest. "You scared me half to death."

"Sorry," he said.

My fear was turning to joy, but my feet stayed plastered to the floor.

He moved toward me. "I needed to see you. It was driving me crazy, you sitting there, us not being able to talk about anything."

"It did feel like an awfully huge secret," I said.

Concern flashed across his face. "It's nobody's business."

"I know." I agreed with that. At least, conceptually, I agreed with that. But Sophie was a pretty close friend.

He framed my face with his hands. "We don't owe anyone an explanation."

"I know," I said again.

His smile was tender. "Tasha doesn't explain."

I reached for my Tasha-ness. "Tasha does whatever she wants."

He gave me a slow kiss that curled my toes.

He moved his lips half an inch from mine. "What does Tasha want to do?"

"You," I said with bald honesty.

I wrapped my arms around his neck and put my pent-up desire into a kiss.

"Oh, yeah," he whispered, wrapping me tight and propelling us to the door.

I fumbled for my key, struggling to slide it into the lock until Jamie's hand closed over mine to steady it.

"You okay?" he asked.

I nodded. "Fine."

"Nervous?"

The very last thing I felt was nervous—excited, energized, aroused. I felt all of those things.

"I'm not nervous," I said.

"Good."

The key slipped into the lock and the sound of the tumblers turning seemed to echo.

Jamie turned the knob and pushed the door open.

"I'm not nervous, either," he said as he closed it behind us.

I couldn't help but smile at that.

"What are you?" I asked.

"Happy."

"Me, too."

"I missed you," he said.

"So did I."

He smoothed back my hair and gazed into my eyes. "I missed this."

He kissed me tenderly.

A sigh coursed all the way through me.

He pushed the sweater from my shoulders and tossed it on a chair.

I did the same with his suit jacket.

"But not just this," he said between kisses. "I don't want you to think—"

"That it's all about sex?"

"It's not."

"I know. We've had sex exactly once."

"Twice," he said. "Did you forget?"

"I meant one night."

We'd definitely made love twice that night. The second had taken a long time, a really, really long and wonderful time.

"Okay," he said.

I pushed the buttons of his dress shirt through the holes, gradually revealing his bare chest.

He stood still and let me work.

I parted the two sides. I kissed his chest, tasting the salt of his skin.

He sucked in a breath.

"I really want to go slow this time," he said.

"Me, too." I pushed his shirt from his shoulders and let it drop to the floor.

"I'm not just saying that," he said.

"Neither am I."

I lifted the front of my dress and drew it over my head. I tossed it aside and stood in my bra and panties. They were a pretty set, translucent white lace with shiny silver details.

"Don't move," he said.

I stilled.

He took a step back, and his gaze traveled from my boots to my eyes.

"My work here is most definitely done," he whispered.

Judging by the glow in his eyes, he didn't mean the sex was over, so I smiled.

He moved in and smoothed back my hair. "You are hands down the first and only woman who men will point at from across the room."

"If I'm dressed like this, they probably will."

"If you're dressed like anything."

"I think your judgment is clouded right now."

I was thrilled Jamie was so sexually attracted to me. I was absolutely attracted to him.

"Take off your pants," I said to him.

"Demanding."

"If you get to check me out, I want equal time."

"Yes, ma'am," he said.

He kicked off his shoes and stripped out of his pants and socks. He was down to his black boxers.

I pretended to consider him for a moment.

"And?" he prompted.

"I'd point," I said.

"Good to know."

"Other women would point, too."

"I think I need to flash a fancy car and a big credit card to guarantee their interest."

"Oh, no, you don't."

I came close enough to trail my fingers down his chest. "You've got pecs and a six-pack."

"Lots of guys have that."

I came closer still, setting my hands on his shoulders. "And really broad shoulders with that confident stance."

"I have been practicing."

I touched his chin, moving it to one side and then the other.

"Why do I feel like livestock at an auction?"

"Strong, square chin," I said. "You can't buy that."

"With the right plastic surgeon, you can."

"Not like yours. And your eyes…" I felt myself falling into their depths.

"What about my eyes?"

"*Best* blue eyes ever. They show off your intelligence, and they glow when you smile or when you make a joke. Women like a sense of humor."

I meant all of it. I meant everything I was saying, and the power of my emotions scared me.

"My lips?" he asked on a whisper.

I set aside my fear. "Kissable."

"That's exactly what I was going for." He kissed me.

He pulled me close.

Our bodies meshed together, every bulge met with a corresponding hollow. We fit. We fit so perfectly.

His hands roamed my body, arousing every inch, igniting passion along every trail they took. He peeled off my bra and cupped my breasts, sending tiny shock waves through my core, making my limbs twitch in anticipation.

He stripped off my panties and then his boxers.

He lifted me to perch on the back of the sofa, easing between my thighs.

"Condom," I said.

"Got it."

I hugged him close, surrounded him, absorbed his kisses, took his caresses and gave back with my own.

Our bodies were slick as we moved together.

I was hot. His skin was hotter.

His scent surrounded me. His kisses enveloped me. His caresses made me gasp with pent-up desire and burning anticipation.

"Now," I finally groaned, completely out of patience.

"Slow," he said, but his hand kneaded hard on my lower back.

"Too slow."

"Okay." He shifted me. He moved. He eased inside.

I felt the world stop. Every molecule of me was focused on him.

He pressed deep, and I spiraled upward. Again and again and again, until I lost track of time and space.

I kissed him over and over. I clung to his shoulders, ran my hands down his back, pulled him against me and into me, climbing to the top and then finding more.

When I hit the edge and fell, I called out his name.

"Tasha," he groaned. "Tasha, Tasha, Tasha."

I was limp, and he carried me to my bed, flipping back the covers and climbing inside.

We made love again. Slower this time, more sweetly, less passionately, a soft and satisfying echo.

Later, when I felt Jamie move, I realized I'd fallen asleep in his arms.

I opened my eyes to see dawn barely filtering into the sky beyond the window.

His body was warm, wrapped around mine from behind. He put a featherlight kiss on the back of my neck.

"Again?" I muttered.

That would make three.

"I wish," he said, a low chuckle in his voice.

I shifted, settling to a more comfortable position.

"Maybe," he said with a teasing lilt.

"Optimist."

He was quiet for a moment, his breath caressing the hairline at the back of my neck.

I savored the feeling, clung to the moment. I wanted to stop time and never leave this place.

"You should come with me," he said, his voice a low rumble.

My first thought was no. I didn't want either of us to move, ever, not even an inch.

"Where are you going?" I asked after a minute.

He rose onto his elbow and rolled me so he could look at my face. "Los Angeles, remember?"

I did.

He'd been offered a job in O'Neil Nybecker's head office. Their head office was in Los Angeles. I knew that. It just hadn't been foremost in my mind.

Right now, I thought he'd meant breakfast. But he didn't. Jamie was leaving Seattle.

"Come," he said, an eager light in his eyes.

The single-word invitation swirled through my brain, hitting synapses, gathering data, analyzing and comparing to known information, seeking meaning.

I was afraid to hope. But my blooming heart colored my thoughts.

Was he saying…?

Could he possibly be suggesting…?

Did I dare hope he was asking for something more than friendship, something romantic? Was it possible that of all the adoring women in the world, Jamie might be interested in me?

My head was nodding before I thought it all through.

His grin went wide. "Great. We can carry right on with the house hunting."

I hesitated. Wait. What?

"I want a wild and exciting Tasha-and-Jamie type house."

A house? He wanted me to help him find real estate? Like any good friend would do? I would have laughed if it didn't hurt so much.

"You up for that?" he asked.

"Sure," I said, trying desperately to match his smile. Then I eased away from him.

His arm went quickly around my stomach. "Where are you going?"

"It's almost morning." Cuddling with my friend-with-benefits had suddenly lost its appeal.

"What time do you usually get up?"

"It takes me a while to shower," I said.

He kissed me again.

I kissed him back, and it felt good. But it was a bittersweet good. Last night we'd reached the pinnacle, and there was nowhere to go but down.

I didn't want to give up our friendship. But I knew it would never be the same.

And that was my fault.

It was all my fault.

Jamie had stuck to the rules of the game. I was the one who had broken them.

On the plane to Los Angeles, Jamie showed me our latest stock portfolio numbers.

I was surprised to find we were flying first-class. Not that I didn't like it. I liked it a lot. But it seemed like an extravagant waste of money.

So he'd pulled out his phone.

I'd stared at the numbers, thinking there had to be a mistake.

He'd laughed at my astonishment. Then he'd teased me about having too little faith in Jamie's instincts for trading.

Then he'd given me a half hug and told me he'd booked a five-star hotel.

So here we were at the Chatham-Brix Downtown, checked into a suite with a sweeping view of the city.

I had mixed feelings about sleeping with Jamie again.

Oh, I wanted to sleep with Jamie again. No matter what else was going on in our relationship, the sex was off the charts. And I hadn't had a lot of off-the-charts sex in my life. I'd really never had much at all.

I'd certainly never had any that came close to Jamie.

But the friends thing was hard. I was lying now when I called us friends. My feelings for him had gone way beyond friendship. And when the sex stopped, when everything stopped, as it would as soon as he moved to LA, it was going to hurt so much.

I'd done heartbreak once, and I had no desire to do it again.

I told myself Tasha could handle it better than Nat. But myself didn't really believe it. It was going to be even worse this time because what I'd felt for Henry was nothing, nothing compared to what I felt for Jamie.

"Marnie arranged all three viewings for this afternoon," Jamie said, coming in from the wraparound balcony. "Traffic looks busy, so we better get going."

I knew the houses we were going to see. I'd helped Jamie pick them out on the real estate website before we'd left Seattle. They were all in Santa Monica. One was even on the beach.

We ended up going to the beach home first. It was a sleek modern condo on the ground floor with a patio walkway to the lush green lawn across the road from a sandy beach. It had a lot of white walls, glass features and stark marble countertops, both in the kitchen and bathrooms.

The master bedroom had a gas fireplace, which I loved. And the patio had a fun wraparound sofa and gas fire pit. I could see it would be cozy on cool evenings. But the neighbors were pretty close, as was the traffic noise.

When we saw the second house, I thought I understood the real estate agent Marnie's strategy. Away from the beach, you could get a whole lot more for your money.

The second house was bigger. It was private, with a big yard and hedges that screened the neighbors. There was a pool and patio out back, and beautiful landscaping in the front. It was also on a quiet street.

It had a white interior with lots of archways and some wrought-iron features. The floors were beautiful hardwood with scattered area rugs. Paned doors and windows into the backyard let in enormous amounts of light. And the kitchen was a dream, tons of counter space, cupboard space, and glass-fronted feature cabinets. An octagonal breakfast nook stuck out into the backyard. I could picture Jamie having coffee there in the morning.

The master bedroom was roomy and beautiful. But I couldn't bring myself to linger there. While I could picture myself in the bed with Jamie in the hotel room, here in what might be his new house, I could only picture faceless, nameless other women in his arms.

I pretended to check out the guest bedroom.

Marnie had assumed we were a couple, and Jamie hadn't corrected her. It made it worse when she talked like I'd be cooking in the kitchen or swimming in the pool, or showering in the en suite. But I tamped down my flailing emotions and played along. What else was I going to do?

The sun was setting by the time we made it to the last house. My first impression was of warm lights on the palm trees decorating the front yard. Around and above the front door were two stories of glass walls. The polished maple ceiling colored the glow from the entry hall.

The house was a roomy open concept. Walls were painted white, but the maple trim and maple flooring warmed the atmosphere. The kitchen had stainless appliances and gray speckled countertops. It opened to a big, furnished deck with a built-in fireplace, barbecue and kitchenette. You could see the ocean in the distance.

I could imagine entertaining here. I could see friends and family—Jamie's friends and family, of course—spilling out from the family room and kitchen, onto the deck on a warm summer night.

The master bedroom had a peaked maple beamed ceiling and its own private sundeck. I told myself not to linger in it, but my toes curled into the plush carpet, and I kind of fell in love with the steam shower and gloriously huge bathtub.

"What do you think?" Jamie asked, coming up behind me.

"There's a lot to like," I said.

"Values in this neighborhood have steadily climbed for the past three years," Marnie said. "There's no end in sight."

"What do you like?" Jamie asked me.

"What do *you* like?" I said instead.

He glanced around. "It's the new me."

I told myself Jamie deserved this.

Whatever came his way next, he wasn't the James who'd been left at the altar. He was confident and decisive, great looking and a very exciting man. He had a new job, soon a new house, all his new clothes and hobbies. I was sure they had rock climbing in California.

The world was his to enjoy.

I had to be happy for him.

"I think you'll love entertaining on the deck," I said.

"Do *you* love the deck?"

"I do," I said. "And the yard. There's room out there to garden and to lounge. And you can't beat that en suite." I gestured to the attached bathroom.

"Is it a buy?" he asked.

"It's pretty expensive." It was also really big for one person.

"That's the beauty of short-term trading," he said. "What was unaffordable two months ago is now completely within range."

"I have you to thank for that." I was thinking I really would go condo shopping back in Seattle. It would give me something to focus on for the next few months.

I was going to get through this.

I knew I was going to get through this.

I'd refuse to do anything else.

"We'll take it," Jamie said to Marnie.

She looked shocked, but she recovered quickly. "I can help you write up the offer. Did you have a price in mind?"

Jamie looked at me. "Should we start low?"

"Do you want to dicker?" I wasn't a fan of the negotiating process.

Maybe Tasha would like to bargain. I didn't really know. It was getting hard to tell what the Tasha me would want versus the Nat me.

"Not really," Jamie said.

"If you go twenty-five thousand below asking, I can pretty much guarantee they'll accept."

Jamie looked at me.

I shrugged my shoulders. The game was over. It was his decision, his money, his life.

"Done," he said to Marnie. "Write it up."

"Subject to financing?" she asked.

He smiled and shook his head. "No need. I'm sure I can arrange the financing."

Marnie beamed. "Then congratulations. I'm guessing you want an early closing date."

Jamie squeezed my hand. "The earlier the better. They want me to start in the LA office on Monday."

I forced myself to smile, to keep up the facade for Marnie's sake.

I wanted to cling to Jamie and never let go. At the same time, I wanted to get the heck out of LA and never look back. I knew in that second that I couldn't stay the night. I couldn't make love to Jamie one last time in that opulent hotel suite. It would kill me.

"I'll get started." Marnie dialed a number as she left the bedroom.

"This is terrific," Jamie said to me.

I pretended my phone buzzed and pulled it from my purse. "I should take this," I said.

"Sophie?" he asked.

I nodded. I don't know why I thought a silent lie was better than a verbal lie, but I did.

I moved a couple of paces away. "Hi," I said into the phone.

I waited a minute, feeling terribly, utterly awful about what I was doing.

I scrambled for a viable reason to leave.

"She did?" I said into the phone. "Uh, okay." I looked at Jamie to find him watching me. "I can. If you think so."

"What?" he mouthed.

I held up one finger, trying to stall as I solidified my plan. It was shameless. It was probably unforgivable. But I didn't have a better idea, and I was running out of time.

"As soon as I can," I said into the phone. "Bye."

"What?" Jamie asked.

"It's Brooklyn," I said. "I don't know what's going on, but Sophie wants me to come back to Seattle."

Jamie clamped his jaw.

I knew he wouldn't ask about Brooklyn. It was the one thing he'd stay miles away from.

"I'm sorry," I said.

"Don't go."

"I have to." I wanted to cry. I wanted to collapse into a puddle of guilt. But mostly, I wanted to throw myself into his arms for as long as he'd have me.

We could hear Marnie's muted voice outside the room.

"You don't need me for this part," I said.

He opened his mouth, but I kept on talking.

"I'll book a flight in the cab."

"You're going *now*? Right now?"

"I'm sorry," I said again.

"How soon can you come back?"

"I don't know."

"You'll come back as soon as you can."

I nodded, another silent lie. I'd come up with more excuses later if Jamie pushed it.

He might not push it. He probably wouldn't push it. He'd get settled here in this great new house, with his great new job, and a great new girlfriend within a week or a month, surely not longer than that.

He'd have the life he'd wanted, just like we'd planned.

"My assistant has started on the paperwork," Marnie said brightly as she came back into the master bedroom. "We can swing by the office and sign, and I'll present the offer tonight."

"Good luck," I said to Jamie. I was already calling a cab.

Twelve

Five days, thirty texts and seven missed phone calls later, I decided I had to bring Sophie in on my deception. Jamie was more persistent than I'd expected, and I was afraid he might reach out to Sophie. If he did, he'd discover my lie.

I didn't want him to know I'd lied. For some reason, that was important to me.

I poured Sophie and me each a glass of merlot.

"We got another big order today," Sophie was saying.

She'd kicked off her shoes and curled up on one end of my sofa.

"Congratulations." I thought about recorking the bottle, but I had a feeling we'd finish it off before the evening was done.

"Japan was for sure the place to go. Cash is starting to flow in, and we've gone into actual production. Ethan's looking at expanding the facility to the space next door."

"I'm so glad it's working out." I really was.

Sophie's success was a bright spot in my dismal-feeling life.

"I'm not ready to quit The Blue Fern yet. Neither is Bryce. But we're talking about approaching the general manager with a proposal to job share. We'd each work half-time, and hire another person to take up the slack. That way, we don't need to take a full salary from BRT, but we'll have more time to devote to building up the company."

"That sounds like a good idea." I wished I could focus on Sophie's company, but I was painfully distracted.

I handed her one of the glasses and took the other end of the sofa.

My shoes were already off, and I turned sideways to face her, leaning my back against the arm.

"What about you?" she asked.

"What about me?" I told myself to take the opening and plunge right in, but I didn't know how to start.

"What's going on?" She took a sip. "Oooh. That's good."

"It's not too expensive," I said, taking a drink myself.

Inwardly I was kicking myself for being a coward. I had to speak up already.

"I did something," I said.

Sophie's brows went up, and she stilled. "Do tell."

"I lied."

She looked surprised by that. "To me?"

"No. Not *to* you. But it was about you."

"What did you say? Something good, I hope. Did you tell some guy I was really smart and rich and hot?"

I knew I shouldn't smile, but I did. "No."

"Too bad. I could have faked that, at least for a little while."

"You are smart and hot."

She coughed out a laugh. "Maybe a little smart. And maybe a little hot. I'm sure not rich."

"Not yet."

"No, not yet. But back to your lie…"

"Right." I'd been framing up my words for the better part of a day. I didn't know why I was trying to rephrase them on the fly right now. "I lied to Jamie about you calling me to say Brooklyn had a problem."

"Who's Jamie?"

"James. I mean James."

Sophie looked completely baffled. "What are you talking about?"

I took another drink. "I've been seeing James." Okay, that had come out all wrong. "I mean, not seeing him, as in seeing him. Just, well, with Brooklyn leaving him, and Henry leaving me, we kinda got to talking one day, and we've done a few things together."

"What kind of things?"

"Rock climbing, for one."

"You?"

"Yes."

"And James."

"Yes."

"*Rock* climbing?"

"We did. We took lessons and everything."

"Why didn't you tell me? How is that a secret? Was it illegal rocks? Were you trespassing? Did you steal something from… I don't know… Olympic National Park? A treasure or something?"

"We didn't steal anything."

"Well, that's a relief."

I knew I had to get to the point. "While we were in California, I—"

"You and James went to California?"

"Last weekend."

"Okaaay…" She drew out the word. "Did you, like, climb some California rocks?"

"No. He has that new job. We were house hunting."

Sophie sat back. She took a drink of her wine. "You do know you're not making any sense at all."

"I know."

"Tell me more about the lie."

"In California, in LA, I pretended you phoned me. I pretended Brooklyn had a problem. I knew he wouldn't ask any questions about Brooklyn, so I thought I'd get away with it."

"Did you get caught?"

"No. Not yet."

"I don't know, Nat. You're acting like this is a big thing. It doesn't sound like a big thing to me. I'll lie for you if you want me to. I'll tell him anything you say."

I knew she would, and I loved her for it.

"But why did you lie? What did it get you?"

"Out of there."

"Out of LA."

"Yes."

"You needed an excuse to leave?"

"I…thought I did in the moment."

Sophie sat forward and stared at me straight in the eyes. "What happened?"

I shook my head. "Some things I can't tell."

I wasn't sure if Jamie wanted to keep our makeover plot a secret. It didn't seem like such a big deal if we told people at this point. But I didn't want to break my word without getting his permission.

"What things can you tell me?"

"Jamie and I became friends."

"Jamie? He's Jamie now?"

"It's a nickname."

A knowing light came on in Sophie's eyes. "Like Tasha is for you. What *have* you two been up to?"

"Nothing… I mean…" I couldn't look at her.

There was awe in her tone. "Holy cow."

I could feel my face heat up.

"You slept with James Gillen? Nat, you slept with Brooklyn's fiancé?"

"They weren't engaged anymore. And it was nothing. It was a friends thing, friends with benefits thing."

"You have benefits with James?"

"Only a couple of times."

"Is that what happened in California?"

"No. It didn't happen in California. It would have. If I hadn't left."

"And you didn't want it to."

I wasn't sure how to answer that question, so I moved on. "And now he keeps texting and calling."

"Hang on," Sophie said, holding up a finger. "It sounds like you're saying you *wanted* to have benefits in California. So why did you leave?"

An ache formed in my stomach. "I didn't mean to tell you all this."

"Of course you meant to tell me all this. You must have been dying to tell me all this. Why did you wait so long to tell me all this?"

"It was a secret. It was a thing. It was a secret thing."

"James wanted to have a secret affair with you?"

"It wasn't an affair. Neither of us is with anyone."

"You were kind of dating Ethan."

I gave her a look. "Please."

"Okay. I guess you weren't really dating Ethan."

"It wasn't romantic," I said.

To my embarrassment, my voice cracked.

Sophie's eyes filled with sympathy.

"Oh," she said. "You mean it wasn't supposed to be romantic."

I struggled to breathe. I was afraid to try to talk. The heartache I'd been suppressing was fighting to get out of my chest.

"But it got romantic."

A whisper was all I could manage. "Only for me."

I blinked against the threat of tears. I wasn't going to cry. I wasn't going to let this make me cry. That would be a whole other level of pain.

"Oh, Nat."

I shook my head, and I swallowed hard. "I'm fine. I just… I didn't want Jamie to ask you about the phone call and have him find out I made it all up."

"Yeah, because *that's* the biggest problem here."

"I'd be embarrassed," I said.

"He's the one who should be embarrassed. What was he thinking? Sleeping with you, swearing you to secrecy. What kind of a man does that?"

I realized I'd mischaracterized our relationship. I hadn't been fair to Jamie. This wasn't his fault. It was my fault for letting it get out of hand.

I should have pulled the plug earlier. I recognized the signs. I'd have to be an idiot not to recognize the signs that I was falling for him.

A knock came on the door.

I wasn't expecting anyone.

"Do Bryce and Ethan know you're here?" The last thing I wanted was to deal with anyone else right now.

"Maybe it's Brooklyn," Sophie joked.

I couldn't find the humor in it.

"Too soon?" she asked.

"I think it is."

"Tasha?" a voice called.

It was Jamie.

Sophie's mouth dropped open. Her voice dropped to a whisper. "I'm guessing nobody else calls you that?"

"Tasha, open up. I can hear you're in there."

I looked to Sophie for advice.

She cringed and shrugged at the same time.

"Tasha?" Jamie sounded frustrated. "This is ridiculous."

"She's coming," Sophie called out.

I shot her a look of astonishment.

"You can't hold him off forever."

I opened the door.

"*What* is going on?" Jamie asked.

"Sophie's—"

"You don't pick up the phone. You barely answer my texts. You said you were coming back. Why didn't you come back?" He barged into the apartment. "There were papers to sign."

He spotted Sophie.

"Hi, James," she said.

He clamped his jaw and glared at me.

"I can leave," Sophie said.

"No," I said.

I wasn't ready to be alone with Jamie. Okay, that was a lie. I was dying to be alone with Jamie. But that was a bad thing, a very bad thing.

Seeing him now, I wanted to grab him and hold on to him. I wanted to be wrapped in his arms…like…forever.

It was worse than I thought.

I was in love with Jamie.

"We need to talk," Jamie said to me.

I backed away from him. "She knows most of it anyway."

"What do you mean she knows most of it? What does she know?"

"*She's* right here," Sophie said. "Listening."

Jamie ignored her. "What does she know?"

"That we slept together."

"You told her that?"

"I pretty much guessed," Sophie said. "And why would you ask her to keep that a secret anyway?"

The question seemed to stump Jamie for a second. When he spoke, it was to me. "I didn't think you'd want to tell people. I don't care if anyone knows."

The conversation felt surreal. "Well… Sophie knows."

"Fine," he said. "Why didn't you come back? What did I do?"

I found the question more than absurd. "You moved to California."

He seemed puzzled. "Yeah…and I asked you to come with me. You said you would."

I almost laughed at that. "You asked me to help you *buy a house*."

"Uh-huh. A house. That we both loved. That we could live in. Together."

"Whoa," Sophie said. She came up on her knees and watched over the back of the sofa.

"You did not," I said to Jamie.

If he had…well… I would have… I didn't really know, but it would have been something different than what I had done.

Now my brain and my heart started fighting again, trying to work out what Jamie had meant, what Jamie meant now.

He took a few steps toward me. "Tasha, what did you think was happening between us?"

"Makeovers," I said. That much I knew for sure. "We wanted to attract the opposite sex."

"Really?" Sophie asked.

"We did attract the opposite sex," Jamie said. "We attracted each other."

I waved my hand. "You know what I mean. We were friends."

"With benefits," Sophie said.

We both looked at her.

"Should I go now?" she asked.

"Don't bother," Jamie said.

He took another step toward me. "I don't know how it went off the rails. I wish I'd said or done something different." He came closer. "I don't know how you feel about me, Tasha. But I have to think there's something there. I can't be in this all alone. It doesn't make sense. I'm wild about you, *wild* about *you*, intellectually, physically, romantically." He leaned in. "I want to be your best friend. I want to be your lover. And I want to do it all forever. Rock climb with me, dance with me, skydive with me, buy tuxes with me. It can be in LA. It can be here. It can be anywhere. I don't care about any of that." He took my hands. "I'm in love with you, Tasha."

"Swooning over here," Sophie said.

"Marry me," Jamie said.

My brain—which was already struggling to process his words—fogged completely over. "Huh?"

Jamie grinned at my baffled expression. "I think you have to give me a yes or no to that."

"Yes," Sophie said. "Say yes already."

Jamie cocked his head in Sophie's direction. "I like her. I always have."

"Yes," I said, barely believing it was happening. "I love you, Jamie. I love you so much."

He pulled me into a hug, and then a kiss, and then a deeper kiss.

"I'm out of here," Sophie said.

This time she didn't wait for either of us to answer.

Ours was going to be the simplest wedding in the history of weddings.

We both wanted it that way.

And we tried, we really did. But Sophie insisted Layla had to be there.

It was hard to argue that Jamie's sister shouldn't attend.

And if Layla was coming, Max had to be included. If Max

and Layla were going to be there, it seemed churlish not to invite Brooklyn and Colton. Especially since Jamie was adamant that he didn't hold anything against Brooklyn.

He told me if it hadn't been for Brooklyn breaking up with him, he never would have found me. And he realized now that what he'd felt for Brooklyn had been puppy love. He'd hung on to it for so many years, he didn't know how to let it go, even when they grew apart.

He also said if it hadn't been for me, he wouldn't have grown from James into Jamie.

I believed him. I felt the same way. I wasn't Nat anymore. I wasn't only Tasha either, but I had a lot of Tasha in me, and I loved it.

Our parents had to be included, of course. Mine had traveled up from Houston.

Jamie's parents spent the winters in Fort Lauderdale now, but they were happy to put off their travel plans for a wedding.

Me, I just wanted to be married to Jamie. I didn't much care where or how.

We found a rustic resort on Waddington Island, an hour's boat ride from Seattle. It had a chapel overlooking the ocean, a five-star dining room, and cottages for everyone to spend the night.

I wore a short white dress, with a lace overlay and a scalloped hem. The lace neckline was scooped and detailed, while the underdress was strapless. I wore a little diamond pendant that Layla had lent me. Jamie had once given it to her for her birthday. I matched it with diamond stud earrings.

I felt pretty. I didn't think I'd ever felt this pretty in my life.

My shoes were sleek, heeled pumps, white with blue soles. Something blue. I liked that, too.

When the music came up, Sophie started down the aisle in front of me. She wore a simple aqua dress that let her beauty shine through. She looked amazing, as she always did.

I saw Jamie at the front of the chapel. He wore the tuxedo we'd bought together.

I smiled, and he grinned back, gesturing to the suit.

Yeah, I'd take a guy with a perfectly cut, perfectly fitting, owned tuxedo any day of the week—especially this guy.

"Nice touch," I whispered to him when I got to the front.

He took my hand. "Not as nice as you."

"Brookswood Bridal Department."

"Seriously?"

"Where else would I shop?"

"Friends…" the preacher began.

I sobered and stopped talking.

We said our vows, promising love and laughter and adventure forever.

When we kissed and made our way down the aisle, I thought my heart would burst open with joy.

In the garden out front, Layla hugged Jamie. Then she pulled me to her.

"I can't believe it," she whispered. "I'm *so* happy to have you as a sister."

"I love Jamie very much," I told her.

"I know you do. And I can see how much he loves you. You're perfect for each other."

Brooklyn was next.

I hesitated in front of her. We hadn't spoken since she'd left Jamie at the altar.

"Congratulations," she said. It was clear she was as nervous as me. I thought of all the platitudes I could offer.

"This is so weird," I said instead.

Her expression relaxed. "Isn't it?"

"I don't know how it happened this way. But I'm so glad it did." I pulled her into a hug.

"I do love James," she said into my ear. "Just not in the right way."

"I love him in exactly the right way."

She hugged me tighter. "I'm so happy for both of you."

"Thanks for leaving him," I said.

We both laughed.

"Do you think he wants to talk to me?"

Her question was answered before I could say anything. Jamie was there beside us.

"Hello, Brooklyn."

She looked up at him and stepped back from me. "Hi."

"Thanks for coming," he said.

"Thanks for inviting us."

They both fell silent.

"I'm sorry," she said.

Jamie shook his head. "I'm not. You were braver than me. I'd have gone ahead and made a mistake for both of us."

Brooklyn looked startled.

"You were right to walk away." He paused. "Okay, maybe you could have done it a day or a week or a month before the wedding. But at least you did it." Jamie took my hand and drew me to his side. "And I'm the big winner."

"I'm so glad you feel that way," Brooklyn said.

I caught movement out of the corner of my eye as Colton approached.

I couldn't tell the twin brothers apart, but from the expression on his face, I was pretty sure this one was Colton, not Max.

He firmly stuck out his hand for Jamie. "Congratulations," he said.

"To you, too," Jamie said. "You have an amazing wife."

"I hear you lucked out, too." Colton looked to me.

Jamie wrapped an arm around me. "She's the best. I'm not sure I deserve her."

No one seemed to know where to take the conversation from there. I didn't want to leave it at this. Brooklyn was one of my best friends, and I was deliriously happy at how things had turned out.

"Thank you," I said to Colton. "I appreciate you stealing Brooklyn."

It was clear he had no idea how to react.

I let him hang for a second.

"I…uh…" He gamely stepped in. "It was my pleasure."

I looked around the circle. "We all agree it turned out right?"

Everyone enthusiastically nodded.

"Great. Then let's quit being so weird about it."

Jamie leaned in. "Way to go, Tasha."

"Tasha doesn't mess around."

"Yes," Brooklyn said with enthusiasm. "I'm through being weird."

"Okay by me," Jamie said.

He gave Brooklyn a hug.

They were both smiling when they pulled back.

Colton looked happy, too. He looked relieved and happy.

Other people came forward with their congratulations. We cut the cake, threw the bouquet and danced the night away under a full moon and the scattered stars.

Later, at our cottage on a point of land overlooking the rolling ocean, Jamie carried me across the threshold. An open window had the sea breeze flowing into the pretty room.

Jamie set me on my feet, his arm staying around my waist. He smoothed my windblown hair. "I love you, Tasha Gillen."

My heart was big and full in this perfect moment. I touched his face, stroking the rough whiskers that shadowed his chin. "I adore you, Jamie Gillen."

He smiled as he leaned in for a kiss. "I'd point at you across any old room."

* * * * *

COMING SOON!

We really hope you enjoyed reading this book. If you're looking for more romance, be sure to head to the shops when new books are available on

Thursday 6th March

To see which titles are coming soon, please visit
millsandboon.co.uk/nextmonth

MILLS & BOON

MILLS & BOON

MODERN

Power and Passion

Prepare to be swept off your feet by
sophisticated, sexy and seductive heroes, in
some of the world's most glamourous and
romantic locations, where power and
passion collide.

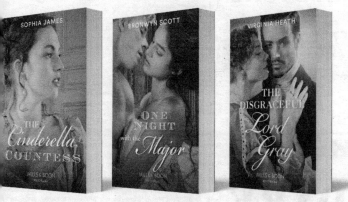

MILLS & BOON

THE HEART OF ROMANCE

A ROMANCE FOR EVERY KIND OF READER

MODERN

Prepare to be swept off your feet by sophisticated, sexy and seductive heroes, in some of the world's most glamourous and romantic locations, where power and passion collide.
8 stories per month.

HISTORICAL

Escape with historical heroes from time gone by. Whether your passion is for wicked Regency Rakes, muscled Vikings or rugged Highlanders, awaken the romance of the past.
6 stories per month.

MEDICAL

Set your pulse racing with dedicated, delectable doctors in the high-pressure world of medicine, where emotions run high and passion, comfort and love are the best medicine.
6 stories per month.

Celebrate true love with tender stories of heartfelt romance, from the rush of falling in love to the joy a new baby can bring, and a focus on the emotional heart of a relationship.
8 stories per month.

Indulge in secrets and scandal, intense drama and plenty of sizzling hot action with powerful and passionate heroes who have it all: wealth, status, good looks…everything but the right woman.
6 stories per month.

HEROES

Experience all the excitement of a gripping thriller, with an intense romance at its heart. Resourceful, true-to-life women and strong, fearless men face danger and desire - a killer combination!
8 stories per month.

DARE

Sensual love stories featuring smart, sassy heroines you'd want as a best friend, and compelling intense heroes who are worthy of them.
4 stories per month.

To see which titles are coming soon, please visit

millsandboon.co.uk/nextmonth

JOIN US ON SOCIAL MEDIA!

Stay up to date with our latest releases, author news and gossip, special offers and discounts, and all the behind-the-scenes action from Mills & Boon...

 millsandboon

 millsandboonuk

millsandboon

It might just be true love...